KALTENBURG

KALTENBURG

Marcel Beyer

Translated from the German by Alan Bance

Houghton Mifflin Harcourt
BOSTON   NEW YORK
2012

First U.S. edition 2012
Copyright © 2008 by Suhrkamp Verlag, Frankfurt am Main, Germany
English translation copyright © 2012 by Alan Bance

For information about permission to reproduce selections from this book,
write to Permissions, Houghton Mifflin Harcourt Publishing Company,
215 Park Avenue South, New York, New York 10003.

www.hmhbooks.com

First published as *Kaltenburg* in 2008 by Suhrkamp Verlag,
Frankfurt am Main, Germany

Library of Congress Cataloging-in-Publication Data
Beyer, Marcel, date.
Kaltenburg / Marcel Beyer; translated from the German by Alan Bance.
p. cm.
ISBN 978-0-15-101397-5
I. Bance, Alan. II. Title.
PT2662.E94K3513 2012
833'.92 — dc23
2011051596

Printed in the United States of America
DOC 10 9 8 7 6 5 4 3 2 1

The translation of this work was supported by a grant from the Goethe-Institut,
which is funded by the German Ministry of Foreign Affairs.

Oh, just a small bird—no special name.

—Vladimir Nabokov, *Speak, Memory*

I

1

LUDWIG KALTENBURG IS always waiting for the jackdaws to return, right up to his death in February 1989. Even in his last winter, he confidently tells visitors that one day a pair of the white-eyed corvids which he loves, which he admires, will choose his study chimney for their nesting site and found a new colony of jackdaws with their brood. "I know they won't start building their nest for a few months yet," he tells his guests, disciples, or journalists who have driven for nearly an hour from Vienna through the snowy landscape of Lower Austria. The future is clear to him, he says. Wrapped in a woolen rug, the great zoologist Ludwig Kaltenburg sits at the window, plaid pattern, full white hair. His hearing is very poor, but his mind has lost none of its sharpness.

"Birds shy away from smoke," he says, and that's why he's against keeping the small stove in his little annex burning all day long: electric heaters frame the late-period Kaltenburg. His mood is relaxed. "I'm fully aware that the young jackdaws will have to manage without me."

Before his guests can politely protest that the distinguished Herr Professor will outlive them all, Kaltenburg describes how a so-called chimney jackdaw makes its way down to its nest in complete darkness. After some hesitation and a few trial runs, the bird dives beak-first into the entrance of the artificial cave, rights itself, spreads its wings to get a hold on the rough chimney walls,

3

stretches out its legs, and pushes off with its claws. Then on it goes cautiously, step by step so to speak, two meters or more down into the depths. Loud flapping, scraping, scrabbling. Snapshots of this procedure, taken many times over a day, give the impression that the jackdaw is plummeting helplessly from a great height, but the opposite is true: every movement demonstrates considered action and extreme skillfulness.

Nobody dares contradict the professor. His last colony collapsed many years ago, but still no one knows as much about jackdaws as Ludwig Kaltenburg. In icy January he projects for himself and his guests the doings of future generations of jackdaws, and when he spins around in his wheelchair, many a visitor is uncertain whether he is actually hearing the sound of rubber tires on parquet or the quiet call of a jackdaw convincingly mimicking the squeak of wheels. Kaltenburg inclines his head as though listening. The radiators hum. In the chimney a jackdaw's wing brushes across the sooty brickwork.

2

―――

BIRDS SHY AWAY from smoke. Kaltenburg is eighty when he begins to part with his old papers: they feel to him more and more like lumber. Instead of burning all these memos, lecture notes, pocket diaries, essay drafts, and bits of correspondence, he entrusts the papers with relish to his charges, piece by piece. All the preparatory work for his 1964 publication *Archetypes of Fear*, after lying neglected for more than two decades, shut away in a Maria Theresa strongbox, is now put to new use.

Over a few fine spring days Ludwig Kaltenburg distributes the manuscript pages of his draft copy among the resident rodents and waterfowl as nesting material. He hands over half a dozen pages of keyword lists to a young stoat with whom he feels a friendly affinity. Then, in the summer, Kaltenburg sits on the terrace behind the house, looking out over the spacious garden, the pond, the meadow, and eventually takes a handful of notes out of the shoebox on his knees. When the ducklings come home with their parents at sunset, they gratefully accept the activity provided by the woody paper.

He has always regarded *Archetypes of Fear* as a kind of turning point in his life's work. The first book produced back in his native Austria after a twelve-year absence. The first in which Kaltenburg draws openly on observations made during his time in Dresden, although the introduction emphasizes that the idea came to him while snorkeling off the coast of Florida. His first extended study since the end of the Second World War which is not immediately translated into Russian, apart from an incomplete summary that circulates in samizdat form. It is only in 1995, prompted by the sixth anniversary of his death, that a small specialist publisher in St. Petersburg brings out a complete edition, a reliable translation but unfortunately given a misleading title, which in English would read something like *I, Ludwig Kaltenburg, and Fear.* The Soviet Union has vanished from the map, and Russian readers are no longer interested in the writings of a zoologist called Kaltenburg.

The book's very existence was ignored. Its author was passed over in silence. He was loudly condemned. Harshly attacked. Ostentatiously shunned at conferences. Colleagues in the USA accused him of naiveté, colleagues in Europe of dubious methods. Educationalists and conflict studies experts alike were still up in arms in the 1980s about his statement that as a potential lifesaver, fear is a truly marvelous natural mechanism. During a televised discussion, a friend of Kaltenburg's younger days is said to have turned straight to the camera—"Ludwig, I know you're watching right now"—and strongly urged Kaltenburg to concentrate on his own field and put speculation about the nature of man behind him for good and all. With *Archetypes of Fear,* Ludwig Kaltenburg achieves worldwide recognition.

3

─────

ITHIN A FEW MONTHS the edition runs to figures that
would have seemed impossible for a work by a zoologist,
and Kaltenburg reportedly treats himself to a Mercedes
convertible out of the proceeds.

Even the early chapters might occasionally make some general
readers feel uneasy, although initially Kaltenburg seems to have
no more in mind than to unfold a panorama of possible fear re-
sponses familiar to every keen observer of the animal kingdom. It is
known, for example, that young songbirds—the author references
coal tits—are liable to die quickly after hatching, despite adequate
warmth and nourishment, if their nest is continuously subject to
abrupt random shocks. It has been observed that even in the egg
the blind and featherless creatures flinch when a falling twig hits
the nest.

A long passage deals with the phenomenon of the sudden shedding of one or more feathers in reaction to fright. Characteristi-
cally no direct violence is involved, as in the striking case of the
turtledove hearing a shot close by as it flies over open country: it
is checked in midair, dropping some of its feathers, as though the
shot had been directly aimed at it, or even as though the pellets
had pierced its body—only to resume its flight immediately, albeit
visibly shaken and weakened by the loss of feathers. According to
Kaltenburg, this sudden molting represents a kind of survival of in-

fantile shock reaction in adult birds, with the significant difference that only certain individuals exhibit this behavior. Kaltenburg cites one breeder whose chaffinch aviary housed an extremely susceptible female. He had always taken care to handle his birds as gently as possible, but even so, the first time the breeder went to take the sleeping chaffinch out of the decoy cage, a disconcerting number of belly feathers were left behind in the palm of his hand, and afterward the female shed feathers almost automatically every time she saw a hawk or a cat.

The counterpart of his discussion of molting is the section on hyenas. These animals show no tendency whatever to run away from man. They know no fear, and even in the wild an individual hyena will approach so close to men that it takes hardly any effort to kill it with a club. Apparently the rest of the pack watch such occurrences with the utmost indifference.

In the central part of his book Kaltenburg classifies various kinds of fear experience on the basis of fifty years of personal observation, and then, in a chapter called "Fear of Death," he turns to a series of sensational baboon photographs taken under the most adverse conditions in the monkeys' natural habitat and made available to the author by a friendly film director. According to Kaltenburg, the facial expression of a baboon at the very last moment of its life, when the animal realizes in a flash that this time there is no escape from its attacker, differs in no way from that of a human being who finds himself helplessly cornered by a deadly enemy.

Up to this point, as he says, the study essentially confines itself to drawing up a sober account of zoological findings since the beginning of the twentieth century. But what both fellow specialists and scholars from other disciplines particularly balk at is a chapter called "Prospects: The Nameless Fear," devoted to the correspondence of animal to man under extreme conditions. Initial reaction is that here the author has stepped over a line. One erstwhile colleague complains angrily that Ludwig Kaltenburg seems to have forgotten where he belongs.

4

———

K ALTENBURG TALKS ABOUT a prisoner held for years in
solitary confinement who relieves his isolation by befriend-
ing the crows that gather every day outside his cell window. Talks about the common practice of inflicting electric shocks
on working dogs to make them bond more closely with their masters. Talks about rats. About bird-watching outside Stalingrad and
in Leningrad; wonders whether the proximity of death, paralyzing
all their limbs, makes people and animals particularly clear-sighted.
However, the question of where his case-study material comes from
remains open, since Ludwig Kaltenburg fails to name either written or oral sources. Thus he is vulnerable to the charge of using
practically unverifiable information and developing his theories
from phenomena of which he has no personal knowledge.

A case in point is the episode in Dresden in February 1945, when
a horde of monkeys escaped from the bombed-out zoo and a "well-
known acquaintance" or, as we are told elsewhere, a "student" of
Kaltenburg's claims to have had the chance to observe behavior extremely unusual in animals, and lasting several hours. The witness,
still a child at the time, says that all through the night when Dresden was reduced to rubble and ashes, he was wandering about in
the town's biggest park looking for his parents, and that by the next
morning he was still in the same state of literal disintegration, that
is to say, bereft of any sense of self. At the edge of the Great Gar-

den he stopped near a group of distraught people with whom half a dozen chimpanzees or orangutans or rhesus monkeys had mingled—Kaltenburg's witness could not recall the exact composition of the group.

Eyes on the ground, the survivors search for familiar faces. At some point the chimpanzees too begin to scrutinize the features of the motionless figures; you might almost imagine they are looking for guidance from the eyes of the living and the dead in turn. In fact the observer thinks he notices something like relief among the animals when the humans rouse themselves from their torpor, collect the bodies strewn everywhere, and lay them out in some sort of order on an undamaged grass verge. The chimpanzees know nothing about identifying lost relatives, nothing about lining up the dead on the grass, nothing about how you take a corpse by the shoulders and feet to carry it across to its own kind. And yet one ape after another joins in this work, as Kaltenburg reports, without saying who described this scene for him. I did.

II

1

———

WHERE WERE THE old man's urges I was supposed to succumb to, where was the rush of hot blood, where, I wondered, was the sheer panic, combined with the shrewd look of appraisal? And where was the masterful air of the older man that I ought to have been projecting in the presence of a woman who was only half my age but who had nonetheless shown an interest in me, even if it was only in my talk? I was privately surprised to find in my behavior no sign of that ridiculous capering, crowing, and chest-puffing, not the slightest trace of the courtship display that my younger self would have anticipated from a gray-haired gentleman like me.

Now and again I almost long to be one of those men I have often observed doing what's expected of them at their age. I would make a show of fussing around in my pocket to produce a fresh white handkerchief with which to continually mop my brow, and it would not occur to this young woman before me to be in the least surprised, even though it was only the end of March and not at all warm. At most she would ask sympathetically whether she could fetch me a glass of water, and whether we should take a short break, which could only mean that she would allow me some privileged access to her life that is never granted to men of her own age. By inclining my head I could indicate that something of the kind she was suggesting would be very acceptable, while I patted my neck with the damp handkerchief, imagining it was her young woman's hand dabbing the beads of sweat from my skin, not my own.

Years ago I used to pity my young contemporaries constantly showing off their Latin and Greek, even murmuring words like "omnibus" as though imparting some arcane knowledge to the lady beside them. But while those young fogeys may have become wise old gentlemen, silently observing a few blades of grass day in and day out, or fatuously enjoying misquoting their dubious classical jokes, today I'm the one who is flaunting my Latin for this young interpreter: *Carduelis carduelis*, I say slowly, so that she can write it down; her list is gradually filling up. *Carduelis chloris*, I say, and *Carduelis spinus*.

The names of birds: goldfinch, greenfinch, and siskin. "What on earth do you want to learn bird names for?" I had asked when she rang and told me that she had to prepare for a high-ranking visitor from the English-speaking world who was interested not only, as protocol demanded, in informing himself about economic developments since 1990, but—as a seasoned nature-lover—in discussing the local flora and fauna with a few of his hosts. It wasn't the names that worried her, she could easily learn them by heart, but she couldn't visualize the birds. She asked if, to put her mind at rest, I could spare a couple of hours to go through the English, German, and Latin names of the mounted specimens on display.

The collection I used to work in was formerly located in the old town but is now housed at a new site: it was there that we arranged to meet. The old building had a view across to the castle ruins. Tourists came to admire the mural, the *Procession of the Dukes*, and in summer voices drifted up from the street to my room, Russian babble, Swedish babble, then the unvarying harder tones of the tour guide. And in the evenings I used to stand on the banks of the Elbe to watch the gulls flocking above the Court Church. Here in the new building I have been given a little room in the corridor where the offices are. I still come nearly every week. I'm drawn to the mounts. One of my colleagues had directed Frau Fischer to me.

"And don't forget," I managed to call down the phone before she rang off, "you'll have to go out to Klotzsche, the Zoological Collections aren't in the former House of Assembly anymore."

I met Katharina Fischer at the top of the stairs. We turned from the open corridor into the collection area, through the glass door from daylight to artificial light, past the notice NO FOOD IN THE COLLECTION ROOMS, PLEASE. Silence. The whitewashed walls, the heavy iron doors, the composition floor under our feet, were evenly lit by the fluorescent strip lights. The double door next to the sign saying DRY VERTEBRATES was lemon yellow, canary yellow, and easily wide enough to allow the bulk of a mounted adult elephant to be wheeled into the collection, although nowadays the room behind the door contains mainly animals you would have no trouble carrying in your jacket pocket. I'll never get used to this building, won't have to, the move at the end of 1998 coincided with my leave-taking from the Ornithological Collection.

The increasingly oppressive cramped quarters in the House of Assembly, the smell of carcasses and alcohol and toxins, by turns sweetish and then acrid, that penetrated our rooms from the taxidermy workshops, depending on weather conditions, the damp, the musty walls topped by a temporary roof, the floods during heavy, prolonged rain. Dangers that threatened to ruin our specimens and eventually our health as well, and even the DDT that we personally sprinkled for years over the open drawers: all of this is so closely associated with my work in the collection that I would be hard-pressed to recognize anything in this new space if it weren't for the old familiar animals.

"You weren't born in Dresden, were you?" Frau Fischer inquired cautiously soon after we met. Usually it took her only three sentences at most to tell by their accents where people came from, she said, but in my case she still couldn't make up her mind. "I couldn't even guess at the general direction," she admitted as she took her pens and notebook out of her backpack and cast a first glance at the birds I had got ready.

It's true, I'm not from here, and it was only by accident, or rather because of the state of affairs at the time, that I came to Dresden early in 1945, when I was eleven: my parents had decided to leave the city of Posen and head west. Even before that we must have moved around a lot; I never had a chance to pick up a regional twang at home, let alone a dialect. I think they may even have taken care to choose a nanny for me who spoke clear High German.

I have a mental image of myself in my best Sunday shirt sitting on the bench in our kitchen, and my nanny wiping my bare legs with a damp washcloth. Could my parents have taken the nanny along on the move to Dresden?

Long-term memory, short-term memory. The interpreter had asked for a half-hour break during which she would like to be distracted, in order to test whether all the names she now had in her short-term memory really were lodged in her long-term memory. She wanted me to examine her afterward to find out, but meanwhile in this half-hour break she preferred not to stay around the mounted animals, perhaps because she needed to match the word with the object purely in her mind's eye, or because after a while she had become uncomfortable in the presence of the birds: they perch on their branches as though they've just landed, as though they're going to take off again at any moment, and if people are not used to them they're afraid of scaring them away with a nervous movement. So we had exchanged the windowless room with its egg sets and mounted specimens for my office, which gave me a chance to smoke a cigarette and offer Katharina Fischer a coffee.

She scanned the bookcase; there was a small pile of volumes from our library, I'd been using them over the past few weeks, and next to them my little reference library. The interpreter quickly took in the *Journal of Ornithology, The Bird Observer,* next to *Grzimek's Animal Life* and *Wassmann's Encyclopedia of Ornithology.* By comparison, in this light the hardback dictionaries on the top shelf look older than they are, German and Russian, German and English, editions from before and after reunification, slightly scuffed, darkened with age, as though I hadn't touched them for years. *Archetypes of Fear* is absent from the bookcase.

No, on that night when we arrived in this city, which was in the process of turning into a sea of rubble no longer warranting the name of "city," my nanny was not with me as, wrapped in a blanket, I lay on the grass in the Great Garden. People all around, the whole park full of people, squatting in the darkness, walking to and fro, talking quietly, looking up at the sky without a word, and all of them strangers. Huddled next to me were an old couple; in the bright glow the man's face was lit up as though by candlelight. The rims of his eyes, the furrows around his mouth, and the stubble of his beard turning red, then yellowish, white, then dark gray as the clouds passed over the treetops. The woman was wearing a good but no longer new coat, a broad shawl over her upper body, I can't remember, was she wearing a cap, a hat, her head was resting on the man's shoulder. Exhausted, in the open air, on a February night, they had nodded off. A noise like nothing ever heard before drove the two of them out of my mind.

We sat for quite a while facing the birds I had lined up—that's to say she sat, I soon got up again to stand behind the table and point out to her the crucial differences. Working from left to right, as seen from her perspective, I gave her the German names for the chaffinch, the brambling, the linnet, the twite, the mealy redpoll, let's leave out the Arctic redpoll, it can be annoyingly hard to identify with any certainty, but go on to the serin, bullfinch or hawfinch, though the four stonebirds can be omitted despite their lovely pink plumage, then the scarlet grosbeak, the great rosefinch, the pine grosbeak—enormous compared to the others—the crossbill, the Scottish crossbill, the parrot crossbill, and finally the *Carduelis* finches, the siskin, the greenfinch, and the goldfinch, also known as the thistle finch.

While I walked along the line, she began to draw up a list, the English names first; she had acquired an English bird book and was leafing through her *Peterson's Field Guide*, the section on finches. But watch out, I broke in, that you don't mix up the goldfinch with the German *Goldfink*, which is a brambling in English, or, worse still, group it with the snowfinch, which isn't a finch at all but a sparrow, just as the scarlet rosefinch is not a *Rosenfink* in German; the German for that is *Karmingimpel*, and only the Swedes call the scarlet rosefinch a *Rosenfink*.

Maybe I was overtaxing her a little at the start, but I had known straightaway that any interpreter who prepares so thoroughly for a conversation that may never take place, no, in all probability never will take place in the way she anticipates, must on no account be undertaxed. The *Peterson* Frau Fischer is using is a work I seldom consult: although its structure is conventional, I have always found it a bit awkward to use, because the illustrations, descriptions, and maps are each collected into separate sections of their own. I placed the Svensson/Mullarney/Zetterström next to it; descriptions on the left, on the right birds drawn against the light, silhouettes in a low-lying mist, and Katharina Fischer realized at first glance that it is all about recognizing the birds in their natural environment, not indoors.

To really complicate matters—so began my sentence when I felt she had spent slightly too long poring over the bird books—be careful not to confuse "sparrow" with "sparrow." Depending on who you're talking to, British or American, it means either a true sparrow or our German *Ammer*, one of the New World buntings, which you'll see over here only once in a lifetime as an accidental that has drifted across the Atlantic. So what we call an *Ammer*, the British call simply a bunting: easy to remember.

I was afraid my remarks might have confused the interpreter so thoroughly by now that she might be wishing she had never taken on the job. So I thought I would gradually begin to simplify the business, first of all by eliminating certain finches that never appear locally and that were therefore, I hoped, unlikely to crop up in the conversation when Frau Fischer's assignment required her to start moving birds around between languages. I removed a few examples from the table: the two-barred crossbill, the Sinai rosefinch, the evening grosbeak, the white-wing grosbeak, the red-fronted serin, the Syrian serin, the Corsican finch, the citril finch, the twite, and the beautiful blue chaffinch vanished from our sight, and as Katharina Fischer found, the whole arrangement now seemed much more manageable.

I can see myself sitting there in my white shirt, the beam of light from the kitchen lamp doesn't reach me, my nanny shades me from it, the shirt is crumpled, and if I were under the light you might be able to make out dark stains on the material: mud, colored crayon, dried blood. Maria. She can't yet have been twenty years old.

2

—

THAT NIGHT IN the Great Garden it was only for an instant that my parents flashed through my mind and then, strangely, they vanished from my thoughts, just as they themselves later vanished for good; they were never found. They must have been killed, but against all reason I have often played with the idea that they survived but believed me to be dead, they wouldn't give up, and the authorities could not shake them off until, in a fit of the most extreme brutality perhaps, they went so far as to show them the body of a young boy disfigured by the flames, and since they could do nothing and nobody would help them, after a few weeks they moved on. I know that I have always clung to this notion whenever I recall the elderly man and woman squatting right next to me on the grass. They might have been my parents. And in the darkness I simply didn't recognize them. Two figures, aging from one instant to the next, with burns on their faces: I had never seen anything like it. How would I know my own living parents from so many dead? After all, when I first saw myself again in a mirror, this face bore no resemblance to the one I knew from photos and memory.

What have you let yourself in for, you poor girl? I blurted out at one point, and as soon as I said it I could have bitten off my tongue—what a job the interpreter had taken on, trying to learn by heart the whole of the local birdlife here in March, of all months. If the foreign guest had only put off his visit until the winter or even until high summer, if only he had waited just a few weeks, but as it was she would have to take into account all the overwintering species, the breeding birds together with the summer visitors, because not all of the former had left yet, and not all of the latter had yet arrived.

"So then you got stuck in Dresden?"

You could put it that way, I got stuck here, although after leaving Posen we were only passing through Dresden. As far as I can recall, my father, who was a botanist, met some colleagues, and my mother showed me around the city where she had lived for a while before I was born, perhaps the happiest time of her short life. I thought I sensed that as we strolled through the old town together, if you believe an eleven-year-old could sense such a thing. I think we retraced her steps as a young girl, and she never used the new names, she persisted with Theaterplatz, Augustus-Strasse, Jüdenhof, and Frauenstrasse, whenever we stopped for her to tell me something, in the bright, mild weather, a kind of false spring surrounding us that February. In the afternoon we would sit in a café and watch the life around us, Wildsruffer Strasse, Scheffelstrasse, Webergasse, they all still existed then, the city was full of people, and I tried to make eye contact with this or that refugee girl, or an older, limping man, even if I never forgot what my family had drummed into me—although our family had nothing at all to fear—once when we were safe from observation: never look an SS man full in the face.

For me it was—I know this sounds strange—a proper holiday, although a little incident took place of which I was ashamed, and as an adult, truth to tell, went on being ashamed for many years. Coming from the Theaterplatz, it must have been in the morning, we walked past the House of Assembly, and then we were taking the steps up to the Brühl Terrace when I came across a sign: JEWS NOT ADMITTED. And, yes, children find it hard to suppress cruel impulses, children sometimes behave like maniacs, but all the same there's no excuse, I don't know what came over me: I stopped and was gripped by a feeling of triumph, halfway to the top I looked up, then again at the notice, and strutted—I wasn't walking now, I was strutting—up the remaining steps, we're allowed onto the Brühl Terrace, we're not Jews. At the top I turned around, saw the Court Church, Augustus Bridge, the Italian Village below, and then my mother, who had reached the landing. She stopped too. I can remember it as though it were yesterday, I looked into her suddenly narrowed eyes, and I could sense that, at the end of her sleeve in the heavy winter coat, her hand was twitching: my mother, who had never hit me in her life, came close to slapping my face in broad daylight.

So my nanny really did not travel with us after all, the white Sunday shirt with dark stains, a young boy on the kitchen bench seat, utterly dazed. Perhaps my parents fired her that very evening.

On that Shrove Tuesday my mother even wanted to take me to the zoological museum, which she had often visited in her Dresden days, but when we turned from the Postplatz into Ostra-Allee we could see immediately that the building was no longer there, it had been flattened in an air raid the previous October. My mother obviously knew nothing about that, just as I could not know then that I was standing in front of the ruins of an institution which I myself would work in, many years later.

At lunch my father was still with us. We were sitting at a first-floor window somewhere looking down on a large square, so we had probably turned into the Old Market, the sunshine was pouring in, almost blindingly, and we three had a window table to ourselves. The light was strange, pallid; the mashed potatoes on my plate were steaming, as though the sun's rays were heating them. I also had peas and a ground-meat "German beefsteak," no doubt eked out with a large quantity of breadcrumbs, which I had taken a bite out of and then left. Beefsteak. I had only just learned this word for "meatball," at home we said *Frikadelle*, the new word seemed strange to me: when I found it on the menu I had thought it both promising and off-putting, and if I decided to risk it when we ordered our food, it was not so much because of an appetite for meat-balls but because I wanted to see, and taste, whether my father's explanation was right, or whether—despite its related appearance and similar taste—there was something quite different about a "beef-steak." No, it wasn't the same thing, even if my parents did insist, almost despairingly, that it was just a different name.

Until the food arrived, my mother left her wonderful dark otter-skin cap lying on the table. As always, my mother seemed very elegant to me, she attracted attention, but on this day in this restaurant there were also black looks coming from other tables, my father noticed it.

"Please, can't you put your otter cap away?"

But she behaved as though she had seen nothing, heard nothing, and tugged at his tie, which was always crooked, improving the knot, examining the collar, and looking into my father's face. He turned away and grimaced, but she knew he liked it, just as he liked her putting on her jewelry, the pearl earrings, the bracelet, and the little chain necklace; we weren't refugees, we were people out for a meal in the metropolis, and the woman opposite him was his wife, and it didn't matter what other diners made of her outfit. She in a simple dress, with her shoulder-length hair elegantly cut, and he in clothes undecided between a visit to the big city and a country ramble, with his rough mittens which embarrassed me a bit when I saw other gentlemen with their buckskin gloves placed neatly at the edge of the table. My mother ran her fingers through his always unkempt mop of hair, that's the kind of thing they played at in my presence. I looked down at the square, I looked into the sun, the food arrived, I put the otter cap on the windowsill.

My father ate his stuffed cabbage with great gusto. I don't know what he had been doing that morning, the meeting with his botanist colleagues wasn't due until the afternoon. I paid no further attention to my parents' conversation until my mother suddenly dropped her voice. Now, I thought, she's telling him what happened at the Brühl Terrace, but she made no mention of the incident at all, she was talking about the zoological museum.

"It's a shame, I couldn't show him anything, no great auk and no 'World of Beetles.' The museum is closed. No, not one of its closing days. The museum is no longer standing."

My father shook his head, the air raid last autumn, utterly deplorable, but my mother wouldn't leave it at that.

"Now you see what they're capable of, so something good has come out of our canceled museum visit after all."

Not a word about who she meant by "they," whether my mother blamed the Allies for this destruction or perhaps those who had rejected the precaution of evacuating the exhibits, because they liked to think that a city like Dresden was immune.

My mother turned to me, and almost seemed to be enjoying a certain satisfaction: "You see, people are capable of anything, you'll remember this day for the rest of your life."

She turned out to be right. I thought of her words again in the years after Stalin's death, I was well past my twenties and learned that the collection had definitely not been completely destroyed after all, the most precious items were still in their secret depository. It made me think of my parents, and I caught myself thinking, *Your parents didn't have a clue*, while it seemed to me that I was old enough by then, that we were all old enough at last to find out at least half the truth, even if only from a hushed aside. The great auk: the last British specimen of this bird variety was caught in 1840, the very last Icelandic breeding pair on the third of June 1844—I could recite the dates like a schoolboy when I was approaching fifty and saw our Dresden great auk for the first time. I had already lived far longer than my parents did, but I could still hear their words, and to this day the great auk is inseparably linked with the memory of our last family lunch together.

"Are you sure you don't want any more of the *Frikadelle?*"

I shook my head, the mashed potatoes and peas were more than enough for me, and so my father, who had been eyeing my plate throughout, fell upon the German beefsteak. It was when they came to pay that my parents began to whisper to each other, we were already getting our coats on and they still hadn't settled the question: he, who publicly ate unfinished rissoles from other peo-

24

ple's plates, and she, who left her otter cap lying openly on the fine tablecloth without caring what anyone thought—these two grownups who were my parents, sophisticated people as I thought, who were my guides through the big city, were unsure how much to tip, whether it was even the thing to do in a good restaurant like this, in Dresden. I had never seen my parents like this, positively nervous, and it was only once we were back down in the Old Market that they regained their self-confidence.

My father, who will have seen the Botanical Garden on the northern side of the Great Garden in prime condition, early in the afternoon of the thirteenth of February, with its beds and plots and neatly winding paths. My father, who was apparently going to meet colleagues there, who was expected. My father among a group of botanists, all alive, all still healthy, their faces perhaps already beginning to show optimism as they talked quietly about the summer ahead. By that evening, reunited with his family, my father would be back in the Great Garden, in the spacious park, soon to be strewn with craters, uprooted shrubs, shattered trees, and the many dead, to whom he himself was going to belong.

My father the botanist, who was drawn back to botany again at the unforeseeable end of his life. Did he take us to the Great Garden because he knew the way from that morning, or because he looked to the protection of trees and fields and flowers, which always had a calming effect on him, or was it that he followed the crowds escaping from the flames in the inner city, hoping by some miracle to snatch his family from certain death?

To this day I, the son who survived, have not made a single visit to the Heide cemetery to stand at one of the mass graves and conjure up an image of my parents. Instead, I go to the Great Garden, across the meadow on its western edge, and stand under an English oak for which Dresdeners have a special name: the Splinter Oak. It must be some three hundred years since somebody planted it in this spot, as a border marker, they say, the park hadn't been conceived of then. If you come from the zoo side, you don't notice anything: just a tall, gnarled tree with beautifully striated bark. But if you walk around the trunk, the skin of the tree seems suddenly to burst apart, revealing the bright, open, light wood, framed by thick, knobbly protrusions. Looking up, crooked branches, as though their growth had taken place against solid, tormenting air resistance, the broken places, and below the thick foliage of the crown a torn-open area, splintered, shattered, fissured. It takes a while to realize that the scarring across the entire trunk is uniform: this is where the bomb splinters are embedded in the bark, they're still there. On that side the wood has taken on an unusual, lustrous brown hue. Dead wood lies on the ground, it powders when you kick it, rotten: for years a fungus has been spreading through the inside of the stricken tree, a late consequence of the bombing. It survived that night, but eventually it will be destroyed by the sulfur shelf mushroom. At the Splinter Oak I have a memory, my parents are standing there in front of me.

3

———

WHEN THE INTERPRETER asked what made me choose my specialty, she added that she supposed if your father was a botanist it was not unlikely that you would take to ornithology. It is true that from an early age I have had a certain conception of nature; the self-evident receptiveness of my parents to the world of living things was bound to rub off on their child. But I was not willing to claim that coming from such a home I was more or less bound to end up as a biologist, let alone set my heart on becoming a zoologist, least of all an ornithologist. I went through a phase in my childhood when I didn't like these creatures at all. For a long time I was fonder of the cat that brought in the bird than I was of its present to me, laid at my feet with excitement and pride to claim my friendship.

Mother and Father surmised that my aversion was due to an experience I can barely recall, though they often told me about it. It seems that once when I was alone in the house a young bird blundered into our drawing room, and I was infected with the panic of the young creature, which for some reason could not find its way through the open French window and into the garden. I wanted to get away from this agitated, flapping thing that made such awful noises, but just like the ruffled bird, instead of running out into the garden or simply opening the door to the entrance hall, where I would have been safe, I huddled in a corner. When I was eventually found between the stove and the sideboard, I must have been a picture of utter confusion; I don't remember, but that's how my parents described it to me.

All I can recall is this unpredictable creature caught up in the dark curtains, I'm staring at the striped edge of the shiny rectangle of cloth, apparently stirring idly in the mild afternoon air, though in fact its motion results from the frantic movements of the young bird, which cannot shake the heavy material with commensurate force. Its claws gripping tightly, the bird climbs higher, and the next moment it is hidden in a fold, but I know it's still there, the hem of the curtain silently brushes the parquet floor. Did it really enter the drawing room of its own accord, or did the cat bring it in? In my memory the bird more and more assumes the form of a swift—even while the ornithologist in me says that a swift would never fly through an open door into a house, and if it did its flight velocity would make it smash headfirst into a wall, and if it survived it would not be able to get off the floor to bury itself in the curtains.

The next minute I was sitting completely dazed on the kitchen bench, hardly hearing my mother scolding the nanny, who had gone off to enjoy herself in the fields with an admirer, leaving me alone in the house, and who was now wiping my bare legs with a damp cloth. Yet it was all my fault. I had begged her to leave me playing in the drawing room after lunch and go for a walk by herself, I wouldn't tell my parents, I had kept my promise on previous Sundays. Eventually I had a temper tantrum, thrashing around wildly but taking care not to hit my nanny; I may have been screaming too. No, before I got to the point of screaming she would give in, relieved on the one hand, on the other worried about going for a walk by herself, though both of us knew, without ever saying so, what "by herself" meant on a Sunday afternoon.

I was left in peace, playing my solitary games in the cool room with its half-drawn curtains, while she had to worry about me, whether I would be up to any mischief, she didn't know what I did when she was away, whereas I had some idea what her admirer would be up to with her in the distant meadow. So that, as I was later to realize when I was grown up myself, her worry about being with her lover would be combined with concern about neglecting a child.

I had goose bumps, the cloth which had been pleasantly warm from the water and the warm hand running it over my legs got cold from one minute to the next in the unheated kitchen, the cool evening air. When my nanny came back from her outing I said nothing, didn't answer any questions about why I was cowering in the dusk between the stove and the sideboard, why I was keeping my arms so tightly crossed, why I couldn't put one foot in front of the other like a normal boy. She didn't notice the dark stain on my trousers, didn't notice the swift, which was still lying on the carpet with a wildly beating heart, as though paralyzed, the last time I saw it. I was able to keep everything back from my nanny, but not from my parents, who returned at dinnertime from a visit, and now I was sitting in nothing but my Sunday shirt on the kitchen bench with a wildly beating heart, I had wet my trousers out of sheer terror.

I could hear the noise, but I didn't comprehend a word that was being said, my blood was roaring so loudly in my ears. Silently my nanny let my mother's reproaches and her unusually rough language wash over her, as she knelt in front of me she kept her eyes lowered, didn't look at me, just as I would have given anything in the world not to meet her gaze, although I didn't dare close my eyes and wish myself away from this scene, away from the tiled kitchen with its horrible echo, back in my quiet bedroom. My mouth was dry, I couldn't even swallow, let alone confess my guilt, call out, "It's all my fault, please leave her alone, she hasn't done anything." Perhaps I have never since then experienced such a powerful sense of injustice and torment, the young swift, my wet trousers, and the nanny I was fond of.

I have a dim memory of lying in bed, I had been there for ages and should have been asleep, while my mother kept repeating the same phrases over and over to my father, scraps of sentences that reached me from their bedroom, though I couldn't make much sense of them, things like "the poor thing," and "with his bare hands," and "our own son," and then later, if I heard correctly through the half-open door, again and again, now almost in a whisper, as though she had no strength left, maybe because she was so disgusted: "The eyes."

What happened to the swift afterward, I can't say. It's possible it didn't survive, that it expired after my father gently released it from its purgatory and ushered it toward the garden, though without touching it with his bare hands. Or it died, exhausted, toward evening on the soft, patterned carpet. Just as it is possible, although unlikely, that despite its experiences it had a long life before it, an airborne life which would bring it back for just a few weeks year after year to our latitude, to the neighborhood of dark curtains, cool drawing rooms, and cruel children, which, as though it had learned its lesson on that Sunday afternoon, it would take note of only from a great height, from a safe distance.

I learned my lesson too, though without realizing as much straightaway. It took me until the next morning, when I emerged from an uneasy sleep and my stupefied condition, and went the way I had gone the day before out of my room, along the corridor, then down the broad staircase, into the kitchen, where I was given a drink of milk, and finally into the drawing room, to the site of my downfall. All traces of the struggle had been erased, not a mark on the carpet, the curtain hung as neatly as if no swift had ever become entangled in it. However, the discovery I had made the afternoon before but only grasped now when I glanced across the empty battlefield hinted that I was destined to be an ornithologist: I had seen the legs of the swift.

To this day, there is a widespread notion that this is a bird that possesses neither legs nor claws; it spends most of its life in the air, and is said to lack such equipment. A bird that you hardly ever see close up, that impresses the viewer on the ground with its dexterous wing strokes and rapid flight, sometimes swooping low enough to make you instinctively duck, and lingering immediately afterward at a great height, an almost imperceptible dot that seems gradually to glide off into space. You never see a swift sitting on a branch, it never moves about on the ground. With such a creature it's not surprising that ignorance shades over into superstition. People used to be convinced that swifts came straight from the moon.

Abhorrent as the young swift was to me, something connected me with it, my enemy and comrade in fear on a long Sunday afternoon in the drawing room: I had wrested knowledge from it which it tried to keep hidden from humans. For the bird to have clung to the curtain material, it must have had the necessary claws. And when it lay on its back on the carpet, close to death, with wings outstretched and helplessly twitching, I saw with my own eyes, from close up, the short, admittedly rather wasted-looking, but certainly existing legs of the swift. Legs such as all birds have. That made it anything but the mysterious creature of fable endowed with marvelous powers.

I raced from the drawing room across to the kitchen, where my breakfast was ready, shouting again and again, "The swift has got legs," breathless, I wanted to go into all the details, but my nanny, pushing the plate of open bread rolls toward me when I finally sat myself down on the kitchen bench, just shook her head sadly.

Something was broken. I still have this vague feeling today, even though it has never become quite clear to me what happened. The look on my nanny's face, her head moving gently from side to side, her bright, loose hair against the light, caressing her chin and cheeks. Was that the last breakfast Maria would ever serve me? She sat opposite me as though she knew something far more significant than my basic discovery about the swift, a terrible revelation hardly bearable even to an adult, let alone a child.

Did I idolize Maria? As a small boy, yes, certainly. And it only struck me years later that her head-shaking might have had more to do with her lover than with her possible dismissal. But at the time the effect on me was, must have been, to make me connect my nanny's secret knowledge with the incident of the swift the day before.

On the one hand, I thought, I must try with all my might to work this creature out, and then I, who was to blame for her despair, would discover what was making my nanny so miserable on this morning, but on the other hand I couldn't stand the idea of ever taking a close look at a stray young bird again. Because, but for the swift, this depressing breakfast scene would never have happened, I would never have had to sit helplessly opposite my nanny, unsure, torn this way and that, sad but a bit disappointed at the same time because she wasn't interested in the admittedly puny legs of the swift.

I chewed silently. My nanny said nothing. As if I had contributed to the extinction of the swift. As if the day before I had taken the decisive, irrevocable step of making this bird species disappear from the earth forever. As if I had the last living specimen on my conscience.

4

——

S TRANGE YOU SHOULD ASK that particular question, I said
to Frau Fischer, because I've always wondered about it myself: Didn't I have any school friends of my own age with
whom I could play in the fields after school and spend long Sunday afternoons? Friends from my early schooling? I can't remember any.

Over there on the edge of the forest, a herd of deer whose out-
lines you could only make out gradually after sunset in the field
against the dark background: sometimes my father took me with
him on his study outings. In the summer, when the evenings stayed
light far too long for me to sleep, he came into my room to see if I
was still awake and allowed me to get up and get dressed again. I
was never a good sleeper.

Possibly because I thought of these twilight walks as an extraordinary reward—even if I never knew what for, because they were
always bestowed on me out of the blue and no doubt on a whim
of my father's—on these outings of ours I was always particularly
obedient and keen to learn. I learned from my father how to move
silently through the undergrowth and, instead of constantly talking, how to listen for the most distant sounds. Did he dislike going
alone? Was it a ruse on his part, to do with his idea of education?
If we set off late in the evening there obviously wasn't much to see

anymore, and so I learned to concentrate on faint impressions and seemingly trivial phenomena.

We did not speak. He went ahead, gesturing toward a wallow or teeth marks on a birch tree. We crept to the edge of the wood and waited. Eventually, just as I had been promised at home while hastily throwing on my clothes, deer began to appear in the forest. The animals, I learned, talk to each other almost continuously; they often talk to us too, but we rarely notice what they're saying, not realizing they mean us. The animals address themselves to us, from a distance, hidden in the leaves of the trees above us, from the thicket beside the path, they ask questions or they curse us, they are letting us know "I am aware of you." But even to get anywhere near certain animals, to detect them in the first place, you have to know how to be silent; if you want to catch sight of them, these talking creatures, there's one thing above all you mustn't do: talk to them.

As I say this, there is after all a shadow that passes across my mind, but not the face that goes with it. I had a friend of my own age in Posen, our neighbors' son, I ran into him occasionally in the street. We weren't particularly close friends. It could be that whenever I had anything to do with him, curiosity and repulsion balanced each other out; a certain amount of pity came into it too. Was he retarded? He seemed very awkward and clumsy to me, there wasn't much you could do with him. He didn't talk a lot, and when he did his speech was indistinct but very loud. Drawn-out sounds that he produced with an effort, trying to make complete words out of them. When I was with him I was a bit scared. But at home I mimicked him.

He knew about our twilight excursions. He wanted to go with us. He begged his parents until they eventually let him. We didn't have much to do with our neighbors, but I remember them asking my father in: Yes, he did sometimes take me out at night to the fields with him. And yes, the neighbors' boy could come with us one evening. It's hard to know whether his parents thought the boy was making it up, or maybe they wouldn't believe my father until their own son reported back to them from one of these expeditions.

On the evening in question the boy came over to us, but he was too shy to come into the house, he stayed by the door. And I had never seen him so excited. This poor creature, at other times practically unable to utter a word, could not stop talking. An annoying evening, as my father and I agreed afterward. We didn't sight a single animal. They must all have retreated silently at the approach of the babbling youngster.

Otherwise, nothing. No one else comes to mind. As though that first night in Dresden had wiped out a whole host of other images, as though the onslaught of those impressions alternating abruptly between extremes of brightness and darkness had driven out of my mind memories shaped in a more subtle light.

"What about your grandparents?"

I shook my head.

"Uncles, aunts, cousins?"

None of them either. Presumably my parents didn't care much about keeping in touch with their relatives. Who knows, perhaps they were glad to escape from their family background by moving to Posen.

"Well, can you remember your parents' friends or acquaintances?"

Only those I met again later as an adult. That could well have seemed rather unreal—being afraid that however hard you tried you might not recognize anything about a person, after a gap of ten, fifteen years. I did feel disoriented, helpless for a moment, but fortunately, before I had time to lose my equilibrium completely, the new faces brought back to me these people's younger features, voices and movements that I was familiar with as a child.

"In an earlier life," as the interpreter put it.

In an earlier life, you could say that. But knowing myself as an adult to be surrounded by these figures meant that I had preserved something from that life.

5

―――

THERE WERE TWO MEN in uniform in the house. I clung
to my nanny's wrist, to her forearm, even if only with my
eyes, since at that moment I couldn't literally hold on to her
because she was balancing a platter of meat in one hand and holding
fork and spoon in the other while she served two slices of roast meat
per person onto five large, ivory-colored plates of our best Sunday
china, plates with a lime-leaf green border, a tendril that began nowhere and ended nowhere, though I was always trying to find its
starting point nonetheless. Then, still holding the fork, Maria gave
everyone some gravy, without dripping any of it, calmly but deftly,
always leaning in over their left shoulders. She had begun with the
guests, then served my parents, the steaming roast beef hanging
for a moment in midair next to faces, ears, almost in front of people's eyes, but no one noticed it, it didn't bother anyone, everyone
around the festively laid table went on talking, apart from me, to
whom my nanny came last. I was hoping that, as she usually did,
she would have saved a particularly good slice for me, totally free
of the gristle which you would chew in vain and wouldn't be able to
swallow but which you couldn't put back on your plate in front of
guests, so that you would have to park it in the back of your cheek
until the meal was over and you could get to the toilet. Then Maria
lifted the lid of the potato dish and my father spoke into the rising
cloud of steam: "Please help yourselves, gentlemen."

There were two men in uniform in the house, and I was allowed to address them familiarly as *Du*. Earlier, when they arrived, I heard my parents greeting them at the door. I was sitting on the rug in my room, wanting to finish my game; light, friendly voices reached me, and then my mother was calling me down to say hello to Herr Spengler and Herr Sieverding. When I saw them in the hallway, there was some chat about our house, my mother was stroking my head, I was shaking hands with the guests, it was their boots I noticed first, clattering on the stone floor like nothing we had ever heard in our house before. I still didn't know what to make of it, two uniformed men whose voices didn't match their boots at all, they came up to just below their knees, so highly polished you could practically see your face in them. I stared at the boots, the grownups' eyes were also drawn to the soft, black, gleaming boot tops, and one of the men began to laugh: "That's not my doing, you'll have to congratulate Martin here for that, he's got the knack of losing himself for a whole afternoon in boot cleaning."

"Well, run off and wash your hands": my father didn't know what else to say.

Martin Spengler, the younger of the two, could hardly have been any older than my nanny, the other one was called Knut Sieverding, I turned the soap over in my hands under the tap, that name is harder to remember, Knut is the older one, but both of them are much younger than my parents, I was still twisting the soap over, but holding on to it with slippery fingers, I don't want to forget those names, Spengler and Sieverding, Knut laughs, and Martin polishes boots, but both of them make the same clatter with their boots on the stone floor, how cold the water gets when you let it run, the tall, thin, quiet man is called Martin, the shorter one with the untidy hair is Knut.

"Are you coming down? Time to eat."

My nanny was knocking at the bathroom door.

A splash of gravy had cut through the green border. I didn't have any gristle or stringy bits. Although there were visitors, I was still allowed to mash the potatoes on the plate with my fork. Knut was the one sitting opposite me, Martin the one to his left. My father had announced he was inviting students from his lecture for the evening, and now two men in uniform were sitting at the table with us. They came out from the town, we lived a long way out, the wood behind the railway embankment, fields all around, and I wasn't sure that our road didn't quite quickly turn into a track, an overgrown path that petered out somewhere in the fields. I never went that far. We didn't have many neighbors, in summer the green growth was so dense that you'd hardly suspect the nearest house was there. At the back, toward the stream, my father's greenhouse, I used to hide down there in the bushes. From the terrace side you could walk into the drawing room, on the floor above my parents' bedroom to the left, mine to the right. I knew every corner of our house, and there were many dark corners that nobody went to but me. What happened the week before had long since been forgotten. Today I was allowed to have dinner with the grownups. Maria took the meat around again, winking at me without anyone seeing. She smiled. Then she smiled at Martin.

"Hermann, are you listening?"

My father looked across at me from his place at the head of the table, then at Knut. He had laid his cutlery down on the edge of the plate. Maria was holding the serving platter up in the air, with both hands. What had Knut—Herr Sieverding—asked me, my mind went blank, I tried to imagine what he might have asked me, there were no potatoes steaming on anybody's plate by now, I couldn't think of anything.

"No, it did have legs, I saw for myself. The swift, I mean."

"But he's asking what class you're in," murmured my mother in my ear.

By this time I couldn't say a word.

"Oh, well," broke in Martin, who cleaned the boots. "School isn't important at all, not that interesting, don't you agree? Unless you're very lucky, you hardly learn a thing, at least nothing important, nothing about animals, plants, or cameras, for example. Things that interest a bright boy, paper and pencils and everything you need to take a good photo. I bet you'll have a hard time finding a biology teacher who is aware that swifts have legs."

"But the bird is called *Apus apus*," said Knut, "and its footless condition is mentioned in its name, twice in fact, as though to confirm it or to indicate that there is nothing else to know about it, that it's distinguished by nothing except its lack of feet."

"You see, I'm sure you didn't learn that at school."

"No, you're right. I only just managed to scrape through my leaving exams. Instead of studying, I used to go off all on my own looking at wildlife, and when I passed my exams my parents were so relieved, they bought me the movie camera I had been coveting so that I could film animals. Yet it was my love of observing animals that made so much trouble for me at school."

It was getting dark outside. My nanny was in the kitchen preparing dessert and coffee. My mother had laid her hand on my knee. Everyone had forgotten how embarrassed I'd been about Knut's question.

"Nobody would know now that you weren't a model pupil," said my father, "if you don't mind my saying so. Getting invited at twenty-one to Berlin for the anniversary of the German Ornithological Society—I thought you would have been top of the class, Herr Sieverding."

"Not a bit of it. I was too busy observing the bird world. And I couldn't have made the film I showed in Berlin about snipe in the Königsberg area if my parents hadn't given me the camera."

"You're a real professional when it comes to birds," said Martin, nudging Knut with his elbow. "Tell us again about the first lecture you gave, back home in Königsberg."

"God, I was so nervous. What I knew was the remote world of birds out on the Courland Spit, and here I was about to give a presentation on it, using my own photo material, in the lecture theater of the Zoological Institute. My hands were sweating. My parents were there. Seasoned ornithologists were there. Fortunately my lecture went off very smoothly, there was even an article in the *Königsberg Daily News*, the first one about my work: 'Camera Reveals Family Secrets.' Of course, I've got to say there were also some critics, who had expected something completely different. I simply wanted to show the world as it was, whereas they wanted me to explain the world to them, a bit like a grandmother explaining the world to her grandchild."

"As if showing anything were that easy."

Knut and my father laughed. Martin took a drink of water. Now that I had been paying attention again for quite a while, something dawned on me beyond all the stories about school, birds, and filming: it was entirely for my sake that my parents had invited these two men, Knut and Martin, with their pleasant voices and black leather boots.

6

———

THE WAY I SEE IT today is that my parents were worried about me after the incident of the swift. Obviously they noticed how slow I was to get over my confusion, how I was becoming more withdrawn as the week wore on, preferring to spend my time alone in my room and answering encouraging questions with a scarcely audible yes or no, or showing no reaction at all. Since they connected my depression with the swift, though not with my equally depressed nanny—who was punished by being ignored for a few days—my parents made a plan: with guidance, I was to learn about the world of birds through direct, intensive contact.

What seems to me in retrospect so endearing, my parents worrying that their only child's not very significant encounter with a young swift might have serious repercussions in his later life, at the time aroused contradictory emotions in the child concerned. On the one hand, I was proud to be the center of attention, even more than usual the world seemed to revolve around me, they had even invited young ornithologists to dinner just because of me. But on the other hand, I also felt betrayed, because plans had been hatched behind my back to rescue a creature who was being kept just as much in the dark as if he were a small animal.

It is no doubt a matter for dispute whether my parents were being particularly progressive for their time or, on the contrary, old-fashioned and exceptionally strict: the conclusions they drew from the incident to help me conquer my bird phobia expanded step by step into a large-scale program of education. Knut and Martin suited their purposes right from the beginning.

My father had noticed them in his lectures for different, in fact opposing, reasons, which in itself says something about the friendship of the two young men, four years apart in age. Martin, the younger one, the boot cleaner, behaved badly, not to say rudely, one morning in an upper tier of the auditorium during an "Introduction to the Foundations of Botany" lecture. My father was obliged to ask him to be quiet, because as he was taking notes he was frantically shuffling his papers, and even groaned aloud at one point when my father came to cell structure. After the lecture, as my father was to tell my mother with forced jocularity, perhaps with a trace of bitterness, it wasn't the disruptive student who came down to the podium to apologize, as you might have expected, but his friend Knut, the older one, who begged with exquisite politeness not for understanding, but for forgiveness, while Martin remained unmoved, brazenly lolling about up there on his bench and following with lowered gaze as Knut, on his behalf, repeatedly bowed his head to my father down there by the blackboard.

It transpired that both were in the Luftwaffe training school here in Posen, and Knut was a regular student of biology and zoology besides. Martin only occasionally accompanied Knut, his immediate superior, to the university. Martin, a lad who was not quite of this world and who tried to overlay his insecurities with a rough manner, a questing spirit, dreamy, you might say; others would call him impudent. Knut by contrast steadier, altogether more mature, he knew exactly what he wanted and was a good influence on his younger companion, a bit like an older brother.

Knut came out to show us his bird photos from the Courland Spit. He brought his camera with him, Martin and he allowed me to take them on secret paths through the woods, I showed them where we found deer.

"Up there—can you see it? A woodpecker."

"Green or spotted?" I could hear it, but I couldn't make it out yet.

"Now he's moved off to the other tree."

There on the ground was some sticky stuff, a ball of feathers, Knut poked around in it with his stick: "That's where a long-eared owl has eaten a small songbird and spat out the remains." He looked at me inquiringly.

"That's what you call a pellet."

And Martin: "Now I wouldn't have known that."

Sometimes Martin came to see me by himself. Soon the pilot, who wanted to become a pediatrician after the war, was a regular visitor to our place, even when my parents were not at home.

A gust of warm wind stirred up dust from the road, for a moment I couldn't see anything. Somebody was coughing. Then Martin emerged from the dust cloud, his hands covering his mouth, nose, and eyes. As soon as he recognized me he waved. How dusty his boots were. Despite the sunshine, Knut had stayed behind to prepare for the next day's classes. We had this afternoon to ourselves. But first Martin needed a big glass of cool tap water from the kitchen, to quench his terrible thirst. Maria was standing by the table peeling vegetables, and as soon as she saw who had come in with me she wiped her hands on her apron and beamed. If anybody else came into the kitchen with dirty shoes, she would go crazy. Martin had struck up an understanding with Maria immediately, in fact I sometimes thought there was a closeness between them, as though they hadn't just met at dinner the other evening, when they could only exchange a few polite words in any case since Maria was serving the food. It almost seemed to me as if they had known each other for some time.

With Martin I spent whole afternoons in the countryside. He said he found the city too oppressive, not because of the streets and houses but because of all the people. We took nothing with us to the fields except a sketchpad and pencils. We just drew what happened to be in front of us: panicles, lumps of clay, beetles. Martin was utterly calm as he watched my efforts, his sleepy, then suddenly alert glance. He commented on this or that pencil mark, the strength, depth, darkness of the line, he saw the way the color covered the background, followed the direction of a movement, a turn or stroke as it tended out beyond the edge of the paper. A hare didn't have to be a thing with long ears, if the seemingly shapeless collection of lines on the page squatted or leapt like a hare. He never minded that I drew a hare when he asked me to draw a bird.

I took my first snapshots, with Knut's camera: in the garden, my parents with friends, an early summer's evening, everybody looking up at me from the table, in the corner on the right you could see part of the greenhouse. Knut, half hidden in the grass while we waited for partridges. Martin, a snap I took of him on the road a long way from our house, and no, it didn't peter out in a narrow track between the fields, it led, quite recently paved with granite, to the next village. In the sky in the background were dots, migratory birds, geese, you could tell by the formation.

So autumn came. And one event from that time particularly stands out for me, even though the central feature itself escapes my memory. Somebody—Martin? my mother?—at some point suggested that Knut should show us his film about the snipe which had been mentioned at our dinner together. To begin with it was no more than a persistently recurring notion, but how could you carry out such a bold venture, you'd need a hall to show it in, then there would be the problem of a suitable projector, and anyway, Knut was here with the Luftwaffe and as a student, he didn't have the film ready to hand.

Gradually, though, everybody became quite carried away by the idea. If necessary you could rig up a makeshift projection room here in the house, the drawing room with its heavy curtains would do quite well. Once the others showed they were really serious about it, then of course Knut would gladly make sure we obtained the film. Martin would ask around about a projector, but without attracting attention. I had never seen my parents so feverish. However, they insisted I should not go around talking about it. They didn't like their son trying to impress the neighboring children by boasting about family matters. Martin had found a suitable projector, which he could borrow for a day. My parents kept reminding me of my promise. Knut dropped in to tell us that somebody would soon be traveling to Königsberg and would visit Knut's parents to collect the film and bring it safely back to Posen. I couldn't wait for the weekend, I would no longer have to restrain myself.

The night before the great occasion I hardly slept; my parents were very excited too, I could hear footsteps on the stairs until very late, and voices coming from the kitchen through the open door. But the only thing I can remember about the snipe film itself is one word: "Rossitten," and that didn't even come from the film, which was silent. "Rossitten": Knut used it in his commentary, describing the ornithological station up north in East Prussia.

The next morning I was woken by the preparations: on the ground floor chairs were being dragged to and fro across the parquet, my nanny was taking out a large bed sheet from the linen cupboard in the corridor to iron for use as a screen. I could hear the curtains being opened and closed again a few times, then my father went shouting through the house that we needed dark blankets. Our drawing room was being got ready for the screening. The stove and sideboard had disappeared behind the improvised screen. My father stood on a ladder pushing woolen blankets down between the window frame and the curtain rail.

In my pajamas I sat down at the little table that had been pushed back against the wall for the screening. I could hear my nanny in the distance, my breakfast was waiting for me in the kitchen.

Why don't I remember anything about the snipe film? I think I was rather disappointed that Knut did not feature in his own film. My expectations had been pitched too high, how could it be otherwise, but apart from that my expectations were completely wrong from the start. Don't ask me how a child of six or seven who has never been to the cinema and never seen a film arrives at his fixed idea of a film, not open to doubt and impervious to adult comment, as though he had already seen all the films in the world. If you had asked me what to expect from this film, I would have replied without hesitation: obviously it would show Knut moving through his home landscape looking for birds. You would also see Knut with a bird on his arm. And Knut watching a dark swarm, pulsating in the air, as it slowly disappeared over the coast into the sunset.

The film had been loaded onto the projector. My father turned out the light and joined us in our semicircle. My mother on the left, with me next to her. Over there my nanny and Martin. The projector clattered, the screen went black, there were just little hairs fluttering brightly at the edges. A short leader strip, and yes, to confirm what I had expected, there it was: KNUT SIEVERDING, his name in large capitals. There was no soundtrack, Knut delivered the commentary standing beside the projector. I don't know when it first occurred to me that his name was like that of a variety of snipe, *Calidris canutus*, the knot, known in German as a *Knutt*.

Reeds swaying in the wind. A wide sky dominated by shining masses of clouds. Then back to ground level—reflections in water, spikes of grass—there was something moving. Knut was about to appear in the picture. I waited. There they were, the snipe, then the landscape again, sky, clouds, grass, I heard Knut's voice explaining everything precisely, in real life, here in our drawing room. But Knut had yet to appear in the film. I was so impatient that I didn't take a proper look at the birds.

Considering how many wildlife films I have seen since, as an adult, including films by Knut himself, and how inspiring I have found them, often far more so than those with a human cast, I'm still surprised by how little I gained from seeing my first wildlife film, in fact the first film I had ever seen in my life.

The screen had reverted to a brilliant blinding white, our motionless figures could be made out in the darkness, still looking toward the screen, as though comparing the image left on the retina with what we had just seen. But the film was finished. The reel turned a few more times, and then it was empty, the celluloid strip tapping against the sprocket, a regular, quiet clicking, like a clock measuring an infinite expanse of time, and apart from that nothing moved. Three more revolutions, three more disturbing clicks, and the projector lamp went out, the whirring gradually died away, then ceased altogether. Somebody switched on the chandelier lights and somebody cleared his throat, we viewers were clapping, Knut took a bow. He stood right next to me, but I hadn't seen him in his film.

7

———

OUTSIDE, A SPRING SHOWER, the sky had blackened, it looked as though there might be a storm. The world beyond the window was deep blue: the approaching cloud front, in the distance the wall enclosing the grounds, where the gateway gave onto a long concrete drive that led right up to the building. On the left by the entrance the tall beeches, in summer the foliage is so dense that it looks like a forest, and on our right, behind the old storehouse, the birches on the gentle slope: all covered with a blue shimmer. Big puddles had quickly formed in the mud, the arc lamps in the car park were already lit.

We had been discussing Martin's work, exhibited in all the big public galleries, the drawings with their characteristic combination of roughness and fragility. We talked about Martin's room installations, partly manic and partly pedantic in their effect, composed of everyday objects and sculptures which only a few art lovers were prepared to see as sculptures. Long rows of shelves, preserving jars, boxes, with stains on the floor where a dark, sticky-looking liquid had been spilled: as though someone had broken into a zoological collection.

Traveling with her parents, she had regularly been taken to exhibitions, Frau Fischer told me, and whenever they planned a trip she could always count on spending at least one long day among contemporary works of art. At that time she had always felt uncomfortable in Martin's rooms, not to say intimidated by things. The material was enveloped in a dangerous stillness, at once dead and alive. Whether it was just a sponge, or a piece of sacking, or a completely ordinary old pair of tailor's scissors, it would never have occurred to her to touch these objects.

"Soon I didn't want to travel any distance at all during the holidays, and I swore that when I was older I would never go abroad. Then I became an interpreter."

Our empty coffee cups, the half-full ashtray. If we had been sitting in a ground-floor room, in the bluish half-light, we could have seen the steam rising from the grass, seeming to do battle with the falling raindrops. They were huddling out there, protected by the leaves, hunched, feathers puffed up, without a sound, waiting for the cloudburst to end.

"Didn't Knut Sieverding make a film about a hamster too?" asked Katharina Fischer, recalling a winter morning when the first-years were led by their teacher into the biology lab, full of anticipation but also a bit unsure; from their primary school years they were used to being read a story on the last day before the Christmas holidays. Here in the high school the class teacher busied herself with a video player, muttering to herself, and not until the cassette had been pushed home did the pupils in the back rows quiet down like the rest.

"There was one scene that sent shivers down our spines."

A stoat crawls into a hamster's burrow, and Katharina Fischer remembered as though it were yesterday how tense she felt watching the intruder, because she knew the nest contained a litter of young. The stoat moves in further and further. The mother hamster clearly notices changes taking place somewhere in the intricate system of runs, perhaps the soles of her feet have picked up vibrations from the ground, or she may have sensed unusual air movements through her whiskers, or maybe it's simply the smell of the stoat—the hamster's head jerks up, she stops for a moment, as though she has to arrange these irritating sense perceptions into

49

a picture. She turns, runs up along the tunnel, and suddenly the hamster and the stoat confront each other face-to-face.

Yes, she had seen Knut's film.

"Our teacher, in the semidarkness next to the screen, completely unmoved."

Not a coldhearted person, surely.

"No, but in that situation it just disturbed us even more, the stoat attacking a young family of hamsters, and the teacher not even flinching."

She knew the outcome of the confrontation.

In the end the stoat withdraws from the burrow. The whole class was relieved. Such death-defying courage. All the same, the image came back to Katharina Fischer for a long time afterward, the puffed-out cheeks of the mother hamster, the sharp teeth, the little claws.

"What would Knut Sieverding have done if the defense had failed, if the stoat had got to the helpless young hamsters in their nest?"

Knut Sieverding would never have imposed that on children. A dead mother hamster and an unprotected nest, never.

"Did he look for a particularly tough hamster?"

It took him weeks to train the stoat to go so far and no further into the hamsters' burrow, stop, and turn back after a while. The scene was planned down to the last detail, you could say it was staged, and it didn't matter to the stoat whether a mother hamster turned up to drive it off or not.

Frau Fischer nodded absently. "A tame stoat meets a tame hamster."

Meanwhile, far more than the intended half-hour had elapsed, we ought to be getting back to the birds. The rain was becoming heavier all the time. Anything that had not found its way into Frau Fischer's long-term memory would have to be revised.

I unlocked the door to the egg collection again, the big yellow iron door, which I always think opens only against a certain resistance, as though higher air pressure prevails in the room behind it. As soon as the door shut behind us we could no longer hear the drumming of the rain, what pressed upon our ears now, subdued, a fine carpet of sound, was the steady noise of the recirculated air.

The walls are lined all around with display cases, you are looking into glass birds' eyes everywhere, but the shining buttons are no more than crude indicators of the location of the sense of sight in life, uniform dark points instead of the infinitely varied, subtly shaded colors of the iris. In the short space of our walk back to work we passed countless specimens whose eyes seemed to follow us attentively right into the small square left clear for table and chairs. Here were birds of paradise in a thousand variations, the color combinations, the form of the plumage, the pose, and there house sparrows, whose varieties reveal themselves only to the patient observer: every single bird has been carefully treated to create a lifelike impression. Even a habitual visitor can occasionally succumb to the illusion that he is surrounded here not by mounted specimens but by silent observers: I sometimes experience this when I stand lost in thought at a display cabinet and discover with a shock a bird that has fallen from its base.

We sat down again at the wooden table, on two angles of a corner, close together; Frau Fischer sketched a finch in her notebook, then flipped back to the beginning of the book and looked at me, concentrating completely on the matter in hand. This I took to be my signal to stand up. I positioned myself behind the table, my thumb in the English bird book, and examined the interpreter as you would a schoolchild. We moved briskly through the Turdidae family, we touched on warblers, chats, redstarts, and thrushes, Frau Fischer had retained everything very well, I presented her with the English names and then the Latin ones, and she reeled off both German and English equivalents as though she had always known them. Just as quickly, we put titmice and sparrows behind us and came back to the finches, where we had started.

I laid a gentle finger on the gray head of a bird slightly smaller than a sparrow, with a crimson forehead and breast, its back cinnamon-colored. The answer came without hesitation: the *Blu-thänfling*, the linnet, Latin *Carduelis cannabina* or—very confus-ingly—also *Acanthis cannabina*. She made a note, "unusual white edges to primary feathers," and drew an arrow from it pointing to her linnet sketch.

The teacher posed the questions, the pupil answered, but after a while a third voice intruded into our dialogue: "If we ever go to Vi-enna together, you must remind me to show you the crown prince's last eagles."

The voice of my teacher, Ludwig Kaltenburg. He taught me to observe mounted birds as you would live creatures.

If you're ever in Vienna, I said to Frau Fischer, you must go to the Natural History Museum and take a look at the two sea eagles that Crown Prince Rudolf of Habsburg shot a few days before his suicide. It would be hard to find such strange mounted specimens anywhere—the pose, the expression, the plumage—and remem-ber, the taxidermist will have had not just two dead birds on the ta-ble before him as he went to work but another death on his mind, and so the two eagles, not to say the one double-headed eagle of the Habsburg emblem, became in his hands two birds with drooping feathers, bowed down with grief as though they knew on the day they were hunted that the man who ended their lives would soon take his own. They are anything but proud heraldic beasts, and per-haps that's why the little explanatory tablet was added, otherwise such taxidermy might have been regarded in 1889 as an insult to the Crown. They're beautiful, these two eagles from the Orth region, the wide, marshy Danube meadows, they're far more beautiful than many a superb, lavishly spruced-up eagle specimen.

"Your teacher—was that the same Ludwig Kaltenburg who wrote *The Five Horsemen of the Apocalypse?*" asked Katharina Fischer.

Yes.

"The author of *A Duck's Life?*"

The very same.

"Didn't he write *Archetypes of Fear* too? And *Studies of Young Jack-daws?*"

As a young academic he made a name for himself with his work on jackdaws.

I shouldn't have mentioned Ludwig Kaltenburg, not at that point, because now the interpreter was no longer so focused, constantly mixing up goldfinch and goldhammer, thistle finch and yellowhammer, despite the mounts in front of her. Nor could she get the names for *Carduelis chloris*, the greenfinch, to stick in her mind. Either she couldn't connect one name with the other or one of the names did not match the bird.

"The goldfinch—isn't that this bird here with the bright yellow head and yellow belly?"

No, that's the yellowhammer, *Emberiza citrinella. Citrinella*, lemon-colored, that ought to be easy to remember. The goldfinch is what we call the *Stieglitz*. The ending of its German name betrays its Slav origins. It's onomatopoeic, supposedly, and no doubt that's why it eventually managed to establish itself on equal terms alongside the old Germanic name *Distelfink*, thistle finch. A bird translated, you might say.

But this still wasn't enough to imprint the goldfinch on the interpreter's long-term memory, her gaze seemed to be held by the cardboard boxes on top of the cupboard, DAMAGED NESTS, NO LABEL, NEST STANDS, perhaps she was avoiding looking at me. The goldfinch, strikingly colorful with a red face against its black-and-white head, brown body, the rump again white, the tail and wings—they have a yellow band, hence the "gold"—are black.

We had begun by discussing the fact that my voice had never taken on a local timbre, despite the sixty years I had spent in Dresden. Certain everyday expressions, of course, one or two constructions, and unconsciously, especially when I'm tired, a slight slurring of my speech. But for me Saxon has remained a foreign tongue. Sometimes I secretly envy people who are at home in a recognizable dialect or even just a regional inflection, I've always listened carefully, acquiring a tone here, a touch of red, a few words there, which in time ran together to form a yellow band, and I've mixed them all into my total speech picture, my parents' white High German, the

53

darker coloration of my surroundings here. You could say someone like me has a goldfinch accent, with a bit of local color picked up in every quarter.

"So I'd have to think of you as a goldfinch."

I asked the interpreter to point out the thistle finch on the desk for me.

"This colorful one," she said and drew a circle around her drawing of a goldfinch.

"And Ludwig Kaltenburg was your teacher? Of course, it's easy to forget that he taught zoology in Leipzig for years. Because he was an Austrian, I always think of him as someone whose whole life was bound up with Vienna. His famous Dresden Institute. When did he leave the GDR?"

Shortly after the Wall went up. Although I'm not quite sure that Ludwig Kaltenburg ever really was in the GDR, or whether he insisted that he lived in Dresden and simply made a few excursions from here to the GDR.

"But he left for political reasons, didn't he?"

He would have shrugged that off. "I don't understand the finer points of ideology. I'm a zoologist. Everybody contributes in his own way." And if his interlocutors should happen to shake their heads or put their finger to their lips or even look at him askance, Kaltenburg was always ready with a disarming smile, adding, "As a zoologist, however, I know that there can be no going back to conditions that have already been overcome." He would have invoked Darwin, talked about "difficult struggles" and "victory over the counterrevolution," he would have recalled the Dresden zoologist Adolf Bernhard Meyer, a passionate advocate of the theory of evolution, and finally, with expressions like "historical necessity" and "not by chance" and "in this time and place," he would have returned to his own specialization without having blotted his copybook.

Yes, there were political reasons. Or else Ludwig Kaltenburg left out of desperation.

"You got to know him as a student, in Dresden?"

It was a renewed acquaintance. Early fifties. My parents already knew Kaltenburg. If we hadn't had a shared background, he would hardly have noticed me: one of the many young people strolling along the Elbe and looking up at the Institute site in Oberloschwitz where the great Ludwig Kaltenburg lived with his animals. A not particularly gifted student in a full lecture hall whose name needed to be spelled out to you again at exam time.

8

———

POSEN MUST HAVE BEEN a strange city in my childhood. It would never have occurred to me that I was in Poland, I never heard anybody speaking Polish on the streets, Polish was prohibited in public, and I never heard the language at home either, there were Viennese, Königsberg, and Rhineland accents, but not a single word of Polish. All the roads had German names, and even the castle that you approached via Sankt-Martin-Strasse was naturally a German building. I don't know why my parents insisted on taking this route when we went into town, past that monstrous edifice, somewhere between giant prison and baronial keep. Over that short stretch of road I became completely silent and kept my head down, the distance across the square with its pond and Bismarck statue seemed to me endless, and when we went that way I fixed my eyes on the projecting, square castle tower at the end, a stone box that was always surrounded by scaffolding, just as the castle always seemed to be undergoing building work and renovation and modification, as though it were a medieval structure that had gradually fallen into disrepair through time and war and weather, perhaps in danger of collapse, certainly always under threat, while it in turn seemed to be threatening me: the walls might not be about to fall down, but two sinister bailiffs were going to leap out from the gateway, seize the nearest passerby, and drag him off to their dungeon. A dark, prehistoric fortress, and yet the castle was hardly more than thirty years old.

Everybody knew this was where the local Gauleiter was settling in, for my parents that would have been a reason to avoid this route, I don't know whether it was defiance or some compulsion that made them take me past the castle every time, grim, withdrawn, it had to be done. You didn't have to be a child to be mystified by the immense deliveries of sandstone, marble, and granite to the site. Once, I remember, we were stopped, a workman was blocking the footpath, but my father wouldn't give in, no one was going to prevent him from picking his way, hand in hand with his son, between the massive building blocks. There was almost a row, I think, we stopped, or maybe my father couldn't find a way through the stone blocks: that was when I discovered, in a polished slab of marble, my first embedded sea snail.

What a contrast to the world of the shopping arcades, how differently they greeted me, with their comfortable temperature in summer or winter, the light, the voices, where I couldn't get lost. The space was covered by a glass roof, and pigeons sat up there on the girders. I was in town with my mother, and while she was flitting between shops, soon going back to the first place she had tried, unable to decide in her search for a winter hat between rabbit, otter, and fox, I was allowed to play in the arcade: half in the open, half indoors, the daylight made the pigeons' necks shimmer as the birds swooped down from above, just over the heads of the grownups, and then flew noisily with their rather clumsy-looking flight action out onto the street.

I had time to look at everything. For a long time I crouched in front of a young beagle waiting for its mistress to return, after I had established from a safe distance that its lead was firmly tied to the ring and there wasn't too much slack in it. I knew my mother's shopping wasn't going to be a quick business, she had been at the furrier's, and now she had disappeared into the haberdasher's. I wished I could defer for as long as possible the moment when I heard my name being called, right through the arcade, people turning around to look at me, salesladies coming to their doorways to see who was missing, I would thread my way through to the familiar voice, and then as usual we would finally go over to the department store, which supplied the things we really needed.

She had chosen the otter skin. At long last my mother had also found herself a new pair of suede gloves. The climax of the department store afternoon was when we took the escalator up to the fourth floor, from one department to another, every time I looked down I felt butterflies in my stomach. Finally we had selected my warm winter underwear, they were predicting a hard winter. I wanted to go home, at last we were walking down the stairs, the last stretch, the way out, now nothing could pull us back into the showrooms that you could only see as though from a distance on every floor going down, the display stands, people, the noises, but here on the stairs, our footsteps echoing, we were no longer affected by all that activity. My mind was already fixed on the tram stop, the journey home, our kitchen, and my nanny when, just as we had almost reached the exit, there was Professor Kaltenburg coming toward us, a university colleague of my father's.

We had to say hello to him. My mother stopped on the landing, and he too, who had been purposefully striding up the stairs as though he wanted to get to the menswear department as quickly as possible, didn't just raise his hat in passing, he halted, held out his hand to my mother, stroked my head. and smiled, saying "What a surprise" and "My dear lady" and "Well, my boy?" I was pulled in different directions, I already saw myself back in our drawing room, why couldn't Professor Kaltenburg go home with us? I thought, but the two of them had already begun—a child picks this up after the first few sentences—a longish conversation in the bare, windowless staircase. Of course it had not escaped me that Kaltenburg was attracted to my mother, but then he was attached to my father too, and to me. While he was paying my mother compliments, he was looking at me: "And if you don't mind my asking such a prying question, what nice things have you been buying, then?"

She didn't show him my underwear, thank goodness, but my mother carefully took the cap, which the professor loudly admired, out of her bag, and when the gloves emerged from their tissue paper, he had an idea. He wanted to give a lady a pair of leather gloves for Christmas, could my mother spare a minute to advise him on his choice?

There he'd been, rushing upstairs, and now he had turned right around and we were going back to the beginning of our store journey, to the ground floor, from which we had long since escaped, and once more the saleslady was taking out one pair of gloves after another.

Why, I asked myself later, did this Professor Kaltenburg not use the escalator like everybody else to go upstairs in a department store? Yet another mystery about this man. Professor Kaltenburg, the first man I ever saw wearing sunglasses, Professor Kaltenburg, who came to see us on his motorbike, Professor Kaltenburg, about whom I would continue to unearth new secrets, Professor Ludwig Kaltenburg, who has had such a decisive influence on my life. He kept his secrets until the end, from using the stairs where there was an escalator to expressing radical, albeit mystifying, self-criticism in his last letters, which reached me from distant Vienna at the end of the eighties.

His keen glance, the laughter lines around his eyes. His movements, quick and exact when it came to precise actions, but at other times awkward, unsteady, seemingly given to chance fluctuations, as though his body were performing grotesque contortions without its owner's knowledge. Ludwig Kaltenburg, a falcon poised to swoop, wishing it were one of those gentle birds of passage moving steadily along in a great flock.

Now he was picking up a pair of dark tan gloves as though they were exactly what he'd been looking for all along. And then with a laugh he was pushing them back into the pile. Then he was glancing sidelong at my mother while she was pointing out the quality of the leather and solid seams of an expensive pair.

"You've got to run your hand over them carefully, here, turn the glove inside out."

I was afraid we'd never get home for supper. In the artificial light of the store it looked to me as though the day outside had ended long before. The suede leather. The animal smell. I could hardly stand the smell there.

"No, you must have got something wrong, Professor Kaltenburg is not a colleague of your father's at the university."

"But isn't he called Professor?"

"He is a professor, only in Königsberg, not here in Posen—but you know that, don't you remember, he was talking about Königsberg back there? And he's not a botanist."

I knew Königsberg, that's where Knut came from.

"So what's he doing in our city?"

My mother hesitated for a moment. "Professor Kaltenburg is a zoologist who takes care of confused people in a big mental hospital here."

"Confused?"

"Not just confused, of course—they're seriously ill."

I could tell my mother was not happy with her answer. She reflected. Then she spotted something, and: "Give the lady your seat."

I got up off the seat, a woman pushed past me as though I didn't exist, took my place without so much as a nod.

"And who was he talking about when he said he needed a nice pair of gloves for a lady?"

"His wife, of course—who did you think?"

I was standing in the gangway now, the tram was getting fuller all the time, my mother was holding on to me with one arm, the other was clasping the bags and boxes on her lap.

"Look, it's raining." And: "We'll soon be home."

But the words could not be wiped away. A zoologist who worked in a mental hospital. The smell of suede, and now the tram had stopped again, the damp steaming off the passengers' coats. Hadn't I watched a veterinary surgeon at work in a cowshed, the blood and the bellowing, the crude, bright instruments? I could see Professor Kaltenburg in a white coat, using his zoological expertise on the patients. The tram's electric contacts were sparking. Hadn't I watched badly injured people being carried on stretchers into courtyard entrances in the city, hadn't I seen bandaged heads, heard cries of pain and the "Quick, quick" of the ambulance men? Professor Kalten-burg in the posture of a falconer, his gaze turned upward and his arm outstretched: I can see him—was I already seeing him like this even then? Where does a child get such imaginings from?—in solid leather gloves, adjusting some medical apparatus whose thick cables run to a patient's bed.

9

I'D LOVE TO TAKE a close look at the bird."
With this parting sentence outside the department store
Professor Kaltenburg invited himself over to our house. My
mother had told him about our starling, which, unusually for a starling, had refused to integrate into the family, did not seek company,
didn't eat properly, and showed no sign whatsoever of the ability to
talk, a point my father had used to make me keen on the bird.

This starling wasn't our first bird, and my father had taken them
all to his heart, every single time. If you keep a careful lookout for
nests, if you find helpless nestlings that have fallen to the ground
and are either still just breathing or already completely dried up, if
you cannot get enough of the sight of a bird nursery in late spring
and the brood's first attempts at flight, sooner or later, like my father, you will bring birds into the house. It may be that he simply
couldn't resist them, or maybe it was part of his plan to gradually
accustom me to the presence of birds: soon we had our first fledglings in the conservatory, went collecting worms, gathering seeds
in the greenhouse and using them for feed, and from then on, apart
from the injured birds we took in, every spring we had orphaned
youngsters to hand-rear with egg yolk, hemp seed, linseed, and
poppy seed. Barley groats or bread rolls soaked in milk, groundsel
and chickweed, lettuce. My father in the kitchen: "No, for this one
I've got to mix some water in with the milk."

I watched my father, and the birds, but I never fed them, never cleaned their cage, I didn't even whistle, let alone touch one of these creatures. The blind, croaking, featherless, wrinkled animals in a box lined with wood shavings: I never quite dared approach them, always kept a certain distance.

"I'd love to take a close look at the bird." By the time Professor Kaltenburg came to see us, Martin had long since left. Sometimes we still got postcards, from Erfurt at first, then from Königgrätz. He always addressed them to the family, never just to the professor of botany, and their contents were intended for all of us too, the words meant for the adults, his frequent sprinkling of little drawings aimed at the child. Then the greeting cards stopped, the last one—but I may be wrong about this—came from the Crimea, about the time when the peninsula was cut off and was being vacated, so probably in November 1943.

I noticed the dust cloud from quite a distance, a motorbike was heading from town and racing at a crazy speed down our road. I rushed around the house, my father must be in his greenhouse at the back, my mother was lying down after lunch. "There he is," I shouted from the doorway, "he's here," although I couldn't see my father anywhere in the greenhouse. His head appeared at the side between the grasses, he wiped his hands on his trousers as he came toward me, and just as he was asking, "The professor?" we heard the motorbike in front of the house. Kaltenburg switched off the engine and heaved his NSU into our driveway; he was wearing leather gloves, a leather jacket, and dark glasses against the sun, which was very low in the sky at that time of day.

My nanny stood at the kitchen window. Professor Kaltenburg pushed his glasses up onto his forehead, took off his gloves, waved toward the window, glanced around as though looking for my mother, then held out his hand to my father and laughed.

"Where's our little patient, then?"

I followed Kaltenburg and my father into the conservatory. It was almost as though the starling had been waiting for us, it was hopping around in a lively manner in its cage, and as soon as my father opened the little door it jumped onto Professor Kaltenburg's

63

hand and then straight onto his shoulder and then his head. Professor Kaltenburg wasn't in the least taken aback, even when the young starling messed up his hair and started investigating the sunglasses, tugging at them until they finally fell to the ground, Kaltenburg laughed and talked to the creature. I stood to one side with my father, and later I realized that from that afternoon onward the memory of my father began to fade.

Today I know so much more about Ludwig Kaltenburg's life than I do about my own parents'. Admittedly, over the decades Kaltenburg frequently talked to me about himself, right up until his death, presenting particular episodes in varying lights—my parents were not granted that much time. But I think it started that afternoon when Kaltenburg first visited us. He was soon telling me how he had reared animals even as a child, how at that moment in Posen he didn't have the company of a single living thing, how he nearly became director of a zoo, and how in America, where his father sent him to study, he had spent all his time going to the beach to collect marine specimens, since he didn't understand a word of the lecturers' English. Kaltenburg came from Austria, was a full professor in Königsberg, and spent some time in Posen. The places where my parents had lived—I can't think of any apart from Posen, except for our stay in Dresden. Where did they grow up, where did they meet, where did my father study? Where did we live before we moved to Posen? Did they share a common past in Dresden? I knew nothing about any of it.

In Posen they must have been regarded as outsiders, otherwise it's hard to explain why I have so few pictures in my mind of my parents' social life. I can't remember any social occasions at home, it may be that my father really was rather isolated among his colleagues. Perhaps that was why he put so much effort into cultivating Kaltenburg's friendship, just as Kaltenburg did into gaining his. Although they were both in their late thirties, I envisage my father as the younger man and Kaltenburg as the older of the two, no doubt because of later images, snow-white hair framing a tanned face radiating health.

"Is it really true," I asked him, "that you took some live ducks with you to Königsberg, and all the other professors were amazed?"

"Yes, I did, by the crateful, and I lugged fish over there as well, and kept them in the institute."

Professor Kaltenburg has become world-famous, but I have never yet discovered whether my father was a leading light in his subject, and in later years, to spare myself painful memories of him, I have never looked up my father's books or articles. As an adult, however, I have been comforted to hear from Knut, Martin, and others who attended his lectures at the University of Posen that he was a good teacher who inspired enthusiasm in his students for the plant world. And given the unspectacular nature of most botanical phenomena, that is no mean feat.

Kaltenburg inquired in detail about the feed we were giving the starling, about its care, my father answered obligingly, Kaltenburg nodded, Professor Kaltenburg shook his head, he asked whether my father had caught and reared the bird himself, no, he had bought it, Kaltenburg wanted to know who from, while the starling was continually looking for new places in the conservatory from which to fly at the professor, my father named the dealer, and Kaltenburg shrugged: "I know him well, of course, and I've got to say he's reliable enough."

The two of them arranged that Kaltenburg should take care of the bird himself for a few days so that he could observe it. They looked at me as though my agreement mattered to them, I nodded, I didn't mind, I wasn't attached to the bird. Privately I hoped Professor Kaltenburg would succeed where my father hadn't, and teach it to talk.

Our guest didn't want any tea, at any rate not just yet, perhaps later, my mother would join us. But he would be interested in a tour of the greenhouse. He let my father show him his favorite plants; Kaltenburg kept giving him a sharp, or rather surprised, sidelong glance while my father immersed himself in his plant world. My father was attracted by the less conspicuous, often overlooked grasses, herbs, flowers, his interest wasn't sparked by the cultivated type, and ultimately not even by any that grew from seed sown by human hand. Then it was my father's turn to suddenly raise his head and take a sidelong look at Kaltenburg as the latter examined a plant which had recently been brought in. Two men, as it might have seemed to an observer, who were doing some cautious footwork around each other for the moment, as though unclear whether this was leading to a friendship or was just preparation for a fight.

Striped goosefoot and fat-hen, spreading orach, redroot amaranth, black nightshade, and smooth sow thistle: my father showed me them all on our walks, I can still recite them by heart, but soon I'll have forgotten them again. Oblong-leaf orach and flixweed or tansy mustard, wall rocket, prickly lettuce, Canadian horseweed: my father regularly audited the railway embankment not far from the house. "Look, we've never seen these tiny flowers before, and the panicle there." He crawled around in the grass, carefully freeing the roots with a trowel. And up there on the embankment the slow-moving trains, made up of a few passenger cars and countless cattle wagons, in which the animals never stirred, where are they heading for? I asked my father.

"To the east—don't you know your compass points?"

I learned to distinguish white from black henbane, my father held up two stalks with hairy leaves and small flowers, "You must never, ever touch this plant, or that one, do you understand?" Whether it was black or white henbane, "I warn you—if I ever catch you with either of them," the green, yellow, white, black flowers, my father warned me, but he never got as far as a threat.

What kind of mental picture was that? I wonder suddenly, flocks from beyond the Urals and from the plains to the west, the beautiful dusky plumage, here shimmering like freshly boiled pitch, there matte black like tar that has become brittle with cold, and then in places this fine ash-gray layer, like that on smoldering old wood that no breath of wind has touched for a long while.

Professor Kaltenburg took enough birdfeed with him for the next few days. We fussed over fastening the blanket-covered cage to the luggage rack of his motorbike. All three of us were waving: my father, my mother, and me.

When the starling came back to its familiar surroundings it seemed a different bird, so interested and alert as it investigated the plants, its sleeping quarters, the whole conservatory. But it never did learn to talk.

10

—

I HAVE TO FORCE MYSELF to recall the last clear visual memories I have of my father, as though I were afraid, as I was then, of meeting his eye. I stand there hanging my head—the stone floor of the hall, the wooden boards in the conservatory, the carpet in our drawing room—and I can no longer see my father's face. Shame? Certainly I lowered my eyes because I felt shame, I was ashamed because my father had been shamed. Pain too, for sure, because if you let pain happen to someone else, if you don't protect him and then don't even ease his pain afterward, you yourself feel hurt. But worse still was the betrayal. I didn't look my father in the eye because I had betrayed him, and knew that he knew it as well as I did.

I was hanging around in the conservatory with our tame starling. When can that have been? Kaltenburg's first visit took place in the late autumn of 1942, and from then on close contacts developed between the two of them. My father was going to meet Professor Kaltenburg in town after his lecture. No, Maria had better count him out for dinner, he had arranged to see Kaltenburg, who had promised to give him a copy of his latest article. "Most interesting as usual, what he's got to say about the differences between wild and domestic animals. But 'interesting' is not the word—this essay will be epoch-making, no doubt about it. And then please remember that the professor is coming over for a meal on Friday."

I have a feeling that Professor Kaltenburg even spent a Christmas with us. So it went on, for at least one winter. And then, in spring, or by the summer of 1943 at the latest, if not 1944, at home the name Kaltenburg was deleted from our vocabulary from one day to the next.

The bird sand crunched beneath my feet, I was leaning on the back of the armchair between the indoor palm and the rubber tree trying to keep quiet, moving my mouth silently as though still trying to teach our starling to talk. His cage, its door usually stood open, and in the corner the box with the injured blue-throat, and then all the equipment, feeding bowls and water bowls, pipettes, wooden rods, seed mixtures, accumulated over time to form an immense armory. The door of my father's study was ajar, the low voices of two men in the background, and by concentrating hard I could make out a sentence here or there, especially when Professor Kaltenburg was speaking.

"I can give you a cast-iron guarantee."

The starling—didn't we ever give it a name?—was pecking around in the pot of the rubber tree, it wasn't particularly interested in me, it never landed on my head as it did with the professor.

"In that case, I feel reassured."

My father, more quietly, speaking as though he and Kaltenburg were not sitting in the same room. I was still trying to guess what they were talking about, all the while ready to make out that I was busy with our starling, in case anyone came in.

"As far as the other matter is concerned, well, we've talked about that often enough."

They laughed. Then my father was obviously waiting for Kaltenburg to go on.

"The blue-throat."

"Yes?"

Did the starling really have to poke around in the dry rubber-tree leaves at that precise moment? I was powerless, because if I shooed it away I would be discovered. I reached out for it very slowly, I still didn't know whether I was actually going to take hold of the bird, but then it fluttered away, into the palm tree. My father and Professor Kaltenburg were now talking more loudly.

"You know my opinion, and I'm sticking to it."

"Please, that's ridiculous, just because of a blue-throat with a broken wing."

Up to that point their talk had seemed half joking, but now I wasn't so sure. Somebody walked restlessly up and down, was it my father, was it Kaltenburg, somebody lit a cigarette, somebody closed the window.

"Yes, it's harmful to take on injured animals, I don't mean for the animal, but for your boy."

"Kindness to the creature is harmful? Just tell me, where's the harm in arousing a child's sympathy for the suffering of a living being?"

My father's voice faltered. Kaltenburg, on the other hand—it seemed that the more agitated his interlocutor became, the calmer he was.

"You want to help, but you can't. An animal that has no chance of surviving in the wild won't do so under your well-meaning but misguided care either."

"But all the same, it's absurd to talk about an atmosphere of death."

"An atmosphere of death": that was the first and only time I ever heard my father use that phrase. It was a Kaltenburg expression. My father did his best to sound as though he were putting it in quotation marks, a dubious construction that could have come only from an Austrian. He imitated a Viennese accent, trying to wound Kaltenburg, to silence him. But Kaltenburg was not so easily hurt; indeed, Professor Kaltenburg found it easy to ignore such attacks.

"Tell me straight out, and then I'll forever hold my peace: has there really been a single occasion when you succeeded in rescuing a sick or injured animal, have any of these birds ever survived, have you managed to return any of them to the wild?"

My nanny was calling me. Otherwise it was quiet. Kaltenburg

was genial, he was waiting, he was in no hurry, my father should take his time before answering. He wasn't interested in scoring a point in this contest between two grown men, what he cared about was "the boy," me. I could see him sitting at my father's desk, his hands resting on the leather writing mat, to his left an open botanical reference book, an ashtray on the right. Kaltenburg leaned back while my father, a guest in his own room, searched for an answer.

For a long time, neither man spoke. Kaltenburg stood firm. The atmosphere of death, he insisted, would affect me, might determine my relationship with the world.

My father was no longer walking up and down. Then he said, almost inaudibly, "No."

Maria was calling. I found it hard to take my eyes off the blue-throat in its box. Eventually I was being called from the kitchen for the third time, I turned away. It wasn't until I was an adult that I gradually began to grasp what Kaltenburg, who refused to be put off by my father that afternoon, meant by "atmosphere of death": he told me about his time as a POW, or the thoughts he had about Dresden in his darker hours, and how he had always shrunk from certain people, certain places, as though scared of being exposed to a pathogen for which there was no effective remedy. When I was listening from the other room that day, "atmosphere of death" simply hovered in the air as a mere phrase with which I associated as little as I did with those opening sentences I had heard through the open door, Kaltenburg's friendly words: "I can give you a cast-iron guarantee," and my father's reply: "In that case, I feel reassured."

Is this the atmosphere of death? I wondered in bed that night, because Professor Kaltenburg did not stay as planned, my father spent the evening in his study, he came out briefly to eat. The two men had parted with a handshake but without saying a word—did that mean we had been plunged into a permanent atmosphere of death? I had to keep reminding myself that this was all over nothing but a sick blue-throat, but nonetheless after Kaltenburg's departure something weighed heavily on the house.

My mother looked in on me. She too was agitated, I could tell by the way she fiddled with her blouse as she sat on the edge of my bed trying to explain the argument to me: "We know we're not running a veterinary practice. But the professor has no right to interfere in your education, that's our job, you are our child. How do we know what other views Professor Kaltenburg holds that might influence a young boy—a boy who is basically a stranger to him—without the parents ever finding out about it? But this outburst of Kaltenburg's probably has nothing to do with birds or with you, he's simply over-wrought. No, this awful animal business isn't important—which makes the rift between your father and Professor Kaltenburg all the more tragic."

An image of crows, I can't quite place it, flickers briefly in my memory: at first you see a single scout, loudly croaking in all directions, and the next minute the sky blackens. Enormous flocks from Siberia. Flocks from the Elbe region. Rooks, hooded crows, carrion crows, they join forces in winter.

The way he pulled on his helmet, got on his motorbike, disappeared over the horizon: as if Kaltenburg—who had wistfully stroked my hair just one last time—was leaving us to our fate, as if all his efforts to persuade had been in vain, and we would never see him again. But I wanted to see Professor Kaltenburg again. I haggled with myself—if I nodded at the professor's words, even if I could barely comprehend them, did it mean that I was betraying my parents? Did I have to declare myself either for my father and mother or for Kaltenburg?

A blue-throat with a broken wing: if I'd had my way, we would have put the bird out in the garden, Professor Kaltenburg would come back without hesitation, the friendship would be renewed, and this depressing day forgotten.

Siberian crows love being swept along on the first flurries of a snowstorm, their wings spread out on the wind as black as briquettes, the snowflakes dancing around their plumage. And there's something glowing, a red glow, a bluish glow, as well as a soft brown. A jay that memorized the whereabouts of its food caches in its sleep.

Ludwig Kaltenburg was to initiate me into the laws of the animal world, show me what they could do and where their limits were, where we humans make unreasonable demands on animals and are disappointed when they don't live up to our expectations. Why is it that children turn so willingly to such minor players as Professor Kaltenburg and are prepared to forgive them everything? Since he was competing with the professor, my father had not the least chance of prevailing with his own son.

It wasn't until three decades later that I discovered the real cause of the break between Kaltenburg and my father. I wasn't trying to find out, it simply hit me in the face one day, I couldn't avoid it, and to this day it gives me a stab of pain to the heart whenever I think how late the discovery came, too late for me to apologize to my long-dead father and take his side.

11

WHERE DID I FIRST SEE that image of crows? In its density, its darkness, a flock of uniformly black rooks, among them a few hooded crows, I could easily make them out by their gray markings. And now the gray patches were wheeling away, drawing the black ones with them, the cloud lurched to one side and out of the picture.

"They said on the radio that Paris has been liberated."

My father tapped the cigarette ash on the side of his cup. It sizzled in the cold tea. Astonished, he raised his eyes from his newspaper and pushed the cup aside. "Not a word about these things outside this house, remember, not to your friends, not at school," he said to me, as though he'd given too much away.

I can still see the way my mother laughed, though I can't remember why, I can see her freshly starched white blouse. Was it the same one she wore for Kaltenburg's last visit? Irritated, my father folded the newspaper.

"What an unbearably stupid rag."

And my mother, getting a clean cup from the cupboard: "Oh come on, don't take it so much to heart."

By then it was a long time since we'd had any visitors. Professor Kaltenburg was on active service, from what we'd heard Knut must be in Crete, and we had no idea where Martin was. My father lit another cigarette, glanced out at the garden, suddenly the room was filled with bright sunshine, the stove, the edge of the armchair, and the triangle on the carpet, my father narrowed his eyes as though hatching a plan.

There they sat with their son in the drawing room, this ill-matched couple, my parents. My mother, with hair pinned up, was brushing at the cloth on the small table as though there were crumbs to sweep away. She was always drawn to the city, and at first she may not have been altogether keen on this house at the edge of the fields. "But just think of the child," my father will have said, and she had given way, her husband needed to be close to nature, in the concrete desert among so many people he would wither away, and it wasn't that far to the tram terminus, to the stores, cafés, and arcades. Building work on the castle had stopped some time before.

Another event comes to mind—when was it, on the same day he mentioned Paris, did it follow Professor Kaltenburg's disappearance, and was there some connection between the two things?

Of course, at that time my father had to work on useful plants. Cereal yields needed to be increased. There was a feverish race on to replace petroleum with vegetable oils. New medicines were required for the wounded. But his private greenhouse was his own domain, for a long time my father had succeeded in fending off all claims on it. His wild grasses he owed to the wind, to the animals, and to travelers who unwittingly brought back seeds from all over the world, on their shoes, on their sleeves. And the specially heated corner for exotics—I can remember the times when I was allowed to put my hand into the glass casing, very still, warm—and my father was scared that even a grownup like Professor Kaltenburg might be careless enough to break off a bloom.

Yet now, in the wake of the intensive educational measures introduced for his son's benefit, the botanist had become passionate about bird life. Which, as one can well imagine, created considerable problems, since birds do not just perch picturesquely on branches and savor the amenities offered by plants, rather in the manner of museum visitors; they are also inclined to feed on this attractive display. All the same, my father continued to bring birds into the house, and never once complained as, in the course of time, they devoured everything. It even seemed to me that he actually encouraged the birds to help themselves to the rarest specimens in the botanical inventory, and derived immense pleasure—verging on insanity, as I now think—from seeing whether a native bird enjoyed the flavor of a foreign flower. But perhaps he was pleased because, like any other child, I took a boundless delight in this destruction, not, as some people would imagine, out of childish brutality, but because of a child's certainty that this world, which for adults is solid and fixed, is continuously changing. When I think what our conservatory looked like toward the end . . .

Presumably at some point, from one day to the next, my father was forced to replace the collection he had painstakingly assembled in the greenhouse over the years. That's how I see it today. A moment which must have represented a great defeat for him. To me it was a riotous plant-feast. Perhaps that helped my father take his mind off the despair.

Early in the evening he came to fetch me from the kitchen, where I was sitting as my mother and nanny were planning the coming week. He put a finger to his lips, I was supposed to slip out of the kitchen unobtrusively—yet everybody except me was surely in the know about what was going on. I followed him into the conservatory, which scarcely warranted its name of "winter garden," since by then it contained hardly any green plants, just bare, half-chewed stems with a few isolated dried-out leaves languishing in their pots. My father told me to entice the tame bird we had reared out of its cage, which always stood open. Was it the nameless starling? Or another bird, a blackbird? I can't remember. Walking through the garden, my father held the bird carefully, only releasing it when we had reached the greenhouse and the door was shut behind us.

Apparently everything had been planned well in advance, my father had made a space by clearing away pots and tools and had brought in garden chairs. Hour after hour, until it got dark, we watched the bird setting about the plants, rooting around in the garden mold, plucking the fresh shoots, and pecking fiercely at the juicy leaves until they were an indefinable green mass, more like chopped spinach. We sat watching as though spellbound, made friendly bets on which plant the bird would move on to next, trying to outdo each other in estimating how much damage an individual plant would suffer.

I woke up in the middle of the night. From the garden came a regular scraping noise, interrupted by a longish pause. I didn't get up, didn't go to the window, I didn't even open my eyes. I knew: my father was sweeping up the plant debris next to the greenhouse. The next day all the beds were freshly laid out with castor-oil plants.

12

I T WAS VERY EARLY in the morning, not yet light. I listened. Nobody in the house seemed to be awake. Ice on my window, not a glimpse of the world outside. But if I was the only one awake, then I was alone, because it meant my nanny wasn't up yet either, and she always got up before us and lit the oven. I left the bedroom in my pajamas, no light in the corridor, and as I was placing one bare foot in front of the other on the stairs, half hesitant and half impatient, a word came to my mind. I didn't know what it meant, I didn't know where I'd heard it, but I could hear it being spoken quietly in my nanny's voice: "*Jerzyk.*"

Slowly, with the word echoing in my ears, slowly I opened the kitchen door: my nanny was sitting at the table under the lamp, her cardigan around her shoulders, she looked across at me: "Why are you so surprised? Still asleep? Aren't you going to say good morning? Or has something happened?"

I shook my head and went to the stove, where she laid out my clothes every morning. This must be a scene from the winter before we left Posen. So my nanny can't have been fired after all.

Maria. I don't have as many memories of my nanny as I should. And this is the last of them. Besides, they are rather hazy, shot through with doubts, nor have they gained in clarity with age. I have no idea what became of her. Maria's arms were soft, and I was always surprised just how soft such slender arms could be. I can remember her scent, I would recognize it anywhere today. As if she ate fruit whose aroma permeated her skin and filled the air. Her hair—I remember Maria having very fine hair, I can see every strand of it above her small ears, how it hugged her head, combed back and pinned down. But its color—my memory ranges between brunette and black. As if memory depended on the angle of the light. Maria's hair in the late afternoon when she was urging me to do my homework. When I was allowed to play out in the garden until dark. Maria's hair when she put me to bed. The way it shone in the early morning over the stove with the glow from the iron hotplate.

I got dressed, Maria made cocoa, shoved a log into the range fire, it was almost ten to seven by the big kitchen clock. I stood at the cold window in trousers and pullover, snow was falling. It would soon be light, the snow on the ground had a violet shimmer, as if illuminated from inside. I could no longer hear the half-sung Polish word, the voice had stopped perhaps when Maria spoke to me from her place at the table as I came in. Soon the roof of the house next door would be indistinguishable from the sky, and the snow a deep blue expanse. It would rapidly turn light blue like the coverlet on a child's crib, and under a blue-gray sky it would finally take on a white coloration. Then the day's first Siberian crows would let the wind carry them in the gentle snowfall.

"Come on, your cocoa is ready."

I turned round. Only then did I notice the suitcases in the corner by the kitchen bench.

13

———

Jerzyk. the swift. My first Polish word, as I realized years later, talking to a Polish colleague. Maria must have uttered it on the evening of my confrontation with the swift in the drawing room, while I sat huddled on the kitchen bench bewildered by what was happening to me. That childhood experience had changed me, no doubt about that, but I'm sure I would have regarded it as no more than an isolated incident but for another bird encounter shortly after we arrived in Dresden. Once again my parents were absent, and this time they probably never found out about it. Although, it now occurs to me, they might have experienced the same thing at the same time, if they were alive.

I am talking about the birds I saw that night in the Great Garden. In the darkness I couldn't be at all sure it was birds, which made these objects, these things, these clumps all the more sinister. I didn't understand what they were until the sun had come up, pale sun, hidden behind black, gray-black clouds of smoke that covered the horizon and towered high into the sky.

That night, as I was wandering through the park, something hit me hard on the shoulder. Not a punch, not an animal pouncing on me from behind, nor a broken branch spinning through the air and splintering on the ground. The sound was both muffled and solid, and when the object touched the ground it rolled on for a bit. I picked it up, rather sticky, crumbly, its surface rough, I lifted it to eye level, a lump of tar perhaps, or just a cinder. I put my nose to it—but in a reflex reaction I hurled it as far away as I could. What I had smelled was burned flesh.

The next blow was to my head. I raced off. I tore around between the trees and craters and people in the clearing, and the longer I raced, the more desperate my situation seemed, these clumps were falling everywhere, and even when I thought I might catch my breath, at the exposed root of a massive oak or in the shadow of a freestanding wall, I could hear them hitting the ground all around me, getting nearer, closing in on me, these birds falling dead from the sky.

Woodpeckers that had escaped from their hole in a burning tree. A tawny owl on the hunt torn out of its normally stoic, deathlike calm by the outbreak of fire and the noise of the bombers, flapping wildly in an effort to put out the flames that had moved from its tail coverts to its secondary feathers. And wood pigeons which had shot up into the air when the din started, to fly toward the Elbe, and in those tremendous temperatures had been incinerated in midflight even at high altitudes. The many ducks, crowded together in the ice-free area of a pond, where they felt safe from all enemies: how could I tell a spoonbill from a teal, or a widgeon or a tufted duck, or a goldeneye or a pochard, since all were burned on the water at the same time?

Maybe some animals in the Great Garden were simply vaporized. Crows, of course, enormous flocks of rooks, hooded and carrion crows, roosting up in the trees. There may have been one or two bramblings among the birds. And waxwings, which, arriving from the north in the depths of winter, were unexpectedly roasted that night.

The entire stock of birds spending the night in the park appeared to have gone up in flames, one after another. I thought I could identify the remains of some species next morning despite their disfiguration, insofar as the heat had not reduced them to formless matter, to ashes, or to nothing at all. The migratory birds, it seems, had come to a considered decision to take off in the autumn, as if they wisely foresaw what was to happen here in February.

A singed mute swan with a featherless neck and bare wings, apparently no longer fully conscious, fell tottering onto its side as it tried to stand up, stayed there in a daze for a while, and then tried to get up again—it was then that I noticed it simply had no feet.

Flamingos too, if I remember rightly, I saw a row of bald, deep gray flamingos, which must have fled from the bombed-out zoo into the Great Garden. The firestorm must have burned off their gorgeous pink plumage, they were only just recognizable by their large bills, charred and slightly twisted. The burned-horn smell, bags of skin, like leather, but still keeping their shape, as though a shock process had drawn off all their body fluids, which is in fact what had happened. Mummified creatures, the flamingos required only embalming and binding with cloth to become bird mummies like the sacred ibises of ancient Egypt.

I ran. And I talked. I must have been talking aloud to myself while I walked next day, the fourteenth of February, through this city I didn't know—and on that morning it would not have been recognized by its long-term inhabitants. The day before I had quietly followed my mother as she pointed out an architectural detail here, remembered an episode from her Dresden years there, and when we sat in the café in the afternoon I simply gazed with astonishment at the street scene as I was spooning up my cocoa. But now I was wandering through the streets talking loudly, and perhaps if I had kept my mouth shut I wouldn't have been noticed and subsequently picked up, for on this Ash Wednesday there were countless people walking around Dresden, looking for relatives or for their own houses. I have no memory of the third air raid, at midday: did I follow the crowds to the Elbe meadows, did I try to shelter beyond the station? All I know is that everywhere I went it was burning, from dawn to sunset. Buildings were collapsing, the howling in the air, and yet aboveground an almost rural stillness spread through the city, no shouting or calling, people staring silently into the flames as if mesmerized by the crackling. It's possible that by the noon air raid I had long since put the city behind me and was wandering through a suburb, in the direction of Heidenau: a lone figure who wouldn't stop talking when spoken to or questioned. I don't know what I was saying or who spoke to me, or what their questions or advice may have been—perhaps that's why to this day I have no memory of the last hours of my parents' lives, perhaps it was fully explained to me that same evening or soon after, and not a word of it sank in.

14

———

WHATEVER HAPPENED TO my mistrust? It had evaporated the moment Katharina Fischer stepped into the Zoological Collection. I told her how Ludwig Kaltenburg had warned me repeatedly, "Watch out for female interpreters, especially the young, pretty ones who are amenable to a private conversation outside official talks, even if it's only a few words. Yes, they keep their eyes open, all the time, and they are better listeners than anybody else."

I would put the birds I had lined up back in their glass cases later, and before I went home I would linger for a while in the windowless room with our native finches. Frau Fischer had collected her things, notebook and pencil; I handed her the *Peterson*, which she had nearly forgotten. The loaded backpack was slung over her shoulder, I locked the egg sets away.

"Have you followed your teacher's advice, then?"

For forty years. Sometimes Professor Kaltenburg struck a confidential note, at other times he proclaimed his warning with burning intensity. And yet it was completely unnecessary, in my case at least. Unlike Kaltenburg, I have never led a delegation, and I've never been offered the services of an interpreter for my own personal use—after all, I'm no great authority, I've never been the guest of honor anywhere. And anyway, he wasn't revealing any secrets to me. An interpreter had to be reliable, absolutely trustworthy, dedicated, attentive, and communicative. Everybody knew that.

"If everyone was in the picture and choosing their words carefully, was there also an unspoken agreement among colleagues not to be distracted by the finer points of ideology, as Ludwig Kaltenburg put it?"

Neither by the finer points nor by the crudeness. Naturally there are always people who don't feel bound by agreements. But without international exchanges we and our subject would have gone under a long time ago. At this very moment, for example, as we stand in this normally quiet corridor, countless birds are traveling around the globe, no longer under their own wing power but in padded envelopes, while our specimens lie on desks in distant foreign institutes where colleagues are studying them intensively. Observing and collecting go on everywhere, all the time. No matter what the conditions, you might say that an ornithologist is someone committed, first and foremost, to the world of birds.

There was one more thing I wanted to show Katharina Fischer before she left. She followed me into the skin collection, which in contrast to the egg collection may initially have a sobering effect on the visitor: there are no old glass cases or wooden cabinets here, no mounted specimens and egg sets on black cotton wool. The rows of compact fitted pull-out cupboards give no clue to their contents. Close to the door, the first big worktable, there are others stretching right back to the end of the room. Your eyes search involuntarily for somewhere to rest in this space.

Frau Fischer viewed with interest what was lying at the front of the table: the latest arrival, which had come in the day before from the taxidermist, a young greenfinch sent by a private donor, its neck probably broken by a windowpane. Your eyes range over the yellow propoxur flakes used to control museum beetle, over the transparent bags used for freezing the birds, which are then taken one by one out of the deep freeze for treatment, and over the array of letters requesting loan items.

There is a regular exchange, so that if a colleague indicates, however discreetly, that he is afraid he is about to go mad, then without any ifs or buts you will send him the assistance he needs. Especially as it often takes only a small gesture to help the endangered person, perhaps with a supply of bird rings. This was the request from a British ornithologist, interned in a POW camp in Bavaria, sent in 1944 to his colleague Reinhold in Berlin. In order to keep himself occupied and avoid his fellow prisoners' dull activities, he had begun to observe the barn swallows in the camp. From morning till night he kept an eye on the nests the birds had built under the hut roofs, watched them as they brooded, as they reared their young, and he hit upon the idea of using this empty, open-ended time to do some research. But in order to find out which mating pairs used the same nest for their second brood as for the first, he had to ring the swallows.

"Reinhold sent him some bird rings?"

Yes, even though he was not very pleased with our wartime opponents, especially since they had dropped a high-explosive bomb on the songbird hall of his Natural History Museum.

The interpreter shook her head, as though emerging from a daydream back into the real world. Perhaps outsiders always need a little time, some quiet moments to get used to this unusual room, before you can show them some carefully chosen specimens. A bird skin—I had picked up the young greenfinch from the table—must feel good lying in your hand, when you see it you should really want to hold it. But however well the specimen is prepared, painstakingly stuffed with wadding, its feathers perfectly preserved and carefully dressed, the most important thing about it is the label. The species name, of course, date and place where found, the finder himself, data on size and sex, sometimes the taxidermist's name and any toxic material used in the preparation—if these details are missing, then even the most superb skin ceases to be a research specimen and becomes a mere decorative object.

"So an individual bird not only supplies information about itself and its species but will also tell you something about the people who discovered, named, and prepared it, and possibly last saw it alive."

The name of Gustav Kramer on a label will remind any ornithologist that this colleague discovered how birds navigate by a solar compass, and he will also be reminded that Kramer was killed in 1959 during a mountain tour in southern Italy trying to climb up to the nest of a pair of rock pigeons.

I led Frau Fischer to a pull-out cabinet and opened a drawer containing sections of our finch collection. The birds lay tightly packed, finches from Russia, finches from Italy. A rock sparrow from Kazakhstan, where our own thistle finch and their gray-head meet and intermingle. Our last large consignment of finches came from Görlitz, where the customs people had confiscated the birds on their way from Belarus to a Brussels restaurant. All those already dead on arrival at the German border were passed on to us. In a second drawer there were Saxon finches from the last one hundred and fifty years. The offspring of a linnet and a thistle finch, next to it a cross between a finch and a canary, such as breeders commonly used to produce.

"So when you look at bird skins you see people you know."

Or used to know. Friends. I felt that more keenly than ever before during the preparations for the move from the city center out to the collection's new building. During the few weeks I spent going through all the holdings, I examined skins that I hadn't seen for years, and while I was packing up in one department after another I found that beside the systematic organization of the collection a completely different network of connections had developed. Birds I had first come across in a film by Knut Sieverding turned out to be in the same drawer as a species discovered by the aforementioned Reinhold—and it was Reinhold who had helped Knut to land his first big filming commission. Night herons, great tits, birds of paradise, magpies, starlings, a crow from Ludwig Kaltenburg's Institute, lay next to a glassy-eyed crow collected by Christian Ludwig Brehm in 1810 and personally prepared by him: I found new interconnections everywhere.

And then, installing everything here in its new space, I noticed two bird skins which had lain peaceably side by side for more than half a century. One was a representative of a subspecies of reed bunting, unfortunately no longer officially recognized, on which someone—no doubt one of my predecessors—had bestowed the binomial second term *kaltenburgi*, in honor of Ludwig Kaltenburg. The other was an ordinary local reed bunting prepared by Eberhard Matzke, whom Kaltenburg would later stubbornly insist on seeing as his powerful adversary.

"I can imagine it sometimes feels a bit uncanny when you know the birds so well. Or is it the other way round—the more you know about them, the more familiar they become?"

I pushed the drawer back into the cabinet. Katharina Fischer still had to pick up her coat. If I had observed correctly, in the course of the afternoon the birds had become more familiar to her too, although we hadn't done much more than bandy names around and keep our eyes carefully fixed on the row of finches as we did so. I asked her if she remembered the chaffinch sitting on a branch.

"Certainly."

That chaffinch used to be Martin Spengler's pet bird. That is to say, it lived in the room Martin used as a studio and where he slept, you couldn't call it an apartment. One day the chaffinch simply dropped off its perch. Such a small organism can't take too much turpentine in the atmosphere. It might now be numbered among the forgotten birds if Martin hadn't bequeathed it to the collection.

As we were about to say our goodbyes, it occurred to Frau Fischer to ask me what had made me take a special interest in goldfinches. "Was it while you were a child in Posen?"

No, not until later, when both Posen and childhood were behind me. For me the goldfinch was associated with Dresden. There was a chaotic time lasting several months, or maybe it was only weeks, when I stayed in various places, and I could easily have finished up in an orphanage but for a family that was prepared to take an orphan along with their own three children. I never really felt at home there, though the parents tried hard. But I suppose by the age of eleven, or almost twelve, you're too old to fit in with a new family. I soon began roaming about in the more deserted parts of the city, the mounds of rubble, the thistle-covered areas, it was the thistles that brought the goldfinches to Dresden.

She nodded, thanked me, shook my hand, and turned to go. The rain had stopped. Then she turned around again in the doorway to say, "If you'd like, I'll phone and let you know how the job went."

It was getting dark, I saw Katharina Fischer getting into her car, she gave me a last wave, her brake lights came on briefly, and the engine started. The car turned out of the car park into the drive, the red taillights disappeared, and while the glass door was slowly closing before me, I recalled how hard it was for me as a child to accept that what we called a sea swallow was not a swallow but a tern, and what we knew as an Alpine crow was not related to the crow family at all but was a kind of chough, and so on with a whole host of names—I just couldn't get it into my head that birds are not attached to their names in the way we are attached to names, even when we know they're misleading. No matter how well my parents explained it to me, they could name as many species as they liked, I simply refused to accept that the mountain finch didn't live in the mountains, the oystercatcher did not live on oysters, and the plumage of the purple gallinule was not purple but indigo through and through. It certainly didn't help when my parents persisted in telling me that my exciting discovery about the swift had been due to the fact that despite its Latin name it does have legs—I didn't want to hear anything about swifts. Today I know all about the bastardized Latin and Greek, about the crude misunderstandings and twisted spellings, the hair-raising mistakes of translation and observation. All the same, I have never quite given up thinking that you have to get to know every single bird individually to learn anything about the unique characteristics of its kind.

III

1

———

ONCE KEPT JACKDAW specimens under my nose for six weeks. It must have been in the midsixties, and I've never forgotten the smell of jackdaw since. You won't know what I mean unless you know their characteristic smell. Rather pungent. If you filter out the overriding smell of naphthalene, it smells like leather at first. Having pinned down this smell in turn, if you go on holding the specimen to your nose, it will feel more and more as though you have a powder on your tongue that just won't mix with saliva. A hint of burned tar when you rub it between your fingers. But not of cold ash. No, cold ash would have upset me.

A Danish colleague had asked me to check out something for him in connection with our jackdaws, I think beak anomalies were his field, and he was following up some ideas arising from the work he had done on jackdaws in recent years. It was a favor, a routine investigation such as we often undertake for each other; you send a specimen for comparison to someplace on the other side of the world, and only if the colleague there notices any discrepancies do you make the trip yourself to look at the foreign bird specimens. To carry out this friendly act with the utmost conscientiousness will not have taken me long, since I knew our jackdaws so well, but then they lay—while the Danish specimen had long since been returned to its homeland—half the winter long on the desk in front of me. They were Ludwig Kaltenburg's jackdaws.

I can see the jackdaws at play in the Dresden sky above the slopes of the Elbe valley, as though putting on a performance for me and Ludwig Kaltenburg, standing on the big balcony. And Kaltenburg, who must have watched this display countless times, who had surely never known a sunset over the city without the black dots wheeling in the evening sky above, was following their mock aerial battles, nosedives, and antics as if his protégés were showing off their skills purely for the visitor's benefit. Soon he was completely absorbed in the sight of his jackdaw flock, which made its way home at dusk. It was as though he were seeing them for the first time.

I never saw Kaltenburg so concerned about any of his other animals as he was about the jackdaws. I remember him giving me a protracted explanation of why they needed bringing in every evening. Protracted, not because Kaltenburg expressed himself in complicated sentences or because his language wasn't vivid — there was no one who could describe something as clearly as Professor Kaltenburg. No, protracted because while talking to me he was on the roof waving his arms about to call the jackdaws in. I was holding the ladder, just watching his feet on the top rung, and trying to work out which way Kaltenburg would be flinging his upper body next. He stretched up, gesticulating, started to wobble, and at the same time turned toward me as I gripped the ladder tightly down below.

A jackdaw has no innate fear of natural predators, it has to learn from its parents the likely form in which mortal danger will appear. But most of Kaltenburg's jackdaws had been used to people since the day they were hatched, to a human being who had no fear of cats or birds of prey, so if the professor did not want to lose them, he had no choice but to lure his birds back to the cage for the night. It took one or two hours every night — up to a point the creatures would willingly follow him into the room, but then they would take off again, playing with their flightless comrade, trying to draw him up to the roof ridge, until Kaltenburg finally had them all safe inside.

You can't get the smell of these birds off your fingers. You can spend several minutes washing your hands, soap and disinfectant and sand, you can scrub your fingertips until they bleed: it's no use, the slightest trace develops into a tremendous olfactory memory. You mustn't touch a live jackdaw when its fellows are nearby—they invariably see it as an attack. How often had one of Kaltenburg's birds hacked at the back of his hand just because he had gently picked up another jackdaw, which resolutely refused to be led into the cage? And here was I, bending over the dead jackdaws, pushing them around on the desk, with unpecked hands to which their smell was clinging.

Every morning I arrived very early at the collection, setting to work with numb fingers, and every time I had the feeling that the jackdaw skins in their protective feather coats had retained some of the warmth of my hands overnight. While the winter cold seeped slowly out of my limbs, the space gradually turned into a jackdaw room. I postponed the work in hand. Let a colleague go to the bird dealer instead of me. My article on the migratory movements and distribution of the thistle finch was supposed to be submitted by January. I withdrew. There was no space on my desk for finch specimens. When the sun shone on my back at midday, I was enveloped in a jackdaw cloud.

The skins included Taschotschek, a descendant of Tschok, Kaltenburg's very first jackdaw. Naturally I was familiar with all of his jackdaws, I could tell them apart by their faces, though the specimens now had no eyes. Taschotschek was a special case, however, there were more memories connected with her than with any other bird of her species.

I once asked Kaltenburg whether he somehow felt bereaved by the death of a creature he had studied for a lifetime, having perhaps hand-reared it. No, not bereavement. But nostalgia, yes, that was something he felt, like every healthy person. He often thought back to his first meeting with Tschok, in a damp and dark dealer's shop in Vienna that he used to visit as a young man. There was a disheveled, shy young bird sitting in a corner at the back somewhere, the dealer thought it hardly worth bringing it out, but Kaltenburg saw

95

its beak, its eyes, and had to have this jackdaw straightaway. The dealer virtually made him a present of it. It was through Tschok that he had started observing birds closely. His experiences with this bird had opened up a new world for him. He owed his first major contribution to ornithology to Tschok. A close, decisive bond, no doubt about it. But all the same: never sadness.

Did he wish his first jackdaw were still alive? That would be flying in the face of nature. And if he had the choice of going back to the time when he had Tschok around him day and night—no, he wouldn't dream of it, he wouldn't swap the present for the interwar years. In a certain sense Tschok wasn't dead anyway, he survived in his descendants, to his surprise he had discovered Tschok's characteristics in every brood. That was why he had given the young bird who most resembled Tschok the name of Taschok, and called the most similar among *its* descendants Taschotschek, which was followed by a second Tschok—and so on from one generation to another.

My knowledge of the live Taschotschek distorted my view of its skin, which was now a softly stuffed, feathered display specimen like the others. When I was classifying them into groups I was inclined to start with Taschotschek, to look upon her as the holotype of a subspecies yet to be discovered. I pushed the others aside, until only Taschotschek lay on the desk in front of me, and then one by one I added others, relatives of Tachotschek, descendants, but also jackdaws who had found their way to this flock as if by accident and had stayed on.

For Taschotschek attracted other jackdaws. It was almost as if she were recruiting new birds for Kaltenburg, as if she knew how pleased he would be by the increase in his jackdaw flock, and how important it was to him to keep its size constant. Because, naturally, there were losses all the time, two young jackdaws paired off and left, many birds disappeared without trace, simply failed to return in the evening—a careless flight maneuver, a hunter; the other birds couldn't tell Kaltenburg what had happened.

The neighbors must have thought him insane, a man who crept around on the roof in his old sports jacket every evening at sunset to gather in birds and put them to bed. Ludwig Kaltenburg was soon so well known in the city that people brought him dead jackdaws. On one occasion someone came to the door, full of remorse, stammering out a confession: he had run over a bird, and he wondered whether—and here he opened a stained bundle—it was one of the Herr Professor's jackdaws.

In this sack of feathers with legs and beak I saw the movements of the living Taschotschek, saw her look and her behavior that had so often made us laugh, Kaltenburg and me. I saw her jumping onto Ludwig Kaltenburg's shoulder and tugging nervously at his hair if there was a visitor she was doubtful about. Kaltenburg could be a gambler too, he was mindful of limits but sometimes exceeded them. Taschotschek wouldn't have minded if Kaltenburg had followed his jackdaw flock up into a stormy sky to participate in their breakneck aerial maneuvers; in other words she trusted his capability within her own sphere but sometimes seemed a bit skeptical about him as a judge of human character. If someone seemed to the jackdaw to be threatening, and if Kaltenburg moved too close to that person, or the conversation took on a tone that sounded dangerous to her, she didn't hold back as she normally did, at first observing strangers in complete silence, then gradually making contact with them. If there was someone present whom she thought of as the enemy of her friend, she would fly out of the room, perch on the rooftop, and make a racket until Kaltenburg had no choice but to break off the conversation, leaving the dumbfounded visitor alone for a while, and appear on the ladder outside.

This was something I witnessed several times, and in a few cases it occurred to me later that Taschotschek had not been wrong. At one time, when we had just returned from an excursion on which the jackdaws had accompanied us for quite a distance, a man appeared—unannounced—who insisted on talking to Kaltenburg. I didn't know him, Kaltenburg treated him like a stranger too, yet something about this man interested Kaltenburg. Taschotschek scuttled about uneasily on the tabletop, went over to the sugar bowl, seemed to want to block Kaltenburg's view of his uninvited guest, spread her wings and got one of them in the tea—and Ludwig Kaltenburg, who normally never lost his composure over an animal, reacted irritably, brushing Taschotschek roughly away onto the back of the armchair.

Suddenly she didn't just look worried—as far as you can say that of a bird—she looked terrified. And she took off, out through the balcony door, which stood slightly ajar all year round, trying with her wing-flapping motions to entice Kaltenburg out onto the roof. She instantly struck up her usual noise. Kaltenburg went on ignoring the jackdaw's din, until eventually he turned to me: "Could you go and see what's got into her again?"

I climbed up the ladder, Taschotschek refused to calm down for me, wouldn't let me touch her, and as I stood up there, with the old city beneath me in the afternoon light and the agitated jackdaw flapping under my nose, I regretted leaving the room: what was Kaltenburg discussing with his visitor, whom I took to be a stranger, what risk might he be letting himself in for? No, Kaltenburg wasn't the type to let himself in for anything. But why was he so keen on talking undisturbed to his visitor, and why did he want not only his favorite jackdaw out of the way but me too? It's possible that this bird really had more than once helped him out of a difficult situation, and but for Taschotschek it is possible that Kaltenburg would have had to leave Dresden much sooner.

Every morning I had to shake off this kind of sentimentality, had to convince myself: you don't know this bird, it's no more familiar to you than any of the other bird skins that have accumulated in these drawers over the course of a century. If I wanted to study her impartially, I couldn't let familiarity lead me to premature conclusions—once I was on the point of sending my Danish colleague a second letter, saying I'd made a mistake, for I had now spotted a clear anomaly in the beak of this jackdaw skin which I had just prepared myself, simply in order to bring him back from Copenhagen to Dresden and introduce Taschotschek to him. I would have made myself a laughingstock. A good thing pet names don't appear on the labels of such tame birds. No, Taschotschek was no example of a subspecies, I had to keep telling myself, *These skins you've been poring over with such tenacity for weeks without knowing the point of doing so—you'll only get to know them step by step, learning about each one in-dividually and very slowly, their plumage, their beaks, their smell.* It was only later, much later, in the eighties, that some research came out of it on the feather formation of common jackdaws and Daurian jackdaws.

I even deluded myself that Taschotschek's skin smelled slightly of Kaltenburg. Once, late one afternoon when the fog around the building refused to lift, it was traces of his aftershave, and later, as darkness was coming on, Kaltenburg's breath. I shut my eyes, brought the birds at random up to my nose: yes, every time it was Taschotschek I held in my hand. And yet all the skins had of course been disinfected—it was a delusion, Tschok, Taschok, Tas-chotschek, I couldn't get away from this notion, had to break off work for a day.

And then my hands when I went home in the evening. I felt I was spreading an atmosphere of jackdaw around me. I wore gloves, put my hands in my coat pockets, but all the same I wondered—in the tram, people must be noticing that here was someone who spent his days sorting out dead jackdaws on his desk, and not only that, they must be noticing that this man knew Professor Ludwig Kaltenburg in his Dresden years like nobody else.

How proud the whole neighborhood had been at first when they heard that Professor Ludwig Kaltenburg, the great authority, might be moving to Loschwitz. They triumphed over the celebrity district of Weisser Hirsch, over the villa quarter of Blasewitz, and above all they triumphed over Leipzig, where Kaltenburg held his professo-rial chair. In the morning at the baker's they murmured, "Have you heard?" In the afternoons on the Elbe meadows it was, "Yes, he'll fit in well here." And in the evening, among intimates, "Who would want to settle in Leipzig anyway?"

That must have been in the spring of 1951—or had the first inkling reached the city as early as the winter? Twelve years later many a resident was glad to see the back of Kaltenburg, as though a curse had been lifted from the slopes of Loschwitz. They told the whole world, that is to say Blasewitz and Weisser Hirsch, how re-lieved they were that he had finally gone, "that troublemaker," "eccentric," "and so arrogant"—they had found it hard to forgive him his steadily growing reputation on the international stage.

No, Ludwig Kaltenburg did not mourn for any animal that died—for him it represented the certainty of getting to know more animals. But he took the death of his jackdaws quite hard. One evening he got home just before dark; he had rushed away after breaking off one of those interminable meetings that lead nowhere, tore along by the Elbe, over the bridge, and could see even from a distance: there were no black dots whirling in the air waiting for him. He rode through an utterly serene sunset, light blue and red and glowing, a disaster. Panicked, Kaltenburg raced up the narrow alleyways, pedestrians jumped out of the way of his motorbike, Kaltenburg changed gear, he didn't brake, he scraped a wall, finally turned into the entrance—and saw the first birds lying on the grass.

He sent for me to come over that same evening. A small heap of dead jackdaws lay on the ground. Kaltenburg could hardly stand, couldn't make it back up the ladder, I climbed onto the roof and scooped two young jackdaws out of the guttering. Over the next few days we combed through the plots of land stretching down to the river, and except for one or two birds we did manage to find all the dead jackdaws.

During the last few weeks of his time in Dresden I barely recognized Kaltenburg. Then, from one day to the next, he disappeared. I don't think anyone knew about his plans except me.

"And never forget to poison your bird finds carefully." That was what Kaltenburg told me once. Professor Ludwig Kaltenburg, who showed me how to prepare a skin. He favored a solution of sodium arsenite, and if you didn't have a poison license you should use borax and naphthalene. "Always make sure you poison your skins carefully." I have never found out how Kaltenburg's jackdaws actually died. Hardly had he left Dresden before rumors started circulating in the city, many of them harmless, many just plain stupid, today I can only remember the most wicked of them: Kaltenburg was said to have put out poison for his birds himself, in order to make his departure more dramatic.

With a dead bird in each hand I stood there on the balcony, Kaltenburg sat despondently in the gloom of his study, I couldn't bring myself to approach him carrying the two lifeless bundles of feathers. I thought I would look around for a box, but in Kaltenburg's household there was no box that wasn't occupied by a live animal. I was considering stuffing the jackdaws under my sweater, but then I heard his toneless voice, he didn't look up: "Just come in. It makes no difference now."

I suggested burying the birds in the garden. For a long time there was no response. Then Kaltenburg shook his head. "You can take them. Take them away and make good skins out of them. They'll remind you of our time together in this city when I'm gone."

2

———

THE MENU LAY OPEN in front of us, but we hadn't ordered yet. Katharina Fischer was looking out of the window, her expression almost suggesting that it was her own memory that was filling with Ludwig Kaltenburg's jackdaws, because of the images I had shown her one by one.

She had told me on the telephone about her assignment, about a long, no doubt tiring day, which she assured me she had got through all right, despite minor irritations. No, unfortunately, the local bird life wasn't mentioned at all, and the stern head of protocol intervened immediately when she tried to raise the topic of this winter's waxwing invasion with the English visitor during a short break. All the same, our meeting was not without results, for it made her go back to Kaltenburg's works, those battered volumes, full of underlinings and coffee stains, which she had studied intensively in her later years at school, and which at some stage had disappeared into a banana crate to finish up in various cellars every time she moved.

The minute she glanced through the books after so many years, Katharina Fischer noticed that for some reason she had put an exclamation mark after every mention of a place-name. Prague and Paris, where Kaltenburg had said his piece about the events of 1968, not without sharply attacking the Soviet Union as well as the students. Then Königsberg, a place with which Frau Fischer had as little connection in her youth as with the town where she now lived.

Moscow, Paris, Florida, London, Rotterdam—when the interpreter asked me if I'd noticed that the professor never at any point mentioned Posen in his writings, I decided to ask her out to dinner, a simple "certainly" or "of course" over the telephone would not do. She accepted without hesitation, and we agreed to book a table in this restaurant on the bank of the Elbe at Blasewitz.

The river, the meadows, the slopes on the other side, on our right the Loschwitz Bridge—in her mind's eye she was following Kaltenburg as he raced over the bridge on his motorbike. His leather biker's gear, his white mane, and the way the rider bends over the handlebars; it can only be Kaltenburg, even if the steel supports of the bridge cause a rapidly alternating pattern of light and dark stripes to flit across the figure, so that you begin to wonder whether it isn't a phantom your eyes are following, while the professor has long since reached the other bank, is taking the bend, disappearing between the houses on the Körnerplatz.

We debated back and forth on what to call it: a homecoming, an escape, the end of a long farewell, which had basically started with Kaltenburg's arrival? A long farewell which coincided with my leaving school, my studies under the professor, and a few important years as a colleague at his Institute. I supplied him with material for a series of studies, researched pair bonds in the common raven, carried out observations on same-species killing among various types of animal, so that Kaltenburg was able to build up a comprehensive picture of this aberrant behavior. I was allowed to take part in the big research project on night herons, although that was never completed, more's the pity, because Kaltenburg never again returned to this bird, which, far from yielding its secrets after years of observation, actually became more puzzling.

My own research involved the early months of life in the great tit, and it also took me all over the country to find out more about chimney jackdaws. Looking back, though, I must say that I don't see either of these projects as valid in terms of detail, and neither do I find the ideas I had then about the house sparrow's capacity for mimicry convincing today.

No, I replied to Katharina Fischer, go with Ludwig Kaltenburg to Vienna? I would never have wanted to join him, quite apart from the fact that it wasn't an option. For one thing I saw it as my duty to look after the animals in the Institute—although that wasn't ever discussed—now that its head was no longer available. For another, my parents-in-law would have been heartbroken if their daughter had decamped to the West. And I wouldn't have gone anywhere without my wife. When I was lucky enough to find my place at the Ornithological Collection, I don't mind admitting that I felt something like freedom. No, to Vienna, Ludwig Kaltenburg had to go back to Vienna alone.

A bit farther upriver, beyond the bridge which blocks the view, somewhere on the hillside the red taillight of a motorbike will have lit up, Kaltenburg turning into the narrow path, dimly lit by a few gas lamps, which led to his villa. The waiter hovered, he wanted to take our order, and no, no motorcyclist on the bridge, no jackdaws above the hillside, the sun had set, Frau Fischer tore herself away from the view outside, I had been watching her reflection in the windowpane.

3

WHENEVER I ENTERED Ludwig Kaltenburg's study, I was stepping into my father's room. More precisely: my father's room as it would have been if he were still alive. A few details may actually have corresponded: the position of the desk in the middle of the room, the small, uncomfortable cocktail-bar chair with worn arms, selected on a whim for use as a desk chair and then missing from the drawing room, the rickety dark-wood bookshelves behind. If you stood in the doorway looking toward the window, this picture, shifted diagonally slightly to the right, was in the middle of your view. But if you sat at the desk, you saw the passage to an adjacent room, to where our conservatory was. The arrangement of the broad desktop: the leather writing mat, an open reference book on the left, an ashtray on the right, but between them, in no discernible order, dog-eared lecture notes, walnut shells, pencils, a pile of blank writing paper, and on it a portable typewriter.

Entering Kaltenburg's study, for a split second I even saw my father's mail lying there, soft, padded, firmly sealed envelopes, with the address on them in a script which told you that the sender found writing Cyrillic letters easier than writing Latin ones. Little packets of seeds from Leningrad. I had to remind myself: in his day, your father would hardly have received botanical samples from the

Soviet Union, what you were looking at was the present-day desk of a man rooted in the distant past. Still more than the corresponding details, however, it was the atmosphere of this study which created for a moment the illusion of a Posen room in a far-off world, above all in winter, in the late afternoons. The way my father sat there without noticing me, underneath the desk lamp, or rather in shadow, shining hair, only his hands in the pool of light and a white sheet of paper and plant samples he had been studying closely since midday.

Kaltenburg's study did not possess a ceiling light, any more than my father's did: this fact may account for the familiarity of the room. The professor immediately had the ceiling lights dismantled in every room when he moved into the villa, or perhaps one should say, when Kaltenburg's animals commandeered it. Enormous chandeliers, finest blown-glass work left behind by the previous owner—Kaltenburg gave them all away without the least remorse.

The neighbors' amazement when a whole lighting shop was gradually spread out on the lawn by the entrance, and Kaltenburg—"Come on, come on over, choose what you want"—beckoned to the inquisitive folk who had thought they were out of sight behind the bushes. Their sidelong peeks at their new neighbor as they took a closer look at the goods, and Kaltenburg went on encouraging people to lug home some of the "loot," as he called it: "Here, these belong together, so do me a favor and take this decorative piece as well."

Eventually they all left with their booty tucked under their arms, bowing to the professor, thanked him sincerely, placing one foot carefully in front of the other, said many thanks, taking care not to stumble as they walked away backward, thanked him profusely—but Kaltenburg brushed all this aside: "What's the point of me having chandeliers in the house? The animals would just use them as staging posts on their way from one cupboard to another, to stay out of my reach when I wanted something from them, or do gymnastics on the lamps. Then every few days one of these great lumps would come crashing down. That would be a shame. And dangerous, as well."

My father's room: I could never quite shake off the impression, in fact it would become all the stronger later on, when Ludwig Kaltenburg had left Dresden and I was roaming through the deserted house, taking care of the remaining animals. For if anything could have released me from that notion, it was Kaltenburg himself, a figure who was out of place if it was my father's study I was standing in. Kaltenburg always brought me back to reality.

I remember Kaltenburg saying when he arrived in Dresden and we met up again, "You see, my boy, I told you early on you'd never get rid of me."

A sentence that was lost at first in the excitement of the day. After Kaltenburg had given away his chandeliers, was there an announcement of a welcoming visit by VIPs, or did the professor read out a call for peace on the grass behind the house? I seem to remember there were reporters in the grounds, I can hear the clicking of cameras, see Ludwig Kaltenburg answering questions on the steps, then in the aquarium wing, still empty at the time. I brought him a glass of water, a photographer was packing up his equipment—and in the midst of it all Kaltenburg turned quickly to me and remarked, as though we were alone, "I said you wouldn't get rid of me in a hurry."

And then he was gone again, I stood holding the empty glass, a woman journalist from Moscow had beckoned the professor over to the garden gate, the interpreter explained they wanted another picture, in front of the transport containers this time. It was then that Kaltenburg, hurrying obligingly down the steps, began to show the first signs of exhaustion. Normally ultra-polite to young women and always donning the protective armor of joviality for public appearances, he growled in an undertone to the female interpreter, "By the transport containers, I got that. My Russian isn't nearly as bad as you might think."

He was to make up for his slip later, admitting his gaffe and inviting the interpreter out to dinner. They had both been a bit stressed, he was truly sorry, and the interpreter was to fall for his charm. Her name was Karin, he told me afterward, a really great girl, a great woman rather, and I think he even named an animal after her later.

But at what point during the Posen years did Kaltenburg tell me, as a boy, that I would find it hard to shake him off? The question was running through my head that night as I fell asleep, and during the following days, and I could not come up with an answer. Over the years the sentence has often come back to me, and even if Kaltenburg did utter it that afternoon purely on a passing whim, he turned out to be right.

Ludwig Kaltenburg was trying to clear a path for himself to an open transport container. He trod warily and yet firmly, ducks scattering and fluttering, a terrible clucking and commotion, the ducks' instinct was to take flight, finding strangers everywhere irritated them, and they kept returning to their master's feet so that he could hardly move: I can remember the occasion now, it was the day that Kaltenburg's flock of ducks arrived in Loschwitz. For that time it was a spectacular relocation which excited interest right across Europe. "Three Hundred Ducks Find a New Home in Dresden," in Vienna it even triggered a debate in Parliament, and the press headline "Big Loss for Austria."

Almost all the birds had survived the journey unharmed, and only a small part of the population subsequently went missing, a superb achievement. Kaltenburg basked in his success. He had accepted a chair in Leipzig, he had been headhunted by them while Vienna and Graz were still making up their minds, and Kaltenburg was undoubtedly attracted to university teaching, since he loved passing on his knowledge to younger people. In spite of the painful rejection by his homeland, it must surely have given him satisfaction to see that in his—celebrated—case, Austria had lost out through internal obstruction and petty wrangling. But what clinched it in the end was that along with the professorship at Leipzig, Kaltenburg managed to negotiate his own institute in Dresden, he was promised all the support he needed, whether material or moral, and at the highest level.

As a child I once asked Kaltenburg incredulously whether it was true that he had taken live ducks with him to Königsberg—for me as a ten-year-old that was as unimaginable as it clearly was for Kaltenburg's colleagues at the time. And now here I was witnessing at close quarters a far bigger duck relocation, and even giving a helping hand where I could, bringing the professor a glass of water, shepherding a stray flock back out of the roadway onto Kaltenburg's estate, or rescuing a terrified drake, found cowering on the veranda steps as though paralyzed, from the midst of a crowd of humans. In the evening, when the whole show was over, reporters and inquisitive locals having dispersed, I heated some water, took a bucket and scrubbing brush out to the front of the house, and as the sun set cleaned up the garden path, the driveway, and the stretch of road outside the villa. The dark green patches, in fact a whole trail of dark green: out of sheer agitation three hundred ducks had repeatedly emptied their bowels, and without noticing it the visitors had spread the muck everywhere.

Ludwig Kaltenburg had made a brilliant debut, the newspapers carried pictures of a beaming man in knee breeches, the sleeves of his white shirt rolled up, the top buttons open. Kaltenburg crouching among the ducks, Kaltenburg explaining something to the spellbound woman journalist from Moscow, Kaltenburg surrounded by Loschwitz children, showing them the right way to hold a duck: a soothing and refreshing sight for all readers' eyes, which—especially when such momentous occasions were being documented—were used to seeing the same old crew of stiff, aging gentlemen in gray suits, with gray faces, gray smiles, all waxworks molded out of melted candle stumps.

Then one morning a brand-new black SIS limousine arrived outside the house, and the accompanying letter had every appearance of being written by Walter Ulbricht himself, who intended this showpiece from the Stalin Works as a welcome present. But according to the Dresden city council a new homeland went together with a new hometown, so a few days later Walter Weidauer brought the professor an equally brand-new, equally black motorbike, the AWO 425, which Kaltenburg had long coveted. Whether through miscalculation or because the press had not been properly coordinated—at any rate, somehow neither gift resonated with the public to anything like the same extent as the duck relocation shortly before. Later, among friends, Kaltenburg happily recounted how three hundred simple, unsuspecting ducks had upstaged the representatives from Dresden and Berlin.

Nor did I once see him driving the Soviet limousine himself, he could never warm to the somber road cruiser, perhaps because the gift package from Berlin included a driver. "Krause is such a nice quiet man," I can hear the professor saying, "I don't really know what I've got against him."

The car was used only for official business, above all when the professor had to go to Berlin. In Dresden outside the motorbike season you only ever saw him driving around in his little Opel. If anybody mentioned the limousine, he would nod eagerly: true, it was a beautiful car, if a little unwieldy. It was hard to negotiate the narrow alleys of Loschwitz in it, particularly with such a crazy driver as himself at the wheel.

That was the Kaltenburg the Dresdeners got to know, and instantly love. It was in his nature to make every appearance in society a little entrance onto the public stage, whether it was simply changing his gloves at the front door or taking his splendid chow dog along with him or, in later years, demonstrating at a garden party how a shrill birdcall would bring his jackdaw flock over—"You don't believe my birds will do what I tell them?"—from the other side of the Elbe. A certain mysterious charge seemed to build up before every appearance, people waited, anticipated, talking about Kaltenburg's motorbike trick, the trick with the sunglasses or his gloves. Would he speak about the Institute, would he put on animal stunts? Kaltenburg rejected this. "You can't call it a stunt," he said, "it's just natural behavior."

Not many people recognize that a lot of energy goes into little performances like this within the private sphere, and most do not want to know about it. There is always a price to pay for being a lively personality; Kaltenburg needed a retreat, his "household," as he called the villa with all its animals. He could spend whole days in the meadow, you thought, *He's not moving, he must be asleep*, while in fact he was engrossed in observing wildlife. A few ducks had settled around him, on the cellar steps a raven was noisily belaboring a closed box, behind the house the blue-and-yellow macaw was having a fight with the washing line, the dogs raced yapping through the garden. "Life means observing," said Kaltenburg, and you should seek the company of animals.

Much of his life was spent alone with animals, it was a basic need for him, and just as others eventually feel uneasy without human company and are drawn to it in the street, in the theater, simply to be among people, Kaltenburg could never be away from his animals for more than a few hours without becoming restless. It may be that he had got so many of them to imprint on him from his earliest days onward in order to make sure he never lacked their company, and it may be that the reason he performed his jackdaw trick so willingly was that the birds who amazed guests by circling over his head allowed him to escape in spirit, if not physically, from the tedium of a summer reception. The guests thought it a miracle, but the professor knew that his jackdaws were calling him, always calling: "Come with us."

4

———

A LOW CLINKING SOUND, such as I'd heard countless times in Kaltenburg's house when a jackdaw had quietly retreated and was investigating an object somewhere. I could hear a jackdaw beak in the distance pecking carefully away at a loose furniture fitting; I heard a screw falling to the floor, and knew that it wouldn't be long before the brass fitting itself dropped to the parquet with a clatter. But it was only Katharina Fischer's bracelet repeatedly touching the cutlery as the interpreter played with her napkin.

"Every time I see a jackdaw, I'm fascinated by its white eyes. You can't help feeling the jackdaw is fixing you with a piercing stare, that it can see right through human beings."

Or maybe what we see is the jackdaw asking itself whether we're the ones who are trying to look right through it. Direct eye contact with a bird always has a certain suspense about it, something not quite decided, even if you are very familiar with each other.

"As though both parties are waiting for the next move."

However, in Dresden, said Katharina Fischer, she didn't often spot jackdaws. Last summer in the heat wave she had seen two thin crows and two jackdaws hopping around the statue of the Golden Horseman in the Neustadt marketplace, all pretty aimless, with wide-open beaks, you could see their dark red throats.

In Dresden these days you don't find more than a handful of

breeding pairs a year, jackdaws pulled out of the city a long time ago. It was already beginning to happen in Kaltenburg's day, and that's partly why his birds became so well known. And after they died it would probably have been difficult to build up a replacement colony. It's possible that as a youngster I was aware of declining jackdaw numbers myself. But I wasn't bothered while I was surrounded by Kaltenburg's flock.

"That makes it sound as though you were actually living in the Institute."

Almost. I didn't sleep there, rarely had meals—but otherwise, I practically did live there. I went home just to eat and sleep, and later, as an adult, I was sometimes sorry how little attention I had paid to my foster family. The long summer nights in the allotment, visiting relations in the Erzgebirge mountains, our evenings around the kitchen table, with the parents helping each of us in turn with our studies: it feels as though all that time I was making the utmost effort not to imprint any of these images on my memory.

I think I've still got the binoculars my adoptive siblings gave me one birthday, and if I could remember the details of how they came by this good, solid model, I would be able to think of the story today as part of the gift. Not even my foster parents were let in on the binoculars plan, so they were as amazed as I was to hear the risks their children had run just to please their foster son. I remember we were sitting in the parlor, the best china, the tablecloth, there were meatballs in caper sauce, my favorite at the time, and the potatoes tasted wonderful. But it's a shame I can't remember anything about the acquisition of the binoculars except that it involved a school-bus driver, and the youngest child having to summon up all her courage to address him in Russian, while she sat behind her brother on his bike and he kept one foot on the ground and the other on the pedal, ready to scoot off with his little sister at a moment's notice. They were laughing, acting out the various parts as they told the story, imitating the bus driver as though the whole thing were one big joke, although we all knew they had been pushing at the extreme limits of danger. After all, every kind of private contact with members of the Soviet forces was banned, not to mention barter deals, and the draconian punishments meted out to any soldier who transgressed were said to include up to a fortnight in a dark, cramped hole in the ground.

A happy, relaxed evening, one of the few I can picture. I just couldn't bring myself to call my foster parents, to call strangers, "Mum" and "Dad," I couldn't get the words out. The parents would have liked me to call their children "my brother and sisters" — my mind would never accept the "my," and to be honest I hated "brother and sisters" from the first day. For a long time Herta, Gerlinde, and Hans-Georg called me the "foundling," and if we had a row they hissed "bastard" into my ear, their breath hot, when their parents were not around. But looking back, all this sounds unfair, my attitude to my foster family will have been skewed from the very beginning. When I think back to the birthday present, what trouble my new brother and sisters went to, their pleasure when, completely unsuspecting, I began to take the heavy object out of its newspaper wrapping . . .

I always imagined the binoculars had already served their purpose during the advance on Dresden, and as though traces of those events were left on the lenses, I liked to think that something of the landscapes and objects the Red Army officer had trained them on was still attached to the eyepieces. I saw him standing upright in an open jeep, his glance sweeping from a burning farmhouse on the left to a birch-tree copse on the right where German stragglers had still been holed up until a few days earlier. The landscape stretches toward the west over gentle hills, on the horizon a mob of tiny figures, refugees, deserters, Waffen SS perhaps. He keeps the binoculars glued to his eyes, gives the signal for the car to move forward again, and now the tank column following in the rear comes briefly into view.

It is through these binoculars that the officer looks along the Elbe valley, searching out a bridge over the river and finally spotting in the distance a blue-shimmering steel construction projecting above the ruins. And of course on his way into Dresden many a bird enters his field of vision, as they do mine now. During the day he observes the wild geese coming from the south as they break their journey to rest by a lake, and hardly a night passes when he doesn't wake up thinking he hears their wings beating above his billet. Over the weeks the number of empty stork nests declines, at some point he stops counting the occupied ones and only counts nests that have been abandoned. And on one occasion the officer lingers near a group of rooks flocking around a dark, shapeless bundle on the ground, suspiciously at first, then driven closer by curiosity, until one leading rook is bold enough to start cautiously plucking at it. Horsehair perhaps, rotting straw, a bag full of charred papers, a lost eiderdown, from its size you might almost think it was a person.

I regularly went roaming with two friends from school, Klaus and Johann, war orphans like me. Johann was allowed to invite us home, and if he begged long enough his foster parents even let the three of us sleep over in the loft. With blankets, sandwiches, and tea, we climbed up the rickety ladder to camp from Saturday night to Sunday morning among the furniture and household bric-a-brac from the kaiser's time. Candles were taboo.

Together we combed through the dead zones in the inner city, all children were drawn like magic to the rubble, and it was nothing special for us to explore these areas by day. The real challenge lay in finding your way about after dark, which was obviously strictly forbidden. Our parents didn't like it at all when we clambered among ruins threatening to collapse at any time. This wilderness was frequented by some shady types, but we were out to prove our courage, convinced that grownups by contrast were scared at the very thought of the dead zones.

After all, for a long time people believed there were still countless victims of the night of February thirteenth buried in the cellars, but when a body turned up from time to time, it was definitely of more recent date. A man with his hands tied behind his back, shot in the back of the head at close range—that kind of thing was automatically put down to feuding between black-market gangs, and on the quiet there was also talk of old scores being settled. Once the body of a young woman was found in the bushes, with eyes rolled back and strangulation marks on her neck. "Prostitute"—we didn't know the word at all, "unfaithful fiancée" was the current expression—and "streetwalker," a term we had picked up from an adult conversation, meant just as little to us as we wondered why the young woman had put on nice clothes and makeup before she was murdered.

We brought home the material for our stories from the deserted inner city, hauling back trophies, a brittle leather strap, a pottery shard, a fork, adding new items from the world out there to our collection in the loft.

No, the zones didn't seem dead to us then. I wandered about on my own too, my binoculars round my neck, I got to know more about wheatears and crested larks, tawny pippets and little ringed plovers, sparrow hawks and linnets—or should I say I got to know them all over again. As for identifying plants, however, I have never got back to the standard of the embankment behind our house. Flix-weed, tansy mustard, prickly lettuce, redroot amaranth—I hadn't forgotten the names, and anyway we learned in school how to distinguish the three levels of ruderal plants: parsley fern, horse thistle, and henbane ought to have meant something to me. But when I scanned the terrain with my binoculars, all they showed me were leaves, blossoms, and herbs, more or less varied in shape and color, and nothing caught my attention until it was held by a yellow wing stripe, a red head marking, a white cheek, the ivory-colored beak of a goldfinch.

There is a kind of counterpart to my memory of the goldfinches in the thistle patches: a November evening during the Korean crisis, when we were all waiting for World War III to break out. I can remember a torchlight procession in which all schools took part, youth urging the world to make peace, intimidated youth, "free youth points the way," and I was part of this movement, like my classmates, among whom I queued to receive my torch at the assembly point. Silently we moved off, not a fun weekend activity, bravely and stiffly we marched down the Strasse der Befreiung to the Platz der Einheit, the leaders of the procession had reached Bautzner

Strasse long before and were already moving up the Elbe slopes heading for the Palace of Pioneers.

I can see us now turning into the broad open ground, the sea of light beneath the trees. The chairman of the regional Peace Committee gave his speech, then we stepped forward, one school class after another, until we reached the hillside, where we rammed our torches into the earth—or did war orphans take precedence, was I one of the first to stick my torch into the frosty soil? I know that I immediately took a step backward, leaving my classmates behind me, I stood to one side. It seems to me that by that time I no longer had much in common with Klaus, with Johann.

Neither did I have the slightest inclination to meet up all that soon with Herta, Gerlinde, and Hans-Georg, presumably they were in the hall, there were more speeches, or perhaps the seriousness and intensity of the evening had long since given way to dancing. I wandered for a while through the park, up the hillside, looking down into the valley. Nothing much more than a smooth black surface where you could make out isolated pinpoints of light. It was easy to imagine that these signs of life too must soon be extinguished, as though a harsh wind were sweeping across this desolate landscape, and sooner or later those last inhabitants still clinging on would be forced to give in, as the wind drove them before it to the edge of the great darkness.

Not far from me someone lit his cigarette from a torch. He belonged to a group that stood on the meadow, a little apart, almost as though they wanted to demonstrate to the other participants that although present, they had nothing to do with the actual ceremony. The six of them stood in a circle, young men smoking, a few years older than me. One of them, towering above the others, was wearing a peaked cap, all of them were casually dressed, except for—and I had only just noticed her—a woman, her back to me, lit up by torchlight, wearing a black velvet cap. Wrapped in a long fur coat, a well-preserved garment which had been brought safely through the war, and which made a lady of her. Was she the oldest in the group? Voices. Who was speaking? The young men's eyes, like mine, were on the woman. I was the only one who couldn't see her face, only this collar, her cap, her shape in the coat. There was silence. The tall one in the peaked cap raised his head, I had been spotted. And as I avoided his gaze, turned away, I heard a laugh.

It was still ringing in my ears as I entered the hall to look for my new siblings, it was high time we set off for home. Hans-Georg with his angular physique, a hint of his future coarseness around the eyes. Gerlinde with her German plaits. Herta, the oldest, crazy about dancing, but to her regret not very good at it. I was going to stand by the edge of the floor and just watch the dancing figures as quietly as possible, when in the corner of my eye I spotted a flowing movement: the heavy fur coat was gliding through the crowd.

A Russian aristocrat, whose family had gone over to the right side at the last moment. No, that kind of good fortune didn't happen. A delegate from the national Peace Committee of a fraternal country. Someone recruited very young by partisans in the Baltic, perhaps. But I still hadn't caught a glimpse of the lady's face, she passed me too quickly. On her head was the peaked cap the tall character had been wearing earlier, a bit too big, so that it fell over her left ear. So I'd got it wrong out there, it wasn't a black velvet cap that had been gleaming in the semidarkness but her dark hair. The unknown woman disappeared among the crowd at the other end of the room, the corridor opened up by the dancers closed behind her. I turned toward the exit, it was clear that my new siblings had already left the place.

During the long walk home, it didn't bother me that the three of them might have hatched a plot, intentionally disappearing in order to tell their parents that I had left the parade ground without permission, that I had hidden from them. It didn't matter whether I was the one who got the beating, or Hans-Georg for not having kept the crew together. I wasn't even scared that they might be lurking in the bushes somewhere along the route to give me a proper fright by leaping out in front of me with a fiendish yell, with mock-Russian gibberish.

An open, untroubled, inappropriate laugh, which even after it faded away still dominated everything, the circle of grim young men, the meadow and the hillside, the whole ceremony together with its stupid music. The danger of war and our will to peace. The dark past, the dark future, and the present November night in the open air, which hinted at a harsh winter to come, with lingering frost and snow. I didn't know the color of her eyes, I hadn't spoken to her, but this unknown woman's laugh accompanied me as I fell asleep.

5

———

I WOULD NEVER HAVE told Ludwig Kaltenburg about my troubles at home, adolescent problems, it would have been too embarrassing. No, perhaps it wasn't even that—when I was in the Institute foster parents didn't exist, nor siblings to plague me, and in the evenings I always went home feeling stronger. Not a word, yet Kaltenburg must have sensed the strain I was under when I came to him for an hour in the late afternoon, sometimes out of breath, lacking concentration, eyes restless, like someone who has escaped his tormentors and found refuge. Kaltenburg would not have shut me out, I know, he would have listened patiently, but since I didn't talk he chose not to mention my agitation. Instead, I had hardly got my jacket off when he took me to the hamster corner: "Look what he got from the bookshelf last night—a couple of pages of Kant."

Or he would send me, as though I had let my duties slide, into the feed kitchen: "Don't bother hanging up your jacket. The fruit, have you forgotten? They've been expecting you all afternoon."

He watched as I leapt down the steps—but no longer running away. For when I jumped over the wheelbarrow by the side of the path, avoided the gardener's lad, brushed along the hedge, headed straight toward the dozing dogs as though I'd taken leave of my senses, a feeling of calm came over me. The wooden lattice construction devised by the feed manager for keeping sunflower heads dry. The mealworm incubator. As soon as I started picking out the rotten strawberries, as soon as I saw the bucket of apples in front of me for cutting up into beak-sized chunks, yes, as soon as I dipped into the cherries, I had regained my Loschwitz breathing rhythm.

They've been expecting you—this "they" encompassed the long-term inmates as well the fluctuating chance visitors. Animals with whose impulses the professor was intimately acquainted. Animals which had only recently aroused his curiosity. Animals that needed to be studied carefully in the future. Some fresh ones to be researched and others that couldn't be. And the "they" included Ludwig Kaltenburg, included me too.

Whenever he noticed that I wasn't even up to feeding the animals, he would throw on his jacket and "Out we go, down to the Elbe," or, if the weather wasn't good enough for a birding expedition, "I'll get the Opel out of the garage."

Our outings in the car were called "induction by personal inspection." I can remember the smell of calf leather in the little sports car, remember the way Kaltenburg sat next to me holding the wheel firmly with both hands, concentrating on the road. On the spare seat there was always a pile of books and brochures; I reached back with my left hand, read to the professor from the lives of famous ornithologists, while he chauffeured us to their birthplaces and homes, to the sites of their activity. Thus Kaltenburg once took me on a whole-day excursion down the Elbe to Köthen, to see the Ziebigk estate, Naumann's place. We drove to Renthendorf to see the Brehms' house. To Waldheim, where Maikammer was born. To Reichenbach in the Vogtland. To Waldenburg. I can hardly recall anything about the town of Greiz, but on the other hand I have the clearest memory of a portrait of the *pâtissier* Carl Ferdinand Oberländer, who became addicted to collecting native and exotic birds. His expression seems to betray grief and melancholy, the furrowed brow, around the eyes, the mouth: it won't be long before his passion drives him to ruin, he will have to sell his wonderful collection of mounts.

Once, in the most glorious weather, we roamed for a whole day through the landscape of Moritzburg with its many pools, we could have made countless sightings, but Kaltenburg was intent on one thing only, finding a particular pond where, as he said, Hans Steingruber had begun his career. He had been cycling past this spot on a day in March 1923 and had seen two coral-red beaks glowing on the water. Kaltenburg stomped through the reeds on the bank: "At that time he was your age," and red-crested pochards had not been spotted for more than seventy years. Nobody was willing to believe Steingruber, even Reinhold in Berlin was skeptical when the young man came to see him. No, *Netta rufina* in Moritzburg, that must have been a faulty sighting, he was certain of it, Reinhold, the greatest ornithologist of our time.

In retrospect the outings could be seen simply as preparation for meeting live people. The "induction by personal inspection" continued in Loschwitz, costing the professor no effort at all, since authorities from all over the world found their way to him unbidden.

At the same time, Ludwig Kaltenburg could be quite prone to moods, that is to say, I saw him getting irritated above all when people thoughtlessly disturbed his most intimate moments together with animals. He seemed open to everyone, you could have got him out of bed at any time of night to share a sighting with him, yet he often reacted harshly to some annoyance if it came at the wrong moment—a new colleague who wasn't yet familiar with the aquarium wing, a roofer finally arriving to replace a row of shingles on the gable end of the summerhouse.

The first time Reinhold visited the Institute, Kaltenburg happened to be at a difficult point, trying to get birds to follow him, an exercise that stretched over several days because some young jackdaws of that generation were not always ready to fly behind him from room to room. He walked down the corridor, into the kitchen, out again, into his study—and forgot that Reinhold was expected.

I had been hanging around outside the house since early morning, curious to see this man who had inspired so many ornithologists. In the background there was a succession of noises: calls, stamping, flapping of wings. More calls. Silence. A contented murmuring. You could follow progress with the new brood in the garden sound by sound. Then the limousine drew up in the driveway.

Krause walked around the car, quickly ran a sleeve over the mud-guard, opened the rear door, and stood to attention looking into the middle distance: a wiry older gentleman emerged, to me he looked about eighty, although at the time Reinhold was only in his early sixties. I greeted the visitor and took him up to the first floor. Reinhold was far too astonished to be dismayed that his reception was not exactly friendly: "It's not half past twelve already, is it?" Kaltenburg's voice, sharp, because we were getting in his way between cloakroom and bedroom. "Didn't we say half past twelve?"

We ducked, a young bird flew along the corridor, Reinhold just shook his head, smiling, and let me show him around the grounds of the Institute. Whatever I was describing to him, he scrutinized the animals as though ascertaining the facts for himself, and every second I thought he was going to interrupt me: "Monk parrot, did you say? That's impossible. You probably weren't even born when the last monk parrots of the Loschwitz breeding colony left the city."

Two hours later Ludwig Kaltenburg seemed like a different man, he was friendliness personified, was generous with flattering remarks to his guest, and even formally begged his pardon. But Reinhold wouldn't hear a word of it, saying he had known Kaltenburg far too long to be put out: "My dear Ludwig, I would have been more bothered if you had given me priority over your jackdaws."

I experienced such outbreaks too, but Kaltenburg never felt that my presence disturbed him when communing with his animals.

One autumn afternoon—Kaltenburg's first autumn in Dresden—with terrible wind and rain, the villa was silent, and there was silence too as I stepped into the hall, all living creatures had retreated from the weather. Everything in the house was geared to a system that finely balanced the animals' requirements, nearly forty years' experience had gone into the appearance of rooms where the untrained eye would at first have seen nothing but pure chaos. In one room, for example, the furniture stood a little way away from the walls—behind it somewhere was the den of an animal which only Kaltenburg may ever have caught sight of. In another room incredible heaps of lumber, tables and chairs all mixed up, empty book covers—this had been the favorite room of a capuchin monkey long since departed for the zoo, and now the hamsters seemed to feel particularly comfortable in there. Next came a bare, sparse room, the opposite of the last one, in one corner a fine carpet of sand: this was where the timid quails liked to retire. Something Kaltenburg had learned early on about rooms used for nesting was that there should always be the same fixed distance in centimeters between fireplace and cupboard, and he had maintained this ever since a hamster had developed, unbeknown to anyone, a mountaineer's "back and footing" technique to climb to the top of a cupboard and make its nest out of old documents. No ceiling lights anywhere, but unlike the curtains, curtain rails had been left in place in every room; the finches had to have suitable roosting places, after all.

The handrails up the stairs—perches for exotic birds. The carpets and runners—less decoration than thread supplies for the ducks to fall back upon when nest-building. The curtains that originally hung in the drawing room—they never came back from the laundry. A fragile system designed to meet the needs of the animals as much as the human inhabitants—and yet it looked as though Kaltenburg took a secret delight in testing the capacity of the system to destruction, as though every time he introduced a new species of animal into the house he was expecting his so-far-proven system to collapse.

I stood in the study doorway, and no, it wasn't my father's room, there sat Ludwig Kaltenburg at his desk, in front of him a cup of tea, a pile of loaves, and an open newspaper. He didn't look up. Tearing off chunk after chunk from a white loaf, he held the pieces aloft next to him and let them drop. He wasn't disturbed by my arrival, and neither were the two dozen ducks, hardly a glance, just their quiet clucking as they waited patiently by the desk for the next bite of bread to come—they could count on it—from the hand of their master. I didn't try to tell myself the ducks knew me so well by then that I didn't bother them, it was just that they knew nothing could happen to them in Kaltenburg's presence. He murmured something, perhaps a reassuring sound from human to animal, and then his voice became clearer: "Did you shut the front door? That new Alsatian bitch has got to stay outside for a bit, she's terrifically jealous of the ducks."

I nodded, Ludwig Kaltenburg didn't need to say any more, I took one of the white loaves from the desk and started pulling it to pieces for the birds' snack. Hardly a word was ever said in the Kaltenburg household about the bread supply, about provisions for the animals in general, just once I remember the professor telling a visitor, "I don't have the time or the energy to get involved with ration coupons." And also, "It's autumn, my drakes are molting, that's when their feed needs to be especially good, every child knows that."

Over time it became a set phrase. If Kaltenburg talked about molting drakes, then we knew he was pushing higher authority to make up some deficit or other, and sometimes, if he was in a good mood and fancied his chances, he even—"molting drakes"—tried renegotiating.

No, there were no samples of seeds from Leningrad on the desk, just a newspaper covered in breadcrumbs. Kaltenburg picked it up carefully by the edges, formed a chute, and to the joy of his molt-weakened drakes dropped the light flakes onto the carpet.

6

ALTHOUGH HE MAINTAINED that it wasn't necessary, I wasn't going to hear anything new, it was basically always the same, nothing could have stopped me accompanying the professor to his lectures. "You know I won't be offended if you've got something else on in the evening," he always said, after I had told him, "I'll be there listening carefully as usual tomorrow evening." It was almost a ritual between us: "I'm afraid it will be very crowded and you'll have to stand all the way through," while the professor well knew he could count on my presence down there in the hall. "Don't inflict it on yourself," a ritual, a game, it was up to Kaltenburg to bring it to a close: "If you'd rather go and see a movie, with your school friends perhaps, I'll understand," to which I didn't reply, and so with an "If you insist on it," he gave up trying to change my mind: "But don't say I didn't warn you."

During that time I can't have missed a single one of his big lectures. I went with Ludwig Kaltenburg, but during the evening itself I didn't stay near him. We didn't stand together before proceedings began, afterward I went home without even saying goodbye to him, while at the front of the hall the professor was surrounded by his listeners. And I never wanted to be at the front, I sat somewhere in the middle, as though I were just another member of the audience. That was our silent agreement, so that he never saw me among the one, two, three hundred blurred faces.

The hall belonged to him the moment he began to speak, he knew that. All the same, I had to give Professor Kaltenburg my assessment of the audience, he could gauge the general atmosphere from the lectern, but what details had I noticed out there, someone next to me writing everything down from beginning to end, a young couple in the row in front of me getting bored at some point. I looked around, noting a slight cough on the left, and on the right a woman who never seemed to stop hunting for something in her handbag. There was no cause for concern, I sat in the crowd, and the crowd listened to Professor Kaltenburg. For me it was less a matter of paying attention to what he said than of being carried along by his voice, his Viennese cadences filling the room, his distinct articulation, for an hour and a half Kaltenburg addressed the Saxon silence, talking clearly and animatedly and calmly. I never knew him to lose track, as for instance by noticing just in time that the sentence construction he had embarked on could end up in a mess, and he never went in for the familiar sort of muttering all too familiar when people are reading off empty passages from the page, quite simply because such passages did not occur in any lecture by Ludwig Kaltenburg.

In public he renounced anything speculative, even though speculation was of course an important element of the Institute's work, Kaltenburg would not permit himself any "philosophizing," as he called it. He confined himself strictly to the animal kingdom, and his Dresden audience was grateful for it, they found it refreshing that someone was talking purely about observations, solid information, irrefutable facts which no reasonable person could doubt. So in time a regular audience was built up, you recognized more and more faces, people nodded to one another, almost by silent agreement: this evening too will be reserved for the animals and the reality before our eyes.

You sensed how close the relationship between Professor Kaltenburg and his audience actually was in the following question-and-answer session. His answers were never simply polite, let alone brusque. At the end of the year parents always wanted to know what domestic animals were suitable as pets for their children, "No

127

guinea pigs, please," he always replied, most listeners already knew his reasons, but each time Kaltenburg patiently ran through them again.

"And that brings us to the area of unproven facts, not to say assertions that have turned out to be untenable." You might think this would be enough to make the hall hold its breath, but no, the professor then rolled his eyes, almost sank to his knees at the lectern, people were laughing, Kaltenburg caught himself up again, playing the penitent, and said, "The chaffinch."

If you were attending a Ludwig Kaltenburg lecture for the first time, you might then learn from the person sitting next to you that both the chaffinch question and the introductory joke were a standing feature of the evening. The professor had once strongly advised against acquiring a chaffinch, which would only remain a pleasant companion, earnestly singing its heart out, as long as its owner sat motionless in front of it. Otherwise, made extremely nervous by sudden movements, the bird would go on beating against the bars of its cage until its skull cracked.

The audience's rejection of this had been vociferous, one chaffinch owner after another spoke up, Kaltenburg must have observed a badly damaged specimen, or he himself had been going through an extremely neurotic patch. He was obliged to admit defeat, Professor Ludwig Kaltenburg had got it wrong, he didn't mind admitting as much. "I prefer talking about things we know for certain," was what he had always said, so where chaffinches were concerned, he was happy to leave the field to long-term observers.

One evening when the professor was about to dismiss his audience, somebody surprised us by coming up with yet another question. Kaltenburg had glanced along the rows for the last time, had embarked on his usual closing speech: he hoped that for today our questions had been answered, if not exhaustively, since there were unfortunately all too few questions about the animal kingdom that could be answered exhaustively—Ludwig Kaltenburg's discreet hint that he himself was exhausted, that the audience should save its open questions for the next lecture session, please. Among the regular listeners there was nobody who failed to take the hint, nobody who would dream of interrupting Kaltenburg at this point. People had fished out their bags from under their seats, they had their coats over their arms, waiting to applaud again at the end. "In the coming weeks we will all discover new things about the animals around us, and new questions will come up," all that was left now was his "Many thanks once more for listening to me for so long and so patiently" and "I hope you have a pleasant journey home"—two sentences between which Kaltenburg always left a short pause, to savor the attentive silence in the hall for a moment.

"Herr Professor, if you don't mind"—somebody had stood up in one of the back rows, I could hear people muttering, Hey, that's not fair, you can see the professor is tired, anybody asking a question now must be a newcomer, someone ignorant of the rules. "Herr Professor, if you don't mind, I'd like to ask a brief question," and the tone suggested that the speaker was somebody who would not recognize the rules after twenty lecture evenings with the professor, who would never respect them. People were turning round, trying to see this person, only a few noticed how Kaltenburg had raised his eyebrows, as though wondering what was in store for him now.

"If I think of a chick being nursed under its mother's wing, for example—what part of that behavior is acquired, and what is innate, what is due to experience? In short, does an adult bird know that it was taken under its mother's wing when it was young?"

A trick question? Was someone trying to lead him on? Had they planted an agent provocateur on him at last? The professor knew all the tricky types, they too were part of the regular audience. Those who always asked the same question regardless of the lecture topic. Those who always knew better than the lecturer and couldn't wait to pick him up on some trivial detail. And the one who produced an uncontrollable torrent of language that never led to a question mark. We all knew them, but this questioner did not immediately fit into any known category. Was the professor racking his memory for a face that corresponded to that of this unknown young man, was he looking around the hall for me, as though I might help him out at this juncture? I could see he was playing for time, which he did initially by explaining to the audience the unfamiliar German verb the young man had used, *hudern*, for when a chick is taken under its mother's wing.

Hudern: the expression was far from unfamiliar to me. I learned very early on what it meant, and I know who taught it to me. Who helped me with my drawing when I really wanted a picture of the mother hen who strayed into our garden with her brood of chicks one afternoon. Who did most of the work when all I had done was dash a few yellow circles down on paper to represent the young birds. I didn't have to turn around to see that lean figure before me, the taut skin that looked as though it had been stretched over the skull by hand, the high cheekbones, the peculiarly round eyes, whose effect was intensified by what seemed to be a complete absence of eyelashes. And yes, I could have told Ludwig Kaltenburg who the unknown listener was. Someone who had grown up on a farm in the Rhineland, watching from an early age how the hens nursed chicks under their wings, how they spread their wings over their offspring to protect them from rain, cold, strong sunlight. I recognized him instantly from his voice, his intonation. Nothing Saxon about it. A stranger. After you had been listening to Ludwig Kaltenburg for an hour and a half, carried along by his mellifluent Viennese accent, your hearing was sharpened, as though the eardrums had been cleansed of all sorts of guttural, hissing, and oral cavity noises. The question about chicks being nursed had been put by a Rhinelander, in a softly flowing High German, but you sensed he could just as easily have been speaking *Platt*, the Low German dialect of the lower Rhine, the language he grew up with.

Kaltenburg had left the question of nursing chicks far behind, moving on from chickens to the duck family, then touching on spotted nutcrackers, ravens, and nightingales, talking—in grossly simplified terms, as he admitted—about "stupid" and "clever" animals. Possibly still not sure whether he was being set up, he was keen to reach terra firma quickly. He was in the process of building his Dresden jackdaw colony, this was a time when he often thought back to Vienna and his first flock, long since dispersed—for him it was an easy move from here to the topic of tradition-building in the animal kingdom.

A young jackdaw, attached to older birds, would follow the same flyway as its forebears, and this knowledge, if you wanted to call it that, would be passed on to its own young. The sequence of route-training stayed the same from generation to generation, not based on some kind of insight but simply out of tradition. "My tomcat used to hunt regularly in a particular bit of the garden"—the professor leaned forward, resting on his elbows—"and the birds learned to avoid his hunting ground. Years after he died the young jackdaws were still doing the same, keeping the memory of an old cat alive."

With regard to memory itself—Kaltenburg's glance now took in the audience as a whole, whereas before he had been concentrating on the stranger—or, to be more precise, with regard to feats of memory in the narrowest sense, there were significant differences between the species, sometimes in fact between one individual animal and another. Just as there were between human beings, which was why he thought it wrong to see humans and animals as poles apart when it came to the ability to remember.

With this change of direction the professor had finally managed to put an end to the eerie mood in the hall, there was even some laughter here and there, a laugh of relief, the mixture of disquiet and paralysis was dissolved at a blow. It was true that there should not have been any mention of humans, that was the pact between Kaltenburg and his public, but in this particular situation the professor had no choice. There had never been such an atmosphere at a lecture, oppressed silence, uncertainty, doubt, anxiety, the whole evening could easily have been poisoned retrospectively. Ludwig Kaltenburg too looked relieved now: he would never have forgiven himself if he'd had to watch his listeners slope off home hanging their heads. The tension drained from his face, he bowed, the first few people were getting up to leave.

There was no time to lose. I pushed my way along the row to get to the central aisle, the dense crowd: Martin nowhere to be seen. I squeezed through as far as the door: nobody even remotely resembling him. I slipped between an old couple into the foyer: Martin must have altered. But there he was: moving purposefully toward the exit, he was just lighting a cigarette.

7

―

EOPLE AUTOMATICALLY STEPPED ASIDE to let Martin Spengler pass, they didn't dare make eye contact with him, and on the way out he saw nothing and nobody. They shied away from this stranger who had nearly upset the balance of Professor Kaltenburg's lecture evening with a single, late, inconsiderate question. But even as a silent listener among the crowd he would have made people somewhat uneasy. Yes, maybe it was something I grasped at that moment as I chased him across the foyer, drawing attention to myself in the process: wherever Martin Spengler turned up in public he caused a certain annoyance, hard to explain but totally unrelated to whether he was trying to provoke people or not.

The way that Martin once nearly got into a fight with a gang of juveniles, the way that, insecure as he was, he felt challenged by a group of cheeky but fundamentally harmless kids marauding through the rubble landscape, who for their part felt threatened by Martin as they probably did by any adult who crossed an unseen territorial boundary: it must have been one of his earliest, most formative experiences in Dresden. I can see Martin getting out of the train with his portfolio under his arm, leaving the station and walking in the direction of the art academy. But when we met up again by chance, Martin had already been living in the city for quite a while, and perhaps my memory only places this story at the beginning of his stay in Dresden because I have always regarded it as symptomatic of his student years, not to say his whole life.

Martin was received in Dresden by the echo of children's voices, it had to be children's voices, even though from a distance there was something shrill and hateful about them such as you would only want to ascribe to an adult. At first he couldn't make out any words in all the shouting, simply accepting it as a sign that the area was not completely devoid of life. There were no signposts, he had difficulty finding his way through the network of trampled paths and cleared stretches of road. Martin had an appointment, hugged the portfolio of drawings close to him, he had worked at it for a long time, constantly adding new pieces, taking out older ones, so that now it provided an overview of nearly eighteen months' work.

Masses of masonry, dust, a shrub here and there. Not that such areas were unknown to him, but he knew them only from a bird's-eye view, from his cockpit. You could just as well have told him he was traveling through the karst region north of the Mediterranean. Or far to the east. He had seen places, from above the Crimea, where Dresden stretched in every direction, to the horizon. As a fighter pilot Martin had been decorated several times over, but which sorties he got his medals for he could no longer say, there had been too many, and mostly he saw nothing below him but a postwar Dresden. The burn marks on his neck, from the chin to behind his left ear—if you mentioned his scar he would say, "That's what they gave me the gold medal for, 'wounded in combat.'"

No, none of it was that unfamiliar to Martin—it was just that he had missed his way some time ago in the empty city. Children were playing somewhere in the ruins, crawling through half-collapsed cellars, following the course of completely vanished rows of streets from one plot of ground to another, a subterranean network of paths to which no adult had access. Then they would resurface somewhere unexpected, lugging planks out of a cellar and using them to get to spaces you had so far seen only from an insuperable distance, glimpses into secret rooms, across a gaping chasm four stories deep. The children would be egging each other on, thought Martin, while they dragged their plunder with grim determination through the brick debris, or two rival gangs were preparing for a fight, or the excitement was all about some tremendous discovery, the children had found something in the ruins they'd never seen before, something strange to them—but what could be strange to them?—hence all the shouting.

At first Martin wanted to use the children's voices to orient himself. Perhaps he had missed some sign in the landscape where he should have turned off, a particular heap of stones, a gorse bush with a distinctive shape, maybe he hadn't taken in the details of the lengthy directions in the right order, had paid more attention to the tone of the friendly old lady on the train than to the information she gave him. Most of the journey had taken place in silence, actually quite a pleasant silence, he felt, even though he wondered now and again whether he, the stranger, was the reason for the reticence of his fellow travelers, who all seemed to be natives. No, it wasn't his fault, Martin realized as the valley narrowed on either side of the track, the Elbe slopes closing in on the train windows, for as the end of the journey clearly approached, the first quiet conversations started up. More and more voices joined in, he heard mention of people's jobs, place-names, surnames, even a first name, an address. He was relieved, satisfied that during the journey it had been simple consideration for others, a matter of leaving them in peace. You read, you dozed, you lost yourself in daydreams, but now, just before arriving, there was no fear of bothering anyone if you began a conversation.

It was at Weinböhla that the lady spoke to him, gesturing toward his portfolio, and when he began to explain something about drawings, the art academy, his application to study there, the lady nodded as though she had known all along. Her husband had been an artist too, a man obsessed by his art. Precisely in the darkest years he had been driven by an almost frightening compulsion, producing hundreds of drawings, even though there wasn't the slightest prospect of ever showing them in public. On the contrary, nobody could be allowed to see the pictures, and as her husband finished one sheet after another, it was her job to hide them. She had found more and more new hiding places, in the loft between two hideous old farmhouse dressers, behind the wall cladding in the summerhouse, under all the clutter in the tool shed. In a way she had admired her husband, whose work obsession prevented him from looking either forward or back, but she also felt powerless, close to despair as she sewed sketchpads into pillows or wrapped half a dozen pictures in packing paper and laid them along the shelves in the larder like ordinary lining. A few days later the wrapping paper had been torn away, the scraps covered in manic yet almost microscopically fine pencil strokes. Another headache. Her husband couldn't remember anything.

Before Martin could ask his name and whether his work was on display in the art gallery today, whether he was still working at the same furious pace, she said, "All burned."

With that, the subject was closed. "All burned": paintings, drawings, and sketches, or the artist himself together with his concealed work—Martin did not dare ask. The lady composed herself, returned to the art academy, and began to describe the easiest way to get there. It would have been better if he had asked her to draw him a sketch map on his portfolio case, because as she spoke—now fully turned toward her interlocutor—in well-formed, clearly structured sentences about things which did not affect her emotionally, Martin soon had ears for nothing but her way of talking.

They crossed the Elbe, the lady made him calmly repeat all the details, corrected him, went over it again, the train drew into the central station, and as they parted Martin had only a hazy notion of the city's topography, but he had learned his first lesson about Dresden: people here set great store by a cultivated command of High German. "We're supposed to get off the train at the front"—such prompting would have sounded far too direct, an uncouth way of addressing someone, especially if you had only just met them. In Dresden you had to say, "It might be preferable to alight by the door at the front end of the train," and you certainly couldn't have a brusque "We're getting out . . . ," let alone "We gotta get off up there."

Even before he set foot on Dresden soil, he had already learned a new word, almost a foreign word—not a dialect expression, far from it. It was something that went beyond good High German when the lady unselfconsciously wove into her sentences a refined form of the German subjunctive, *wöllte*, and thereby showed Martin what it was to speak Highest German. Admittedly, he was taken aback at first, he had never heard *wöllte* before, but it seemed so familiar to people here that he assumed the children were taught it in the first year of elementary school. He must catch up quickly, Martin resolved, as he helped his kind traveling companion with her cases and took the most polite leave of her on the platform.

While still in the station he witnessed a mother admonishing her child to "stay here, please." Even when a wayward child was threatening to disappear into the passing crowd and one felt one's face reddening with anger, one still used the proper imperative, albeit with a sharper edge. Even the harassed mother over there struggling with her luggage would not let herself go in public with a coarse, rustic "Hey!" Here they had internalized Luther, talking like a book at all times, as Martin realized at once.

When he arrived he knew practically nothing about the forms and the depths of the local language. After a period of disenchantment, while Martin tried to ward off any taint of dialect by employing a harshly correct High German, his growing curiosity led him to become more accustomed to it, and he gradually acquired a command of Saxon, though without ever accepting it completely. In particular, he learned to imitate its Chemnitz variety, in fact he eventually picked up an almost perfect Chemnitz accent, perhaps partly because it could not have been much further from Martin's native inflections. There was not the slightest melodic affinity between the two dialects, so that he didn't have to develop a feeling for fluent, for right and wrong transitions.

Now, however, Martin was lost, confronted by paths branching off between two mountains of rubble, he should have paid more attention to the directions. *Die Ohren* (the ears)—as he wasn't far now from the scene of the action, a sound was beginning to emerge that resembled these words, if anything; the chorus drifted across the empty lots, breaking on the hollow facades. Soon he thought he could make out another syllable, something formed with an *aus* (out), the shouting children were to his left, *raus*, *saus*, or *Haus*, at the next crossroads perhaps he would find out what lay behind this *Ohren aus* (ears out).

Later he could not have said what he caught sight of first, after he had taken the turning: the dozen or so boys and girls perched high above him, excitedly leaning out of the window spaces in a ruined building, poor creatures with scarred knees and mended clothes, shrieking their heads off. Strangely enough, it was more difficult to hear them now, were they suffering from mumps, could it be that the children had lost their teeth?

Or was it the man ahead of him he saw first, down below in the alley, about a hundred meters away, he must have taken a secret path over the wasteland, through what had been backyards, and emerged from a passageway onto the open street without noticing Martin's appearance at the corner of the house? From behind, it was difficult to guess his age, between thirty and forty, Martin would have said. Dark suit, no coat, no hat. Nothing else striking about him. It was hard to imagine what he was doing in such a place carrying his briefcase—perhaps he was just someone who had finished work early and was taking his usual shortcut from office to home.

Martin shuddered at the thought that he might have ended up in a similar job and had to walk day in, day out through the ruins of some small German town or other. There would be monotonous work waiting for him in the surveyor's office, insufferable colleagues, at home his young family would be expecting him, at some point the children would leave home, otherwise things would stay the same for the rest of his life. Not that Martin had achieved much in the last few years. But at least he wasn't carrying a briefcase, he was carrying a portfolio full of his own drawings through the city.

The children were targeting the man from city hall, of that there was no doubt, perhaps they had followed him the whole way. There was nothing for it now, the man would have to pass the screaming crowd of children. He straightened his back. Slowed down. Hesitated. Stopped. Bent down and reached for a stone. The children were so busy shouting at him that they didn't grasp what was going on. No, this rabble simply had no fear. Drawing himself back

137

for the throw, he turned around quickly, saw Martin behind him, dropped the stone. And finally Martin understood: *Ohren* didn't come into it, it wasn't *Ohren* the kids were thinking of, they were shouting in Saxon dialect, *"Oochen aus, Oochen aus"* (eyes out).

The young man in the dark suit, hatless and coatless, was wearing an eyepatch. With only one eye, his tormentors would have calculated, he wasn't likely to hit anybody, the stone would have been propelled with force but not aimed properly, and would have bounced back off the facade somewhere.

"Eyes out, eyes out"—the man with the eyepatch reached the next crossing, the one after that, soon he had disappeared. Martin had not moved from the spot, his portfolio under his arm, now he wished he had called out to the man ahead of him, stopped him and asked the way, involved him in a conversation. There was no point in turning back, the children would be quicker than he, knew the area well. It was quiet now, they were waiting for him to get nearer. What would they shout at him, what flaw would they hit upon, would it be the scar, his posture, his whole figure, his long arms clutching the portfolio with his drawings, his cheekbones, his shoulders, his walk, his hairline, would they discover something else altogether that nobody had yet noticed? Martin knew how sharp and merciless children's eyesight could be.

Suddenly he felt like emulating the one-eyed man. That is to say, he was conscious that he was already looking around for a really big stone, as sharp-edged as possible, it had to be weighty and solid, mustn't easily crumble. No rotten piece of rubble. A good throwing rock. And Martin had no intention of meekly putting the stone down again if somebody suddenly turned up in the street. He meant it seriously. He wouldn't be able to defend himself against the children's superior numbers, he would go down under a hail of stones, but one of the gang at least would have reason to remember this day for some time to come.

As soon as he was two or three houses away, they started up their chorus as if at a word of command. Martin walked on swiftly, straight ahead, not looking up, not hearing a thing. Then the indistinct carpet of sound again. Then half-intelligible words again. He had left the gang behind him, reached the next street corner. The children were hollering, *"Oochen aus, Oochen aus,"* as they had been the whole time, as they had perhaps the whole year through, a monotonous battle cry, but good enough at any rate to intimidate random passersby, and the eyepatch was nothing but an unlucky coincidence.

Martin slowed down, the children hadn't meant him personally, nor the one-eyed man, he had survived his second lesson about Dresden. He looked at his shoes—dust; his trouser legs—dust; sandstone and mortar had combined to form a fine layer. Now he could feel his shoulders, could feel his neck again. He was gripping the portfolio tightly in his left hand, his right hand was empty.

8

———

WE WERE SITTING IN our damp clothes in a small shelter upstream by the Elbe when Martin described his arrival in Dresden to me. The rain fell steadily in front of
us, we had been careless enough to run into a storm that had been
threatening to break for ages, not a soul in sight anywhere apart
from us, but we had both been drawn by the sulfur yellow sky. We
sat on the narrow bench together, the storm had passed overhead
toward the city, and I remember exactly how we flinched when our
clammy sleeves touched, how Martin constantly edged away from
me, as though while he was narrating he could see me only from a
certain distance. Then we left the shelter. Martin had fallen silent.
The fields were steaming.

Katharina Fischer had laid her knife and fork across her plate,
folded her napkin. That atmosphere Martin was surrounded
by—the same as in his space installations. While customers at
nearby tables continued their conversations about the day's events
and their holiday plans, the interpreter was lost in thought for a
while. "It may be that today I would hardly feel the latent aggres-
sion that used to make me recoil when I walked into a space set up
by Martin Spengler. What do you think? Was he aiming to convert
tension into harmony?"

It was hard for me be the judge of that, since from childhood I had known extremely harmonious moments in his company. I can't remember exactly whether he had already taken to visiting the hyenas, I couldn't even say whether the hyenas were already back in the zoo during his student days. But Martin went to the zoo a lot, right from the beginning. Cloven-hoofed animals. Wild cats. The aviaries. I can see him outside an animal enclosure, bent over his drawing pad, working on into the sunset. Soon the zoo would be closing for visitors, Martin enjoyed the remaining time right down to the last minute, hardly seeming to look up as the animal on the other side, the black bear, observed him curiously.

I sat next to him for many hours, absorbing what was taking shape on Martin's page. I especially loved going with him in the mornings, he had permission to start drawing early when the animals were being attended to, it was all intimacy and pleasurable expectation, none of the bustle the day would inevitably bring, no school groups, no families, no bunches of high-spirited art students who regarded animal studies as nothing but a boring exercise.

It was on a morning like this that I brought up the subject of Ludwig Kaltenburg's lecture. When Martin reacted evasively, I thought I detected a note of regret at having confronted the professor bluntly.

"No, no, that's not quite right," he corrected me, in the same friendly tone in which he had addressed Kaltenburg. "I don't feel guilty about disturbing the professor's peace of mind. On the contrary."

He had been completely indifferent to the topic of the lecture. The lecturer himself, however—Martin had come across the announcement in the newspaper, that is to say, he probably wouldn't have taken any notice of it if the name had not vaguely jogged his memory. He flipped back through the pages, the large capitals: "Professor Ludwig Kaltenburg Lectures," Martin stared at the words, there could be no mistake, not even a chance identity of names, and the professor didn't have a doppelgänger, for sure—this was the man, all right. Martin had suffered sleepless nights because of him. Met him? No, he had never met Kaltenburg. He only knew the name. He knew it from the evenly flowing handwriting of a botanist, my father's writing. From letters he had read in another life on the edge of dusty airstrips.

"To be honest, I sat in the audience all evening with one fixed purpose: to entice the great Professor Ludwig Kaltenburg out of his shell. And to do it just before the end, when nobody—least of all the professor—would be expecting a wild, unusual question."

Martin concentrated on a female bison which stood feeding not far away, looking over at us from time to time. On the page he had drawn broad charcoal lines, which he began calmly rubbing.

"You remember your nanny, of course? I sometimes wonder what became of her. She was about my age, perhaps a year or eighteen months younger. When I went to Posen I was still obsessed by the idea of becoming a pediatrician, she was looking after you, there were things for us to discuss. We strolled through the fields, just as you and I did. She even persuaded me to go for walks in the town. Our Sunday afternoons. I was never sure whether your nanny told you about it, she denied it, but I suspected you knew. She couldn't have hidden anything from you."

The animal turned away, Martin tore the portrait he had begun off the pad, it consisted of not much more than a bison's chest in isolation. A quick glance—and he sketched a bison's flank.

"I hope you don't mind me telling you this now. She was fond of you, I'm sure you know that. Though you must have been a difficult boy at times. Perhaps that's just what she liked about you. At one time there must have been a situation where you got her into a lot of trouble, or so it seemed to me, but I could never for the life of me get her to say anything about what you did wrong. She stood firmly by you. Do you remember her name? Your parents called her Maria, but maybe that wasn't her real name at all. I'd love to know whether she's still alive. Where. And what she's doing. Married with children, that's what I would wish for her. I always had the feeling that your parents kept a protective eye on her. Did you notice anything? I don't mean anything about her, but the way people treated her. Why am I asking you this, you were only seven or eight, what could you know? But we can't ask your parents now. Did she go with you to Dresden?"

Flanks by themselves, parts of the chest, the beginnings of an ear—the keeper was coming around now, making one last check on the enclosure, our time was running out. With hurried strokes and without a further glance at the animals, Martin produced a piece of shaggy hide.

"I was jealous when I found out from your parents' letters that Professor Kaltenburg was in and out of your place for a while, then stayed away after an unpleasant scene. For me it was obvious he had made approaches to Maria. She rejects him, there's a big commotion, your parents come out on her side and break off all contact with the professor. I found my own scenario so convincing that I was on the point of literally taking off to come and see you. Where was I at that time, Croatia maybe, Apulia, in the Ukraine. I had no idea how I would manage it. Just clear off with the plane. Desert. The enormous distance almost made me lose my mind. So one morning out of a clear blue sky a plane lands on the dusty road in front of your house. You have been sitting drinking cocoa. The noise. Maria joins you at the window. You see me climbing out of the cockpit. A professor who is barely forty, a fanatical motorcyclist to boot, that kind of man can be dangerous. It was only then that I found out I was really keen on your nanny. And you can't imagine how intensely I loathed Herr Professor Kaltenburg."

The first school groups had arrived at the entrance. Martin said goodbye to the ladies at the ticket office, and then the zoo and our undisturbed morning were behind us.

"Did you know that for Maria—that I made some drawings of her? My private name for the work I did then is the 'Posen Block,' and if it's ever exhibited anywhere you've got to remind me of that title, okay?"

Frau Fischer inquired whether the drawings still existed.

Certainly. They survived the Posen years, the war, Martin preserved them carefully in a number of portfolios, and somehow he even succeeded in smuggling them out intact to the West. Today they are among the most important works from that early period.

"As the 'Posen Block'?" She had never heard of a body of work with that title.

No, in fact the "Posen Block" has never been exhibited as such. Memories of a nanny—but in the catalogue it's called "Russian Nurse," a restrained sketch on a tear-off drawing pad, the soft hair, the cap with a cross, only the eyes and nose are executed with a stronger pencil line. Another drawing: "Three by the Fire," a very consciously chosen, vague title, two dark human figures contemplating an aureole, and on the left the contours of a bright figure with long hair, crouching, eyes downcast. The young woman, a suppressed fantasy perhaps, which recurs in the late work.

On the other hand, many of Martin's student pieces stuck out like a sore thumb, it occurred to me, after I had asked Katharina Fischer if she would like some dessert, a coffee. In retrospect you can see in his student work the pressure he was under: sometimes he dutifully tries to please his teachers, at other times he is really untrue to his own hand, his own vision. Presumably he left most of it behind in Dresden, if he didn't burn it. But I've kept all of Martin's bison sketches.

9

IMPORTANT AS LUDWIG Kaltenburg was for me, it wasn't from him that I first heard the name Hagemann, but from Martin Spengler. If I visualize him in his Dresden period, it's not in group photos at the college, not among a circle of laughing students, not at a carnival party. Martin in Red Indian costume, Martin at a dance, Martin as a member of a bowling team—unthinkable. For me he belongs at the Hagemann family dining table, he belongs in their drawing room. I can see Martin in the little room behind the kitchen, a space crammed with books, painting equipment, drawing pads. A narrow bed, two stools, an old bureau: this accommodation had been fixed up for him by his favorite professor, a friend of the family and also the first patron of this independent-minded art student, whom outsiders usually considered taciturn. As far as I can recall, in Dresden Martin didn't show his hyena drawings to anyone but this professor, the Hagemanns, and me.

The Hagemann family was pleased to have Martin in their house, it could easily have been different, as with the elderly couple and their middle-aged son who had been allocated quarters on the first floor. When they first moved in there was talk of having met previously, during the war, the man even announced his service rank as though that made him the new head of the household. But

Herr Hagemann did not wish to be reminded of his former superior officers, least of all by one of those officers himself.

Contact was limited to the essentials, they said hello to each other when the Klein family crossed the hall with disapproving faces to disappear up the stairs to their domain. The daughters of the household soon dubbed the Kleins "the Super-Tenant family," and eventually the parents caught themselves using this secret nickname themselves now and then. "The Super-Tenants again"—Herr Hagemann with pocket diary in hand—"I've got to get the cardboard laurels out of the cellar." Whenever the opportunist veteran appeared on the stairs on the eve of some official anniversary celebration, commemoration, birthday, or death day, silently reminding Herr Hagemann to put the decorations out, it was all the head of the household could do not to warn him, "Herr Super-Tenant, you're definitely going too far."

If the Hagemanns were having a reception, Martin made himself scarce in a corner of the drawing room and didn't budge all evening. The world of art and academia frequented the Hagemanns', the company often including foreign visitors. Martin listened, he studied. Faces, hands, ashtrays, armchairs, shoes, curtains, the stucco rosette on the ceiling: wandering around the room, his gaze often fell upon a small dark spot, up there between the hook for the chandelier and a stucco sunflower leaf. A housefly stiffened in death, but Martin wouldn't have been all that surprised if on closer inspection the empty exoskeleton had turned out to be a tiny hole. And he pictured to himself three people with wry faces upstairs crouching together under the kitchen table, with father, mother, and son silently fighting over whose turn it was to apply their ear to the hole punched through the linoleum.

Once the guests had all left and the family had gone to bed, Martin crept out of his room again back into the drawing room, enjoying the silence, sitting in the green armchair, Frau Hagemann's favorite. In the darkness he looked at the walls.

"These walls are a world in themselves," he said once. At the Hagemanns', hyena art hung everywhere.

Every time I met Martin, he told me about the Hagemanns, and

146

I soon felt I knew the family personally, as though I had enjoyed their company for years, the parents, the two daughters—Martin, who got on well with them from the beginning, passed on some of his intimacy to me. I particularly remember one of his stories, perhaps because I never found out whether Martin invented it for me in the telling, or because it took place in the Great Garden, or perhaps quite simply because Klara Hagemann was the central figure in it.

One day, during a Sunday walk in the park, without warning Klara left her family standing on the path. A figure in the distance, an unusual movement, had caught her eye, and before her parents or sister had time to notice that a man holding a dog lead was about to beat his animal with it, Klara had raced off. She ran straight across the field, screaming, a stream of words never heard before in this spot and probably never heard there again. The dachshund owner knew he was being accosted, looked around, couldn't work out at first what was happening, had no idea what was coming at him, just saw a screaming girl in a Sunday dress. For a moment he forgot the existence of the scruffy, whimpering animal cowering in the grass at his feet—and lowered his arm. Klara Hagemann had been eleven or twelve. Straight after the war. Her parents' hearts must have stood still.

Martin said, "She was still quite small at the time."

Half of Dresden looked on as a girl in a white dress with knee-length socks and sandals delivered a telling-off to a dog owner, a total stranger. The Hagemanns had no idea where she could have acquired such language.

He said, "She's quite different today."

As though he had been present himself, Martin described to me how the father took a deep breath, took his first step into the field. Seen from the path, his walk, his shoulders, looked a little stiff. Once over there he looked the man in the eye, speaking two, three short sentences. They shook hands. Then Herr Hagemann and his daughter were back. He took off his hat, wiping his brow. He was sweating: "Not another word. We're going for a coffee."

The two girls ran on ahead. Ulli, the older sister, always one step behind Klara. His wife took his arm. Her expression said, *Klara was right*. He was powerless against it. Herr Hagemann had been looking forward to a peaceful family walk. But Klara was his daughter. He was the father of Klara Hagemann. A perfectly ordinary, mild Sunday afternoon in 1946 or 1947.

As can be imagined, I was pretty curious about this girl, or I should say this young woman, and was looking forward to being introduced to her by Martin. The trouble was, he knew me well enough to be aware that I was quite capable of wrecking a carefully planned arrangement at the last minute, I wouldn't have cared a jot about embarrassing Martin, I simply wouldn't have turned up at the rendezvous. He had no choice but to simply take me by surprise, and so he told me, as he packed up his things at the end of an afternoon together at the zoo, "By the way, I forgot to tell you — we're going to see Klara."

The further we walked down Tiergartenstrasse, the more agitated I felt. Martin remained cool. "She'll be waiting for us" — he turned purposefully into the Great Garden — "She's always over-punctual, you know." He walked faster, pulled my sleeve, pointing at the ruins of the palace: "What did I tell you, the woman over there in the blue dress, do you recognize her?"

We shook hands, and Klara greeted me so politely that I almost expected a curtsy. But there was a spark in her green eyes that seemed to warn me not to go thinking her good manners were for my personal benefit. Martin pointed to his portfolio, then at me: "Hermann was with me in the zoo."

"In the zoo?"

With raised eyebrows, Klara fixed her gaze on me with the air of someone who vaguely remembered going there a long time ago. At least I was in Martin's company — obviously it wasn't thought strange he should go to the zoo regularly, and he was much older than I. In fact, she insisted on assessing Martin's new work before anything else, we found a place under the trees, and she hadn't even ordered a drink before Martin was made to open his portfolio. "Mineral water or a soda — no, I'll have water"; she didn't mind, the drawings lay spread out on the table in front of us. Klara, who didn't appear to be interested in animals, compared the hare with the graylag goose, pulled a series of eagle studies closer to her, the line on this page, the fine hatching over there, as though just breathed onto the paper, a bird in motion, and then — "Could you move that glass, please" — that line on the head of a resting bearded vulture.

"Tell me, do either of you know which house Kokoschka stayed in?" Martin pointed across at the palace pond. "Is that the one? The one in front, maybe? Or is it one of those that was bombed? I'm sure you can tell me, Klara."

Klara shook her head, as though she knew exactly. I, on the other hand, didn't even know the name Oskar Kokoschka, I was hearing about this painter for the first time, and especially about the life-sized doll he got someone to make in the image of the woman he idolized, an ugly, crude monster puppet which Kokoschka hoped would inspire him in Dresden.

"I have heard that the doll was found one morning soaked in red wine and with twisted limbs somewhere here in the garden. I'd love to know where, precisely."

A policeman on his beat had thought at first that the limp figure with the dead face was a real female corpse, Martin went on talking, and I was grateful to Klara when she interrupted him in mid-sentence: "I hope you don't mind, Martin, but I think that'll do."

We sauntered around the palace pond, to the Flutgraben — that is, I saw Klara strolling next to Martin, saw the toes of her shoes, yes, Klara was strolling through Dresden as though demonstrating how you should move in the distant future along the boulevard of an imaginary metropolis. Her ankles. Her dark, very slightly wavy hair.

"Martin has told me about your episode with the dachshund owner," I dared to address her.

"Oh, that old story" — amused, I thought, or perhaps like someone tired of hearing the same anecdote repeated. And I wasn't expecting that Klara, acting as though Martin were suddenly in the way, would drop back a step and smile across at me.

Martin suggested hiring a rowboat. Apparently the idea appealed to Klara too, he was inviting us to take a boat ride, I could see Klara and me sitting next to each other, Martin facing us on the oarsman's seat. But when we got in, it was "No, no, Hermann, you've got to sit at the front." We both looked questioningly at Martin, he shrugged his shoulders, "Enjoy the trip," he pushed the boat off, "Water makes me nervous," Martin stayed behind on the landing stage: "We'll meet up again in an hour's time, in safety, on dry land."

Klara and I on Lake Carola. Martin followed us on the bank. That is to say, he had to keep stopping because my rowing was so bad that we hardly moved from the spot. I was on a collision course, all around us boats were gliding smoothly through the water, all of the strong young men oblivious of the labors of their upper body, their shoulders, their arms, their hands. The evenness of the oar movements was impressive, everything working like clockwork, each one of them enjoying a trip with their beloved could concentrate on taking a close look at those eyes, those lips, that nose.

I succeeded in steering our boat under the bridge without capsizing, the narrow part of the lake was behind us, for a while we were moving toward the fountain. And that was when Martin appeared again, Klara spotted him as we passed the restaurant, mixing with the families at the feeding place, Martin in a flurry of ducks, hopefully he wouldn't think of waving.

Martin waved to us.

Hordes of children squatting on the bank looking for fish in the shallow water, children, half scared and half overconfident, holding out dry bread for the ducks to take, parents watching over their offspring—they would all turn instantly to look at the waving man in their midst, would follow his eyes across the lake, point to a boat, and have to laugh, the splashing water, somebody snatching hastily at the oars. But Klara didn't turn a hair. I was rowing with my right arm, I wanted to bring the boat around, Klara was directing me. I was gripped by ambition, I was aiming at least to circumnavigate the little island with the swan's nest. I no longer noticed the other boats. Once I had to push us off again from the bushes onshore. Once some twigs brushed Klara's hair. And precisely when I was thinking with relief that Martin could no longer see us at this point, she said, "Made it."

No, Klara wasn't laughing. But as we moved more or less calmly between the island and the bank, and I didn't even have any trouble maneuvering the boat a little so that Klara could get a better view of the white plumage over there in the bushes, I could have sworn that sitting facing me was an unknown lady I had heard laughing one November evening long ago. The woman in the fur coat wearing a peaked cap, the way she held her cigarette on the dark Elbe hillside, how she swept past me in the hall, and Klara in her blue dress, her hands holding on to the gunwale to get a good look at the island in Lake Carola: one and the same person, I could have sworn to it.

10

K LARA STOOD BAREFOOT in the doorway, in her blue
summer dress which I knew from our boat outing in the
Great Garden—the blue formed a very striking contrast to
the green of Klara's eyes. It could be the way the light was falling,
I thought, evenly shining through the leaves of a big beech tree by
the entrance. Klara watched me calmly as I approached, she might
have seen me standing at the iron gate reading the nameplate, the
Hagemann property, the path through their garden, the house
where Klara and Martin live. I went up the steps to the entrance,
the blue dress, the green eyes, Klara's bare feet on the threshold, I
really didn't know where to look.

I had come to pick up Martin, it was all arranged—in my confusion I may not even have said hello.

"Oh, really? He's not here. Perhaps he'll be back soon. As far as I
know, he was going down to the Elbe. You can go and look for him
if you want."

Even as she was saying this, quickly, decisively, as though to
get rid of me, she stepped aside in the doorway. I followed her, we
crossed a small anteroom, more a ventilation chamber, and Klara
pushed open a swing door as if unaware that somebody was behind her. The wings of the door sprang back, I was just able to slip
through.

"The door nearly caught me."

"Oh dear, you poor thing."

I assumed she was going to take me straight to Martin's room, where I could wait for him, but she paused: "We used to play around with the swing door, Ulli and I, every evening after supper, we used to run back and forth in our nightgowns from the corridor to the vestibule and back. Our parents shouted that we shouldn't romp around near the cold entrance, and we shrieked every time one of us had been hit on the head by the door. Out of breath, overexcited, faces flushed, just the state to be in when you're meant to be going to bed."

The "vestibule," not "a ventilation chamber" or "a small ante-room" — for me the word is inextricably linked with that afternoon, when I heard it, from Klara, for the first time.

"A lovely house, with this swing door." And I must have also said something like "You've got lots of space."

"Well, we're not the only ones living here — but don't worry, they're not around."

I don't quite trust myself. Neither the surprised, stupid adolescent trotting along behind Klara in the hall nor my present self claiming to remember. Klara's cool, almost rude behavior at the beginning, only to take a friendly interest in me scarcely two minutes later — it would sound more credible if Klara's tone when I turned up unannounced at the door had been consistently polite, if rather distant. First careless, then slightly too pert, that's not Klara — and did she really ask, "Are you scared of me?"

I don't know to this day whether Martin's absence was accidental, whether he had forgotten our arrangement or deliberately gone for a walk by himself. It's also possible that he may have been in the house the whole time, having a midday nap or engrossed in his work, and Klara didn't want to disturb him — one possible explanation why she didn't take me to his room, no, to the "maid's room," as she called the room behind the kitchen.

We had hardly sat down in the drawing room when Klara remembered that she had a book for me: "A present from my parents, and because Martin told me you were interested in swallows, I thought it might be something for you."

Not swallows—swifts: did I call that out to Klara as she left the room to fetch the book, or did I manage to suppress such a redundant correction? You think you never see the world so clearly as in such situations, and then you have to concede that out of sheer excitement you had eyes neither for yourself nor for the person opposite.

Klara handed me a hardback volume. I opened it at the title page and was shocked to see a familiar name: LUDWIG KALTENBURG. Shocked, because I had never heard of the book, according to the title a guide to living with animals.

"I know him."

"You've read the book already?"

"No, not a word of it. I'm just surprised. Because I know the author."

"Another book by him?"

"No, that's not it. I had no idea that he wrote books like this. I've known Professor Kaltenburg forever, since I was a child, but he didn't write popular handbooks then, only academic works."

"Oh, academic works, I get it."

I was on the point of surrendering. Klara didn't miss a thing, she picked up the slightest alteration in my voice as well as the deceptive casualness of a throwaway sentence, sensed a touch of arrogance as well as the little lie that had preceded it. She didn't let go.

"You know Professor Kaltenburg personally? I don't believe you."

As though suddenly sorry for her brisk tone, she asked, "Would you like a glass of cordial? You could browse through the book until I get back."

I felt as though Ludwig Kaltenburg had let me down. When I asked him about his manual the next time we met, he brushed aside this "little effort," as he called it, with a shrug. A straight money-spinner, Kaltenburg's financial worries in the early postwar years, no prospect of a suitable post, all the animals that needed feeding every day. When he was writing it he had also been driven by a certain anger, he was maddened by the countless bad animal books on the market, he said, wanted to sweep away all that senti-mental, hypocritical garbage: no more cute little noses, no more round, astonished, sleepy eyes, or should one say bedroom eyes, and no more cuddly creatures that were nothing but humans in plush costumes. Nobody would have believed at the time that Kaltenburg's book—which, incidentally, was followed by a num-ber of sequels—would be such a notable success. He would never have dreamed that his collection of experiences with animals would reach such wide circles, even including Dresden society. He was still writing occasional little articles of that kind, he said, newspa-per editors pestered him for them, obviously readers couldn't get enough of unadulterated animal-watching. For him they were re-laxation exercises, in the evenings when he didn't have the con-centration for serious work he would sit down and compose, with a light touch, for an hour at most, until the last feed. "And you've known all the stories for years, you heard them from my own lips. But of course I'll give you a copy, you know I really love you to read every word I've written."

When Klara came back from the kitchen, I talked to her about her parents. She said they were certainly kindhearted people who refused to let anybody destroy their belief in human goodness. I was holding my glass, Klara emptied hers in one go—but as chil-dren she and her sister had sometimes suffered for this belief. The pressure to be good despite all the challenges.

"A child can't keep something like that in mind day and night. Once Ulli and I raced through the house shouting nonstop some phrase we were making fun of, I can't remember what it was, some political chant perhaps."

She sat down next to me on the sofa, hugging her knees.

"Suddenly my father grabbed me fiercely by the arm, he came shooting out from nowhere, pulled me under the stairs, and hissed, *You know perfectly well the kind of people we've had foisted on us upstairs.* His eyes staring, his lips trembling, and before he let go of me he whispered one word: *VORKUTA.* That night we could hardly get to sleep, although of course our father's hint about Siberia was lost on us. Vorkuta to me meant the bruises on my arm that I covered up with a long-sleeved blouse."

The fine hairs on her arm. Klara stroked her left foot.

"If you know Professor Kaltenburg so well, you must have been to his Institute in Loschwitz?"

Naturally—the door to his Institute, and even to his private quarters, was open to me day and night. But what kind of an impression would it have made if I had blurted out everything I knew about Kaltenburg? I knew every corner of his villa, I knew the man's every emotion—a pale young man basking in the light of his fame. So I steered a course through Kaltenburg's world as well as I could without sounding boastful, I took a back seat, telling her that what impressed me about Kaltenburg when I was a child was the way he had with gloves. Often he carried several pairs around with him, the thick calf gloves for the motorbike, the finer ones for the car, the mittens made of thick felt for a walk in the woods, the "torn ones," as he called them, a favorite old patched pair he wore in early autumn down by the Elbe and sometimes in the evening, on his way down into the city, then his buckskin ones for unavoidable social occasions, which he took off to greet people.

Klara asked me that afternoon, "You want to be famous too, don't you?" And when I came up with no answer she added, "Or at least notorious."

The sun, which had moved around the house, was now shining through the big veranda windows straight into the drawing room. Our empty glasses on the table. The carpet. My dusty shoes. After a while Klara said, "By the way, I enjoyed our time on Lake Carola."

"It was the first time I'd ever sat in a rowboat."

"That was obvious. But I loved the way you simply ignored people when they started laughing at us."

She blinked, jumped up, and said something that I didn't quite catch, something like "This isn't getting anywhere." In two steps she had reached the window and begun to close the heavy curtain. First the left half, dark and heavy as a fur coat I had once followed with my eyes. Klara reached for the right half, carefully guiding the hem behind an indoor palm with her foot. I followed her movements, followed the strip of light as it got narrower. The dark hair on the back of the head of a strange woman. The bright chink had disappeared, and for an instant I was blind. Then I saw Klara's face, right in front of mine.

11

———

THE LAST PLEASURE BOAT had glided past sometime before, we could count only about two dozen dinner jackets and evening dresses under the festive lanterns, down below the band was playing for two or three couples self-consciously dancing, most passengers stood together in little groups on deck to take in the evening air over the Elbe one last time before the trip ended. Not a sound to be heard. It had gone quiet here in the restaurant as well, the steps creaked, the waiter came up to serve our coffee, took the empty dessert plates away. Frau Fischer lit a cigarette.

I had tried to describe my excitement when, at the end of my first afternoon in the Hagemanns' house, I had asked if I could take her to the cinema. And how Klara, no doubt just as excited, answered with a decisive nod of the head and a firm "Friday." As though it had been settled long ago: from now on she would be going to the cinema only with this boy called Hermann Funk.

My excitement then, a few weeks later, when I had my first invitation from the Hagemanns. I knew the drawing room from my afternoon with Klara, I knew the receptions at the house from Martin's description, but all the same I can barely remember the evening itself. I can't even recall Klara there, that's how excited I must have been. Fortunately, at the time I wasn't aware that there was a good deal more associated with the name Hagemann than Martin had conveyed to me on our outings. Yes, if my parents had been Dresdeners and I had grown up in the city, I would have known about the family name, would probably have heard it mentioned at home when I was a child.

Among their extended family there was a line of academics, there were landowners, the car-business Hagemanns, Klara's grandfather had been a cigarette manufacturer. Older gentlemen in their circle still praised the quality of certain brands, the Turkish Mixture, the Pure Virginia, and when they shook Herr Hagemann's hand they did so solemnly, with dignity, as though they were still expressing their condolences decades after the firm had gone bankrupt and Grandfather had been consigned to the attic. Klara's father felt uncomfortable in such situations — granted, there were such things as family virtues, hard work, conscientiousness, and an artistic vein, but Herr Hagemann did not possess an estate, nor did he run a factory. It's possible that his choice of chemistry at the university was meant to give him something of an outsider profile in the family, he had gone to Berlin, had met his future wife in the laboratory, toyed with the idea of going abroad, but then come back to Dresden with his young family after all. Perhaps he would have preferred to live where the name meant nothing, but all the same: if you were introduced to Klara's father, exchanged a few words with him, perhaps got to know him a little better, you soon sensed that Herr Hagemann felt an obligation to his family name, especially as all the rest of the Hagemann clan had been decamping to the West one by one since the war.

That was his stubborn streak. His secret wish to restore the good name of the Hagemanns. So Klara's father tolerated it when his colleagues in the laboratory appreciatively called him a "real Hagemann" because in his presence the director of the firm, who was given to violent outbursts, was transformed into an understanding character who didn't mind asking the son of the cigarette factory owner for advice from time to time. He also put up with it when his name occasionally provoked some skeptical scrutiny.

Herr Hagemann knew what he was letting himself in for. He and his wife had spent sleepless nights going through the pros and cons together, but the final decision wasn't made until the landed-gentry relatives sent their first letter from the West. His aunt's childish handwriting seemed to Klara's father exactly suited to the "yoke" and "knout," the "demons" and the "bloodsuckers" she was writing about, as though a defeated military commander had dictated his last testament to her in his madness. Herr Hagemann held his breath. As he read the last paragraph, he began to growl dangerously, Frau Hagemann was considering sending her daughters out of the room: their nephew was of course welcome at any time, they said, to escape to the bosom of the family together with his wife and daughters. He remembered staying with them near Meissen, even as a child he didn't trust his uncle, in fact he was afraid of him, like everybody else on the estate. The oppressive summer days were dominated by fear of running into this unpredictable being, the nephew mingled with the farm workers, went out to the fields with them, hung around in the stables—but the landowner had eyes everywhere. Put yourself in the hands of such people? Of your own free will? Never.

Then there were his good intentions. There was his drive to prove himself. And there was the indulgence toward his daughters, especially the younger one, who had inherited so much from him. You certainly didn't have to do everything they expected of you today, but he really couldn't see any reason to complain about the prospect of a peace demonstration. Klara had earmarked that time for the next volume of Balzac, she was complaining about the wasted hours. Her father shook his head, she needn't make a face like that, and then he felt sorry when she left the house looking miserable. The book was lying on the table. Herr Hagemann had acquired it as a young chemistry student in Berlin, had skipped his practicals, had read from cover to cover all the volumes of the cycle that had appeared in German, and felt quite lighthearted about it, as though he had managed to shake off a whole load of Hagemann obligations he had imposed upon himself.

"Then there was no further contact between the Hagemanns and the family in the West?" asked Frau Fischer.

Klara had never seen her western relatives. She wasn't allowed to receive so much as a parcel of books from the uncle.

"So there were some limits to his indulgence toward his younger daughter, then."

I don't think the threat was ever made openly, but neither do I believe that any of the longed-for new books from the West ever got to Klara. Books she wasn't allowed to read—no, it was more to do with his fearful imaginings, her father trying to give concrete expression to his loathing of that branch of the family.

In the first summer of the war the parents took their two daughters on a trip to Leipzig, Klara had just started school, Ulli was two grades above her, their father was in the uniform he detested, he cherished every minute spent with his family. His "three women," as he called them, gave him protection, and protection for him meant the illusion that he was a civilian. So he took his family to the zoo, took them for a coffee, and in the strange city even his daughters forgot for a while that their father was no longer living with them at home. And then—whether it was an idea that occurred to them over coffee or the parents had planned it as a way of rounding off the excursion—they tacked on a visit to the National Library. Ulli thought it a boring idea, even more books than at home, a whole building just for books. She began to whine, she had enough to do with her reading primer at school, here was a whole lifetime of books she would never master, and she saw malevolently grinning authors who enjoyed writing, filling page after page, book after book, and every time they put their difficult-to-read names to a title page they leaned back, stretched themselves at their desks, narrowed their eyes, and trained their sights on Ulli. They filled shelf upon shelf, room after room, while Ulli laboriously formed her letters one by one, wrestling with sentences, toiling away at her exercise books and yet bringing them home every time covered in red ink.

What did her little sister know of the abysses of reading and writing? Speechless, Klara stared at the imposing, shiny row of lettering on the facade. She stood speechless in the entrance hall and was speechless while being shown the catalog, the reference works, the loans desk. And everybody here was carrying books under their arm, all eager to start bending over the open white pages with the black signs, day and night. When you were reading, you no longer even wanted to sleep. Speechless, Klara let her mother drag her away to the train station, she still hadn't found her tongue when the train pulled into Dresden, at night in bed Ulli talked about the cocoa, talked about the animals, then worked out how many days of the holiday were left and fell asleep.

The Leipzig experience may have faded into the background in the following years; how could Klara know what a librarian was? But reading and writing came so much more naturally to her than to Ulli, no doubt as the younger sister she had an advantage: the younger ones sit quietly with their toys listening while the schoolchild at the table traces the lines of print with a forefinger; they listen to the way that words form into sentences, the parents' careful corrections, and two or three years later, when it's their turn to read aloud, it sounds as though they have taught themselves everything overnight. Klara did her homework without grumbling, then sat down with her parents' library to read her way patiently through the centuries. Soon she had a favorite bookseller in the city, Herr Lindner. He was the one who said one day, almost in passing, "I can't imagine Klara anywhere but a library."

She was no longer the girl who confronted strange dachshund owners in the Great Garden, no longer incited her sister to rampage through the house making fun of political chanting, so loudly that the people upstairs could hear. She had learned in the meantime what it was to be a Hagemann, she knew that when she wanted to achieve a goal it was not enough to be more hardworking than the others, brighter, cleverer, if you didn't have the necessary instinct, the so-called ability to learn. It was definitely not easy to keep a tight rein on herself, how often she bit her tongue, how often she rolled her eyes when somebody came at her with "truth" and "historical necessity" when all she could see was stupidity. But she made the effort, kept her aim firmly in sight, had even forced herself during her training to read the collected works of Johannes R. Becher, minister of culture.

It even went so far that Klara was mistaken for an ardent admirer of the culture minister, and I can still clearly remember a distant relative reciting a few lines of Becher at our wedding to please Klara. There we stood in front of the assembled wedding guests, all eyes were on us, I can still feel Klara's moist hand in mine, how she flinched when she recognized the lines, how she held on to me tightly, as though she could not survive the solemn recitation of that harmless versifying without the man beside her.

"The relatives from the West weren't there."

No, of course not.

"It sounds weird, this strict ban on contact simply because of bad childhood memories that Herr Hagemann was unable to put behind him."

The parents kept it close to their chest. They wanted to foster Klara's and Ulli's belief in human goodness. But you're right, there must have been more to it.

Not all that long ago, sometime in the late nineties, we had been invited over by an old bird breeder in the Meissen region, Klara always got on well with him too. It was his ninetieth birthday, the whole village was sitting together on this sunny afternoon in the meadow behind the house, there were cakes, there was schnapps, and the more schnapps there was, the more talkative the farmers became. They were cursing the regional authority's livestock-disease insurance scheme, flies hovered around the half-eaten custard cakes, people were exchanging stories about animal diseases, the cream for the coffee clotted as it was stirred, and soon they were competing around the table to impress us townies with descriptions of worm-eaten sheep and suppurating cows' eyes. Typical butcher's-yard stories, a rough tradition, but this kind of thing never makes either me or Klara feel bad. Then the name Hagemann came up.

The oldest man at the table, who had so far sat quietly listening, looked around at everybody with his light-colored eyes, let his young neighbors know what he thought of their animal stories, cleared his throat, and began telling us about 1945. He had not been drinking. He pointed to the surrounding hamlets, hills, copses, the number of skeletons that were buried there, he wasn't just talking about illegally disposing of a few sheep or cows. "The Russians are over here"—the man brought his right hand down on the table—"and the Americans are here"—his left hand came down not far away. "Nobody knew which of them would arrive first, but everybody was certain of one thing, the great, decisive battle involving our secret armies was not going to take place on Saxon soil, if at all."

Slowly his hands moved closer together as he described the landowners' nocturnal meetings. "They didn't want any trouble," many of them were scared for the first time in their lives, "they had to come up with something," there were shotguns around, and foreign forced laborers who could tell more stories than the farmers liked to think. "So they took their Poles and Ukrainians into the woods."

He named the collective farms, the former estates, listed old names for us, among them there was a Hagemann. The table fell silent. The palms of his hands met. "And that was that."

Klara's maiden name—and what a relief it was to both of us that the name Funk was associated only with the ornithologist and his charming wife who had such refined manners, who could listen attentively and react almost without batting an eyelid to the farmers' coarse tales.

I had paid the bill, helped Frau Fischer on with her coat, a little too heavy for the weather at the time, we were about to head for the taxi stand, on the ground floor the tables had already been laid for the next day, the waiter opened the door for us and said goodnight. The gravel crunched beneath our feet, the night air, the bridge ahead of us, the river to one side, the water shimmering on its way to the sea, and Frau Fischer said she would like to slip down to the riverfront once more for a moment, to take a look across at Loschwitz.

12

———

A RE YOU OUT of your mind?" This was always the prelude
to one of Kaltenburg's fits of rage—as I well knew, but so
far none of his outbursts had been directed at me. "What
do you mean, you're not quite sure yet what to do with your life?"

I didn't relish mumbling and stammering in front of the professor, so I looked at the floor in silence. He had not expected an answer. "What a disappointment. I've got to sit down."

I wasn't sure whether he was groping theatrically toward his
armchair or whether he was genuinely overcome with a sudden
weakness. "The biggest disappointment of my life. You don't know
what you want to do"—he adopted a droning voice, the voice of an
annoying brat—"as if we're playing in the sandpit and you're asking me what you should be, a fireman or a train driver."

He lowered himself heavily onto the cocktail-bar chair, sitting
on the arm, leaning back as though he were going to slide to the
floor. "How long have we known each other? How long? Tell me."

"Ten years?"

Silence.

"Longer?"

"And after more than ten years you still don't understand a
thing? My God, what sort of amoeba have I picked out?"

He passed a hand across his brow, pure play-acting, and in the
next instant his eye caught mine and held it, his gaze boring into my

skull. "You're going to study zoology, no question. You'll be one of my disciples."

He collapsed in the armchair, completely drained, shaking his head as though talking to himself, as though there were no point in addressing me, the amoeba. "Don't know why you didn't think of it yourself."

And then, after another long pause—I was wondering whether to call the doctor or simply go home—he raised his eyes to me again in a typical Kaltenburg twist, almost affectionately, now was the moment for his long-planned surprise: "My boy, we have a study place for you."

Ludwig Kaltenburg was in his element when he could pluck a surprise out of the hat, especially if no one knew what effort had gone into it. The professor was only really pleased with himself when he seemed to have been inspired by a sudden brain wave, a crazy idea, and in a flash had come up with an elegant solution to the toughest problem. You might suspect the struggles behind the scenes—but you couldn't say so, because for a Professor Kaltenburg it was all child's play.

I was supposed to fall upon his neck, to jump for joy. But I could neither move nor speak. The surprise had succeeded. Afterward, I hoped he would assume I had been struck dumb with delight. It looked as though Ludwig Kaltenburg was fulfilling wishes I didn't even know I had.

When I look back on that afternoon, I am overcome with rueful feelings. I'm ashamed to think that I almost feel sorry for Kaltenburg. His outburst, his surprise, the staged attack of weakness—as though he were covering up a real state of weakness, as though contrary to appearances he had shown that he could be hurt, that he had in fact been hurt by me. The "greatest disappointment of my life": just as I was previously unwilling to tell him about my foster family, so I had not confided in him about Klara. He wouldn't have held it against me that I didn't visit him so often, no longer came over to Loschwitz in a tearing hurry and left again soon afterward muttering some excuse—it didn't take much imagination to work out that a date with a woman lay behind it. Kaltenburg was prob-

166

ably waiting for me to tell him about Klara. But I didn't. He was offended. He was afraid I would slip away from him. And that is how, always willing to try anything that would turn the threat of defeat into a triumph, he came up with the idea of the study place.

Those clear, plain sentences of Kaltenburg's that run through my life—they've always been a puzzle to me: his definite "It's the boy I'm worried about" in the discussion with my father that I heard from the conservatory. His "I said you wouldn't get rid of me so quickly" between two interviews outside the Loschwitz villa on a radiant afternoon. The sentence he tossed out to me which forbade contradiction, no, which belonged in a world where Kaltenburg simply couldn't be contradicted: "You'll be one of my disciples." And at some point, arising out of his despair, half self-surrender, half challenge to me: "Then you'll always remember me."

Right into the eighties, in his late letters, there was a whole series of such sentences, and in situations where my courage threatened to fail me I muttered them to myself, hearing Kaltenburg's voice, his confidence, his irrefutable phrasing. How clear and predetermined was the life—and, with the best of intentions, the life of others—he saw before him, stretching into the future: the world as created by Ludwig Kaltenburg. Whenever I couldn't see any way forward I willed myself to take heart from his sentences, but as soon as I heard him speaking, the words had an uncanny ring to them, as though someone were trying to teach me to be afraid. Kaltenburg's confidence has been alien to me throughout my life.

Had he in fact made a plan in the early forties, when he was in and out of my parents' house, and had he, the falcon poised to swoop, spotted with his sharp eyes a creature down there on the ground that looked promising to him? Did it simply suit him that after the move to Dresden the youth seemed as attached to him as the child had previously been, did he feel, rather than plan, at that moment that he should take care of the war orphan who was wandering aimlessly through life, steer him, make something of him? It may be that he was at pains not to destroy my childhood image of the great Professor Kaltenburg, perhaps he himself needed to make a supreme effort to maintain it after what had happened to my parents. Naturally he always had a weakness for youth, he couldn't help turning toward a youngster, supporting him, so long as he spotted in his eyes the least sign of a sharp mind. And once he had committed himself to someone, he wasn't going to drop him again in a hurry.

It must have been clearer to him than to anybody that I did not have the makings of a world-class ornithologist. All the same, I was "his candidate." I can remember that—though it was none of my doing—I even came out ahead of a school leaver of about my age who had more ability and stamina than I, was harder-working and brighter. But the less ambition I demonstrated to Kaltenburg, the more privileges I was granted, the easier everything was made for me.

In the grounds of the Institute I was the only one Kaltenburg addressed with the informal *Du*, while I stuck to the formal *Sie* for him. That alone made me stand out in his surroundings. I helped out here and there, I was around when needed, but it was always clear that I was free to come and go as I pleased. And the director of the Institute always had time for me. Scientists came to visit, old friends of Kaltenburg's, they called each other *Du*. Young people, assistants, researchers starting out were called *Du* at first, but at some point Kaltenburg moved without much fuss to the *Sie* form. With colleagues and people from politics or culture, it was *Sie* on both sides. Kaltenburg would call me over: "Can you [*Du*] give me a hand with the stickleback tank?" and I would say, "Do you [*Sie*] need rubber gloves?" That's how it was during my time as a tenured member of staff at Loschwitz, and we kept it up after the Institute closed, right until the end, in our last letters.

I had been given the chance to study zoology with Professor Kaltenburg in Leipzig. He didn't want any thanks, however, or at least he waved away the words I had scraped together when he was briefly called out of the room by a colleague. When Kaltenburg came back—"We must go down to the garden"—he seemed to have put the preceding scene out of his mind completely. "Yes, you're welcome," he growled, "what did you expect from me," and, full of impatience because he might be missing some new observation, "Now, let's go and take a look at the geese."

All the same, I did not become a disciple of Kaltenburg's. At least, if he could look back and survey my path from today's standpoint, I don't believe that he would want to describe me as "his disciple." I would have had to share his views, at many stages of my life, and that was a situation which was often painful for me. Especially just before his death, when I had to look on from a distance at the kind of followers he had around him. Among them were some whose rather clumsy, not to say small-minded, efforts to defend their honored professor hardly improved matters when they fought back against public attacks with the blind fury of wounded epigones, only to attract even noisier criticism of the professor. Suspicions which Ludwig Kaltenburg, left to himself, would have defused with some calm words. It's possible that, while not reproaching me, he was revealing a trace of his disappointment that I never became his disciple when his later letters referred to the "lickspittles" and "idiots" who surrounded him.

The interpreter followed my pointing hand, lights in the Weisser Hirsch district, lights in Loschwitz, the roads showed up as dotted lines running up the hillside, that's where Ludwig Kaltenburg used to live, up there on the right. No, I wouldn't have wanted to follow him to the West. Even assuming I hadn't met Klara, hadn't run into Martin again, I had long ceased to regard Dresden as a mere stopping-off point, a place where I got stuck for a while due to unfortunate circumstances. And it was the professor I had to thank for that.

The water swirled at our feet, we were only a few steps away from the place where countless ducks and swans gathered during the day expecting to be fed by walkers. Unfortunately, I couldn't pick out the villa itself over there, perhaps it was unlit because it was now empty, or perhaps it was too long since I last stood here for me to be able to orient myself in the dark on the far side of the Elbe. You would have to come back in daylight or, better still, as Katharina Fischer suggested, drive over to Loschwitz and take a close look at the former Institute site.

Once he said, as we were standing on the balcony watching a handful of hooded crows mixing with the flock of jackdaws above the Elbe slopes, "It doesn't matter to me in the least if people see me as an eccentric uncle figure who tells anecdotes that are sometimes amusing and sometimes completely incomprehensible but who is basically not quite right in the head. If strangers see my household and way of life here as weird, even dangerous, that just tells you more about them. It's a risk I take, I know that. But if—God forbid—I ever in my life become predictable to others, if I ever finish up being predictable to myself, foreseeing today what observations I'll be making tomorrow morning, then that will be the moment I die, that much is certain."

On one hand, I believe I can clearly remember that this was one of our first conversations on the balcony, in the early fifties. But on the other, it sounds as though for some time the sky had already been closing in over Kaltenburg's head, and that would place it somewhere in the second half of the decade. Perhaps I'm merging together several discussions, a series of critical utterances over the years in which he revealed some of his hidden worries. Hearing them at first with amazement—after all, Kaltenburg was a rising star in Dresden, people sought his company, and nobody would have dreamed of treating him with anything but the deepest respect—I came to realize as time passed, perhaps realized only after he had vanished from the city, what had been going on in Kaltenburg's mind, the fears he had lived with from day one.

"And don't forget"—he fixed me with a sharp gaze—"never forget that here"—his hand swept around, vaguely taking in the hillside—"in that house over there, or further down, wherever you look, things are going on all the time that are much crazier than you'll ever find in my place. Sheer hidden abysses. Menacing things. Revolting things. Believe me. I have looked into some of these abysses. That's why I don't mind if they weigh me up. Let them take me for a fool, I couldn't care less."

On one occasion Ludwig Kaltenburg said to me, "I can get along perfectly well with a Professor Baron von Ardenne or a Field Marshal Paulus. They have seen a few abysses opening up at their feet during their lifetime too. It's the petty-minded people who worry me."

And one winter evening, as I was leaving: "One has to stay vulnerable."

Sometimes, he said, he had people in the house who clearly thought him not entirely sane, although they would never admit it to his face. Not a single chair available for guests but any amount of space for his animals, the jackdaw colony in the loft, the basement reserved for the fish. A cockatoo had the run of all floors, and its infernal cawing echoed through the whole house whenever an unwelcome guest blocked its usual flight path up and down the stairs. Dogs strayed around in the rooms, which annoyed some people more than did the ducks sitting there on the carpet making a low gabbling noise when the resident tomcat strutted past as though only he and his master were present. And not forgetting the hamster. On the desk a pile of gnawed papers on which it had been working the previous night, but the animal itself was nowhere to be seen. "I force myself not to let on that for the past few weeks it has been residing in the kitchen."

As Kaltenburg had established, there were precisely two groups of such visitors: those who — fear in their eyes, fear of the zoo, the professor — had to make such an effort to hide their horror that they could hardly bring themselves to utter a syllable, and the others, who compensated for their fear by becoming downright rude. Not that they made insulting remarks, it was the tone of voice they adopted: *And what is the point of keeping animals, if one may ask?*

"Do you know what I say then, casually and clearly as the occasion requires? *I'm studying.* Period. That's all."

Then you had to wait for them to come back at you, as you knew absolutely for certain they would. Some of them, who hadn't understood a thing, did so immediately. Others swallowed a few times before they could manage to utter, *What's worth studying about sticklebacks or about this* — meaning Taschotschek — *this bird here? What's so interesting about these animals?* Then, acting absentminded, surprised: "About these animals? What animals? It's you I'm studying."

IV

1

———

FRIDAY THE SIXTH of March. In the morning the news of
Stalin's death had been announced. In the evening I was due
to visit the Hagemanns with Ludwig Kaltenburg. Arriving
at dusk in Loschwitz, I found the Institute site unusually silent, and
I encountered nobody except Herr Sikorski, Kaltenburg's cameraman. When I asked him how people here had taken the news, especially the professor, Herr Sikorski just shrugged: it had been very
quiet all day. Even the birds were less lively than usual. However, as
for the professor, there was no knowing what he was thinking—he
had retreated to the aquarium section that afternoon and not reappeared.

As I went down the stairs to the breeding and collecting tanks
located in the rooms built on the side facing the slope, I felt a for-
lornness that I had never before experienced in this house. The
walls seemed damp, my tread echoed on the stone steps, not a human voice anywhere, not an animal in sight. The cold light in the
antechamber, the barrel vaulting over the aquariums placed close
together, the quiet hum of countless circulation pumps.

The cheerlessness was not even dispelled by the sight of Ludwig Kaltenburg's shock of white hair between the tanks. He was
shuffling in rubber boots down the gangway at the other end of
the room. Through a series of glass panels, the masses of water, his
face was scarcely recognizable, blurred. As though Kaltenburg were

walking across the seabed. Then it was gone, hidden by water mil-
foil, then flashing into sight again, dissolving in a whirl of air and
water, finally regaining its shape, the clear eyes, the beard, the un-
ruly hair.

On the worktop a bare reserve tank with a shoal of cichlids
swimming in it. It appeared that Kaltenburg had spent the afternoon refurbishing the perch's customary aquarium, trying out one
new plant and one new arrangement after another until at last he
was satisfied—that is, today the exercise had served him first and
foremost as a distraction.

"Of course, I had to call the colleagues together and give a little
speech," he said, and, "Fräulein Holsterbach, you know, the dark
Ph.D. student, was crying."

I had no idea what was going through Kaltenburg's mind. Together we put the cover back on the aquarium. He took a step back,
rubbing his hands and surveying his creation. A truly beautiful
world of water.

Slowly he cleared up the work area, took off his lab coat; he was
wearing his black suit underneath, his black shoes stood ready polished on the cellar steps. We were moving toward the exit when he
stopped in front of one aquarium and pointed out a male stickleback
that was busy at the bottom of the tank. Kaltenburg's finger moved
up and down the pane of glass to show me something. The other
fish hovered inquisitively behind the glass, following the finger to
right and left, and only that particular stickleback took no interest
in whether it was feeding time.

The professor tut-tutted, chewing on his lower lip. "Too early,"
he muttered, "it's much too early, strange, the beginning of March
is not the time."

We were watching a male showing off its gala colors and building a nest, even though the spawning season had not yet begun. Its
blue-green back, the red, glassy, almost transparent-looking flanks,
the emerald-green eyes—Kaltenburg put his hand on my shoulder:
"We should be on our way."

It was the first time he had been invited to the Hagemanns', and
you could see from his reaction when I delivered the invitation that

he felt truly honored. You might almost think, low-spirited as he now seemed to me, that he was worried Stalin might yet spoil his pleasure at the last moment.

On our way down into the quiet city a limousine drove toward us, laboriously negotiating the lanes up the hillside. Kaltenburg stopped to let it pass: "I know you can read my expression like a book. It's true, I've been a bit concerned all day. Everybody would have understood if the Hagemanns' reception had been canceled—but I would have regretted it, all the same."

He had released the handbrake, changed into second gear again, concentrating on the narrow traffic lane. "Or do you think it would have been more fitting for me to send my regrets? Do you think the Hagemanns would prefer to spend this evening in their close family circle?"

I shook my head.

Kaltenburg smiled, looking ahead through the windscreen. "You're right. You don't just turn down an invitation to the Hagemanns'. Apart from that, I'm really keen to know what this friend of yours, Martin, is like. And above all, of course, I'm curious about the Hagemanns' younger daughter, what's her name again?"

"Klara."

"You see a lot of each other, don't you?" And as I didn't reply: "Come on, what do you take your old Ludwig Kaltenburg for? I'm not blind, you know."

It turned out to be a quiet evening; a number of guests had indeed called that afternoon to say they were not coming, others simply didn't come. But I didn't have the impression that Kaltenburg was disappointed by this, he chatted for a long time with an archaeologist couple, with Klara's parents, with Ulli, with Klara herself. But Martin listened, silent as ever, to these conversations, his eyes riveted upon the professor. That evening, in this company, nobody would have dreamed of putting any pressure on Kaltenburg, nobody demanded that he should report on the Institute, nobody begged until the professor took his guests into the garden to wake the sleeping magpies and coax them down from the oak tree onto his shoulder.

On the sixth of March 1953 we sat up until well after midnight, just the four of us in the end, Professor Kaltenburg, Martin, Klara, and I. We were exhausted, we simply lacked the energy to break up the group, but we all knew we wouldn't be able to sleep anyway.

"So he's no longer alive, Comrade Stalin," Kaltenburg quietly threw into the middle of a longish pause in the conversation. "It's a good five years since I last saw him, an eternity. It never occurred to me then that this might be the last time we looked each other in the eye. In the end it didn't do him any good to get rid of all his doctors in succession, his suspicion that they all wanted him dead and buried was completely unfounded. Comrade Stalin didn't need anybody, didn't need help, he managed everything himself, and so now he's died by his own efforts. That was something he could do better than most, arrange for a death. Or was he helped? What say the rumors?"

He looked questioningly around the circle. Klara shook her head: "There was no mention on the radio of any outside intervention. Two strokes, so quickly one after the other. He didn't regain consciousness after the brain hemorrhage. The second stroke the day before yesterday, which attacked his heart and respiratory system. Then by half past nine last night it was over."

"With their usual lunacy, they're probably blaming Beria, just wait, I can hear them sniveling, That snake Beria has killed our beloved little father."

Kaltenburg waved away the cigarette smoke.

"I lived so long under Stalin's watchful eye that his face is indelibly stamped on my memory. The bushy mustache. The coal-black eyes. It's true that he has, no, had a more penetrating gaze than I've ever encountered in anyone else. You can't really know what it felt like if you haven't lived for years with the sensation of him staring down your neck, watching your every move."

"Are you talking about your time in Chalturin as a POW?"

"Near Kirov, yes. I was running a ward with six hundred beds, all of them neuritis cases. What a place. It was the same later in Oritschi, then Dzoraget, Amalmy, Sevan, and Yerevan, the inevitable portraits of Stalin hanging on the walls. He wouldn't take his

178

eyes off me during my time in Armenia, and finally Krasnogorsk near Moscow—he followed me everywhere. And the funny thing was, that gaze of his brought us all closer together, POWs and Red Army soldiers, Germans and Russians, doctors and patients, because we all had him to live with."

It was as though something had been dammed up in Kaltenburg during the day, no, over the years, that needed to break out in that late-night session. He looked down as he talked, gazing at the ashtray; after his first few sentences none of us dared raise a question. We all knew that portrait, but Ludwig Kaltenburg showed us Stalin as we had never seen him before.

"You're giving a wounded man his medicine, and Comrade Stalin is watching to see you don't hand out the wrong treatment by mistake to the poor devil lying there hardly able to move, or maybe give him the rations meant for the sad case in the next bed. You distribute vitamin C, and his stern gaze stops you from lacing it with a poisonous powder—well, you're a doctor, so you would never dream of it anyway, but Comrade Stalin's look gives you a bad conscience from the start. You search your soul, as well as you can when you're permanently under surveillance, asking yourself, *Have I done anything wrong, have I done my best at all times, haven't I ever once toyed with the idea of sabotaging the hospital, sending the whole lot of them to their maker at a single stroke?*

"And when you've done your work properly, your mind is at rest and you know that Comrade Stalin has reason to be satisfied with you, you even imagine that he is mildly lowering his eyelids, just for a split second, as though expressing his benevolence toward you. You know it's a delusion, but you can't help it. If you try to catch him out—don't ever think of catching Comrade Stalin out—and turn around as fast as lightning to stare him directly in the face, his eyes are open as always, vigilant, for he knows that if he gives way to his goodness and lets you out of his sight even for a moment, you'll think you can deceive him. A delusion, nothing else, just a picture on the wall that faces you every morning when you arrive in the ward.

"After a long day you fall into bed, but he doesn't sleep. A day filled from the sun's first ray to the last with screams, operations, a lot of blood and dying. He has watched every single fight for a human life, you could almost say he has lived through it. You're finished, your eyes are closing, but he can't afford to rest. He knows that now more than ever he has to watch over you.

"What sights Comrade Stalin has had to witness in his lifetime. And what, more rarely, has he been privileged to witness. I remember that on one occasion I entered into direct dialogue with him to ask his advice, eye to eye, with me at the far end of the ward, him on the wall at the front, and between us a patient who had gone on hunger strike after we amputated his leg. What, I asked, fixing my gaze on the portrait, would you do in my situation, what would Stalin do here and now when things are desperate, to change this emaciated patient's life-threatening condition for the better?

"I didn't spend long thinking about it—Comrade Stalin never needed much time to make his mind up either—but fell into an instant diabolical rage, I flailed around with my arms, stamped with both feet so that the floorboards trembled, the whole hut, I yelled and roared, spat, threw the crutches out into the aisle, and screamed directly into the face of the pathetic bundle of humanity in front of me—barely twenty years old and from Vienna like me—that I was going to make mincemeat of him. That did the trick. In short, all I had to do was behave like an ape, and the poor amputee let me spoon-feed him soup as though I were his father and he the sick child. After that I actually managed to feed the wounded man so well that he was fit to be released. It was this man who took my family the news that I was alive. He smuggled a note out of the camp—in his mouth. A dazzling success, and it was Comrade Stalin who helped me achieve it.

"He grew tired, he was bound to become tired, since he never once took his eyes off us. At the end, perhaps, opening his coal-black eyes wide again, in his last great struggle he looked around the room to register precisely every detail, every face, and since he must have sensed—Comrade Stalin sensed everything—that there wasn't long to go, in his last minutes he wanted to gain a comprehensive picture of his surroundings and take it with him who knows where, the table, the chair, the telephone, the ceiling, then his friends around him, enemies, doctors, snakes, he wanted to look out of the window too, he made an effort—Comrade Stalin never spared any effort—summoning up all of his remaining strength to take in the rectangle of window, the light, the light, but his view was blocked. The heads of these hypocrites, these murderers would have to roll to fulfill Comrade Stalin's last modest wish, to see the daylight in the window one last time, even if it had long since got dark out there, early March, half past nine in the evening. It may be that at the end his eyeballs popped out of his skull because he wanted to catch a last glimpse, and yet he probably saw no more than a diffuse, blinding brightness, before somebody in the circle of intimates, of traitors around his sickbed, deathbed, closed his eyes forever.

"His coal-black eyes held an oath of loyalty: Don't worry, I am following you and your actions, wherever you go, I will follow you to the ends of the earth. And I, was I worthy of the endless vigilance and unconditional loyalty of Comrade Stalin? I received my discharge papers from the camp beneath his gaze, I packed my things under his gaze—turning away without taking my leave of that so-familiar face. As though from one moment to the next all the looks we had exchanged over the years had been forgotten. I turned toward the west without visualizing how the firm gaze was boring into the back of my head, scowling at first, as though he had not yet lost me, as though his knitted brows still had the power to make me turn back. Gradually his stare must have become angry, despairing, in the end melancholy, marked by deep sorrow, since I was traveling inexorably toward my homeland heedless of whether I would ever again see this man who had looked into my eyes night and day for four years. And now suddenly it's over."

Kaltenburg stretched, raising his arms above his head.

"Children, it's very late, we'd better be going"—and he stood up from his chair as though he were leaving the field hospital block, as though taking off his white coat, to reveal the black suit once more.

But after he had dropped me off at home and I stood for a while in the dark street, I could see a doctor again, white coat flapping as he walks down the central aisle of the hospital barracks, turning his head to left and right and tossing a few words of German to one patient here, some Russian to another over there, he corrects himself with a laugh, the flock of nurses in his wake laugh with him. The aisle between the beds vanishes into the distance, but the doctor shows no sign of fatigue when he reaches the door, he has pronounced on cases, encouraged and exhorted, three hundred times. And he knows every single face.

He steps out into the cold, clear air. He breathes in deeply. On the horizon a thin haze covers the hills, the nurses stand there shivering and smoking. The Russian woman doctor at his side has offered him a cigarette, but he needs to breathe in the pure air, he must quickly erase all those patients' faces from his mind's eye before tackling the next ward.

2

——

A FINE FILM OF cloud had hung over the city since the morning, now it was beginning to drizzle. Katharina Fischer said, "Stalin's death loosened Ludwig Kaltenburg's tongue," and her voice sounded as hushed in the silence that surrounded us as if Stalin had died only yesterday, as if nobody quite knew how to deal with his death, as if behind every window silent, tear-stained, dejected people sat around the radio waiting in case the solemn music that had been playing for the last twenty-four hours was suddenly interrupted by an announcer, audibly struggling to maintain his composure, bringing a newsflash: Moscow has just reported that the great Stalin is awake again.

The pavement glistened, a dry smell of dust mingled with the dampness. I was showing Katharina Fischer around Oberloschwitz, pointing out the houses, paths, gardens that were so familiar to me in Kaltenburg's day that I felt connected to every paving stone, every gap in a fence. Not much of all that was left, whether because the old wooden fence was missing here, the pavement was gone there, or because, as I hadn't been up here since 1990 or 1991, it wasn't easy to locate the reference points in my memory.

"We can't let our animals go hungry because of a death, however great the deceased may be," said the professor in measured tones next morning. Later it was said among his colleagues—who knew nothing about our late-night session at the Hagemanns', and were never to know—that his inner conflict was obvious, his deep emotional upset making it hard for him to answer the call of duty. Others were convinced that the reason Kaltenburg had been speaking more slowly than usual was that the vodka the night before hadn't agreed with him. Many later remembered the sentences: "We must think of the animals, we owe it to him," as the professor proceeded to the normal business of the day. Certain breeding programs could not go unsupervised even for an hour, hatching times were near, some of the duck flock was suffering at the time from a nasty rash—but the present occasion called for some colleagues to be released from their duties: who was going to take care of the black ribbon, the banners, and the large portrait above the entrance to the house? Kaltenburg advised against flower arrangements. However tastefully done, anything made with plant material would look absolutely pathetic in a very short time: "Animals have no piety, nothing we can do about it."

Another suggestion was received with an unappreciative shake of the head: someone suggested piping solemn music into the enclosures. No music. Who would answer for the possible negative effects, territorial battles, premature births, general lethargy, no, the risk was simply too great. Ludwig Kaltenburg had a lifelong aversion to funeral marches.

Eventually he even sent one or two colleagues home, either out of sympathy or because he detested their overemotional tendencies. The various jobs were allocated, and Kaltenburg withdrew to his study to write a newspaper article. He had promised to contribute a page entitled "Stalin, Friend of Animals," but when I looked in on him later at teatime the sheet of scrap paper still bore only the title, and the article never got beyond the concept stage.

Yes, Stalin's death did loosen the professor's tongue, but it seems that with his long monologue about the coal-black eyes that chapter was closed for Kaltenburg. The Stalin portrait at the Institute villa, pictures of Stalin all over the city: Kaltenburg passed the portraits without looking up. Whatever nightmares his experiences in the camp may have caused him, and whatever mistrust Ludwig Kaltenburg had to live with at that time, after Stalin's death he seemed liberated. In a single night he had freed himself from the vigilant eyes of Stalin. Furthermore, it was as if Kaltenburg knew that in the future a path would be open for him to return to the Soviet Union.

"A sigh of relief?" thought the interpreter, as we turned into the little street that led to the Institute.

But people would go on disappearing, and would go on being referred to only in hushed tones. A short breathing space, perhaps.

While the professor was talking at the Hagemanns' about his encounters with Stalin, Martin did not look once at the black dot on the ceiling. Not that he had forgotten about it, certainly not. It was rather that under Kaltenburg's influence he had managed to put the spot between chandelier and sunflower leaf out of his mind. Whether it was only a dried-up housefly or whether every word was audible in the room above: Martin could cope with the uncertainty.

The Institute villa itself was now screened on the street side by a high wall, it could not have been built very long before, the whitewashed surface showed no sign of weathering, and the footpath had been freshly laid too, no moss, not a blade of grass between the slabs. We walked up to the wide gray iron gate and had the feeling we were being caught on video cameras as we examined the polished brass plate, two names by the bell, only two: LORENZ and DR. LORENZ—it looked like an accommodation address, or at any rate not like the names of real residents.

"Do you think we should just ring?" asked Frau Fischer, reaching out, her index finger poised above the bell, then she hesitated, and I laid my hand on her forearm, "I'm not sure," and looked at the circular pattern of perforations in the brass plate, I didn't know if I could bear to listen to the crackling, the hissing, and the tinny voice that would issue from this crude showerhead: "No."

Earlier there was just a garden gate here in a crooked fence, hardly waist height, who would have wanted to intrude on the grounds, who was there to escape from the Institute, and if you heard a distant, barely intelligible voice, you knew it was the professor calling his animals behind the house. "No, come on, we'd better leave it," I said to Frau Fischer, and I had the impression that she understood me very well as she followed me across to the other side of the street, which might at least give us a view of the upper part of the villa.

"On the far left, the first-floor window—that was Ludwig Kaltenburg's bedroom, the only room in the house I never went into, or rather I didn't until the professor had left Dresden. The small window next to it is the bathroom. Then the archive and the library, then the staircase. But the important rooms were all on the side facing the slope—kitchen, study, the balcony, the jackdaws' quarters in the loft."

The Institute was constantly growing, it soon spread far beyond the villa, the summerhouse, and the tool sheds, taking in neighboring houses and above all plots of land for colleagues and animals. Huts for long-term guests. Barracks were built to house specialists along with their families, biologists, psychologists, scientific assistants, keepers to look after the birds, and the aquarium staff. Then there were the cleaning ladies, mechanics, carpenters, technicians, caretakers, administrators. The cook. The feed manager, ruler of three kitchen domains: for mammals, birds, fish. And the cameraman. Kaltenburg's chauffeur, who was also in charge of the entire transport fleet. Almost a housing development.

Of course, you couldn't compare this with the size gradually achieved by Manfred von Ardenne's research establishment above Loschwitz, in Weisser Hirsch, where the number of employees and colleagues eventually reached four hundred—but even a tenth of that is a considerable figure, not counting the families of the researchers living on the premises.

Tense negotiations, applications, secret discussions, the group photos with politicians, with officials, with foreign academics—Kaltenburg often came home exhausted, especially when he had been to Berlin with his driver, Krause. He just wasn't one of those people who make routine committee meetings more bearable by simply blocking out the speeches and reports and discussions, getting through the time of hollow words as though deaf, and speculating whether some influential man or other, this or that party official, might spare a few minutes for a friendly chat with them afterward. Though I must say that Kaltenburg never complained to me about the tiring sessions he sat through as if in a vacuum. In any case, if he felt like complaining, he would shun human company altogether and go off to be with his animals. No, not a hint of exhaustion, no doubts, or despair, in front of colleagues at the Institute, the professor radiated an energy that inspired everybody. And in return, the zest for the work that he saw around him gave strength back to Ludwig Kaltenburg, helped him through self-critical spells, helped him overcome occasional bouts of depression.

"Knowing the professor as I do now," said Katharina Fischer, only to correct herself immediately, "I mean, knowing what you've told me about him, I'm puzzled by one thing: did he have any animals when he was a POW, or at least observe them?"

Ludwig Kaltenburg *not* surrounded by animals? Unthinkable. Probably there was a dog's nose or a beak on his passport photo.

"How about on the night after Stalin's death—did he really not mention a single animal?"

I didn't realize that until years later: Martin, Klara, and I had witnessed the first long Kaltenburg monologue without any reference to the animal kingdom. Till all hours he talked about a human being as if he were talking about an animal.

People were in mourning, everywhere you could see eyes red from weeping—but Kaltenburg took his example from a man who knew no tears. When *Archetypes of Fear* appeared a decade later, Klara and I agreed that his work on the book had begun then, on the sixth of March 1953. Covertly—for Kaltenburg would surely not have formulated a plan by that time, in the years before his departure the most he would have done was to jot down a few cryptic, seemingly disparate notes. Nonetheless, the evening we four spent together was the occasion for a shift of perspective. Only a minimal change in the angle of vision at first, as if the professor had become aware of a gentle movement on the margin of his visual field, all the harder to ignore the longer he insisted he hadn't noticed anything.

Gradually Kaltenburg was to turn toward a new area of observation. Our clandestine session in the Hagemanns' house had brought him together with the first subject of his incipient researches, in fact the two had sat opposite each other for some hours. However, much to the professor's regret, for the moment this future object of research showed no interest in submitting himself to observation. "The animals? It's you I'm studying," was what he claimed to have thrown at unwelcome visitors—later, there was no one the assertion fit better than Martin Spengler.

"Why not Klara Hagemann?"

He must have thought of Martin as an open challenge—a person who resisted being seen through by Kaltenburg. And Ludwig Kaltenburg had a masterly ability to coax people's secrets out of them. Secrets they themselves were not aware of. Some were grateful to him: under his guidance they had plumbed depths into which they would never have ventured but for the professor. However, Kaltenburg didn't want to hear about depths. Others felt betrayed: in his presence they had given away something that nobody had a right to know. But Kaltenburg did not believe in any case that you could successfully go on concealing something from the world. Whether depths or involuntary revelations, everybody agreed on one thing: basically the professor had done the talking, interrupted only by questions and comments that sounded to the listener in retrospect like incidental confessions. Kaltenburg's gift for talking and observing—however, as far as Klara was concerned, I'm not sure to this day whether she was a challenge that defeated him or whether he never took on the challenge.

"And Klara's impression of the professor? I think I would have felt a bit uneasy about this man after a first meeting like that."

I don't know if it was shyness or embarrassment, but she wouldn't really say anything about him. It may be that she wasn't sure whether it was admiration or contempt that Kaltenburg felt for Stalin, and it seemed to me that she had to reach a clear verdict on that before she could decide whether to admire or despise the professor. After all, Ludwig Kaltenburg never made any secret of his love for all things Russian. It went right back to his youth in Vienna, did not go cold in captivity, survived the move to Dresden, and perhaps only flourished properly after Stalin's death. For a few months he even preferred to eat lying down when, at the end of an intensive working day, long after the usual big meeting of all the colleagues, he indulged in a late snack. "No, it's not just a fad, it really is more comfortable when you've been on your feet all day": the great Professor Kaltenburg stretched out on his sofa with a plate of fruit, with tea and bread and a leg of roast chicken. Perhaps he dreamed of Karelian birch furniture.

One of his favorite words was *Durak*, "*Da, da, durak*," he would say when he couldn't make sense of something he had observed in his ducks, "Yeah, yeah, stupid," when he simply couldn't make a coherent connection between two series of movements: these were his first words of Russian, taught him by a Red Army soldier to whom Kaltenburg surrendered after an inept attempt to escape at the front. Then there was his love for diminutives and terms of endearment acquired in the field hospital, where they were lavishly employed, and in general his choice of names for his charges. There was a Ludmilla, a Turka, an Igor, and I wondered whether lurking behind Taschotschek there wasn't a Natalia, a Natasha.

As though she had found a reasonable compromise for the time being, Klara began to make little jibes at Kaltenburg, to which he always reacted with a smile, with a good-natured growl. In fact very few people were allowed to tease him, but Klara had not only spotted at first glance a weakness in Ludwig Kaltenburg, she had also found the right tone, she had the gift of being able to talk mockingly to him without making him feel he was being mocked.

When she said in sepulchral tones, "I think I can see Stalin's coal-black eyes glowing," the professor had to laugh, and from the looks he shot at me I realized he would let her get away with anything, because his weakness was none other than a weakness for Klara. If she had wanted to, she could have twisted Ludwig Kaltenburg round her little finger.

"He respected her."

Enormously.

"Because he noticed she was studying him."

And not only him, Professor Kaltenburg. He must have gathered at a stroke that at barely twenty she was ahead of him. Studying human beings came naturally to her, and at an age when he was still concentrating fully on his jackdaws, his ducks and small mammals, when as yet Ludwig Kaltenburg knew nothing at all about the faces of his patients in the field hospital or Josef Stalin's gaze.

3

———

H E INVITED US — strangely enough — to a café. He came on foot down the hill in Loschwitz, whereas usually when meeting young ladies he preferred to present himself on his motorbike. He wasn't wearing gloves. And of course the first thing Klara wanted to know was how he had come by the scratch on the back of his hand. Nothing important, nothing earth-shattering, just the kind of mishap that was a common occurrence when dealing with animals: Igor, the tame magpie, couldn't stand Kaltenburg drumming impatiently with his fingertips on the tabletop during breakfast while reading his paper.

"Sudden rustling of paper — I'm familiar with that."

"Aren't magpies pretty dissolute birds, cowardly and devious?"

"That's what everyone says. It's just that they're too intelligent for most people."

It was the first time I had ever sat in a café with Ludwig Kaltenburg, his idea of a suitable place to take a young woman, a young woman whose admirer, whose future fiancé, you have known since childhood. To left and right of us elderly ladies and gentlemen having afternoon coffee, families, children behaving so politely that their parents must have promised them a second piece of cake if they would stop staring at the famous animal professor.

Klara asked him about the types of animal he had in his collection, all of which she knew from me, and carefully counted them off along with him as Kaltenburg strolled from room to room, peering into the stairwell, the loft, the basement: "Cichlids, or have I mentioned them?"

"They came first, when we were at the aquariums."

"The goldfish, Fritz."

She asked him why certain animals had names and others didn't. I had already explained this to Klara on one of our first dates, it was the hand-reared specimens and those closely involved in research work that were given proper names. She wanted to hear it again from the professor, he didn't mind, he enjoyed it, we hadn't touched the cake on our plates.

Where in Germany do people eat tart and where do they eat "*Torte*," what is the difference between bread and pastry, and exactly what dessert dishes do the Austrians include under the heading of "*Mehlspeise*"? We had never had such discussions before, but we sat in the café, all equally out of place, our polite behavior, our nice conversation, after a quarter of an hour of this we surely deserved at least an extra helping of whipped cream. We might have been ready to move on if Kaltenburg hadn't jumped in with a story that was new even to me.

"If my parents are to be believed, I began life as a tumor."

The painted eyebrows of the old ladies over there by the window shot up. Kaltenburg's parents married late, nobody thought pregnancy was in the cards, in the first instance they may have been almost as shocked by this news as by the earlier misdiagnosis.

"Fortunately I wasn't born prematurely, otherwise my father would have seen me as a questionable gift for the rest of his life." The professor laughed. "I came into this world—and turned their lives completely upside down."

His upbringing was all the more careful, his parents looking after their unexpected son as though they had a bad conscience about him, the father even accepted the son's ambition to become a zoologist instead of continuing the line of eminent surgeons named Kaltenburg. He shook his head in bewilderment, but he didn't object. So, for his sake, initially Ludwig Kaltenburg went into medicine.

Klara nodded appreciatively. "But he must be very proud of you today."

"Even if he were still alive, he certainly wouldn't be proud of a son who voluntarily moved to Dresden."

"Your parents are no longer alive?"

"My father didn't even find out that I had survived the war and been captured by the Russians."

"The patient who hid the note in his mouth arrived too late."

"Yes, he arrived too late."

Klara ate the rest of her cake, the professor looked on.

"Shall I order some more coffee?" He lifted the lid of the pot as though inspecting it carefully to see whether a small mammal was nesting there.

"Animals are just messy, the old man used to say."

"Messy? Nothing new for a surgeon, surely."

Somebody at the next table cleared his throat, the ladies at the window put down their coffee cups.

"And was it a childhood dream to become a librarian?" The professor avoided addressing Klara directly, he didn't know whether to say *Du* or *Sie* to her. "That's certainly the way Hermann puts it, at any rate."

She told the story of the family outing to Leipzig, Kaltenburg listened, Kaltenburg was moved, and Klara didn't seem to know what to make of his emotion, over a slice of cake, with my Professor Ludwig Kaltenburg in a café.

We were all relieved to be standing outside again. The professor's choice of a café was certainly a considered one—later he was to tell me, "On principle I never invite young women into this desolate-looking animal household." But outside in the fresh air, free of the audience in the café which was impossible to ignore, the conversation between Ludwig Kaltenburg and Klara could have been steered in a different direction, just as it would have taken another course altogether if we had been invited to Kaltenburg's villa. The professor quickly said goodbye, he had another appointment, much less pleasant, but such appointments were unavoidable, and then I saw him hurrying away, an unusual picture: Professor Ludwig Kaltenburg on foot on a paved road in the middle of the city.

"Was I too forward?"

"Forward? No, honestly, you weren't. And anyway, you must have noticed yourself: the professor has a soft spot for self-confident young women."

"Too well behaved?"

"All three of us were well behaved."

"So I passed?" Klara didn't wait for my answer. "All the same, I had the impression that the professor thought I was trying to keep something from him."

"He would like to have gone on listening to you: the Hagemann family, your salon, your guests."

"What could I do, with all those people around us?"

"He shouldn't have taken us there if he was keen to hear Hagemann stories."

"I'm going to tell my parents to invite him more often."

And the professor did indeed become a regular visitor to the Hagemanns'. But he came too late, only after Stalin's death. He had missed certain decisive years, conversations and guests on whom he could have sharpened his powers of observation. Yes, the people themselves would have opened up worlds to him which he was never to know.

Kaltenburg should have come to Dresden right after the war and been in touch with the family, he should not have had to wait for me to get to know Klara Hagemann and to bring him his first invitation to the Hagemanns'. Klara was ahead of the professor, and she would always be ahead of him: with the best will in the world, Ludwig Kaltenburg would never be able to make up for that gap of seven years.

Take a figure like Paul Merker, I said to the interpreter: that name does not figure at all in Kaltenburg's world. A member of the Central Committee secretariat and of the SED Politburo who was removed from all his official positions in 1950, expelled from the

Party, and banished to the provinces in Brandenburg—at most the professor would have remarked laconically, "Ideologists put nooses around each other's necks." And added portentously, "A side effect of every ideology."

It all had a different ring in the Hagemann salon. I learned to distinguish between those functionaries who had gone underground in 1933 and those who owed their worldview to a determined course of reeducation as POWs. I learned that you shouldn't confuse those returning from Moscow with returnees from Scandinavia, those coming back from Mexico with others coming out of the German camps. One was said to have betrayed several members of his resistance cell, another to have spent years in hiding on a smallholding, and a third was reputed to despise people who feared for their lives. Here was a former SA man, once a lanky type, an excellent horseman, whose eyes were now sunk deep in his fat face, and there a gaunt character with an agitated look, as though forever assessing which figure in the inner circle should be pushed out next. They might use the same language, shake hands, slap each other's backs, even hug: for the Hagemanns this was simply the solidarity born of necessity, and that kind of solidarity is notoriously unpredictable.

"Now they're putting nooses around each other's necks": it was this same Paul Merker who, aware of the death camps, was talking in 1942 of a "world pogrom," and—as a number of the Hagemanns' guests thought—in doing so incurring the distrust of his comrades in arms. After his return from exile he could easily have joined the ranks of antifascist veterans without another word about those whom the new jargon described merely as "the persecuted." But mindful of the "world pogrom," Merker urged—and he enjoyed great respect for this at the Hagemanns'—that reparations should be made to all survivors, regardless of whether they had been avowed Communists or had been forced to wear the Star of David on their chests.

On one occasion, when the conversation centered on a Berlin theater premiere, a woman suddenly asked, "Has anyone heard from Luckenwalde lately?" She looked keenly into each face in turn—Klara's father shrugged his shoulders, other guests shook their heads, everybody had understood, nobody had any information, so there was nothing for it but to return to the previous topic. They focused on the stage design, moving on to what could be done with trompe l'oeil painting, I looked across at Martin and could have sworn that he had missed the intervening question. I had no idea what "Luckenwalde" stood for. I would have understood references to Moscow, or to Leningrad, or, on that Advent Sunday of 1952, to Prague, because not an evening passed at the Hagemanns' without some discussion of the Prague show trial of Rudolf Slánský and his fellow conspirators, singled out by the authorities only after the most painstakingly detailed investigations.

But what lay behind Luckenwalde escaped me until later, when on my way to the toilet I saw someone going up to the woman in question, and noticed the change in her expression after she heard him say, "Luckenwalde is supposed to have been wiped off the map."

After the last guests had left, I was helping the two sisters in the kitchen, Ulli washed, I dried the glasses, Klara put away the dishes. "Did you notice anything about Frau Koch? She looked so distracted as she was leaving."

Ulli had noticed her husband slipping his arm under hers on the path to the garden gate. "She was quite unsteady on her legs."

"Like an old woman."

Herr and Frau Koch: for the Hagemann daughters they were "the English couple"—they had spent many years in London, and had hesitated to return to Germany, to settle in Dresden. The West was out of the question for Herr Koch. As for his wife, whether here or there, she didn't want to be reminded of the time of the "world pogrom."

"Maybe I misunderstood, or perhaps it has nothing to do with it, but somebody took Frau Koch aside and told her Luckenwalde had disappeared from the map."

"Who said that?"

"I don't know his name, that shy medic."

"Domaschke," Ulli helped me out.

"Luckenwalde?" Klara reflected. "Did you hear any more?"

"No, that's all. It gave her quite a shock."

"That means Merker has gone into hiding."

"Do you mean Paul Merker, the Politburo member?"

Ulli handed me a clean glass. "Politburo, that's all in the past."

"Or they've arrested him." Klara looked at her sister. "Because they need someone to go after."

"They have him running a grill in Luckenwalde."

Impatiently Klara took the polished wineglass out of my hand. "That's neither here nor there at the moment. They've arrested him, haven't they?"

"I'll do the rest tomorrow morning." Ulli put down the sponge and emptied the water from the sink.

"That's what it means. It can't mean anything else. They want to make an example of him."

One sister was leaning against the kitchen cabinet. The other was looking at the floor. I didn't know where to put the dish towel.

"If that's true, Ulli, you know what will happen next?"

"Don't scream. Yes, I do know."

"If they put Merker in the dock and turn him into the great Zionist conspirator, then the Kochs will pack their bags. They'll be off. We'll never see them again."

4

—————

"Ulli, quick, there are two real English people here."
Klara peered out into the hall, a couple stood there talking, the sentences flowing quickly, foreign and clear,
Klara couldn't understand a word. The cadence of their speech was
what had struck her, a different cadence. Klara in her nightdress
hid behind the slightly open door waiting for her parents to move
away, her mother went to get glasses, her father had gone ahead
into the drawing room, now Klara could take a look outside. The
woman was adjusting her delicately patterned stole in front of the
hall-stand mirror, the man was fishing a packet of cigarettes out
of his coat pocket, perhaps they were talking about Herr Klein,
the Super-Tenant, who had just gone upstairs. Klara didn't even
know whether her parents knew English, whether any of the regular guests would be able to converse with the couple.

"Come on, Ulli, or the English people won't be there anymore,"
hissed Klara in a stage whisper over her shoulder, but before her sister could get out of bed the woman had caught sight of Klara in the
doorway, she laughed, suddenly she was speaking German: "No,
my dear, we're not real English people."

Klara nodded. Went red. And shut the door. It was the first time
in her life that she had seen émigrés.

She was still a bit embarrassed about having behaved like a small child, Klara confessed to me when we were discussing the new faces that had appeared in the Hagemann circle after the war. A little girl from Dresden who knew foreign countries, foreign languages only from books. At the time Klara even acquired a few words of English to make up for it, so that the following week she could greet the Kochs as though she had grown up in London herself, as the couple appreciatively agreed.

Ashamed she may have been, but she took a particular liking to her "English couple," and for their part the Kochs never failed to look in on the girls before they went on into the drawing room to greet the other guests, the adults. Herr Koch would stand by the window while Frau Koch sat on the edge of Klara's bed, only for a few minutes, and yet as the sisters drifted off to sleep there was a faint aroma of cigarette smoke and eau de cologne.

The Kochs alerted Klara to cadences. The mere memory of the sound of a foreign language out in the hall was enough later to make Klara aware when there was a cool atmosphere between guests, when someone was covering up insecurity or close to losing self-control, when the drawing room conversation took a turn nobody had anticipated.

One evening in the summer of 1948 she was at the door when the Kochs happened to arrive at the same time as a man Klara didn't know. Clearly the Kochs didn't know who the man was either, for as Klara took their hats and coats to the hall stand, she heard, "My name is Koch, and this is my wife."

Looking for spare hangers for the coats damp from the light summer rain, she missed the new guest's answer.

"Sorry, help me a bit here — the philologist, the philosopher?"

"The last living Proust translator, if you like."

Was he offended? Was he just being modest? Was he joking at his own expense? Herr Hagemann appeared in the drawing room doorway, Frau Hagemann called Klara into the kitchen: "Could you take care of the rest, please?"

Ulli was slicing cucumber; Frau Hagemann took off her apron, washed her hands. "Who's here?"

Klara shrugged and set about preparing the radishes. Flashing eyes, theatrical voice—but for that mincing walk, the man would have been a frightening phenomenon.

The next day she searched her parent's bookshelves, in the French literature section she found two volumes with the titles *Auf den Spuren der verlorenen Zeit* (*In Search of Lost Time*): opening one at the title page, *Der Weg zu Swann* (*Swann's Way*), she read the name RUDOLF SCHOTTLAENDER. She struggled with the book for two or three evenings but couldn't get past the first fifty pages. There were passages that remained obscure to her, she came across oddities, expressions she didn't understand, she could have asked her parents about them, perhaps even the translator himself, but then she was distracted by something else she wanted to read, and soon Proust disappeared under a pile of books on the dressing table: forgotten were the long scene where a lonely young boy falls asleep, the visit of a certain M. Swann, the "bioscope," the "rooms in winter," and, in parentheses, the sea swallow so elaborately busy building its nest.

A year later Schottlaender's name came up again. By this time the sisters were allowed to sit up with the guests for half an hour after they arrived, but the strange man who translated that strange book into German had obviously not appeared again. "A difficult person"—that was all Frau Hagemann would say about it.

"Have you seen what they're saying about Professor Schottlaender in the newspaper?" asked Herr Koch one light summer evening.

"Quite a problematical case." Domaschke, the young internist, sprang to Klara's mother's aid, knowing she didn't like making unkind remarks about guests. "If a university professor fails to march on the First of May, is he really obliged to justify himself in writing afterward?"

Herr Koch: "Naive."

"What do you mean, naive?" His wife sounded irritated.

"I mean all he's done is give them the material they wanted."

"You might as well say 'and played right into their hands'—but after all, they will have started collecting material long before yesterday."

"Do you mean documents?" Domaschke didn't dare ask directly. "Do you mean official papers from the past?"

"What do you think? If somebody like that was in a camp without being a political prisoner?"

"Now you're exaggerating." Herr Koch laid his hand on his wife's forearm. "And anyway, Schottlaender was not in a camp."

"Be that as it may, he had to think of his wife and little daughter. You would have done the same."

"For me there would have been no question of going to West Berlin, though."

Klara took up *Swann's Way* again. The edition had appeared in 1926, and Rudolf Schottlaender was not yet fifty when Klara heard him calling himself "the last living Proust translator" while she was busy with damp summer coats and coat hangers at the other end of the hall. Had Herr and Frau Koch nodded silently to show they understood what he was talking about? Even if there was not much to connect them, as readers of detective stories, with Marcel Proust, they nodded when Schottlaender looked them in the eye as though subjecting them to examination: "It was only about eight years ago that we were still at full strength."

Klara was soon reading about Gilberte, who was either frivolous or timorous, reading once more about Swann, a name she had known for a long time but that seemed to her now—as the most commonplace words seem to many people suffering from aphasia—like a new name. She read about acacia avenues, about a forest from which, wearing a sleek fur coat and with the lovely eyes of an animal, a hurrying woman emerges, only to vanish again in the next sentence without leaving a trace.

Having finished the book, Klara went to Herr Lindner's bookstore to acquaint herself with the German that Walter Benjamin and Franz Hessel bestowed on Proust. For a quarter of a year she was carrying around with her the first two volumes of *In the Shadow of Young Girls in Flower*, printed by Hegner in Hellerau. At Christmas 1951 Herr Lindner surprised Klara with a copy of *Pleasures and Regrets*. This would have given her the opportunity to compare Ernst Weiss's language with that of the other translators, but what intrigued her above all was the third part of the novel. Every time there was a card from Lindner in the mail with the brief message "Fresh goods. Regards, Lindner," she hoped he had found the longed-for volume, published by Piper.

Apart from Ulli, no one knew how Klara had come across this author, and no one would have been able to understand why they took turns reading each other a few pages before going to sleep, as though, if only they studied the same sentences often enough, they would find out something about their own relatives, about whom their parents would tell them nothing.

"That man Schottlaender was right," Klara interrupted once when she had lost the thread while listening to a reflection on ladies' hats.

Ulli looked up from the open page and blinked in the beam of the bedside lamp. "With his story about the dead translators?"

"Herr Lindner knew the dates of their deaths: the first one died in June 1940, the second in September, and the last in January, shortly after New Year."

"Here?"

"In France."

"All three of them?" Ulli leaned forward to make out the face of her sister in the darkness on the other side of the room. "June—wasn't that when the Germans marched into Paris?"

"I think they committed suicide."

"You'll have to ask Herr Lindner again."

"I'll do that next week. Where were we?"

"The grandmother has a teacher with an illegitimate daughter."

"I thought it was ladies' hats? Go on, read."

"No, that's enough for tonight."

Ulli put the book down, turned off the light. She was still looking across to Klara's bed.

"Did the translators all know each other, do you think?"

"Do you mean was Schottlaender friendly with the others? I don't think so."

"I wonder what he was doing during that time?"

"We can ask the Kochs."

"And none of them died of old age. Did he really tell you that?"

"I don't remember. Let's go to sleep now."

The English couple could not agree. Herr Koch said Schottlaender had worked in an arms factory, but his wife thought she remembered him looking after an old lady. Moving between the hall stand and the drawing room, Frau Koch halted in her tracks: "Or was he translating for the criminal police?"

"I think you're wide of the mark there. Schottlaender never did slave translation labor."

When we got to know each other, Klara was still waiting for the continuation of her Proust. For months the main topic at the Hagemanns' had been the sensational trial of Philipp Auerbach: nobody there could possibly condone the police turning the state-appointed representative of victims of Nazism into the victim of a car chase on the autobahn, as though foiling the last-minute escape attempt of some enemy agent. Nobody thought much of the charges that took Auerbach to court. And nobody could forgive the expert witness who said that the accused was incapable of distinguishing between delusion and reality. But opinions were divided about the verdict.

"The man is innocent," said Herr Hagemann heatedly. "He was in the camps."

His unconditional support for the accused—even his wife couldn't quite fathom it. He would allow no room for doubt about the man. When he referred to a "show trial," there was a sharp intake of breath from one of the guests.

"You've only got to look at the judge. The assistant judge. The state prosecutor."

His daughters had never seen him so angry. "I know this type of person, I know them," cried Herr Hagemann, and both Ulli and Klara were convinced he was on the point of divulging something about their own relatives, if Herr Koch hadn't interrupted him: "Herr Hagemann, we all know this type of person, but some of us also know Herr Auerbach."

Frau Koch got up, excused herself, left the room. Klara went after her. She knew that Frau Koch was not so much concerned about Auerbach's character as she was disturbed because they were discussing a trial taking place in the West.

And then, a few days after the verdict in Munich, Philipp Auerbach took an overdose of sleeping pills. Frau Koch didn't want to know whether he was buried according to Orthodox rites, didn't want to know whether a rabbi was present when the scuffle broke out at the cemetery. Whether the police really had used batons on the angry mourners, whether a water cannon was deployed. She didn't want to know. For a while it looked as though the Kochs would stay in Dresden. Until Merker disappeared from the scene.

5

———

A S I RECALL, THE domestic offices were on the other side
of the street, directly opposite the Institute villa. Often
when I left Kaltenburg, I dropped the dirty washing off at
the laundry, I can see myself crossing the road with lab coats covered in green algae stains, with matted winter pullovers, but now
I wonder whether I didn't find a secret path, for the buildings that
most resemble the former laundry and joiner's workshop are situated two house numbers further down the road, half hidden behind
a hedge.

"Did the Kochs go back to England?" asked Katharina Fischer
as we left the Institute villa behind us.

For a while, it's possible that they thought about doing so. Rudolf Slánský was executed, at the Hagemanns' somebody expressed
the fear that the Prague show trial would have repercussions here as
well, and in fact the first house searches and arrests were soon under
way in Dresden. It seemed that they were only waiting for the nod
from Moscow to start uncovering a Zionist conspiracy, since they
already held the ringleader, Paul Merker. In January, Stalin—they
could always count on Comrade Stalin in Berlin—gave the signal:
among the doctors in his entourage he had discovered agents working for an international organization, possibly even for Israel, who
had designs on his life. Stalin gave full vent to this last delusion, accepting the confessions, satisfied to stack them up on the desk in

front of him, there was no need for him to read a single one, after all he had often issued warnings about the Jews.

The first absences occurred in the Hagemanns' drawing room. And the English couple no longer hesitated. They celebrated Stalin's death in West Berlin: Charlottenburg.

Archetypes of Fear would have been a different book. Kaltenburg didn't notice the gaps, I'm sure, until at least the first draft of his study. But you notice them when you're reading the book: when he mentions "how people are crammed together into the most restricted spaces," when he talks about "dehumanization"—you don't quite expect a critique of living conditions in the modern city. At one point he mentions "heat death"—you can imagine the professor recoiling the moment he has committed this term to paper, you can see him reflecting, crossing out, looking for an alternative, until "heat death" comes to mean something about as innocuous as a warning against hothousing a child. Just when you think that Kaltenburg is finally beginning to face up to the gaps, writing how difficult it is to make someone understand "that a culture can be extinguished like a candle flame," then you turn back a few pages and find that this chapter is devoted to a lengthy treatment of the war between the generations.

I remember how, in that same year, Klara once clashed with a representative of the Cultural Association. It was at a summer festival we were allowed to attend with Ludwig Kaltenburg. The effect on the professor must have been like watching the unfamiliar ritual of a newly discovered species. The two were discussing literature, initially it was hardly more than one of those conversations you have with a stranger in a large gathering. And Klara's interlocutor was in no way an unfriendly sort, an elderly gentleman who looked as though he had lived through a great deal, even if he hadn't achieved much of what he set out to do. Now he felt obliged to look to the future, and so for Klara's benefit he lauded examples of the latest activist writing, naming names that are forgotten today, that were soon to be forgotten even at the time. Privately he may have been a Stendhal admirer, but whatever names Klara put forward, he dismissed the authors out of hand. Inwardly seething, he worked himself up to the point of praising the most dubious tractor-versifier, in his blind zeal he would even have betrayed his beloved Stendhal. Klara did not give way, she went for broke: Proust. A body of work, she maintained in a completely unwavering voice, that was practically without equal in our century.

Klara was being foolhardy, she knew that, but in such moments everything was eclipsed by her fearlessness, not even Vorkuta existed. It took her interlocutor a second or two to compose himself. A word like "debauchery" sprang to his lips. He suppressed it. What came out was "decadence."

But whatever attack he launched against Proust, Klara had an answer to all his phrase-mongering, and of course she let slip that she had read a few hundred pages by that decadent, debauched author. The Cultural Association representative could have broken off the altercation, could have sought out different listeners. It was as plain to him as to anybody else who was following the exchange of blows that he was not going to convince this "defiant," articulate "girl." But he could not tear himself away. Something pinned him to the spot. Some voice he didn't recognize was telling him to go on arguing with Klara. Finally, all he could do was exclaim, "We don't need anyone like Proust. We don't need any Proust here."

Like all of Klara's admirers, Kaltenburg was dazzled by her energy, grateful that this young woman had dared to banish Vorkuta for a while, as though she had the power to turn the place back into a blank spot on the map. Afterward, though, he asked me in all confidence, "Tell me, this Proust, is he really one of the greatest?"

He was aware of the years he had missed at the Hagemanns', for sure. If he had been able to envisage those faces, recall those conversations when he began work on *Archetypes of Fear*, then there would be no uncertainty today about precisely what he meant by "atmosphere of death." Perhaps after more than two decades Kaltenburg might simply have dropped this favorite phrase of his, might have replaced it in new editions of older works with another, clearly delineated term. Or he might, once and for all, have struggled through to a definition of the shadowy expression "atmosphere of death." Whatever the painful experiences involved in such an undertaking, Kaltenburg would not have shrunk from it, would not have turned his head away.

"Are you really sure?"

He must have realized he had missed something.

"But are you certain that he would have seen things differently among the Hagemann circle? Would people like the Kochs, Rudolf Schottlaender, or Klara Hagemann have led him to revise his ideas?"

That's what I would have wished for him, at any rate.

It had stopped drizzling. The narrow road ran gently up the hill, and Katharina Fischer was wondering whether, at his age, Ludwig Kaltenburg really would have welcomed a rethink.

"And after all, at that stage the Cold War tensions were gradually beginning to ease off."

There wasn't much to stop him, in fact—all he lacked was a lifetime ahead of him. If he had been a younger man or, as he once wrote, a "representative of a future generation," he would have approached the phenomenon of fear from a completely different angle.

"Under pressure from younger colleagues?"

I think that's unlikely. Nobody could have forced him to make discoveries.

So the "atmosphere of death" in his writings remained to the end a barely definable field that was the setting for a series of varied, insufficiently delimited phenomena. The "atmosphere of death" encompasses injured birds as much as countless field-hospital patients. According to Ludwig Kaltenburg, it includes in equal measure "the displaced," "the homeless," and "those ground down between ideologies." And although the professor may gradually have become uncertain while working on his manuscript whether he was using the expression appropriately at any given point—in fact eventually he could not have said what he meant when he originally coined it—the "atmosphere of death" spread without distinction across slaughterhouses and flocks of dead jackdaws and military bands playing funeral marches alike, and had long since claimed a child wandering through the Great Garden during a night of bombardment.

But what use would a term like "world pogrom" have been to Ludwig Kaltenburg?

6

———

T O OUR RIGHT LAY some derelict land where for a while a few huts had stood, which, if I remember rightly, were torn down in the late fifties. Workrooms and dormitories, enclosures, and an infernal stench that pervaded the surrounding area when warm air crept up the hillside.

Ludwig Kaltenburg was very keen on a close bond between the researchers at his Institute. That's not to say they all had to have the same outlook on the world, the world of animals included: far from it. But I won't go into the experiments with hearing-impaired rhesus monkeys with which Etzel von Isisdorf began here.

"A hut full of rhesus monkeys?"

Yes. And even as a student at that time, when I was allowed to participate in the big evening meetings, I didn't take in his daily reports. I'm sure I wasn't the only one. Perhaps that's why the rhesus monkey section gradually developed into an institute within the Institute. Almost as soon as von Isisdorf accepted an appointment in the USA, the professor had the temporary housing demolished. After all, Kaltenburg argued, the neighbors — the non-animal-loving neighbors, that is — were already under almost inhuman pressure, without imposing that stench on them.

While Katharina Fischer walked silently at my side, I was trying to shake off some unbearable film images that had been running through my mind since I had brought up the name of Etzel von Isisdorf. A monkey's empty eyes, the bared teeth, the broken impression the animal makes on the observer, the look of a terrible presentiment running through it as it turns inward to listen and hears nothing. Its lips tremble as if filmed in slow motion, although the sequence was shot at normal speed.

When we reached a crossing, the interpreter pointed to a corner building: "Did that belong to the Institute as well?"

Maybe. Although it's quite a distance from the main Institute site. The numerous many-angled extensions, the clutter under the awning: at first I didn't associate anything with this building, but then we turned off to the right, and there was the small window in the side wall of the garage, the wall was piled up with rain barrels and garden tools, I saw the curtains, and then I remembered: this was where Knut stayed when he had work to do in Loschwitz.

"In the house?"

No, in the garage.

"In that poky den?" Katharina Fischer couldn't believe it.

Here again I read the nameplate next to the bell, it bore the same name as it had then, and once more I was loath to ring. Frau Fischer should have seen the garage before it was converted into a place for Knut to stay. The little window, the curtains—in reality I knew it wasn't possible, but I had the feeling they were the same curtains as fifty years ago.

The garage was leased, that is to say it was used by the Institute, and in return Kaltenburg sent his workmen along. They fitted the garage out so that you could stay there overnight, put in a window, insulated the walls. Afterward they carried out repairs to the main building, and as I recall they even put in a sauna. A pretty high price to pay for the use of a drafty hut in which you couldn't even have kept your coach horses with a good conscience. Kaltenburg thought wanting to live here was something of a fixation on Knut's part, but then again, he had a soft spot for fixations, he was no stranger to them himself. Nonetheless, Knut couldn't have cared that much about the garage, perhaps it was just that in the villa or one of the outbuildings he would have felt hemmed in, he enjoyed walking a few hundred meters after a long day's work in the Institute grounds.

The fresh night air over Loschwitz, not a soul around by then—the location and comfort of his lodgings were of secondary importance.

They put down linoleum, installed a bed that was much too wide, a bench, and a table; Knut was grateful for the accommodation. Except that, if it had been up to him, they would have made the window a bit larger. The workmen thought they were doing him a favor, the cold at night, the winter cold—whatever tales Knut had to tell about nights spent out in the open, nights on Lüneburg Heath as well as by the Black Sea, he was talking to workmen from Dresden, here we were in Loschwitz, and all they knew was that it can be bitterly cold at night in Loschwitz.

How proud Kaltenburg was to announce one morning that, in the intervals of a conference, he had persuaded Knut Sieverding to use the grounds of the Institute to make the hamster film he was planning. The open-air shooting had been completed, now filming was to proceed in an artificial hamster burrow. There were plenty of hamsters at the Institute, Knut would be able to take his pick from golden and black-bellied hamsters, tame animals gone feral and hand-reared wild animals. There was time, there was space, and all that Knut needed to bring with him was a few sacks of cement to build a proper hamster's burrow in the garden.

"A pane of glass two meters square? We enjoy excellent relations with a first-class glazing firm, Herr Sieverding."

There would probably have been enough cement at the Institute too. Knut asked no questions, however, but promised to take care of it. For all his pride at having engaged the aspiring young nature-film maker, Kaltenburg may have seen the requirement to supply cement as a little test of Knut's serious intentions. But when a truck appeared outside the house and the professor watched Knut struggling with the cement sacks, hauling them off the loading platform and trundling them on the trolley into the garden, there was no doubt about it: with this man, Kaltenburg had made a good choice.

Knut Sieverding's working methods were always a model of patience and attention to detail. He himself would have said that this was not exceptional in his line of work, since anyone who didn't possess these qualities wouldn't be making films in the first place but looking for some other kind of job. If I'd had the same attributes as Knut, it would have been hard for me then to decide whether to emulate him or the professor. Calm. Physical self-control. On good terms with sleep. And naturally his ingenuity in constructing blinds. The professor may have envied this ability in particular. When Kaltenburg worked with animals, it was always face-to-face. Film footage from the early days of the Institute shows him with ravens on his head, his forearm, and his knee, or on the Elbe shore with his young flock of jackdaws giving a demonstration of flying, or in the company of his ducks: the iridescent markings of the parent birds, the light, downy plumage of the chicks, and then a thick white shock of hair—a shot of a pond, taken almost at water-surface level, reeds swaying in the background. By contrast, in the countless open-air sequences Knut filmed in the course of a lifetime, not a single human being ever appears, although a specialist would know there must have been other people present because Knut often situated a number of cameras to capture an animal scene from a variety of perspectives.

He never appears in his own films, you don't see him in a studio setting, or prowling around the landscape in search of a hidden breeding site. Knut may not have attached much significance to this, but it takes me back to his earliest bird shots, the period of his youthful excursions when, with camera and binoculars, he explored a small peninsula in the Frische Haff from early morning till sunset, for months on end, left completely to his own devices. There was no one there to photograph Kurt in the presence of birds, nervous as they were of human contact.

He invited inquisitive school friends to help him build a shelter; they laid a waterproof sheet across a framework of birch trunks, arranging twigs and grasses as camouflage, then squatting with Knut for two or three hours in his blind—increasingly restless, under an increasing strain as they peered into the landscape ahead, until they reached a point where they politely asked Knut for permission to leave him to it. He waited until they had left the breeding area, until even the lapwings felt safe, then carefully moved his observation post another half-meter closer to the nest.

Later he was surrounded by assistants, cameramen, and lighting specialists who could easily have helped him to make small appearances: Knut Sieverding lying in wait at dawn, Knut Sieverding pointing, Knut Sieverding surveying the mating ground, and here Knut Sieverding watching the ruffs at their ritual display. "What a waste of valuable film time"—that's all he would have said. Even when his protagonist was a completely tame animal, he didn't dare raise his voice above a whisper as he worked, staying motionless beside the camera, and sometimes for an instant you feel the stoat is looking offscreen for eye contact, the young woodpeckers are becoming impatient, because Knut Sieverding is not reacting to their pleading. His view was that the author should be out of shot, present only as a voice. As though he were still working under the conditions of his early days, or had derived from them something like a commitment to staying out of the picture.

I am one of those people privileged to have witnessed Knut in action, I have seen him in those moments where everything has to move very fast, where everyone is in place, where a scene is successful or goes even better than hoped for, when everybody feels like cheering but must hold back because animals can't stand the sound of cheering. I have seen him full of self-doubt because of an unsatisfactory day's work, bad weather, running out of time. I have retained even more powerful impressions from the preparatory phase of work on Knut's full-length films, from those months partly filled with excited anticipation, in part characterized by depressing setbacks, when many a film project has collapsed because the director's nerve has failed.

The way that Knut presented his plan for the hamster burrow to me, drawn on graph paper, in the tones of an engineer but with the air of someone rolling out a map of hidden treasure, and suddenly said, as though we had been discussing Kaltenburg all along, "You know how important you are to the professor," then returned immediately to his design. Not "I've noticed" or "It's obvious": Knut said "You know," as though he merely wanted to confirm that I had arrived unaided at an insight that had been in the offing for years.

"The last thing I want to do when I'm trying to film an encounter between animals is interfere," he explained one day during the tedious business of training the stoat. I can see him sitting in the meadow, wearing an angler's waistcoat as usual over his checked shirt, its pockets containing not hooks or worms but light meters, pencils, bits of film stock. Laughing, he let the stoat have the end of a flex. No, he wouldn't interfere, but he did take the necessary precautions to prevent a fatal clash between his performers.

Then we crouched in the darkened tent in front of the camera-ready hamster set, together with Professor Kaltenburg and Herr Sikorski, the cameraman. For one last time Knut let his flashlight sweep along the passageway behind the pane of glass. From outside we could hear the sound of the mother hamster beginning a tentative exploration of her new quarters. The beam of light tracked down to the sleeping den, while the hamster was enjoying the pieces of carrot, wheat grains, and ears of rye that had been scattered over the miniature field. We saw the food storage chamber lit up, the escape tunnel, a side tunnel with bays—it was as though Knut were once more mentally rehearsing each individual scene he was planning to shoot. Now somebody was telling us that the hamster had discovered the entrance to the burrow, and Knut turned off the flashlight.

We pulled back carefully. In the world outside there was penetrating spring sunshine. The following weeks would be entirely devoted to getting the hamster used to a spotlight in her underground world. No hamster before her had ever lived permanently under two-thousand-watt lighting.

The film about the hamster was just the beginning. Three or four big projects were carried out at Kaltenburg's Institute, aside from a whole series of shorter films that Knut made for schools, and after his Congo expedition, when he was in tremendous demand everywhere, he fled to Dresden to write the film commentary in peace. For several weeks he left his lodgings for only a few hours a day, sitting with the professor, letting himself be persuaded by Martin, Klara, and me to go on an outing—but he soon felt the pull of his manuscript again. Hardly anyone knew he was there, hardly anyone ever found out, he sat hunched over his desk for three weeks, crammed in between the bed and the corner bench, a pile of paper in front of him, he didn't need books or any other material, Knut had all his Congo footage in his head, thousands of meters of it. "The shadowy world of the jungle is hostile to filming," he wrote in the nocturnal quiet of Oberloschwitz, and while he was waiting for the next sentence he could hear rhinoceros birds, spoonbills, marabous, saw himself surrounded by giant pangolins, okapis, aardvarks, gorillas, and cheetahs.

In this cramped garage, frequently dank and cold in winter, Knut and I often sat together, or in a trio with Klara, sometimes with Martin too. In the garage you could put a distance between yourself and the Institute without altogether cutting yourself off from it, and for a while after the Institute had closed down Knut was still allowed to go on living there whenever he came to Dresden. Until, citing their new car as an excuse, the house owners began to hum and haw, then ripped out the linoleum, burned the wall insulation, stowed the furniture under the awning in the backyard. Until they no longer wanted to know anything about the past Kaltenburg era. But they seem to have left the curtains in place.

7

———

KATHARINA FISCHER TOLD ME that recently, coming home exhausted one evening from an assignment, she had turned on the TV and happened upon a group discussion in which, along with a number of lesser lights, Knut Sieverding was taking part. At first she had not taken much notice of the program, went into the kitchen to heat up some goulash, her husband was away on official business abroad, after a hard day she simply wanted to have a few human voices around her without having to translate their words into another language. The unctuous presenter, notorious for his powers of empathy, was doing his best to contain an aging actress who was holding forth in shrill tones about her boundless social commitment, for Katharina Fischer this was just background noise, until she heard a voice familiar from her childhood saying, "I don't give a damn what you call it. It's obvious to me we're going to get it in the neck."

She missed the context in which Knut Sieverding made his remark, but she remembered all the more vividly the horrified faces of the studio guests she was just in time to catch as she came back into the living room, before the presenter turned with a nervous smile to the nature-film maker. Knut was so relaxed as he submitted to questioning, his wild boyish mop of hair contrasting with his deadly serious, almost pitying look as he nodded benignly, correcting inaccuracies on the presenter's part but otherwise largely ignoring the interviewer. Knut Sieverding declined to tell anecdotes about celebrities, he confined himself to animals—with one exception: prompted by the name Kaltenburg, he spoke euphorically about his time at the Institute, about a wealth of important experiences, and constantly reiterated how grateful he still was for the chance to work with the professor. Then the presenter read out a Kaltenburg quotation from his cue card: "More fantastic than taking a box at the opera," the professor had rhapsodized after seeing the first rushes of the woodpecker film.

"And do you know how Knut Sieverding responded?" asked Katharina Fischer. "A strange comparison, he said, considering that the woodpecker film was the first wildlife film ever released without the benefit of stringed instruments."

It's true. No music—the idea came to Knut and the professor one afternoon on the balcony at Loschwitz. The opposite of Hollywood. And as for the box at the opera: I can't remember Ludwig Kaltenburg ever setting foot in an opera house, at least not to see an opera, and once when the three of us clambered around in the ruins of the Semper Opera House, that was to do with Knut's idea of making an educational film on cave-nesting birds in the city.

Kaltenburg may not have been able to show it openly, but he had reason to be grateful to Knut too. It was Knut who succeeded in luring Martin to Loschwitz. Another way to put it would be that Knut Sieverding smoothed the path to Kaltenburg for Martin, who had become curious but was still a bit recalcitrant—he told him he would learn far more about animals from him than at the zoo, nobody would be looking suspiciously over his shoulder while he was sketching, and anyway Knut could use some more help with his filming.

"Were you really made to tell your friend all about Anastasia the chow dog?"

"Martin wanted to know everything—he'd never seen a chow before."

"Everyone's fascinated by that blue-black tongue."

"But I reckon he's even more fascinated by the dog's owner."

"If you really think he might benefit from my modest knowledge of dogs, then by all means bring him to the Institute sometime."

It's possible that on that first visit both the professor and Martin were still somewhat self-conscious. We toured the site, Martin was amazed by the dog's tongue, impressed by the aviaries, but when Knut left to go back to work, all three of us watched him as he departed, as though we had just lost our most important playmate. I was the one whose inspiration—if you can call it that—saved the day: why didn't Martin sketch Taschotschek?

Kaltenburg placed Martin with his back to the balcony door and Taschotschek in the middle of the table. Inquisitively the jackdaw surveyed the sheet of paper laid out, the tin box that hid charcoal and pencils, fixed its eye on the stranger who was blocking its exit. Martin talked to the bird, spoke to it reassuringly, and innocently began to draw. And Kaltenburg, sitting with me on the couch to one side, kept out of the way. He was much too thrilled to interfere, no doubt more excited by the encounter of man and creature being played out before his eyes than by the portrait. He followed the tentative hand of the artist, Taschotschek's hesitant steps, his glance jumping from one to the other, weighing up the relative chances of Martin and the jackdaw. As though he had made a bet with himself about who would win: Martin, by managing to capture the bird on paper, or the jackdaw, by reducing its portraitist to despair.

Taschotschek emerged victorious. Kaltenburg sat watching the scene calmly. You couldn't tell by looking at him which party he had backed.

Martin was to make many attempts to sketch Kaltenburg's favorite jackdaw. He never succeeded; after its own fashion the bird always joined in enthusiastically, and the better it got to know Martin during the sittings, the better it was at taking the lead. It took Taschotschek only a few minutes to work out how to open the tin box. With almost equal speed Martin grasped what charcoal meant, a human hand clutching something shiny black—enough to infuriate any jackdaw. A few drops of blood, a ripped-up piece of paper.

No, Martin would have had to draw Taschotschek from memory, and perhaps he actually did so in later years. It's just that it wouldn't necessarily occur to anyone that a line curving across a paper tablecloth was an image of a jackdaw, a jackdaw called Taschotschek capable of driving Martin Spengler mad for months on end when he was a young artist in Dresden.

So, strictly speaking, it wasn't Knut or me that Kaltenburg and Martin had to thank for their friendship, but a bird. Taschotschek's willfulness. Taschotschek's curiosity. At some point the drawing sessions became just a welcome chance for a chat in the presence of the jackdaw.

In *Archetypes of Fear* there is a fairly long passage, which Frau Fischer clearly recollected too: Kaltenburg is speculating about the relationship between fear and hallucination. About the human capacity to escape out of hopeless situations into another world. "If I understand him correctly, it's possible not only to alleviate feelings of fear and hopelessness, but to shut them out altogether by overlaying them with fantasy images," she recollected, and, "Wasn't it rumored that Kaltenburg was making use of findings by American military psychologists from the Vietnam War?"

Ludwig Kaltenburg as a renegade whose reward was access to secret experiments for use in his own studies — that sounded quite ludicrous even at the time. People simply didn't want to acknowledge where he acquired most of his observational material: here.

One evening I had finished checking the aviaries and was going to say goodnight to the professor when I heard him talking to Martin in a low voice in the study, as if not to wake the animals that had retired for the night. Kaltenburg seemed surprised when I appeared in the doorway, I hesitated, he hesitated, I was about to retreat, but then he beckoned me into the room. On the table: Taschotschek, pattering about indecisively on a sheet of unmarked white paper. Knut was sitting on a stool, Martin on the couch.

"So there I was, lying trapped under the wreckage of our plane after we had taken a hit in the northern Crimea and lost control of the machine."

Martin glanced across at me and moved over a little to make room for me. Kaltenburg had drawn up his cocktail-bar chair. I was in the picture straightaway.

"I didn't know that my copilot had been killed, that his remains lay scattered in the snow, flesh, bones, skin, and cloth. I wasn't feeling any pain, I had no idea who or where I was, I wasn't conscious of the frozen ground."

The bird regarded each of us in turn. Ruffled its feathers. Drew its third eyelid across its eyeball. Turned away.

"I regained consciousness for a moment. As if someone had woken me up. And in fact I wasn't alone, my skull, my limbs, my joints—somebody was checking my bones, looking for fractures, abrasions, flesh wounds. My mind was brought to bear on individual parts, my knee, my shoulder. But I wasn't aware of anyone touching me. Then I drifted back into darkness."

A scratching, a gentle clattering sound, Martin had let Taschotschek have his empty tin box. The lid was opened, closed, opened, the box pulled from one end of the table to the other. Apparently the jackdaw regarded it as Martin's job to keep it amused by hiding interesting objects such as colored pencils or erasers.

"The next time I came around, I knew these were the eyes of Tatars. As though the Tatars had not simply observed the crash site timidly from afar but had examined me at close quarters, then run their hands over my body, then taken me along with them. I could smell it, smell their skin, this indescribably comforting aroma, with a slight trace of fish oil."

"And this was all just in your imagination?"

Professor Kaltenburg ignored the clatter now coming from the hallway; Taschotschek had dragged the tin box outside and was pecking at the hinges.

"It must all have been in my mind. I only lay there for a few hours, then I was picked up by a search party. Can you imagine, my comrade Hans was almost pulverized. I think about it sometimes when I'm grinding earth colors in the mortar, when I'm mixing pigment. Doesn't man consist of carbon too when the fluids have evaporated? It doesn't take long to render down that little bit of protein. Pulverized, fragmented into the tiniest particles. Nothing left."

The jackdaw was now on the couch between us, looking up at me, eyeing Martin, and since nobody was paying it any attention, it plucked an old bus ticket out of his trouser pocket.

"There's a photo of me standing in full uniform in front of our wrecked plane. That time, that moment in time, is lost to me. It was somewhere near Freifeld, in that area. That much I can remember. But I've got no recollection at all of being photographed. If they had indeed pulled me out unconscious and half dead from the wreckage, I could hardly have stood up to pose for a photograph. So the picture must have been taken later. I had been patched up somehow, they put me in the jeep and drove me back to the crash site. But why? There were more important things. Getting back to health. The next sortie. Saving your own life. Maybe I insisted on it."

"You wanted a picture to take home with you. Wanted it to send to your parents."

"Probably, yes. But then my injuries can't have been as bad as I remember: double fracture of the skull base, practically no skin left on my body, no hair. Everything full of splinters, hardly any nose left."

Martin stumbled over his words, went quiet, you could only hear his lips moving. At that moment Kaltenburg, Knut, and I were nothing but shadowy Tatars. The professor poured tea for us. Taschotschek hopped onto my lap.

"Herr Spengler, or may I say Martin?" Kaltenburg hovered with teapot and teacup. "I should tell you that in principle I don't like talking about the phenomena they call self-healing powers. Particularly where human beings are concerned, people often make it too easy for themselves. All the same, I've seen some unbelievable things in that field."

"But that photograph—if you take a good look at it: a scab-covered cut at most, my eyebrows perhaps. And I must have been thoroughly concussed, of course. Yet Hans had ceased to exist. What they could find of him was buried in the nearest village cemetery."

"No doubt." Kaltenburg spoke as if he had already said too much.

"No doubt": any deeper insight into his own experience of illness and hallucination might have been destabilizing for the young man, with his Tatar memories.

In the hallway Knut almost trod on the tin box. The lid was missing, I could see a pastry fork. By the hall stand the professor remarked, "Really interesting are the hallucinatory states that occur when self-healing powers are activated. There's still practically no research into that. At any rate, I've never come across any convincing answers."

He accompanied us to the front door, quickly scanned the Institute grounds to left and right, nodded goodbye, and shut the door as we reached the garden gate. Knut set off for his garage. As Martin and I were walking down the hill, I looked back frequently — the dim light of a desk lamp filled the upstairs window that I knew so well, until Kaltenburg's villa was out of sight.

A few days later the professor took me aside; he was fascinated in equal measure by Martin and by his own shrewdness, as though surprised to discover new capabilities in himself at his age. Almost in a whisper, he told me, "I knew it would provoke a reaction in him sooner or later," without clarifying whether the "it" in question was Martin's acquaintance with Taschotschek or the long Stalin monologue. And Martin was to say to Klara at one point, "It's possible that it was some such figure as Kaltenburg who spoon-fed me soup. I was always in and out of field hospitals, though it was before I was taken prisoner, and maybe Professor Kaltenburg wasn't unique. Spoon-feeding soup, extraordinary. But I couldn't swear it didn't happen to me."

Time and again the two of them together — in the garden, in the kitchen, on country walks — analyzed Martin's experience of crashing in the Crimea. Went over the tragic loss of his copilot, the Tatar eyes, the smell of fish oil, coming around in what must have been a tent, since Martin found an expanse of rough material stretched above his head. He had spent hours staring at the fabric in the dim light, not knowing where he was, who had brought him there, yet feeling not at all unsafe.

Martin became more and more absorbed by this image, soon it hardly mattered to him that his spells in field hospitals occurred long after the professor was taken prisoner in Russia, and perhaps it was Kaltenburg's story that inspired Martin to give that early drawing of his, in which I thought I recognized my nanny, the title "Russian Nurse." The spoon-feeding, Kaltenburg's fit of rage by an amputee's bedside, Comrade Stalin's coal-black stare—when Martin's public performances in the sixties and seventies unnerved the public with their soft violence, I invariably recognized elements in them that reminded me of that evening. I think on one occasion he even incorporated the note tucked away in somebody's cheek.

8

A SUNDAY IN DECEMBER. Ludwig Kaltenburg stood by the window in the winter light, we were in the zoological museum, in the workshop of the Ornithological Collection. It was my first visit to the building. I no longer saw the professor very often by himself.

I couldn't make out whether Kaltenburg was looking me in the eye or scrutinizing the half-finished bird skin lying on the table in front of me. He betrayed no sign of impatience, standing with arms folded, nodding.

"Still looks a bit swollen." Kaltenburg pinched the sparrow carefully. "But much better than your first effort this morning. There's a world of difference."

I pulled the cotton wadding out of the skin again, rolling it between my palms.

"But you don't want to make it too hard either."

I started tweaking with the tweezers a clump at the front, then another, then one a bit higher, toward the tail. A bright wad, meant to reproduce the shape of a bird's body. Looking at my handiwork, I realized that I no longer even knew how big the sparrow was before we removed its skin.

"You won't get anywhere that way, you'd better use some new wadding."

And then promptly: "Stop, not so much. You've got to decide in advance how much you need."

A few minutes later: "Perhaps you could sew it up now. Have you got the skull in? Just start sewing, then we'll see what sort of customer emerges. And as I said, don't make the seam too tight, otherwise the bird will burst open again."

I didn't want to know how many sparrows Kaltenburg had brought along for me. "Even if you never learn to enjoy skinning, you've got to be able to do it in your sleep. You must develop skill and an accurate eye, otherwise you're lost."

It's not unlikely that he had me in for "extra coaching" because he found it embarrassing to talk about a student as a future acolyte when that student couldn't even produce a well-formed sparrow skin. I was on my second attempt when Kaltenburg—by the window, arms folded—made a mistake. That is to say, he winced, and I knew he wished he hadn't spoken.

"And they've gone on the hunt in the Great Garden, in this weather."

"Who has?"

"Our comrades from the Society for Sports and Technology." Kaltenburg's voice as he said "our comrades."

"And why on the hunt?"

"Haven't you heard? The Great Garden is closed to the public, the SST is shooting animals—threat of rabies."

"Foxes?"

"Stray dogs, they said, cats, wild rabbits."

"In fact, everything in their sights?"

"Magpies, crows, jays can all transmit rabies, of course."

"A regular slaughter?"

Kaltenburg came across to the table, leaning over as if to scrutinize my face.

"I'm afraid so, yes."

I laid aside the half-skinned sparrow body. How could Professor Kaltenburg summon me on a Sunday to the zoological museum to calmly teach me the proper way to prepare a bird skin while at the same time in the Great Garden an army of lunatics was engaged in disguised target practice? There was no doubt that their victims would also include birds from Kaltenburg's household, hand-reared creatures that frequented the Great Garden during daylight hours. As they did every morning, they had taken off all unsuspecting from Loschwitz to fly across the Elbe, while Kaltenburg was shaving, dressing, drinking his tea. Perhaps he had watched a flock of them circling one last time outside the window before the birds gradually disappeared down the valley, shapes, black dots mixed with white, isolated snowflakes, then becoming nothing more than a memory of movement in the air. Kaltenburg knew about the impending disaster, he should have used his influence, taken some action.

Leaning on the table, he looked at me. "Do you know what happened at the beginning of the century when they started ringing birds at the Rossitten observation post, fully believing it would help protect them?"

I wasn't in the mood for guessing games. I didn't even bother to shake my head. To take my mind off what I'd just heard, I picked up the scalpel and went on loosening more of the sparrow's skin, as far as the neck, prior to pulling it away over the body. As more and more of the inside of the skin appeared, I sprinkled it repeatedly with the mixture of potato flour and plaster Kaltenburg provided that morning.

"People went out shooting birds. They brought down massive numbers in the hope of bagging one from Rossitten."

Carefully I bared the skull, pushing back the skin of the neck and slowly easing it over the cap of the skull. The skin had to be pulled over both rami of the lower jaw at once, and I had to make sure I didn't sever the ear sacs. You could draw them out of the auditory canal with your fingers. No tugging at this point, it would be so easy to tear the skin. One squeeze of my clumsy thumbs could crush the skull to bits. I had to keep in mind the enormous power in my fingers when they enclosed a skull.

"How do you think I lose most animals? People are as keen

on trophy hunting nowadays as they were then, and everybody has plenty of ringed birds by now. I don't suppose I'll ever know whether it's naiveté or ill will. Their pride when they take people into their trophy room, especially if anybody asks them, Is that mount a Kaltenburg?"

The professor paced back and forth, pausing in front of a showcase displaying objects from all over the world—picture postcards, a wooden case with inlay work: a pattern of fish or something abstract. The caiman standing upright with a hat and cane, holding a small champagne glass.

I picked up the blade again and cut through the transparent skin around the eyes until the eyelids were separated from the dark eyeballs. Now for the brain. I made an incision diagonally toward the base of the skull, noting that the neck and tongue were released by the same cut. I lifted the brain out carefully, the eyeballs, taking trouble not to get any secretions or blood on the dead sparrow's feathers. I sprinkled borax over the head and packed the eye cavities tightly with wadding.

Professor Kaltenburg stood by the periodical shelves, randomly pulling out one issue after another and leafing through them. Perhaps he was looking for his own name. I turned the head and neck skin back again with my index fingers, took the sparrow by the beak, and shook the neck feathers back into place. Kaltenburg was restless.

"Do you remember a man coming to the door and telling me he had run over one of my jackdaws? Well, the story simply didn't add up at all. Turns up on an old bike talking about his car. He probably didn't even have a driving license, let alone a car. Didn't it ever strike you as odd? And how would a jackdaw finish up under his wheels? That alone might have set you thinking. I tell you, he got rattled on the way home and lost his nerve."

I introduced the closed tweezers into the eye cavity and coaxed the head feathers back into place. Then the skin was painted with the toxic solution.

"They suddenly turn all humble and come crawling to me, holding out their blood-soaked bags. They're looking for punishment, they want me to bawl them out. But I won't give them the satisfaction, I thank them politely and let them go on their way. I could see at a glance, that dead jackdaw was full of lead shot."

"Can't these people be held to account?"

"Do you want me to shout it from the rooftops? Even the slowest would get the idea. And then we'd have a new popular sport, shooting Kaltenburg's birds. The Institute would be closed within a month."

"You've never told me about all this."

"Naturally I don't tell you everything. I don't want you losing your confidence on account of such things."

So much for the skinning. Now the bird had to be totally reconstructed. Kaltenburg left me working alone for a while, went wandering off through the rooms. When he came back, he seemed distracted: "If we ever go to Vienna together, remind me to show you the two sea eagles in their eerie that Crown Prince Rudolf shot nine days before he committed suicide in Mayerling."

While Kaltenburg was telling me about Vienna, I grew calmer with every hand movement.

"And then if you go to the Natural History Museum in Bucharest sometime, you'll be amazed. The dioramas alone: in the low lighting you have to look hard for the animals between the grasses and bushes."

On his first visit there, standing in front of the display cases on the upper floor, Kaltenburg had almost burst into tears, "You know what that means with me": the exuberant multiplicity of species, subspecies, varieties, although no one—neither a curator nor a bird—was using the display to show off. Despite the great wealth of information, a kind of restraint prevailed, you could almost say tact, which immediately told visitors that here they had pulled off the trick of preserving respect for nature while at the same time offering every possible detail an inquiring wildlife enthusiast could desire about birds, these shy creatures.

"I remember two birds in particular, you've guessed it, a couple of jackdaws, eastern jackdaws, male and female, the label said they had been collected not long before my visit in April 1950 by some enthusiastic soldiers on army land in Bucharest."

Kaltenburg in front of the periodicals, completely lost in thought.

"Incidentally, don't forget to take a quick look at the wall on the landing before you rush upstairs: there's a niche there—you might say a display case—with two urns containing the ashes of the long-serving director of the museum—a student of Haeckel's—Grigore Antipa, and his wife."

The less fat a skin contains, the easier it is to preserve. By the afternoon I had managed to produce a sparrow skin that I was satisfied with. Kaltenburg was too.

"I said you could do it."

Outside, it was rapidly getting dark. Conscientiously I wrote out the label, naming Kaltenburg as the collector, Funk as the taxidermist. The first bird skin I had contributed to the collection.

"They must be just about finished by now."

Ludwig Kaltenburg looked at me inquiringly.

"In the Great Garden, I mean."

It was no longer on his mind. "Are you still talking about the amateur marksmen?" And no, the hunt was due to last only until eleven that morning. "They'll have gathered in their spoils ages ago. Imagine how much work will be coming the way of our curators and taxidermists when the SST comrades start logging in what they've bagged."

9

IF THE INTERPRETER HADN'T asked me about the year the
Ornithological Collection episode took place, I would never
have realized that—although I can remember every word,
Kaltenburg's oddly changeable tone, the sparrow I skinned, and the
gloom of a December day—I couldn't remember whether it was
1955, or a year later, or 1957. It felt as though I had spent a day with
Kaltenburg in a secluded room out of time. I have no date to attach
to my feeling of helplessness to influence external events, let alone
put a stop to the hunt in the Great Garden, for example by wandering all unsuspecting into the park for a stroll and thus forcing the
shooting party to suspend their activities for a while at least.

It's possible that I would have been arrested for disturbing the
peace and interrogated, a refractory young man who, despite repeated warnings, had gained access to a prohibited area; it's also
possible that in the case of such a transgression I would have been
threatened with consequences, declared insane, expelled from the
university because I had insulted upright members of the Society
for Sport and Technology. Perhaps the professor had wanted to
protect me. Or he knew me better than I knew myself and thought
it would be easier for me to bear my own impotence away from the
scene than standing at the edge of the Great Garden, counting the
shots, seeing the birds fall out of the trees in front of me, avoiding
the eyes of the law enforcers.

A Sunday in December: to establish the exact date, all I would have had to do was consult our skin collection. Among countless specimens I would find a young male sparrow, with a delicate bluish sheen to its gray head and distinctly, almost cosmetically rimmed walnut-brown cheeks, whose label bore the professor's name as well as mine. Or I might look among the corvids to identify birds shot that morning in the Great Garden. Then I would be able to put a date to Kaltenburg's exclamation "I don't want you losing confidence," this anxious thought, expressed in an offhand sentence, which I couldn't relate to anything in particular, and which, it seems to me, corresponds to the helplessness I felt that day. Ludwig Kaltenburg and I, spending a day out of time in the ornithology room, both depressed, both trying to look forward to the days, weeks, years that lay ahead of us.

I can at least say with some certainty, without further research, that our time together among the dead birds fell within the period when all the talk was about the return of the Dresden art treasures from secret Soviet collections. Amazed, almost stunned, and a little suspicious, we stood in front of the paintings in the Zwinger Gallery, expecting someone to speak up under cover of the dense mass of visitors and expose the exhibition as a nonevent, a collection of more or less skilled copies. In fact, among the circle of those to whom I talked about things that were not for the ears of strangers, it was Ludwig Kaltenburg who, without taking the precaution of sounding out art historians who knew something about the subject, was the only one not to harbor any doubt whatsoever about the authenticity of these newly liberated Rembrandts, Vermeers, and Raphaels. The professor firmly believed in the sincerity of the new, transformed Soviet Union, and he wouldn't have been Ludwig Kaltenburg if he had been worried simply by finding he stood alone in his opinion.

The professor was so inspired by the return of the art treasures that he sketched an outrageous vision of the future: what if the gallery in the Zwinger Palace was only the beginning? In the light of this unprecedented event, how big a step would it really be to follow through eventually with the missing contents of other collections?

These were the reflections Kaltenburg mulled over on his solitary nocturnal walks through Oberloschwitz with Anastasia, who stayed close to her master. The black sky over Dresden, the dull pavement beneath Kaltenburg's feet—perhaps one reason the professor knocked at Knut's door on his way home was that he was afraid of losing himself in his wishful thinking.

The two of them talked, with Anastasia lying by the stove, about the holdings of the Dresden Zoological Collections missing since summer 1945, about the famous Steller's sea cow and the great auk. Since being transported to the Soviet Union, they seemed to have been erased from memory, very few people ever mentioned them anymore. The name "great auk" could only be whispered, as if one were referring to someone banished and struck from the population register. As if it were not a case of a mounted specimen stored in a secret depository in Moscow, Leningrad, or Kiev, but a living giant bird languishing, despite all rumors to the contrary, in Vorkuta.

So Knut Sieverding knew long before I did where Kaltenburg's hopes were tending in those days, what preoccupied him, and I can no longer say whether it was from Knut or from the professor that I first heard what was going on in his mind when he broke off from work and stared into space: he wasn't dwelling on the activities of a woodpecker's brood in its hollow, or the bloody battle between a ring-necked dove and a turtledove that he had carelessly placed in the same cage; his gaze was plumbing the depths of a secret depository where two custodians were arguing about whether or not to bring the meteorite from the Dresden collection out into the light of day.

"Was it a complete fantasy to hope these things would be returned, then?" asked Katharina Fischer as we walked toward Oberwachwitz, taking a path that Kaltenburg had often used with Anastasia.

Soon we would see, as the professor would have done, a little stand of pines, we would hear that high-pitched, even rush of wind in the trees, the wind that seems to be sweeping through a vast expanse of landscape wherever a few pines cluster together, and then the buildings of the former Soviet field hospital would appear between the treetops. As far as I recall, this is where, soon after his arrival and before the medical facility was transferred to the Garrisoned People's Police, Kaltenburg had installed a huge aquarium.

There was indeed a glimmer of hope. And it's possible that Ludwig Kaltenburg had advance knowledge of developments behind the scenes that the rest of us would have thought impossible. Certainly in those days people thought he was often dropping in on the Russian garrison, that he was on familiar terms with high-ranking Soviet officers.

"Dropping in on the garrison? Don't make me laugh," was his irritated reply when he heard of these suspicions. "It just shows you the limited mentality of people who've got nothing better to do than try and pin something on you."

I can remember that the professor was standing in felt boots in the meadow behind the house, Knut next to him holding a camera.

"In and out of the garrison—and then I suppose I come sneaking out of the grocery store with pelmeni dumplings for my fish concealed under my overcoat? These people's imaginations are as limited as their lives."

It seemed to me that the pair of them exchanged a conspiratorial glance. We walked slowly down the narrow path by the house, Kaltenburg shuffling along beside us—it was obviously the first time he'd worn the boots—then he stopped, let the ducks examine the thick gray felt, and turned to me with an expectant air: "You may not believe it, but I only got back from Leningrad last night."

Knut showed no surprise. I had no idea what the professor was driving at. Knut touched his sleeve, gently silencing him. "Perhaps we should go for a little spin?"

We ran into Krause in the driveway. Saturday morning, of course; Kaltenburg had forgotten. The chauffeur was cleaning the limousine as he did every Saturday, running the sponge over roof and windscreen, mudguards and hood, finishing by buffing up the chrome and the hubcaps, and not even allowing the jackdaws to disturb him as they inspected with their beaks every single screw redeemed from road grime and oil. As we passed him he didn't seem to hear us, lost in his own world.

"Sometimes I feel really sorry for Herr Krause, with all the stories I tell him," observed Kaltenburg as we rolled out into the road in his not quite so immaculately clean Opel. "When I think of him agonizing at night over his reports, not knowing what to write."

He smiled, slipping his boot off the clutch, I think he was still in shock because he had nearly blurted out a secret in the presence of his chauffeur.

"Does Krause force himself to stick to the truth and report the liqueur chocolates that—as I told him—I kept on secretly feeding to an unknown squirrel, or does he permit himself the slight liberty of substituting the more plausible-sounding nut pralines? Whatever the poor devil opts for, he's bound to sweat over it, and he loses sleep because he runs the risk of making himself ridiculous to his readers every time he reports. But let's talk about more important matters—Leningrad."

Kaltenburg took his hand off the gearstick and leaned back. "In the plane yesterday, I was so agitated, I just couldn't sit still. When we landed I had to keep telling myself this was nothing special, just a normal official trip. Krause spotted me straightaway in the arrivals hall, and on the long trip back from Schönefeld to Dresden he tried to pump me a bit, just as I'd expected. It took all my strength to maintain a neutral expression as he kept on looking in the rear mirror."

Now I was the one trying to catch Kaltenburg's eye in the rear mirror. "What do you say, Herr Sieverding? Was I right?" he asked his front-seat passenger, with a nod to me at the same time. "We're going to bring the missing treasures back to Dresden."

"It won't do to get our hopes up too high." Knut answered as though caught up in preparations for a film project against the advice of the entire world of wildlife experts. "We'll have to proceed very cautiously."

"Of course we're just carefully feeling our way at the moment, but I think our talks in Leningrad were a good first step," countered the professor. "We've got a foot in the door, perhaps we can bring it off—even if it takes a while."

This was where his command of Russian came in useful, his love of all things Russian, prone to attract suspicion as much as amusement. Kaltenburg had a plan: he could talk day in and day out, without a single reference to the collection, about the breathtaking landscape, the vast distances, he could go on about the fabulous treatment he had received as a POW. He would also, for example, expatiate on the manuscript he had produced in the POW camp near Moscow, which he had been allowed to take home with him unexamined, because a magnanimous officer had believed Kaltenburg's assurance that it contained nothing political, only observations of animals. There was no stopping Ludwig Kaltenburg as he depicted the forthcoming negotiations and saw himself coming back from Leningrad with a great auk tucked under his arm: "I've been offered the chair of the secret zoological commission. That is to say, I'll be taking it on when the individual commissions are set up."

I think we drove as far as Chemnitz and back on the autobahn that afternoon. Knut had now become far more than the experimental filmmaker who helped Kaltenburg gain insights into previously unknown areas of animal life, more than just a close friend of Martin Spengler's who had brought the artist to Loschwitz and thereby provided the professor with early material for his *Archetypes of Fear*. During this trip it dawned on me: Knut Sieverding had now become Ludwig Kaltenburg's closest adviser.

"You may be able to enter fearlessly into these negotiations, Professor, but you mustn't let that make you think others are equally fearless, otherwise you might be in for a great disappointment." Knut took a skeptical view of "magnanimous officers," he had no vision of a cozily crackling open fire and an evening spent exchanging reminiscences of life as a POW. "They may well listen patiently while you rhapsodize about the Russian landscape, but the longer you go on extolling the virtues of bright birchwood forests, the clearer it will be to you that you're banging your head against a brick wall."

Perhaps Knut was the only realist among us. His voice carried weight, he could even persuade Ludwig Kaltenburg to modify his entrenched views. And so, under instruction from Knut, the professor adjusted to the prospect of bare, windowless rooms at the end of long corridors, hours of waiting until a door finally opens and a museum assistant emerges, silent, diffident, to unwrap a valuable display on the table before the professor. No trace of enthusiasm, no trace of collegial affability—and it was precisely this that Kaltenburg had to overcome, he must not take it personally. "It's better to expect fear."

Fear of showing irresponsible openness to the man from Dresden. The fear that he might find out about stored items of which even the museum director was not officially aware. The fear of inadvertently betraying by a word, a smile, or a nod details whose disclosure could cost you your head.

10

———

WHEN I CALL TO MIND Kaltenburg's feverish look as he reported on his trip to Leningrad, I also see an angry, obstreperous child who had just learned that the family was planning to make a journey westward. I can see myself plucking at the tablecloth, "Dresden," my parents had said, as though it were a magic word: "We can stop over in Dresden." But what did they mean, "stop over," so our real destination was further away? I started to cry, why wasn't my nanny there to comfort me, where was Maria anyway, she had left the house, and we weren't going to come back to this place again either, the garden, the fields, the long winter. Let them go without me. I would manage alone here in our house on the edge of Posen. My father shook his head, "Let's drop it," no one would promise me we would be away from home for just a week or two, "Let's drop the subject," and sure enough there was no further mention of the journey over the following few days.

I did not feel relieved. When my parents withdrew into the study, I sensed trouble. I didn't understand what they were talking about or how serious the situation was, but I sat up next morning when they mentioned an enormous "meteorite from space," a "Steller's sea cow," and the "great auk." These really were magic words, and coming from my father's mouth they sounded as if my mother had invented them and immediately passed them on to him so that he could savor their taste for himself. Perhaps my mother

238

had found them the night before, in the study from which my parents had emerged—as I could see from the landing—for the first time in a long time without looking worried. I knew what an auk was, and a sea cow, but what would a great auk look like?

"As big as an Atlantic puffin?"

"Bigger."

"Like a guillemot?"

"Bigger."

"And where do great auks live?"

"They don't live anywhere, not anymore."

That's all they would tell me: "You'll see when we get to Dresden," and "It's a promise."

They couldn't have enticed me there with a Church of Our Lady, a castle, a Brühl Terrace, but the prospect of seeing a strange creature excited my curiosity. It was more than a ruse to make the journey more acceptable to me, I could see it in my mother's downcast eyes when we stood in front of the bombed-out museum, feel it in her angry tone as we three were having our last lunch together. What did my mother know about the twelve crates of exhibits hidden in Weesenstein Castle since 1942? "Steller's sea cow," she whispered to my father across the table, "great auk," the magic words had lost their power, could not summon up the creatures. And so it was, in that oppressed atmosphere, that I remained none the wiser about their appearance, didn't dare ask, would have had to whisper as well, just as we went on whispering over the following decades.

My parents conferred in my father's study, I listened at the door, there were the usual neatly addressed envelopes containing seed samples lying on the desk, my father was still working on his tests. I heard a rustling sound, my mother had picked up a packet of taiga grass seeds, she held a sample of a Siberian plant in her hand, either the two of them spoke in low voices or I preferred not to hear them, preferred to interpret a plan of escape as holiday planning.

For a good while my imagination had been gradually enlarging an Atlantic puffin or a razor-billed auk, in my mind the bird had taken on hitherto inconceivable dimensions, and I grouped a flock of great auks around the Steller's sea cow, a massive, heavy animal with a shimmering gray and green hide, resting on its short front flippers. In fact I assumed that the sea cow would be a mounted specimen, although I was sure my parents had not deliberately set out to mislead me. In my mind's eye flesh and muscle and skin spread themselves over the skeletal frame as though of their own accord. Perhaps I would have been disappointed if I really had got to see the animal in February 1945, and I can remember not being altogether able to believe it at first when a colleague later explained in passing that the Steller's sea cow in our collection was just a skeleton, not quite complete.

11

I T WAS THE FIRST TIME Klara had heard of sea cows and great auks, she heard the names with slight incredulity, let me describe to her the appearance of these creatures, the cold, deserted areas that were their home. Nor did Klara know anything about the razor-billed auks and Atlantic puffins that had loomed large for whole nights at a time in the mind's eye of a boy in distant Posen before the journey to Dresden. Until she met me there had been no strange seabirds in her life, not even in fantasy to help overcome fear of an uncertain future when lying in bed alone, unable to sleep. Nor had she ever been with her parents to the zoological museum, not that she could remember. When she was a child, she said, regretfully, she had no eye for bird life, for animal life in general.

There were a few she noticed, birds from the immediate neighborhood: she showed me the place on the roof where the redstart took up its post every evening to sing its dry, squeaky song. She was impressed by the bold blackbirds that build their open nests at eye level and seem to hope that their very vulnerability will dispose every enemy to treat them kindly. And she had always liked the great tits that flitted from one treetop to another in the Great Garden, picking off insects from leaves and bark. Their calls of surprise and delight, as though they were directing the girl down below toward a particular tasty find, letting her share their pleasure. In fact, for a long time she had believed it was the same individual bird that waited for her every Sunday in the Tiergartenstrasse to accompany her on her walk with her parents, until she realized that the tits stayed in touch by voice, they conversed with each other, and it was just that Klara could not distinguish one voice from another in the great conversation that ringed the whole park.

But her clearest memory was of the crows in the Wasaplatz, the flock that came back regularly in winter when the beech tree next to the house was leafless and the sisters could see across the square from their room. Perhaps the old spreading chestnut there had served as a landmark for countless generations of crows as they found their way between roosting and feeding places, perhaps a few birds had always detached themselves from the endless moving swarm of crows and landed on the bare branches to take a closer look at the Wasaplatz and search the ground for anything edible. But the first time Ulli and Klara noticed the crows was on a cold, dark morning in the winter before the war began.

Since the turn of the year Ulli had been suffering from a severe cough, which no doctor in Dresden knew how to treat. It came in waves, the attacks went on for a few nights and days, then she had some respite, but it seemed that it was not Ulli but the cough that was getting its strength together, ready to redouble its grip on her lungs, throat, and trachea. Even in the quiet intervals Ulli did not feel inclined to get up, whatever Klara suggested, and whatever lively dialogues she made up for the dolls to engage in on the bedspread—to Ulli it wasn't cheerful conversation but squabbling, and she sent Klara out of the room.

The parents saw their five-year-old daughter coming down the stairs with shoulders drooping. No, Ulli didn't want to play, she wanted to sleep. No, she didn't even want tea. Listless, Klara sat down at the dining table and scribbled around in a coloring book with her crayon.

"Have you noticed—it's snowing."

"I know."

"Would you like to go tobogganing with Dad in the Great Garden?"

"I'd rather stay here."

Meanwhile Ulli had already missed six weeks of schoolwork, as her teacher informed them by letter. The girl was in danger of falling badly behind. Her parents didn't read the letter out to her, they simply said, "Fräulein Weber wants you to know that the whole class can hardly wait for you to get better."

The Hagemanns pulled out all the stops. Friends in Berlin fixed up an appointment at the Charité hospital there. An acquaintance was prepared to drive Frau Hagemann and Ulli to Berlin.

Klara woke up in her parents' bedroom, alone. She ran to the window, scratched ice flowers from the glass: there was a car standing outside the house, two men were talking, their breath condensing, her father and the driver. There was no snow on the ground, you could see a few white patches around the Wasaplatz, with a bluish shimmer in the early-morning light. Klara got dressed as quickly as she could, and by the time she reached the foot of the stairs she was wide awake. Icy air seeped into the house through the swing doors, her father came in, his tired, dog-tired look. He hadn't taken Klara into account, he was about to say something—she jumped in ahead of him: "Where is Ulli?"

Herr Hagemann pushed Klara into the kitchen, "Hush," her mother was standing by the table in the fine dress kept specially for trips to Berlin: "Ulli is still in bed, she only settled down about two hours ago."

Klara remembered the agitated footsteps yesterday, the voices from downstairs, until she had fallen asleep. The fire in the kitchen stove had been burning all night. While Klara put on her shoes, cap, scarf, and coat, her parents carried Ulli downstairs, and like Klara she was in her coat and scarf, but her parents had added an eiderdown to her winter gear. Ulli as if sleeping in bed, Ulli as if about to go on a morning trek. It didn't fit together. Klara was scared.

"Could you hold the door open?"

Ulli began to cough, awake now. Then Klara heard the crows above the Wasaplatz. She saw crows on the ground, not far from the car. Ulli saw them too. For a moment, while the adults were talking, the two sisters were alone. Alone with the crows. Klara pointed at the sky, the silent procession of birds, they flew from the Elbe with steady, sluggish wingbeats, as if they hadn't awakened yet, now and again they called to each other in muted tones. Klara pointed at the top of the chestnut tree, pointed to the birds by the frozen puddle, the birds had turned away from the leftover snow, were observing the two girls with interest, one sister standing with both feet on the ground, the other held up in the air by her father. Klara didn't know whether she felt disturbed, whether she would like the crows to come closer, whether she should hold out her hand. But she knew that at this moment Ulli would not have been able to say either. Then Ulli was bedded down on the back seat, Frau Hagemann got in on the other side, Klara waved, the car vanished into Caspar David Friedrich Strasse.

"Come on, let's go in," said their father.

He had not noticed the crows. One of them had almost reached the front door with Klara. It would soon be light. *Maybe crows will land in the Wasaplatz tomorrow too*, thought Klara.

It was already dark when her mother and sister returned from Berlin. Ulli, who had been asleep on the back seat, was carried straight up to bed. The doctor had reassured Frau Hagemann that there was nothing to worry about, which was all Klara wanted to know, and all her mother wanted to tell her at supper. She nearly fell asleep at the table, and "Yes, we did have a bite to eat before we set off for home"; she said, "I'll sit in the armchair for a moment"; she asked, "And you two? How did you get through the day?"

Herr Hagemann buttered another slice of bread for Klara, he put his finger to his lips, his wife had fallen asleep. Father and daughter cleared the table, and then for the first time in a long time Herr Hagemann slept through the night. No coughing fits, no footsteps on the tiled floor, no concerned voices in the hall. Next morning Klara heard her sister calling from their room: "There they are."

From that day on, over several winters, the two of them observed the activity in the Wasaplatz. On one occasion very early in the morning an acquaintance of the Hagemanns' rang the doorbell frantically, she had just left her husband. Whispering, sobbing, silence, the girls didn't dare to venture out of their room, lay awake, until they heard the first subdued cries of the crows in the distance. Once a long military convoy crossed the Wasaplatz, the penetrating, endless drone of the engines made Ulli and Klara uneasy, they cowered by the windowsill, there wasn't a soul around except for a few soldiers posted at the crossing to direct the traffic, which was practically nonexistent at that time of day. Truck after truck went past, but none of them announced the load under the tightly stretched canvas covers. A soldier on a motorbike stopped at the curb, dismounted, and lit a cigarette, his bored gaze ranging over the trucks, the square, the house fronts. Paused. Looked at the Hagemanns' house. Took his binoculars out of their case. The girls held their breath. But it was only the crows, crows on the roof, which now swooped down, gained height again, and disappeared toward the northeast, as if the combination of binoculars and shouldered rifle had made them nervous.

Quite ordinary crows. No great auk for the sisters, no rare, long-extinct museum bird to stimulate their childish imaginations. Just these mundane birds that hardly anybody noticed, appearing on the Wasaplatz every morning from nowhere. It wasn't easy to tell them apart, in a flock, and always on the move, but after a while the sisters thought they recognized a few birds in the crowd, half a dozen perhaps, representing something like an advance guard, always landing first and always staying longer. At the heart of the group was a hooded crow which soon became Ulli and Klara's favorite. The way it strode through the grass looking for acorns and beechnuts, rooted among leaves at the curbside. The way it grew alert when someone passed by but had no intention of jumping out of the way to safety. Mistrustful, certainly. But also proud: Look at me strolling around the Wasaplatz.

In the war years Ulli and Klara lost sight of the hooded crow. After a second, then a third hooded crow had turned up one morning, the sisters couldn't agree whether it was their favorite bird that was perched on the eaves opposite or the one close to the house, on the path to the stream—though they were able to rule the third bird out completely, the one on the street lamp, because of its noticeably spiky black breast feathers. Before they could decide, the birds left the Wasaplatz along with their uniformly coal-black comrades and joined the great, never-ending stream of birds over Strehlen.

Once Klara thought she had been woken up by the hooded crow calling, it was still dark, Ulli was talking in her sleep, it was much too early for the morning influx of crows. All the same, Klara went to the window to take a look. On the opposite side of the square stood a car with its engine running. No animals, no other signs of life. If the bird had been in the square, it would have trotted back and forth, now taking a few steps on the pavement, then disappearing behind a bare shrub. Inquisitive or fearful, spiteful or serene: the sisters could never agree how to interpret the hooded crow's behavior whenever something untoward happened in the street, when people started brawling and cursing loudly, when a drunk was yelling or a child beginning to cry. It's cowardly, said Ulli, it wants to stay out of harm's way but not miss anything either. Intimidated, said Klara, it's more afraid for the human beings than for itself. And the noise that Klara thought was a crow calling? Some banging. Voices. Now she could see that the black car was partially concealing an open front door, she saw the light in the rectangle, then the silhouettes. A neighbor in his pajamas, and two men in leather coats.

It would be hours yet before the first crows moved in over the Wasaplatz and settled in the big chestnut, the oak, the beech in front of the window, on the rooftop. Hours before they started eyeing the grass verge, the road, the pavement, looking for food and weighing up the passersby, as if nothing had happened between yesterday and this morning.

12

DID YOU KNOW they were not even allowed to keep pet animals?" asked Klara one evening as we sat in Knut's garage. A late, rainy evening in autumn, I think it was the year I had hand-reared five fledglings for Knut's film about the woodpecker. The curtains were drawn, I was sitting next to Klara on the bed. In the dim light the heavy Mongolian bedspread with the pattern of light and dark brown stripes looked like a wine-red, hilly landscape crossed by snow trails.

"No Sunday bike rides. No public transport. No telephone, no radio, and no tobacco products. No walks in the Great Garden. I knew about that kind of prohibition."

Opposite us sat Knut, at his feet and on the desk were piles of firewood. Martin was right by the door on an angler's chair. We sat there with our coats on. There was tea on the iron stove.

"But what a criminal idea, to forbid someone to keep a pet bird—did you know that? No waxbill, no tame robin, and no sparrow taken from the nest. Nothing."

Martin leaned back cautiously against the door. "I did once hear about it, but I thought it was a malicious rumor."

"I'd like to know how one can dream up a ban on songbirds. Who puts such an idea into words. And what happened to the birds."

I offered: "They were taken away? Returned to the dealer?"

"Or abandoned in the wild."

Knut poked around in the fire. "Given away."

"To the neighbors, you mean?" Klara shook her head. "To people involved in the same madness?"

"Anyway, who would want to take on a pet bird like that?" Martin had peeled the bark from a birch log, he examined his dirty fingers, looked at me. When he couldn't stand the silence he would coax us out of our thoughts and back to reality with his birdsong imitations, but this time he was silent. No little ringed plover, no whitethroat, no distant dialogue between two agitated male blackbirds putting their powers to the test in a frenzied struggle over territory—a single wrong note, and he would have reproduced the call of one of those very pet songbirds whose shapes we were imagining in the semidarkness.

There was a knock. Martin got up to open the garage door a crack, and Anastasia bounded in, greeting each of us in turn, shaking her thick, wet coat.

"Are we disturbing you?" Ludwig Kaltenburg ran his fingers through his wet hair, his coat sticking to him, the felt boots gone shades darker. "I walked straight into a puddle."

Knut took the professor's coat and offered him his seat by the fire so that he could warm his feet. "I don't know why you have to walk the dog in the rain," he said, half reproachful and half concerned.

"I couldn't sleep."

"Leningrad?"

Kaltenburg nodded, yes, he'd been waiting for weeks for information about the zoological commission.

"No news?"

"Silence from Leningrad."

I can't remember whether it was Martin or Klara who brought up Shostakovitch to distract the professor, distract ourselves from secret zoological commissions and the ban on songbirds, and soon our conversation turned to string orchestras, funeral music, film music. The rain was beating down on the garage roof. Knut skillfully steered Kaltenburg to a subject that had already been touched on in the summer, when the two of them had been chatting about integrity in wildlife films.

"Hear that? I could listen to it for hours." Rain on a felted roof. The rustling in the trees.

"One of these days we should take the risk of using the soundtrack of a natural habitat as is, just chance it, and ignore this stupid fear that the viewer will think there's something missing."

"How right you are. Here we are showing life on the forest floor, and it sounds as though we've parked an entire symphony orchestra in the treetops."

"You've got to have masses of violins playing all the time—which idiot introduced that law?"

"You'd think it was Stalin's funeral, the way they play, all that sentimental fiddling has nothing to do with the poor forest dwellers."

When the rain had eased and the professor was about to leave, all five of us were so taken with the idea that in our heads we could hear whole sequences of atmospheric noise, scratching sounds. Animal noises. Snuffling. Trampling. Birds calling in the distance.

"That would make a difference. We must try it," Knut said.

"You're wrong, Herr Sieverding—it would be a revolution," Kaltenburg exclaimed on his way out.

But the silence from Leningrad was to last for many years.

The little stand of pines was now out of sight, no garage, no derelict land, no Institute villa, we had reached the slope again and were walking down toward the Loschwitz cemetery, the sun appeared briefly in the west under the clouds. I had already told Katharina Fischer that Kaltenburg's hopes were not to be fulfilled while he lived in this town. The fact is this was Ludwig Kaltenburg's first defeat in Dresden, even though he would never have used that term himself—he probably didn't even know the word "defeat."

What a scene that would have been—you can just hear the breathless tone of the eager radio announcer: Accompanied by a group of Soviet colleagues, Professor Ludwig Kaltenburg presents to the world the treasures of the Dresden Zoological Collections, carefully preserved from destruction in 1945, kept safe in the Soviet Union, and now, thanks to the infinite generosity of our friends, returned to the resurrected city of Dresden.

No. Nothing like that ever happened. Not even Professor Eberhard Matzke, who was undoubtedly involved in bringing the prize exhibits back from the Soviet Union in the 1970s, was able to boast of his great achievement, because the whole transaction took place in secret. In equal secrecy he would have relished his triumph, as a former subordinate of Kaltenburg's at the Zoological Institute in Leipzig, Dr. Matzke the long-serving assistant, the permanent fixture in whom nobody had confidence—until, out of the blue, he began his meteoric rise, to Berlin, right to the top, overtaking Professor Kaltenburg.

"But you never discussed the ban on songbirds with him that evening?"

No.

"Later?" Katharina Fischer looked at me.

No, never.

"I could have sworn you and Kaltenburg had a long discussion about it at one point. There's an obvious connection, anyway."

Suddenly I understood what she meant. I had never thought of it. My father's adopted birds.

Basically, declared Frau Fischer, the matter was clear. My father had taken in prohibited companion birds. She gave no weight to my objections: the advanced date, far too late for people to be looking for a new home for their pet birds, when those people themselves had disappeared from the city of Posen, transported to the camps. Perhaps, suggested the interpreter, the afternoon of the business with the swift wasn't originally connected to birds being cared for in our house. It might be a matter of memory causing a telescoping of events. And like a child who sees himself as the center of the universe, in retrospect I was now arranging widely separated bird images in my mind on one plane. "You're not concerned about the actual sequence of events," maintained Katharina Fischer, "you're only looking for similarities."

Our injured blue-throat, I'm quite certain we picked it up while out for a walk.

"Think about the tame starling. Where am I ever going to find a tame starling in the wild that I can lure onto my shoulder and take it home with me?"

I don't know.

"But of course that's obvious to you, Herr Funk, as an ornithologist."

And finally she asked me a question I had been expecting since we began our walk down to the valley. All afternoon. In fact, since our first meeting in the Ornithological Collection.

"Did you ever see anything in your childhood resembling what Klara saw? Did you ever see a neighbor being taken away before dawn?"

Klara had asked me the same question. No, I had never seen anything like that. And at the risk of sounding odd, almost cruel: today there is something I would be glad to have seen. Certainty, about one moment at least, when Maria left our house—did she leave my father, my mother, because she had been ordered to report at an assembly point? Did my parents go with her, despondent and silent, a little way into town? Or did my nanny disappear overnight because she wanted to forestall difficulties for our family? And yet it was also possible, even if not very probable, that with nothing at all to fear she had gone back to her parents, taken a new job, or indeed, as Martin once speculated, got married, and that she wanted to spare me a long and tearful parting scene. Whether Maria had disappeared at night or early in the morning, I must have been asleep.

"Didn't you ever see them in their leather coats?" asked Klara. "Wasn't there any house on your street in front of which the dark car stopped with its engine running?"

I can clearly remember the fine Sunday when she asked me that question, we had been to the races, had persisted in backing outsiders with poetic names and never picked a single winner, now we were making our way back to the station, through scrubland, allotment gardens. We were walking hand in hand, and I was telling her about the goldfinches I had begun observing in the early months after the war, in this area among others. Thistle territory, rubbish dumps, the embankment on the other side of the Wiener Strasse, I had followed the birds, often near Klara's family's house, thus escaping on hot afternoons from my siblings, who always wanted to go for a swim in a pond—I only went with them a few times. I am eternally grateful to my surrogate parents for letting me go bird-watching instead, even if their voices betrayed a concern that their foster child was in danger of turning into a loner.

"And then in the summer after the war, didn't you see trains taking liberated prisoners home?"

When Klara looked back, for her the area was not populated by finches, she saw no parents feeding their young, didn't hear the cracking of seedpods nor the clamor of chicks, saw no plumage markings, brown backs, red faces, or black wings with yellow bars. The children from her neighborhood used to play on the rail track that led to Prague; the two sisters would take a walk along the line as far as Reick, picking up any strange objects they found on the ballast bed. And Klara could still hear the hum of a train approaching from the main station, the vibrating of the tracks, the faint, reassuring alarm signal that in no way befitted the danger it announced.

One day Klara was dawdling on the sleepers when all the other children had already moved a safe distance away, she saw the engine, pulled up her socks, she was anticipating one of those never-varying freight trains, then the strap on her sandal broke. The next instant she was crouching in the grass barely a meter away from the line, looking up at the crowded cars, looking into foreign faces, hearing foreign languages, hearing nothing at all. The alternation of motion and stillness, noise and silence, was far too rapid for Klara to be able to say later whether the passengers' mood had been cheerful or downcast, and the other children, who now came creeping up, didn't know either. The cars trundled slowly past, in the direction of Prague, to Budapest, perhaps on to Bucharest and as far as the Black Sea. Nobody took any notice of the group of children in the grass, not even the watchful young Russian soldiers standing in the cars.

"Cattle cars?"

No, as far as I can remember, Klara made no mention of cattle cars. Open goods cars, their rusty walls eaten into by coal dust, with a long row of flat plank benches, that was how the trains looked then. But my mind went back to the cattle cars I had noticed on the embankment in Posen when I was crushing leaves between my fingers, when I was identifying, looking for, digging up plants with my father: "To the east, or have you forgotten your compass points?"

V

1

———

SIX WHITE SNOW GEESE were resting in the high grass on the bank near the landing stage; one of the birds, neck outstretched, was keeping watch over its surroundings, peering in all directions, while the others gazed steadily westward, downriver, into the sunset, the yellow and pink and light-blue sky above the city. The castle ferry had just left the jetty on the Pillnitz side, the diesel engine roaring, the little boat struggling against the Elbe current. The blackbird behind me was complaining. The sand martins still darting about.

In the past few weeks, whenever my evening walks have taken me as far as Kleinschachwitz, I have found myself recalling Katharina Fischer's words and trying to clarify my thoughts about the birds we took in. All his life Ludwig Kaltenburg laid great emphasis on zoologists' need to take a critical look at their earlier selves in order to correct past errors of judgment. But in the end, all I see each time is the injured blue-throat in its box in front of me while next door my father is arguing with the professor about sick birds, I can see our starling landing on Professor Kaltenburg's shoulder during his first visit. The story was that my father had bought the starling from a bird seller in town, but he had never actually taken me with him to the breeder's, either because I declined to go or because he had never been there himself but wanted to name someone he knew the great bird expert trusted.

The snow geese were not to be put off by the noise on the water, they turned their heads, gabbling softly, the ferry had reached our side. Cyclists came toward us, then a group of walkers, no one had noticed the white birds in the grass. The ferryman stood on the empty landing stage lighting a cigarette. I turned back upstream to wait by Bird Island for the crows, for the gaggles that would appear from all points of the compass in the fading light, returning from their feeding grounds, cawing excitedly, squabbling inconclusively before they foregathered to roost in their accustomed trees and for a few hours darkness rendered them invisible.

My mind kept going back to Ludwig Kaltenburg, but each time the scenes in Posen were overlaid by a later image. The professor sitting on the edge of the bed, bending down to untie his shoelaces, and tugging the bedspread over with him. His silhouette, the cold morning light on his white hair, he hasn't noticed me yet. Kaltenburg without his jackdaws. The slight creak of the bed, the swish of the bedspread, which leaves a narrow strip of bed linen uncovered, very bright, very fine, not made around here. A little clumsily, he undoes his right shoelace, looks up at me: "Oh, it's you."

No, I never entered the professor's bedroom while he was living in Dresden. I never saw it until after he had left, and even then only because I had to look after the household animals, with which I was nearly as familiar as their vanished master. I kept them company, together we wandered through the deserted rooms. In the bedroom, I remember, there were touches of extravagance out of character with the rest of the Kaltenburg household. An almost full bottle of French aftershave left in the bathroom, an embroidered bedspread, behind the dressing table mirror a pressed cyclamen that had escaped the beaks of generations of birds.

Where the thicket was beginning to get darker, by the riverside path, one icterine warbler responded to another of its kind down among the willow bushes. I could hear whitethroats, magpies, a wood pigeon. Soon the blackbirds would take their places in the treetops to begin their evensong. I was surrounded by voices, and it almost sounded as if my name were being called.

"Herr Funk?"

Katharina Fischer stopped next to me and got off her bike. "So it's you. I thought I recognized you from the ferry."

She went on to say that she would like to go with me to the crows' roosting place, then declared how glad she was to have run into me, because my father's adopted birds had been on her mind ever since our conversation in Loschwitz. Apparently we had each wrestled independently with the question, reckoned we were beginning to get somewhere with it, started to have doubts, then discarded all our previous reflections. By the time my parents got to know the professor, there was no longer any occasion to ban songbirds, at least in Posen: the ghetto they named Litzmannstadt had long since been in existence.

All the same, just like me, Katharina Fischer had found herself caught up in the wish-fulfillment scenario of a secret collusion between my father and Professor Kaltenburg which saw them in a pet shop inspecting, at their special request, birds that came from private households. The previous owners, the dealer would explain, had moved away with no forwarding address. Finding the birds anxiously fluttering about in their cages as his neighbors' households were being broken up, he couldn't bring himself to wring the necks of the aging starling, or the goldfinch, or the yellowhammer that was on display in the window.

Two bird enthusiasts taking up the cause of pet birds made ownerless in the midst of the world pogrom: a wish-fulfillment fantasy, as Katharina Fischer herself must have known. The secret collusion never existed.

"Have you always stood by Kaltenburg?" the interpreter asked suddenly, after we had gone only a few steps.

I can never forget what I owe him. But for him I would never have made anything of my life, it's as simple as that.

"Then I suppose, all things considered, you could be called his most loyal student?"

I thought for a while. I realized that I too had reason to be glad I had met her that evening, otherwise I might never have said this out loud: I had never been so deeply disappointed by anybody as by Ludwig Kaltenburg.

Katharina Fischer shot me a shy sidelong glance, wanted to question me, held her peace.

You might think on the face of it that what really hurt me, what shook me to the core, looks like a simple oversight due to haste or a hazy memory. A mere trifle, a trivial detail that you eventually learn to ignore, especially as it's only a matter of a slight gap. An outsider wouldn't even notice this omission of barely eighteen months, because the professor retrospectively filled the gap with other events, other place, names, and characters. But however much I wanted to, I could never forgive him for this omission: Ludwig Kaltenburg deleted from his CV the period when we were both in Posen.

"As though you had never got to know him as a child?" she asked diffidently. "But why? Did you ever ask him?"

At the time when the famous zoologist appeared to have put our first encounters out of his mind as far as the public, his colleagues, the whole world were concerned, I no longer needed to ask. And Kaltenburg would no doubt once again have pointed at someone else, would have talked his way out of it—as he was wont to do by then—by assigning all responsibility to Professor Dr. Eberhard Matzke.

2

———

W E'VE GOT TO ACT as if we're strangers"—this was the
strict rule for our dealings with each other at the Zoological Institute in Leipzig. We adhered to it all the
more firmly because everybody knew how close we were, even if not
everyone was aware of the particular liberties I enjoyed at Kaltenburg's Loschwitz Institute. Dresden was a long way off, and every
time I made my weekly journey between the two cities I crossed
an invisible line. I never worked out where that line ran, and as
I looked up on the train from my lecture notes, my mind was on
Klara and the past weekend, on Kaltenburg's animals, to which I
had devoted the previous two days, I gazed at the last hills behind
Dresden, the gray, then pale green, then brown, and finally snow-
covered fields, the curve of the Elbe at Riesa, the unvarying plain in
which the settlements gradually merged into a town—somewhere
along the route, I noticed, I had turned abruptly into the Leipzig
zoology student whose life I can now barely recall.

The number of occasions when Ludwig Kaltenburg drove me in
his car could be counted on the fingers of one hand. That was nothing to complain about; on the contrary, our agreement may actually have worked to my advantage, since any remarks I did overhear
referred not to any secret favoritism but to the professor's severity,
from which I particularly suffered, according to my fellow students.
They helped me out, lending me their notes and dropping me little

messages. Nobody had any idea what a strain it was for Kaltenburg himself to play the stranger throughout the week, and how relieved we both were to meet again at the Saturday discussions in Loschwitz.

Once we were standing in a fairly large group in the corridor outside Kaltenburg's office, all wearing sturdy jackets and boots, ready to go on a field trip with the professor to observe passage migrants in the country around Leipzig. It was still early, but we knew the day would soon be drawing to a close. Casually Ludwig Kaltenburg inquired which goose it was that came in both a white and a dark variety, and as if by chance he glanced in my direction. *Anser fabalis* or *Anser albifrons*, or perhaps just *Anser anser*—I looked at the floor, looked at the roughly plastered, white-painted wall, couldn't gather my thoughts. Behind the professor somebody shook his head; it was Dr. Matzke, Kaltenburg's assistant, who came to my assistance by silently mouthing the words until I recognized them: "snow goose."

"All right, then," drawled the professor. "Let's go."

We trotted down the corridor in the cold light, Matzke leading. I always suspected that he saw through the act Kaltenburg put on for his Leipzig colleagues, and that the professor's strict manner toward me simply got on Matzke's nerves.

Dr. Eberhard Matzke was part of the Zoological Institute; nobody could have imagined him anywhere else, he himself least of all, no doubt. This was where he had studied in the thirties, this is where he returned after the war. When they placed a Professor Kaltenburg over him, while he remained plain Dr. Matzke, he took it calmly: for Eberhard Matzke, a Leipziger born and bred, Ludwig Kaltenburg was nothing but a passing phenomenon.

He walked up and down between the microscope tables, slightly bent, helping with a dissection here, moving a slide into the light there. Under his lab coat he wore a cardigan, and in the evenings when he hung up his white coat I always expected to see a few straws sticking to the matted wool. As though Matzke kept animals in a hutch tucked away in a remote corner of the sprawling institute building, animals he had left that morning only because he felt that unless he was peering over our shoulders, we might not go on examining feather structures and sensory cells under the microscope. He went steadily about his duties, that is to say, he spent most of his time at my bench—the Herr Professor must have no reason to complain.

He couldn't understand why many students made such heavy going of these tasks, instead of dispatching them as fast as possible so they could get back into the much more attractive world of living animals. To spur us on as we worked, Matzke told us anecdotes about his encounters with animals, which he was convinced would open up vistas in our mind's eye while in reality we were still struggling with a paper-thin slice of dead tissue. How he had once rescued a golden eagle injured in a fight, how a favorite crow went missing and how he fished it out weeks later from a sedimentation tank—he repeated many of these stories every six months or so, but we enjoyed them all the same because Matzke's slight Saxon singsong and his warm, deep voice soothed us.

"My colleague Matzke should have a medal just for his ability to keep a crowd of students quiet," opined Kaltenburg. We never found out what he thought of him as a zoologist. Possibly the professor would not have believed his "colleague Matzke"—merely an assistant to Kaltenburg—capable of filling a university chair of his own. But he did at least deserve a decoration: "Even if I have to pin it on him myself."

Now and again Martin was allowed to go to Leipzig too: "Just don't go holding the lad back from serious study," warned Kaltenburg, and, half in jest, "Just to make sure, I'll get my colleague Matzke to keep an eye on you." But I was aware that the warning was aimed not at Martin but at me; I was supposed to follow Martin's example in paying keen attention to Matzke's words.

When Martin accompanied me to a laboratory session and Matzke interrupted his story with a long-drawn-out "Aha," I knew that he had got as far as the glass case at the back. That was where Martin liked to sit, concentrating on the display-specimen martens and rabbits that languished there practically ignored. It was a sight I wouldn't have wanted to miss: the huge, heavy man looming over

Martin, and the wiry figure on its folding stool almost disappearing behind a massive back. There was just a glimpse of the corner of the sketch pad, Matzke with arms outspread as though about to devour the stranger, you could visualize his wide-open mouth—but Martin showed no fear, and what came out was only another "Aha."

He was sketching animals, afraid perhaps that if he departed too far from his models in place of Matzke's friendly "Aha," he would get an unhappy shake of the head. At home he had been working for a long time with animal blood, with fat, with tea stains on packing paper, creating beings that few would have recognized at first sight as animals. But Martin himself shook his head when he surveyed his work, he trusted neither what he saw on paper before him nor the figures that had gradually begun to populate the world of his imagination.

I admit we didn't take Dr. Matzke entirely seriously, just as he probably didn't take us entirely seriously either. The heavy, loping gait, the cardigan that had long since lost its shape—and then suddenly, from one day to the next, there was no longer any Dr. Matzke at the Zoological Institute to supervise our small-bird dissections, giving himself a shock when he boomed, "It's a matter of principle here," whereupon he always fell into a half-whispered tone that was meant to be enticing: "And anyway, working like this you'll get to know the bird from the inside out, it's showing itself to you as you'd never see it otherwise."

Matzke turned his back on Leipzig. He had received an offer from Berlin that he couldn't refuse, especially since it held the prospect of a professorial title. At last he would become "colleague Matzke," and a colleague of the famous Reinhold to boot. It was in fact Reinhold who had conveyed the news to us on a visit to Loschwitz. Kaltenburg didn't comment on Matzke's move, he played it down when people said he must surely have pulled strings to advance Dr. Matzke's career when it seemed to be over. And when I asked him once whether the man hadn't always been a bit in the way, he just smiled.

3

―――――

EBERHARD MATZKE REMOVED his cardigan. Gave his hair a side parting. Took over Kaltenburg's former doctoral student, Fräulein Holsterbach. Soon relinquished his Saxon singsong, adopted a clear, almost hard High German, and every time he dictated an article, he asked his assistant to make sure no regional expressions slipped in. By degrees, in his new surroundings Eberhard Matzke even shed the awkwardness that had easily identified him in Leipzig when you were hurrying toward the institute entrance in the morning and saw a distant figure dismounting from his bicycle in the early light. The wider his sphere of influence spread, the slimmer and nimbler he appeared, as though he had learned at every step to avoid an obstacle, even if the obstacle was invisible.

"He's doing well. The Natural History Museum is good for him, the university is good for him." Kaltenburg lauded him when asked about the new man in Berlin. "I'm very pleased that colleague Matzke has found his feet."

The professor had not the faintest idea what was happening under his nose. Perhaps he seriously thought that Matzke would be eternally grateful to him. But in the light of subsequent events, the impression given by Matzke's publications in the second half of the fifties is that he was truly out to demolish Kaltenburg by holding up one theory after another to cast doubt on it, to nullify it. Not that he mounted a frontal assault on the professor, that he never did, but it seems to me that he wasn't fully satisfied with any scientific paper he wrote, any ornithological field observation, even a newspaper article, unless it contained, if only tucked away in a subordinate clause somewhere, a covert little dig at Ludwig Kaltenburg's convictions.

One remark of his instantly made me so angry that I didn't dare show it to the professor. He could not possibly have seen it as anything other than deliberately offensive, an egregiously arrogant departure from the tone of what was otherwise a factual account, attesting to years of zoological research, concerning conflict arising under conditions of imprisonment. I had seen an offprint of the article lying on Kaltenburg's desk and noticed the inscription, "With collegial greetings," in Eberhard Matzke's handwriting, which grew larger from year to year. It's surely no accident that I have such a clear memory of this little excursus—which I couldn't help hoping Kaltenburg had overlooked—for one thing because the author was dealing with the inhibition against biting among wolves, and for another because the offensive remarks touched upon one of Kaltenburg's most sacrosanct principles, frequently expressed to me: "To live is to observe."

Matzke declared it was pure nonsense to maintain, as people had done right up to the present, that in a fight between wolves the weaker will openly expose its throat to the stronger in a gesture that inhibits the latter from biting it. He wrote that he did not know what original observation underpinned this assertion, but by now it had almost attained the status of an article of faith among experts, and in a strange turn of phrase he went on to say that from his own wide experience, at least, the inhibition against biting among canines was just wishful thinking on the part of gullible, peace-loving zoologists. At any rate, word had not yet got around among the parties concerned, he concluded smugly, exposing one of Kaltenburg's most cherished maxims to ridicule. I remember how my temples throbbed as I thought, *I hope the professor did no more than skim through the essay this morning, I hope the ducks distracted him from reading it, that while feeding the drakes he overlooked the tone of his "colleague Matzke" and the effrontery of his pronouncements.*

A committee was restructured—Matzke took over the chair, although Kaltenburg had done much preliminary spadework behind the scenes. There was a post to be filled—by Matzke's candidate. A congress in the Soviet Union—the deputation consisted entirely of Matzke's people. Kaltenburg shook his head; the man was rather overreaching himself, after having failed for so many years in Leipzig to make any real impact—but we, hearing the disappointing news during the morning meeting, looked at the professor and could see he was thinking of Leningrad.

Somebody once claimed to have heard that Ludwig Kaltenburg stomped up and down behind his closed study door shouting repeatedly, "The Party, the Party." To this day I regard this as an invention, some assistant wanting to impress his colleagues, and in any case everybody knew that Eberhard Matzke was not a member of the Party. No, on the contrary, Kaltenburg took every opportunity to warn against jumping to conclusions, took on the role of self-assured intermediary. When the first German students of zoology graduated in the Soviet Union, everyone was afraid that their return would mean our subject would soon be dominated by Party loyalists—but Kaltenburg praised these intrepid young people, stressing the quality of Russian zoology, and "After all, gentlemen, we're all ornithologists together."

He was convinced that even Professor Matzke would calm down eventually. Reinhold in Berlin, getting to know his new colleague at close quarters, thought otherwise, but Reinhold, the grand old man, had often been fearful of his successors, especially when they were keen to strike out in new directions. Reinhold's visits to Dresden became more frequent, he still had relations in his home city, but it looked as though he was visiting his family mainly so that he could also call in at Loschwitz. The phone rang. "Ah, my dear Professor"—Kaltenburg looked across at me—"it goes without saying that you're welcome at any time"; Kaltenburg was making sure he showed the proper respect that, according to Reinhold, was lacking in Matzke; "I'll send my driver," Kaltenburg was nodding in the semidarkness next to the hall stand, yes, Krause still knew the address.

He tried to cheer Reinhold up, to take his mind off things. One day, as the limousine drew up outside the villa, he told Krause to keep the engine running, greeted Reinhold through the open passenger window, pushed me onto the rear seat, and followed me in: "We're going to Strehlen."

The professor made Krause stop at Tiergartenstrasse, he invited us to take a little stroll through the Great Garden, for one thing ideas came most easily when you were walking, he said, and for another I knew that he didn't want anyone overhearing his discussion with Reinhold. They must find an additional sphere of activity for "the young man"—Matzke was all of seven years younger than Kaltenburg. No, not a posting abroad, far away where you couldn't keep an eye on him, but a newly created framework that would satisfy his desire to be the first to break new ground for once in his life. Naturally, it must be a framework within which Eberhard Matzke was kept under careful control. A great undertaking, with a great new title to match for the Herr Professor Doktor—and all, be it noted, under the constant supervision of a worldly-wise international expert, a legendary figure among ornithologists: Reinhold himself.

We walked around Lake Carola, in less than twenty minutes a plan had been hatched, and we went back to the road. The chauffeur got out of the car, held the door open, but Kaltenburg signaled to him that we were going to walk on a bit further, pointing in the direction of the embankment.

"No need to worry. I'll explore the mood among the colleagues, take soundings in the Academy of Sciences and find out what can be done there. You'll see, everybody will support you."

And now it comes back to me clearly, it was the year of Hungary, we had reached the Wasaplatz, I can see the black limousine, Krause driving along beside us at a walking pace as we turned into August Bebel Strasse. Reinhold waving his stick, Kaltenburg gesticulating wildly, as soon as we had set off downhill from the Institute the two had started a debate on the history of ornithology. By now they were on to Georg Marcgraf and Carl Illiger, dropping names like Bernstein, Kuhl, and Boie, not one of them survived into old age, consumption, tropical fever, my eyes were fixed on the barrack gates at the other end of the street. Every step we took was being watched from there, we were moving around the edge of the military security zone, I wouldn't like to know what went on behind those walls at that time, nor what measures might have been taken if Ludwig Kaltenburg had not stopped suddenly and pointed to one of the fairly unremarkable villas: "This is where he grew up."

We were standing in front of the house where Reinhold spent his childhood and youth. I think he was genuinely quite moved, Reinhold in his loose linen suit under a light coat, up there in that attic room was where he had spent his afternoons with grass snakes and lizards he had caught, here in a large enclosure alongside the stable was where the cross-bred offspring of goldfinches and redpolls had first seen the light of day. And as a boy he too used to observe the crows on the Wasaplatz. Ludwig Kaltenburg's surprise for him had succeeded completely. But for my part I was taken right back to the days of our excursions, how long ago was that, all that "induction by personal inspection," only a few years, I was still a boy, collecting signatures for world peace, didn't even know that one day I would be working with Kaltenburg at the Institute, wasn't even sure I wanted to stay in Dresden, didn't even know Klara Hagemann yet, while she was living only a few hundred meters from this spot.

4

———

IN JUNE 1956 A truck drove through Dresden carrying prisoners liberated from the camps. People crowded the pavements,
law enforcement officers kept the road clear. In order to give
as many townspeople as possible the chance to study these figures,
the open truck transported its cargo at walking pace through the
city along the following route: from Dr. Kurt Fischer Platz down
the Königsbrücker Strasse to the Platz der Einheit. From Bautzner
Strasse into Hoyerswerdaer Strasse. Across the Einheitsbrücke to
Güntzplatz. From Güntzstrasse, a right turn into Grunaer Strasse.
The truck followed Thälmannstrasse as far as the Postplatz, the
procession ending at the Theaterplatz.

"I'm sure you noticed it too?" Klara inquired.

"Yes, dreadful." Professor Kaltenburg looked away into the distance.

It had rained a lot throughout the summer, overcast days, muddy
holes all over the city. In the gray light the skin of the prisoners
looked duller than ever, though they were very young, just a few of
them seemed older. Beneath this dirty sky, however, that may have
been a false impression, the hollow eyes, the pinched cheeks, their
poor teeth. No, they must simply have been exhausted.

Kaltenburg listened again to Klara's description of the prisoners'
truck. The inmates' shirts and trousers, the way they hung loosely

from their meager frames. Gray and white stripes. No, no trouser creases. Yes, rough linen. The moment when the driver braked because he got too close to the group in front: the way the prisoners lurched, holding on to each other, for a second you thought they were all going to lose their balance.

"What an awful sight," said Kaltenburg.

Because you weren't sure whether what you were seeing in their eyes was the shock of performers or the fear of camp inmates.

A father pointed with his furled umbrella to a spot far ahead at the crossroads, explaining something to the daughter who was sitting on his shoulders. A family festival. The onlookers waved and called out. A column of trekking refugees came along, with handcarts and baby carriages. At the beginning you could wave to the Saxon nobility, Augustus the Strong under a canopy. The shy young ladies-in-waiting grouped around a model of the Church of Our Lady waving back with their handkerchiefs, the magnificent clothes, the wigs, the powder and lipstick. Hour after hour the postwar rubble-clearing women, flag wavers, apprentice gardeners, fanfares, airplane builders, filed past. By this time you had nearly forgotten the steam locomotive, the horse-drawn tram, and the historic milk cart, along with the float bearing the inscription ALL POWER TO THE SOVIETS, its crew sitting on their bench looking out searchingly from under their steel helmets. Still to come were a combine harvester, the Wartburg vehicle fleet, a car from the animated film studios surmounted by Pittiplatsch, the cartoon figure. One of the last displays of this parade to celebrate the 750th anniversary of Dresden was a huge model of the new brand of cigarette, Jubilar, carried right across the city on the bare legs of six girls.

"Of course it was easy to miss them in such a motley crew," suggested the professor.

Yes, red flags. No, no sewn-on Stars of David. All the same, it was clear that the Jubilee Committee had not been able to make up their minds how to deal with the ex-prisoners. Perhaps the idea had been to have them celebrate their happy release by cheering and raising a fist. But the thin young men didn't smile, their expression was subdued, as though exposure to all these stares was robbing them of their last ounce of strength. And hardly any of the onlookers dared to wave to these figures in their strikingly drab outfits, moving past in silence. You might almost have thought you were looking at real prisoners.

"Hermann was looking for you," Klara remarked. "Maybe you were sitting in the VIP stand in Grunaer Strasse?"

Kaltenburg looked at me, then back at Klara. He hung his head. "I admit it, I wasn't there. I dodged the jubilee parade."

A free day—the prospect was just too tempting, especially as it looked as though the weather might be half decent. In the dawn light the professor quietly hauled his motorbike out of the garage, pushed the machine out onto the road and as far as the next corner. Jumped on, started the engine, and took off before the first of his neighbors could peer out between their curtains. He rode on to Bautzen, he said, the fresh morning air, insects on his goggles, then he turned off south of Weissenberg and, more slowly now, cruised through the villages, the hamlets. Maltitz, Mostitz, all those names, Lautitz, Mauschwitz, Meuselwitz, Krobnitz, and Dittmannsdorf, he'd hardly encountered a single soul.

Goldfinches among the linseed. For a while he had ridden along a path that led straight across the fields, following at a walking pace behind a flock of sparrows in the morning light that was examining a stretch of wheat, acre by acre. So by stages he topped one hill after another, always keeping the birds in view beside him, and at some point, although—being on a motorbike—the professor had no need to pedal, on reaching a loamy valley bottom he found himself out of breath. The tree sparrows took a bath. They disappeared. The lark was singing. Ludwig Kaltenburg was thirsty.

In the midday quiet, he arrived at Reichenbach. Deutsch Paulsdorf, Kemnitz, Russenhäuser. In Bernstadt auf dem Eigen he finally came across a pub, with the strange name The Earth's Axis. He sat there for a long time over his beer, talking to the locals, giving advice, picking up information. An old farmer's wife showed him her geese. He wasn't known here. Kaltenburg in strange parts. He toyed with the idea of spending the night in Bernstadt. It wasn't until late in the evening that he set off for home, without a headlight, the bulb was kaput. He suspected Krause, but he didn't want the day spoiled right at the end by a minor character. He arrived in Loschwitz exactly in time for the morning feed.

5

———

THE WHOLE TIME, a scraggly rook with a bright green-ish-shimmering breast had been patiently worrying away at an uprooted tree trunk. I recognized some fibrous tissue in its beak as it flew off to save its booty from a roving terrier. The rook was skimming away above the water even before the dog had noticed it, its breast feathers shone ever more brightly in the last of the sunlight over the Elbe, shone almost with a petrol-slick sheen.

Like me, the interpreter was watching the departing rook, and now the bird had disappeared on the Pillnitz side.

"Are there any photos of the truck?"

I've never seen any. And if it hadn't stopped right in front of us, we might not have taken much notice of it. Klara and I, Ulli, Martin, Herr and Frau Hagemann, we were all awkwardly placed among the crowd, the parade came to a halt, perhaps somewhere further on a group had got out of sync, the driver hadn't been paying attention, had to brake abruptly, the prisoner figures got a shock, they lurched, tried to steady themselves—and it was this sudden movement that gave us a shock in turn. We didn't say anything, but as Herr Hagemann looked into his younger daughter's eyes and nodded slowly, very slowly, as though only his damp raincoat collar was bothering him, he let it be understood that Klara's parents too were queasy at the sight of such an image.

I don't remember how the rest of that Sunday went. I mean, we probably sat together that evening at the Hagemanns' discussing the Moscow revelations, reading out bits from the West German papers, just as we talked incessantly at that time about Stalin's sudden fall from grace. It was some months later, maybe at about the time of the Soviet march on Budapest, when the Dresden festivities had long since passed into history, that Klara's thoughts returned to the procession. It was only once Stalin's burning gaze was finally extinguished that she got around to asking Professor Kaltenburg about the truck with the prisoners that summer.

On closer consideration, she said, these young people dressed up as camp inmates represented a slap in the face, a slap in the face for all those driven out of the country barely three and a half years earlier.

"And we still don't know the whereabouts of many people who disappeared at that time. Are they still stuck in their prison cells? Being interrogated? Are they still being made to pay the price for the great show trial?"

"Fear," murmured Kaltenburg.

"Fear?"

"I suspect fear behind it, in an unpredictable, highly dangerous form."

"But here they are, parading liberated prisoners before us, the ones that came back, they're showing us survivors at the very moment they have surmounted their fear of death. They're triumphant. And then you think of the Kochs."

"Not that fear, Klara, that's not what I mean," said Ludwig Kaltenburg. "We're dealing here with the kind of fear you use to intimidate others."

Kaltenburg was thinking a lot at that time about his relationship with animals, one evening I even heard him wondering out loud whether it wasn't time for a fundamental reconsideration of the relationship between man and animal. He got Martin to show him the drawings he had made at the back of the laboratory in Leipzig, when Matzke had leaned over him as if to devour the artist along with his drawing pad and folding stool. Although at first sight the professor didn't recognize either marten or rabbit, he was resolved to fathom Martin's concept of the animal, he wanted to reconstruct how you could approach animals without the analytical eye of a scientist.

I believe that at some point Martin, who had gradually come to have confidence in Kaltenburg, even brought to Loschwitz the studies that had evolved from his hyena series, the last works based on his zoo sketches: not portraits at this stage, but a rough pattern of black and rust-brown marks, although you could make out individual backs, flanks, and legs among them. However, the viewer couldn't tell what limb belonged to which animal. Here and there a muzzle appeared, and then a pair of round ears—nothing but a compact block of piebald, quivering fur.

It was a while before the professor could grasp Martin's approach, accept his way of seeing: "So what you do is you make yourself acquainted with the hyena."

"Acquainted? I wouldn't call it that. The more I studied the hyena, the more I doubted anyone's ability to become acquainted with it."

"You give your impression of it. No, hold on." Ludwig Kaltenburg corrected himself. "By making it practically disappear, you've captured one of its traits: a hyena seems to know, like the rest of its kind, that it can make itself virtually invisible."

They exchanged ideas about color perception. They spent hours in front of the Old Masters, wondering about the source of the songbirds depicted in great still-life paintings: Kaltenburg was convinced they were fresh provender intended for that day's table, while Martin thought that from one composition to the next painters would make use of the same particularly well-drawn specimens. They also discussed at length the remarkable shyness that affects young crows practically overnight if the person they relate to is not careful to maintain continuous contact with the nestlings.

"You go away for three days, and by the time you get back the whole brood is lost to you, no further use for observational purposes."

Martin's way of framing questions and formulating his own theories impressed Kaltenburg so much at the time that—how often could he say this of anyone?—he noted with respect that he had actually learned something from their conversation about shyness in crows.

It was the high point of the Loschwitz Institute. I would be hard-pressed to name all the research projects that were going on in that phase of its life, the feed kitchen was a hive of activity at all times. Martin was lending me a hand, helping with the drawings for my study of titmice, Etzel von Isisdorf was devoting himself to his rhesus monkeys, Knut was squatting in his garage working on film commentaries after a year of roaming through the Congo with a camera. Reinhold regularly sat in the garden with the professor, negotiations with the Academy of Sciences over the new research establishment were progressing—and Kaltenburg was not only fulfilling his many duties, but for about a month he entertained the idea of writing a book in his old age about the representation of animals in contemporary art. He was buoyed up by boundless energy and enthusiasm, he would like to have started collecting material straightaway, why hadn't he thought right at the beginning of noting down the key points of his conversations with Martin?

And then Ludwig Kaltenburg lost his head. One day it was all over. The professor banned Martin Spengler from the Institute grounds. Whether he specifically barred him from the house, whether he drove him away or just left him standing, I couldn't say, because I wasn't present at the crucial moment.

"Surely you don't mean it."

"Hermann, don't annoy me even more, can't you see I'm beside myself."

"Martin was equally beside himself."

"That man may be a thoroughly good person, but he shouldn't be allowed anywhere near animals."

"You've got to speak to him."

"Enough."

6

—

NOT ONLY THE PERSON of Martin but his very name was taboo in Loschwitz from then on. Unfortunately, you sense all too precisely when a name must not be uttered, a subject must not be mentioned, so that you can't blithely ignore the prohibition: I never found the courage to break the taboo. Professor Kaltenburg, I noticed, gave me a look if I so much as thought of Martin in his presence. Fits of irritability: he sent me out of the room to perform tasks that could just as easily have been carried out by an animal keeper, the cleaning lady, or his driver, Krause. Or, as quick as lightning, he came up with a theory that he knew would have me enthralled.

Later, in letters—sometimes containing acute analyses of Martin's work—or in interviews when asked about his early acquaintance with the now famous Martin Spengler, Ludwig Kaltenburg readily talked about their time together in Loschwitz, not holding back—he could laugh about it now—from saying that this man had made him furious.

He recalled how he had hit the roof when Martin appeared at the Institute wrapped in a loden coat. All he needed was the knee breeches and a chamois tuft stuck in a little hat to look like a Bavarian hunter. I believe to this day that Martin meant it when he said he thought he was appearing as a herdsman; never in his wildest dreams would it have occurred to him that he was dressed as a huntsman.

I asked him later whether he had ever wondered why it was that nobody at the Institute wore green loden, be it a jacket, a coat, or just a hat, even though he must know how many loden-lovers there were among animal lovers? No, he hadn't noticed. Yes, he could see that now—it was probably a matter of fashion, pure chance, maybe? No, absolutely not. The catalog of commandments, rules of conduct, and—not to put too fine a point on it—laws established at the Institute under Kaltenburg's regime actually did include a ban on loden, albeit an unspoken one. Now Martin had found out at first hand why this was so.

I was on my way to fetch some straw, I was doing a favor for a Romanian guest who had come to Loschwitz to study dwarf pigs, I had just opened the door to the garage where bales of straw and replacement panes of glass were kept next to the limousine, when I heard the sound of the northern raven, one of Kaltenburg's oldest animals. I hadn't reckoned on Martin being at the Institute that day, and I was expecting to witness a confrontation between animals as I moved cautiously past the bushes to the corner, quietly, so that the raven wouldn't notice me. Instead of a weasel or a cockerel or some other animal the raven might have picked a fight with, I saw Martin standing there with his back to me, and quite near me the big black bird that had the man in the green coat in its sights: unawares, he was holding an outdoor broom, no doubt with a view to making himself useful by sweeping the narrow path that ran behind the Institute.

A long, elegantly cut loden coat with staghorn buttons sufficed to upset, if not Kaltenburg directly, then certainly the tame raven and consequently its old friend the professor. "I'm sorry, we can't have this anymore," he said—you might have thought it was the animals that made the laws at the Institute—"There's nothing I can do about it." Ludwig Kaltenburg's hands were tied, he claimed, his animals had simply entrusted him with the responsibility of enforcing the unalterable rules.

Of course, I could distinguish between the raven's combative note or other harmless noises and its attacking cry, but Martin couldn't. And of course I also knew that a raven always launches its attack from behind, because it believes it has achieved a victory, or at least the best precondition for a victory, if it can land on its victim's back. I don't know whether it was too late, but I failed to alert Martin or to distract the bird. The raven hopped sideways, its head down, toward the loden-clad man, its wings spread in order to take off quickly if its opponent should turn around suddenly. But it didn't occur to Martin to do so, he wasn't aware of the situation. Animal cries, birds calling, you heard them everywhere, and part of the attraction of Loschwitz for Martin was surely the opportunity to immerse himself in a restless world of animal noises.

And of course I knew that the raven was allergic to the sight of anyone resembling a huntsman, even from a distance. The robust dark-green material, and then for good measure—the ill-fated combination of two characteristics—a broom: Martin jerked, felt the claws in his neck, fell to his knees, turned around, shook off his assailant, and saw the creature crouching on the ground with wings still spread. Involuntarily Martin had brought the broom up to head height, his eyes dilated with fear, his neck bleeding, he kept his gaze fixed on the bird. Martin was in a state of shock, but the raven gave him no time to recover, it tried to get past the huntsman figure with the leveled gun in order to attack again. Martin didn't understand, whirled around, coattails flying. By the time I had regained my presence of mind and warned Martin that it was far from over, the raven mounted its third attack.

I shouted, "Throw the broom away, take the coat off," but it was no use, the more fervently I urged him on, the less self-control he had. Martin waved the broom handle wildly, hit the raven on the wing, the raven struck at his temple, pulling his hair out, then hacked at the back of Martin's hand.

I shouted, "Hand in front of your eyes," but Martin did exactly the opposite, he put his hands behind his back, making the broomstick describe a wild arc, which took the raven with it and hurled it quite some distance toward the garage. No sooner had the bird pulled itself together than it launched the next attack. Suddenly Kaltenburg was standing between the two opponents. I don't know how he got there so quickly, presumably my shouting and the hoarse croaking of his raven had alerted him.

I heard the broom handle splintering across Kaltenburg's knee, followed by more wood splintering. Kaltenburg didn't utter a sound as he threw the broken bits into the shrubbery, grabbed the bewildered Martin by the upper arm, and dragged him behind the house. Then I heard him roaring: "Coat," I heard, "lab coat," as if this "coat" and "lab coat" were the most crucial words in the language.

The raven flew a little way, up into the oak tree, it took some time to calm down. It preened itself, putting its feathers in order, looking down into the bushes as though it still couldn't quite believe that the broom handle rested there smashed to pieces. At some point it stopped croaking, squatted silently, and surveyed the strip of grass below, casting an eye over a battlefield from which it had emerged victorious, or as leader of an invincible army, albeit one consisting only of a single foot soldier.

I didn't see Kaltenburg again for about an hour. In the meantime I had delivered straw to the dwarf pigs. The professor was still agitated.

"So careless," he burst out. "He could have lost an eye."

I thought he meant Martin.

"Martin?" he snapped back. "Martin could have broken his wing."

I wanted to know where Martin was, but that name had already ceased to exist.

"The raven lost primary feathers," he said, "and as for your friend, I never want to see him on these premises again."

7

———

E VEN LUDWIG KALTENBURG can sometimes misjudge people."

No one could persuade the professor to lift the ban. We certainly wouldn't have dared to raise the topic at the usual morning meeting, but I know that many members of the Institute tried to change Kaltenburg's mind. Admittedly, Martin Spengler had been a nuisance occasionally, pushing his way into an observational setup, for example, or asking questions about what was going on in front of his very eyes rather than relying on his own observation. And hadn't the professor always said that anyone bothered by him should personally take steps to shake him off? But by now everybody regarded the outcast entirely as an asset to the Loschwitz Institute and was not inclined to be judgmental about those moments when Martin had been insensitive in his dealings with animals, or, as Kaltenburg once put it rather bluntly, he had assaulted an animal.

The scientists, keepers, craftsmen, even the feed manager—they all sprang to Martin's defense, although they took good care to avoid touching on the delicate subject of the friendship between the two of them. They left that part to Knut and me. Needless to say, we had no intention of giving in, always thinking of new arguments, and I was almost locked in combat with Ludwig Kaltenburg. I talked about the deep understanding of animals that had inspired

Martin. Certainly he didn't see them with the same eyes as the professor, but Kaltenburg must concede that it was precisely this difference that had first aroused his interest in Martin.

"But how is he supposed to gain what you call a deep understanding of animals without observing them closely? That's a complete contradiction," Kaltenburg objected.

Martin simply did not possess with the same research drive as a trained zoologist, he didn't observe in order to establish functional relations, he let impressions work on him.

"Do you know what? I've long suspected that your friend finds animals—how shall I put it—cute. No trace of deeper understanding there."

But didn't he think there was a certain innocence in that, an attempt to approach the animal without reservation?

"Innocence, without reservation—when I hear that language, I just see red. He's spent too much time reading Brehm's *Life of Animals*."

Knut tried to calm the professor down by admitting that Martin might well have unclear notions of the borderline between animal and human, and when Martin philosophized about "communicating" and an "exchange with the animal," Knut was as skeptical as Ludwig Kaltenburg.

"When he imitates the call of the blackcock, he imagines himself slipping into a blackcock's skin and feathers. When he sits in a cage with a weasel, he sees himself as a weasel. But who better than you to put him right about these notions, Herr Professor?"

Kaltenburg hesitated for a moment, reflected—but no, he had made up his mind.

"You can say I'm limited, you can call me quirky if you like, I can live with that. But any kind of cutesiness makes me furious, even as a kid I hated people using that coochy-coo voice to me."

If he had ever found animals cute, if, as a so-called nice child, he had been drawn to animals because they were nice like him, he would never have become a researcher, he said. Animals are not cute critters, and a child is the last person to be interested in niceness: on the contrary, it was precisely the dignity of animals, their serious attitude to the world, even when at play, that aroused the child's interest.

"That's what attracted me to animals—there's no way an animal can do anything else, it's bound to take you seriously, even if you're a creature who can't yet walk, can't speak, can't even eat properly yet, and come crawling across the field in a diaper."

Dispirited, we made our way to the garage, where Martin was waiting for us. No, we hadn't got anywhere. The professor had digressed into basic principles. And yes, once again he had been careful not to refer to Martin by name. I took Martin one of the young chaffinches we had brought up together in Loschwitz. That was the most I could do.

"I suppose he left Dresden very soon after that?" asked Katharina Fischer.

Meanwhile the crows had made their way to the upper end of the island, far fewer birds than in winter, and yet their noisy competition for roosting spots dominated our whole area.

I couldn't say now how much time elapsed between the two events. When did Knut make his stork film? It must have been 1959. During filming, a photograph was taken that has often been reproduced over time, and if I remember rightly, I was the one who took it, in Mecklenburg, far from Loschwitz and Kaltenburg's Institute. But not with my camera, which is why, as far as I know, it never bears any attribution. The camera must have been Knut's, or Martin's—though I never saw Martin holding a camera. Three men are standing in front of a fence. Grassland scenery. Rough wooden posts with barbed wire stretched between them. Wheat beyond the fence, almost ripe for harvesting. You can see, from left to right, Martin, Knut, and, with his back to the camera, Herr Sikorski, bending down, preoccupied. The photographer has made an effort to include a nest you can make out in the background on the roof of a farmhouse, while Martin is smoking a cigarette and talking. Though his hands are casually thrust into his pockets, Knut looks as if he is being pulled in two directions at once—he is lending an ear to Martin and looking into the lens; I have caught him in a rare moment of impatience.

One of the last shots before Martin left for the West. And I can remember, as if it were yesterday, what it was he was so eager to get across. Knut couldn't wait to get back to work; the stork on its nest looked settled enough, but it could easily decide to take off at any moment. Knut was incapable of concentrating on what his friend was saying, but I recall every word: Martin was talking about Ludwig Kaltenburg.

After what was basically an inexplicable breach, he had gone through all the phases that might conceivably follow such a vehement rejection, had ignored the professor, derided him, rebelled against him. He may have sensed that he would never be free of Kaltenburg's influence. Martin disappeared. Nothing was heard of him for years. It wasn't until the mid-sixties, when I was idly leafing through a few catalogs and picture books one day, that I was struck—because of his slight squint—by a snapshot of a stranger. He was looking past the camera, you couldn't help but stare at that face, as if to attract the subject's attention. The black hat, the white shirt with short sleeves, a shadow in the background, dark shapes, silhouettes, several people, obviously. That wasn't Martin Spengler.

Today I know that the picture shows Martin during a stage appearance shortly after he had tipped a packet of laundry detergent into an open grand piano. It was taken on July 20, 1964, precisely twenty years after the failed attempt to assassinate Hitler in his Wolf's Lair, and at first sight there is something Führer-like about Martin, with his right arm raised. His expression wavers between trance and wild resolution; it looks as if he's grown a little mustache, but then you realize it has nothing to do with hair. Coagulating blood. Martin is bleeding. Blood is trickling over his lips and down his chin. A few minutes earlier a student had smashed his nose.

That wasn't him. And then I did recognize him, after all. Martin in the setting of his large, disturbing art performances which regularly caused public uproar, and he himself took fright at the reactions he had provoked. The point at which other people lose control and blindly hit out, he would fall into a strange state somewhere between rigid self-control and self-absorption. I can see Martin standing on a stage with a bleeding nose, outwardly attentive but inwardly listening: a portrait which, in its very theatricality—the posture, the raised arm, the hand presenting an object—has more impact than the many later pictures in which, though apparently oblivious of the camera, he acts out the role of being photographed.

Did the two of them ever meet again in the West? Not that I ever heard. And I think it's unlikely. All the same, throughout their lives they seem to have moved along parallel lines, and as I corresponded with both of them I kept coming across mysterious coincidences. At the beginning of the seventies, for instance, when the professor began actively to promote the cause of wildlife conservation, he wrote to me one day that he had read out a manifesto in the Munich Hofbräuhaus beer hall, and because of the turmoil in the hall, he had stood on the table to make himself heard—and then I noted the date of the event, a day in July, the twentieth, eight years after Martin's broken-nose appearance.

8

ETWEEN THE BANK and Bird Island the flow of the Elbe
was much reduced, just a rivulet here and there. The gravel
bed was exposed, by stepping from one patch of shingle to
another you could easily get across, but we turned back. Bats had
replaced the sand martins. In a bare, dead tree on the island bank
a night heron sat motionless, watching the unruffled surface of the
water below.

After what she had heard from me, said Katharina Fischer, she
was slowly beginning to see Martin Spengler's appearances from a
different angle. She had always found the artist slightly repellent,
a person who allowed nobody and nothing to share the limelight
with him, who ruthlessly made himself the center of attention on
the stage or in a discussion group. Images of a murmuring, gesticulating Martin Spengler standing his ground for hours on end had
unnerved her rather than attracted her to Martin's world.

"He behaved as if to prove to his audience how easy it is to ignore
people. But now I'm suddenly wondering whether people played
any part at all in Martin Spengler's performances."

And yet in his countless statements about art, man is central.
Martin never missed a chance to propagate his vision of mankind,
which I've never really grasped.

"Of course. Nonetheless, I have the feeling that he was chiefly concerned to move with the patience of an animal observer, as though in his mind he was always communicating with animals."

Then Martin had let it be known, if only indirectly, that he understood the professor's objections. That he accepted them. That he held nothing against him. On the contrary. A quiet echo. An overture.

"Messages directed at Ludwig Kaltenburg."

No, Martin Spengler did not regard animals as "cute" or "nice." That assessment was a crude error on Kaltenburg's part. Since Martin's banishment from the Institute there hasn't been a year when I haven't wondered whether the professor was right to get so deeply involved in the wrangling over the Berlin Research Center, whether he would ever have chosen Eberhard Matzke to be his archenemy, whether in fact he might not have spent the rest of his life in Dresden, if he had been a little more clear-sighted at that time. In Martin he would have had some support to counteract his forays into "zoological politics," as Kaltenburg called it. A book about animal representation in art—it could be that in a weak moment he was afraid such a peripheral work might adversely affect his reputation, or that he heard his colleagues whispering, "Professor Kaltenburg's reaching the age when you take up a hobby," or "His great research days are behind him, he's gone off poaching in other fields." Which was exactly what he did later, and the further he ventured into sociology, anthropology, and history, the more damage he did to his reputation.

As a child I saw my father turning his back on Kaltenburg from one day to the next; in my mid-twenties, I saw the professor repudiating Martin. Both events affected me deeply, neither seemed to me inevitable. An outsider could do nothing but look on impotently. As a result I could never bring myself to break with Ludwig Kaltenburg, though there were times when I didn't want to know anything about him.

The night heron had left its perch. I picked it out again in the reeds on the bank, reflected in the water. Its head lowered, it was on the lookout for fish, its beak gliding to and fro above the smooth, seemingly impenetrable surface. It looked up as we passed. You might almost have thought it wanted to hear what Katharina Fischer had to say.

"At least he didn't regard Martin Spengler as his archenemy."

Knowledgeable as he was about animals, Kaltenburg was unable to see that he himself was fixated on a displacement object. In any case, I'm very cautious when it comes to the subject of Matzke as Kaltenburg's opponent. Perhaps it was Knut—I regret to say—who first put the idea into the professor's head that Matzke was out to get him. Not deliberately, certainly not, I'm not reproaching him, it could just as easily have been me.

"A sideswipe?" asked an astonished Kaltenburg one day, when Knut was expressing his annoyance at an article of Eberhard Matzke's. "I can't believe it."

"After all, it's not the first time we've read this kind of thing, Herr Professor. Don't you remember the brazen words that man dared to utter about the inhibition against biting among canines? Since then it's been one malicious comment after another."

Knut Sieverding, the only realist among us. It was beyond his powers of imagination to foresee the phantasms his matter-of-fact observations might possibly unleash.

"Malicious comments? Colleague Matzke? Aimed at me? But we always got on extremely well."

Knut wanted to proceed carefully, wanted to save Kaltenburg from a defeat, or rather from yet another "small setback" after the professor's failed efforts to bring the missing exhibits back to the Zoological Collections. In Berlin's new Zoological Research Center, Reinhold held the office of director, Matzke becoming his deputy with responsibility for day-to-day business, making it possible for Reinhold to concentrate fully on the kind of large-scale research that had, at least in part, preoccupied him for more than thirty years. We were all convinced that, thanks to Reinhold's newfound freedom, the long-anticipated monograph on avian plumage would now finally come to fruition.

Kaltenburg's plan had worked. Eberhard Matzke, meanwhile,

was clearly on a different track. He did not want to be deputy director. What resulted was the Matzke rebellion, as the colleagues called it, not without a certain irony, since everyone knew that Dr. Eberhard Matzke lacked the nerve for a Matzke revolution. Perhaps Matzke had not expected the Saxon zoologists to rally around Reinhold, perhaps he had pictured them joining forces with him to drive Reinhold out. A Leipziger, a Dresdener—but for Ludwig Kaltenburg's involvement, you could have seen the Matzke rebellion as a purely Saxon affair which happened to be played out on the big stage of Berlin.

"Somebody's got to make him see sense," was the professor's conclusion. "Who else but me could attempt it under the circumstances?"

"Are you sure that's a good idea?"

"Misunderstandings are always better tackled man-to-man."

"Misunderstandings are a different matter, Herr Professor. We're past the stage of misunderstandings. Matzke and Reinhold, the whole setup behind them—the battle lines have been drawn."

"That's just why we need skilled diplomacy, we need to come up with an offer of peace that colleague Matzke, who is prone to bouts of confusion, can accept without losing face."

"I strongly advise you against approaching Matzke in this situation. And with all due respect, I am not convinced that you are the right man for such a mission."

I could see it was a considerable effort for Knut to talk to Kaltenburg about past failings, about Matzke plodding, shoulders miserably hunched, down the Institute corridor under the eyes of the staff, about students in the lab excitedly putting aside their work as soon as Kaltenburg appeared in the doorway, and about the tense silence in the professor's lecture when Matzke took too long to fetch a new stick of chalk for the blackboard.

"But I always helped him where I could."

"I don't deny that. But has it ever occurred to you that Eberhard Matzke has never come to the Institute? Have you ever invited him to Loschwitz? You have people coming and going all the time, with zoologists of all nationalities staying here, and if any up-and-coming young researcher—even a child interested in wildlife—shows the slightest hint of promise, the Institute's doors are open to him."

Kaltenburg growled.

"Have you ever wondered what all this activity looks like to Eberhard Matzke from a distance?"

"I must admit I haven't."

Both were exhausted. Knut paced up and down the room. Professor Kaltenburg sat back in his cocktail-bar chair with arms dangling over the sides.

"Hermann, could you make us some tea?"

As I was on my way to the kitchen, Kaltenburg sat bolt upright.

"Somebody's got to do something."

"Not you."

9

———

W E FOLLOWED THE ANIMALS' example and kept out
of the sun. I think it was a hot August afternoon when I
was informed that I had to renounce my membership in
the German Ornithological Society. I wasn't the only one, we were
all required to renounce membership in a Western organization.
The animals dozed. We were agitated, we were restless.

Maybe this did start out as a crass joke doing the rounds of the
Institute, though in those August days we were in no mood for joking—there was no escape from the enervating heat, whether we
lay under the trees, retreated into the aquarium wing, or sat behind
closed shutters and tried not to move if we could help it.

"Next thing they'll be making us quit the German Ornithological Society."

Professor Kaltenburg, wearing shorts, confused for a moment:
"What are you talking about? Reinhold is sitting there isolated in
West Berlin, and you're wasting your time with that nonsense?"

One of the caretakers was trying all day to get hold of his family, with no success; his wife and children had gone ahead of him
on holiday. Colleagues canceled impending trips to the West. Con-
versely, no prospect of a visit from Knut Sieverding. He never made
the long-planned documentary about house sparrows. Troubled,
Krause washed the car. Or did he come back in the evening from a

trip to Berlin and report at first hand the events that had been unfolding on the streets? No. In any case, we wouldn't have trusted his account.

All at once, the long-running dispute between Reinhold and Matzke was over. Professor Doktor Eberhard Matzke had displayed a frightening degree of ambition, against Reinhold's will he had been made director of the research center, but he still wasn't satisfied. He didn't shrink from using uncouth language to his colleagues to cast doubts on Reinhold's abilities, he blackened his name in the highest quarters, and above all, he declared, there was no place in East Berlin for an ornithologist who lived in West Berlin. It was as if colleague Matzke's complaints and grievances had gained a hearing at some point, for Reinhold's bird collection and library were now placed at Matzke's disposal—the hated eminence no longer able to put a spoke in his wheel.

And then I can see Ludwig Kaltenburg sitting bent over on the wooden bench in his kitchen, his shoelaces dangling in the air for a moment. Gripping the heavy, leather-soled shoe by the heel, he pulls it off with a heave. He sits up again and grunts, "Oh, it's you." Kaltenburg points at the shoe, and as if apologizing, he says, "I went out to get milk."

His beard, his hair, the bench, the tiled floor, are all bathed in the clear light of a mild day. The shopping bag with the bottles of milk is there; I notice the color of Kaltenburg's socks, like mincemeat that's been exposed to air for too long.

I force myself to look elsewhere, the art print on the kitchen wall, the linen cloth on the table, I make the embarrassed old man disappear.

I only vaguely recollect his sending me to Matzke in late 1961 or early 1962 with a peace offer. "Don't forget to have a good shave, you know colleague Matzke can't stand to see a badly shaven man of a morning."

Eberhard Matzke no longer knew me. There was no reply to the peace offer. It will have been around then that the professor finally understood that this wasn't about Reinhold at all. It was he, Ludwig

Kaltenburg, that Matzke had had in his sights all along. From that moment on things went downhill with Kaltenburg.

The jackdaw skins lie spread out before me, a uniform black-ish gray shimmer covers the work surface once the sun goes down. Yes, I skinned Taschotschek. I have preserved it and its fellows very carefully, and in Klotzsche too Kaltenburg's jackdaws will be kept in a safe place.

10

―

THE JAYS ARE GONE," he wrote in his first animal hand-book. "The geese have moved away, to who knows where. Of all my free-flying birds, there remain only the jack-daws." Now they too were gone.

One morning Klara said at breakfast, "The professor is beyond saving."

I left my coffee, put my jacket on. Klara looked at me, she knew where I was going. It was as though Ludwig Kaltenburg had taught us all to sense the slightest change in the condition of certain life forms from miles away.

Half an hour later I turned into the familiar street, out of breath though I hadn't been running. I stopped outside the villa. On the stones of the path leading to the house I saw drops, not rain and not animal droppings, a trail. Right up to the garden gate, as well as on the footpath behind me, I had followed the trail for some while without registering it. At every step I observed these small circles, frayed at the edges, dark, a watery substance, they would soon evap-orate. The door was open, it was always open, there was no door-bell—Kaltenburg said, early on, "You know how it is here, peo-ple continually calling in wanting something from me. If we had a doorbell, my nocturnals would never get any rest."

On the linoleum of the stairs up to the first floor, the marks changed color. White drops on a red background. Step by step I followed the milky trail up to the study. Kaltenburg's socks. An embarrassed smile.

"Oh, it's you."

Kaltenburg sat hunched on the edge of the sofa. He used to eat on it lying back; at night, Martin would sometimes sit there too, as I did countless times. Kaltenburg was struggling with his shoelaces. As though it explained everything, as though on this morning the whole world could be summed up in a single sentence, he said, "I went out to get milk."

His bare hand brushed across the suede leather, the other shoe was standing on the parquet floor in a shiny little puddle. Then it struck me that Ludwig Kaltenburg was wearing socks with holes in them. He raised his head, smiled sheepishly: "I went out to get milk and didn't notice."

He seemed not to know what he wanted to do with the milk. Like a self-conscious young boy. No, to be honest, he looked at me like an old man who has realized that his powers are slipping away.

"The milk was dripping on my shoe, and I didn't notice," he said.

The bag sat in a pool of milk, I took the bottles out carefully, no, there was no broken glass, but one bottletop was ripped off. On the way back from the shop Kaltenburg had spilled almost a liter of milk.

"I'll wipe it up," he said, now sounding like a child wanting to undo a mistake.

I found a bucket in the broom closet, the scrubbing brush, a cloth, fetched water. I started at the foot of the stairs. The same silence as on that evening when we had gathered up the dead jackdaws. Kaltenburg had called for me because no one else was available. He had to wait for nearly an hour in a state of uncertainty until I arrived. It was during that night that Klara first said to me, "You won't be able to save Ludwig Kaltenburg."

His clear look as he talked about the abysses, "There, there, and there," the light spring breeze in his hair, the first sunshine of the year on his weather-beaten face. And yet Ludwig Kaltenburg never really wanted to see that he was surrounded by monsters. Later, people would say that he had gradually isolated himself, that the seal had been set on the end of his time in Dresden long before, but he had been remarkably good at concealing this from himself and the world.

I wiped the milk from the parquet, a trickle running under the desk, the rugs would need cleaning—no, no great store was set by clean carpets in the Kaltenburg household. But with all this milk, there would have to be new carpets.

"Remind me to let you have a key before you go, Hermann."

They took their time, they studied him. And didn't Kaltenburg himself always insist on patient observation? First of all they wanted to acquire an all-round understanding of the subject, sooner or later his weak spots would be exposed, inadvertently he would tell you himself how to throw someone like Ludwig Kaltenburg off balance. It couldn't be done in a hurry—a man like Kaltenburg was able to withstand a great deal, he would fight for his corner, not yield easily. They could have deprived Kaltenburg of his university chair, prohibited him from researching and publishing—he would just have laughed: "Ban me from research? I only have to see to be doing research. You've only got to keep your eyes open, how can anyone stop me doing that?"

Was his gaze fixed on the cleaning cloth, or was he simply staring into space? He sat there motionless, only his toes moving. I wouldn't have expected the holes in his socks. When I had wrung out the rag and washed my hands, I caught myself secretly scrutinizing Kaltenburg as I returned to the room: Had he combed his hair today? Was his collar clean?

"A key, yes, I won't forget."

He said, "Actually, I've always preferred the country."

I knew that for the past few weeks he'd been working on a lecture to be given at a conference in Oslo or Helsinki. And if he insisted on giving me a key to the villa, I also knew that he would not be coming back from this trip.

At that moment there wasn't the slightest doubt. Kaltenburg had dropped many hints, possibly lost on everyone but me. Kaltenburg's fear. The animals sensed you were going to leave them, you moved differently, you approached the animals in a different way,

297

you didn't smell the same: there was no need for luggage in the corridor. It was to be the only time in his life that he would move his household without a single animal.

Professor Ludwig Kaltenburg perched on the edge of the sofa, without looking up he lifted some paper from the desk, scrunched it up, and stuffed his right shoe with it. I almost thought I heard him muttering, "*Da, da, durak.*"

I took stock, reaching for the wadding. I ran my fingers over the pleasantly warm, dark jackdaw feathers. Effortlessly, I filled the skin.

11

THERE WAS STILL a pale orange and blue glow in the sky over the city, a pair of cranes were winging their way up the Elbe, giving voice as they flew, and when we sat down at one of the empty tables outside a long-since-closed snack bar called the Elbe Idyll, Frau Fischer asked what had become of Ludwig Kaltenburg's other animals.

The northern raven disappeared for good soon after its old friend. Some of the exotics went to dealers, some to the zoo, which also took the rare duck species. For some years I didn't dare venture anywhere near the waterfowl ponds, because the older birds were absolutely not to be dissuaded from following me as far as the tram stop. The sulfur-crested cockatoo got away from me one day when I managed to corner it in Kaltenburg's bedroom—it was clearly so disgusted that it wanted nothing more to do with me and went off to look for a new feeding station. Later, it was often spotted by people who were out walking in the Great Garden, and regularly visited the afternoon feeding sessions at the zoo. Taking up its position on a branch or on the large uprooted tree stump which also served the heron as a lookout post, the cockatoo squatted there, less on account of hunger, perhaps, than because it enjoyed the familiar company of the mandarin ducks and pochards, the red-breasted and bar-headed geese, of every kind of strange bird, in fact, whether they were cormorants, sacred ibises, or flamingos.

Like other birds, however, it will have succumbed to the long, hard winter of 1962–63, when the swans were solidly frozen in on the Elbe and the tits were picking at any fresh putty in window frames, attracted by the smell of linseed oil, which was becoming weaker by the day. One day a group of young field ornithologists who spent some years mapping the Great Garden came across a single primary feather in the snow and noted, "Vestige of an escaped bird," then went on, "Obviously brought into the area by visitors," and then, in view of the white parts of the feather, which had a yellow sheen in the winter sunshine, added, "Sulfur-crested cockatoo," followed by a question mark. Because of severe frost damage, among other things, a positive identification would have been impossible.

A few former assistants took over the dogs. The resident tomcat was unwilling to leave his familiar territory, the neighbors went on putting food out for him until the end of the decade. We released Kaltenburg's sticklebacks into the wild and distributed the tropical fish among various aquariums around the city: commercial firms, schools, the sanatorium in Wachwitz.

The hamsters? I can't remember the details of what happened to them. Anyway, I believe two fundamentally different types of hamster must be distinguished in Kaltenburg's life. When he talked about hamsters in the plural, he did actually have in mind the nocturnal animals who kept him company when everybody else was asleep. But when he talked about a hamster, singular, it was just as well not to form too concrete an image of this creature that constantly chewed paper and helped itself to important documents and private letters to build its nest; it wasn't to be taken literally. If the minutes of a meeting had disappeared, let alone unanswered mail from friends, there would soon be a reference to the infamous hamster. And so in time I gathered that "the hamster" in the singular was simply another way of talking about papers that were, unfortunately, nowhere to be found.

Most of the Institute buildings were put to new uses, and I gather there was some idea of turning the villa into a guesthouse. But then it deteriorated bit by bit, the grounds became overgrown, quite a few animals may even have come back to live in this new wilderness. Long after its dissolution, Kaltenburg continued to be very interested in his former Institute, sending me back there time and again to keep him informed. I sent dismal reports to him in Vienna, but he reacted enthusiastically—"Good, excellent"; he was content to know that the Institute he had built up had not fallen into the hands of Matzke.

I wrote to him, "Now the rain has started to come in through your study ceiling."

He replied, "Very good, go on reporting back."

It wasn't until the mid-nineties that the villa was renovated, that is to say, completely rebuilt from the ground up—the crumbling floorboards, the dry rot in the walls of the aquarium wing. The present occupants probably have no idea what sort of place they've moved into, they can't begin to suspect all the things that came to light during the restoration work. Including perhaps a nest made out of scraps of paper, of Kantian paragraphs, and containing little mummified hamsters—it comes to me now that when I was clearing out the villa several adult hamsters fell prey to the buzzard, but as I couldn't find their nest, their last litter must have perished.

Kaltenburg triumphed—in his letters, at any rate. A dubious triumph. It's true that Eberhard Matzke did not succeed in extending his influence as far as Loschwitz, but then again, if he had done so, it might well have been precisely the right outcome: at least the Institute would have been saved, even if it would no doubt have been run along different lines from Kaltenburg's. Until I managed to find a berth in the Ornithological Collection, it wasn't a pleasant time for me, having to see staff layoffs taking effect and difficulties arising with the supply of animal feed. Not long after Kaltenburg left, my days in Loschwitz were numbered too, I found myself responsible for disposing of one familiar creature after another. Dead rooms, a dead garden—the whole Elbe hillside seemed to me bereft.

Meanwhile, near Vienna, Kaltenburg had long since begun to collect new animals around him, in the following years he was to build up colonies far bigger than his Loschwitz flocks.

However many species and specimens Kaltenburg may have surrounded himself with in the West, I'm afraid his Dresden experience always remained on his mind. I see his increasing turn to human beings as a reaction to a painful loss. In fact, perhaps Kaltenburg was driven to turn his attention to human beings because he sensed he would never again be able to give full and unconditional commitment to any animal, having once left his animal household in the lurch. That is my reading of his first book written in the West, his first extensive study of human beings, *Archetypes of Fear.*

Katharina Fischer said that, particularly from reading Kaltenburg's polemic, *The Five Horsemen of the Apocalypse*, she felt she could see the way the author was gradually losing the ground from under his feet. It was as though he were waiting the whole time for someone to hold him in check while he raged ever more blindly. A rage from which no well-meaning assistant, no devoted follower, no human being, could have freed him, because it was directed at human beings themselves. Only an animal might have had that power, observing him from within its own world, with no comprehension of this noisy man who swept everything aside and foresaw a dismal future.

And then the author made a serious mistake, which would soon lead to his pamphlet being popularly known, not as *The Five Horseman of the Apocalypse*, but simply as *Kaltenburg's Gas Chamber Book.* Frau Fischer had heavily underlined the relevant passage in her copy, and to this day I too could repeat it by heart. And yet it's only a matter of an exaggerated formulation, in retrospect just a stupid thing, one of those peculiar turns of phrase used in the hope of surreptitiously erasing some dark chapter in one's past but succeeding only in arousing the reader's suspicions. But for Kaltenburg's indignant comment that nowadays you could hardly talk about the differing value of different people without being accused of wanting to build new gas chambers, and but for the stubborn way he stood by his utterance afterward, it might never have come to light that, long before his return to the West, even long before Stalin's death, he had turned his attention to human beings.

In one of his last letters he assured me that he hadn't actually written the infamous gas chamber sentence himself but that a zealous follower of his had inserted it at a late editorial stage. He wouldn't name him, just as he had given nothing away in the previous twenty-five years, he had taken all the unpleasantness upon himself and had protected the anonymity of his assistant's handwriting. "It's a bitter irony," he wrote at the end of January 1986, after Martin's death, "that in the end we both suffered the same fate. When I think how difficult it was for me at that time to fend off your friend's admiration—only to realize now that both he and I gathered more and more acolytes around us, but, sadly, not independent-minded followers."

He was forced to cast his mind back to his earlier researches. He would have done anything in the world to avoid returning to them. No animal obstructed his view of his own past. Kaltenburg lost the ground from under his feet. Just as I came close to losing the ground under my feet. His early engagement with human beings fell within his Posen phase. He will not have given my father the relevant essays to read. And if on the tram home my mother responded evasively, almost nervously to my questions about Professor Kaltenburg, then it was simply because he himself had nothing very clear to say about his activities in the military hospital in Posen, which remain obscure to this day.

12

———

MATZKE." PERHAPS ONE reason why that long, indeed
grotesquely long phone call in November 1973 between
Dresden and London has stayed so fresh in my mind is
that for the first two or three minutes after I picked up the receiver,
which seemed to me like an eternity, I couldn't match the voice at
the other end to the caller's name.

"Matzke. Can you hear me? Is there someone else on the line?"
It was Ludwig Kaltenburg.

A London conference had been organized to mark his seventieth
birthday. Zoologists from all over the world were gathering in recognition of the life and work of their celebrated colleague. People
were only waiting for the greatest prize of all, from Stockholm. But
it is surely not wrong to see in the London conference a reaction
to the scandal that, beginning with the *Apocalypse* book, had rapidly
become a scandal surrounding the person of Ludwig Kaltenburg
himself. By this time there was also a rumor circulating to the effect that after the annexation of Austria by the Reich, the professor
had immediately applied for membership in the Party, banned till
then in Austria. There was no mention of it in the curriculum vitae
he had put together himself especially for the conference.

"Professor Doktor Eberhard Matzke. Those mudslingers. And
all the papers, even the serious ones, have reproduced this nonsense
spread by East Berlin. But do you know what I did today?"

"Went to see the ravens in the Tower?"

"That was later in the morning. Straight after breakfast I was already giving a TV interview saying once and for all what I think of these mudslingers who make me out to be a Party member. As though I didn't know what's behind it. Who started this rumor. Only Professor Doktor Matzke can be that persistent. With the camera running I said that if that's what the public wants, I can give them a cast-iron guarantee that I was never in the Nazi Party."

It was getting on for midnight, I was lying in bed reading when the telephone rang. And I've got to say I wasn't feeling particularly well disposed toward Ludwig Kaltenburg. I knew he was going to call, but I might not have got up to answer if Knut hadn't been working hard on me for some months beforehand: "I've told the professor many times that he can call on you, he knows how important he is to you, but he's shy about calling you, the attacks on him have made him quite timid." I had written back in a noncommittal manner. Knut's next letter included Kaltenburg's CV. "He's scared that even his closest friends might turn away from him, I've tried to make it clear to him that he needn't fear anything of the kind, especially from you, on the contrary." Knut knew where to put pressure on me, I felt duty-bound, perhaps less toward Kaltenburg than to him, Knut Sieverding.

"Can you hear me?"

"Sorry?"

"I'm going to prove it to them, colleague Matzke and his henchmen, give them cast-iron proof."

Kaltenburg had lied. In his CV he had reduced his stay in Posen to a few months by claiming that in the summer of 1942 he was already a prisoner of war in Russia. But it wasn't until the autumn or early winter of that year that my mother and I ran into him while out buying gloves in town. "I can give you a cast-iron guarantee"—the formulation suddenly seemed familiar to me, like a half-remembered sentence from childhood that you heard through an open door without being able to make sense of it. I lost concentration for a moment, accidentally made a noise, the tame starling was rustling in the rubber tree, I hadn't understood the question, my father was speaking too quietly. In the background, Kaltenburg was working himself up into a fury—"Party, Party, I was never a Party man"—I didn't need a Matzke to tell me that the professor was lying. "Didn't share their worldview," I heard him clamoring, my father had asked him the same question, to which we were now awaiting an answer. I heard "ugly campaign" and grasped that Kaltenburg had used the same words at that time to deny his Party membership, just as his CV was now suppressing information about our shared time in Posen, as though I were the one who was lying whenever I recalled childhood memories, as though I were just making things up.

I couldn't raise it with him. He would have given me some convoluted explanation, about how Matzke was forcing him to make some awful moves in his public life just at the moment, we would have to wait for things to quiet down, and no, of course he hadn't forgotten our earlier meetings, or his acquaintance with my highly esteemed and respected parents. I didn't want to ask Kaltenburg. But he must have noticed that his phone tirades were falling on thin air, and suddenly he was quite crestfallen.

"And I was stupid enough to help this man."

"So you were involved in the rise of Matzke after all."

"Berlin? I had nothing to do with that. Earlier, I mean, much earlier. When he was collecting birds under the most adverse conditions."

"You knew Eberhard Matzke before you came to Leipzig?"

"Oh, yes. That is, I may not have met him personally. But I gave him my support. We knew each other by name. Nineteen forty-two, it must have been."

"He was in the army then—did you make sure he could continue his ornithological studies? Like Knut Sieverding in Crete?"

"Pretty much. No. Worse. Much worse. Matzke was in the camps. A terrible time. The awful nervous strain. He complained, as you can imagine."

"He appealed to you?"

"Not then. Initially he thought he could sort things out for himself, in fact he seriously believed they would grant him an interview with the commandant. Amazing what people's minds can dream up when they're stuck in a hopeless situation. Of course, nothing came of his appointment with the commandant. But Matzke was tenacious. Who knows whether he patiently devised a different tactic or whether he bribed the right person at the right time, whether he went on bended knee to beg or whether eventually they just saw him as a weirdo—but at some point he received a special permit, complete with name, date, official stamp, everything in order, which must have looked odd when the text said something like 'This is to confirm that Eberhard Matzke may observe birds.'"

"But people always say that birds avoided the camps, there was no bird life in the camps."

"Quite right. The smoke. They couldn't stand the smoke. So he had to be able to get out of the camp. He actually got permission to leave the camp for hours at a time. The guards at the gate soon got to know the bird-watcher, they exchanged greetings, perhaps even a few words when they were checking on what Matzke had shot that day."

"He went out with a gun?"

"Of course he did. Was he supposed to catch the birds with his hands?"

"Did he have to pass them on to the kitchen?"

"I don't know. But he did prepare the most interesting specimens."

"And what happened to those?"

"As far as I recall, he once indicated that he'd managed to preserve everything he collected until the fall of 1942. Perhaps he brought the whole collection back with him to Leipzig at the end of the war."

"So he stopped collecting in the fall of 1942?"

"Stopped? Matzke? No, he's an ornithologist. He was posted."

"Posted?"

"What a struggle that was. We ornithologists on the outside wrote pleading letters, drew up petitions, racked our brains, tried everything we could—I spent sleepless nights thinking of this young man, frightened he would go crazy. But our efforts paid off in the end. Matzke was sent to some dump of a place on the Baltic."

"A dump? But there was a camp there?"

"Of course not. That was the point. His nerves were shattered when he left the camp guards. He needed to gain some distance. Matzke spent the rest of the war guarding a secret installation on the coast. In other words, he was allowed to walk up and down the beach, ample opportunity for him to observe his beloved waders. Are you still there?"

"Yes."

"Since you asked about the birds—I'm wondering now whether Matzke lost track of them in all the confusion at the end of the war. Or did he donate them to Vienna? No, sorry, I'm getting mixed up there, he described his night herons and gray-headed woodpeckers in the newsletter of the Vienna Natural History Museum. But listen, are you sure the skins aren't at your place? I seem to remember he handed them over to the Dresden collection, as a noble gesture because they had lost their holdings in the war. Why don't you have a look? You know, night herons and gray-headed woodpeckers above all, take a look at their labels."

I didn't know what to say. Kaltenburg reflected.

"Sooner or later they'll be on to Matzke."

And, after another pause: "I think it's getting light outside. A red stripe on the horizon."

"At four in the morning? Not in London."

"But that's what it feels like. If you hang on a minute, I'll go to the window and check."

"You'd do better to lie down for a bit. Try to sleep. It's going to be a long day."

And, like an echo on the line: "A long day."

Then he said, "There are the gulls."

"The Thames gulls circle all night?"

"They're perched on the windowsill outside, that's where they sleep."

After these last exchanges we hung up. I did actually stay in the room long enough to see the first glimpse of light outside the window. *In another hour the sky over London will slowly take on color too, I thought; Ludwig Kaltenburg will get up, will go over his crowded list of appointments, will see in his mind's eye the names and faces he'll meet in the course of the morning.* Next to me on the table the telephone gradually emerged from the darkness, a gray box on a diffuse gray background. It was as though I had experienced the very last time a voice would be heard through that receiver.

While a flock of geese took off very low above the gravel shoreline, I told Katharina Fischer in conclusion that I never have looked for Matzke's bird skins, and when the collection moved to Klotzsche I avoided looking too closely at our gray-headed woodpeckers and night herons.

In the distance we heard a train, on the other side of the Elbe a guard dog barked, the bell of St. Mary's-by-the-Water was ringing out from Hosterwitz, it was ten o'clock, behind the Elbe Idyll we saw the empty bus disappearing into the deep-green avenue. It was getting cool, and damp, the air was beginning to smell of grass.

VI

1

——

LATER, WHENEVER WE were all together and thinking
back to the fifties, which—since those were our formative
years—we increasingly did as we got older, Klara sat quietly,
not usually her style. When reminiscences were being exchanged,
when we were helping each other out with names, dates, places,
Klara fell silent. As we laughed, argued, interrupted each other, I
could tell it was upsetting Klara, although nobody else noticed. She
hardly seemed to be paying attention, she looked distant while all
the others were listening, each outdoing the last with ever more
precise details or more audacious stories; Klara held back, as if to
stay out of some uncomfortable business.

And that was in spite of the fact that in our circles there was no
danger that an evening might be spent conjuring up all the good
old East German products, such as Leopek cream for sting relief,
or the Fleischfrost range, or films like *Mazurka of Love*. Nobody
talked about Savings Weeks or brought up early GDR slogans like
"By the efforts of our hands" or worked in references to horses as
"oat-motors"—accompanied by a silly wink—in connection with
the rubble-clearing after the war. Klara was under no obligation to
listen to "the Dresden reconstruction lion laughing," let alone people tossing "The enemy is here among us" at her. All the same, she
couldn't stand that sort of evening.

On one occasion, at a party in the house of some slight acquaintances, Klara simply retreated into the corridor for half an hour—the height of bad manners, in her own eyes—in order to escape from a conversation about the seventeenth of June 1953. With the best will in the world, she said later, she simply couldn't bring herself to go back into the room until the last guest had offloaded his memories of that date. She had stood the whole time within earshot, a few steps away from the door, slightly bemused, with her back to a bookcase, feeling a physical reluctance to breathe the memory-laden air in the drawing room.

Somebody recounted how he was just leaving the bakery on the Wasaplatz when he ran into a column of demonstrators coming from Niedersedlitz and stayed with them all the way to the city center, still clutching his bag of bread rolls; another claimed to have marched alongside the strike leader, Grothaus, while a third had memorized a speech to the strikers and recited whole passages from it. As one picture after another emerged, the event became more distinct in the minds of the participants, finally they could all remember meeting in the crowded Postplatz at midday. A moment of silence followed as each of them mentally reviewed the events, and Klara reappeared in the doorway. Nobody had noticed her leaving the room, nobody had missed her.

On the way home—the gathering had broken up soon afterward—I couldn't coax much more out of Klara than that she simply couldn't stand these stories, the poses the narrators struck, as if their memories could help them get a grip, whereas in reality, looking back could only be profoundly disturbing for us, make our present life fall apart.

"We've all got our nightmares, I don't need to be told that," she declared, as if to close the subject, and "We all made mistakes, every one of us, and I certainly don't exclude myself."

As soon as it was evident that the evening was going to descend into reminiscing, Klara would find some pretext for leaving without embarrassing her hosts: exhaustion after a full day, the long trip home, a cold coming on. If she felt too weak to come up with a suitable excuse, she signaled to me that we ought to be going, and I thought of something, citing an excursion, the need to be up before dawn for bird-watching; that was always an unobtrusive way to extract ourselves from the occasion.

If there was no way out, if Klara was asked point-blank what events she particularly associated with the fifties, she categorically insisted that she couldn't remember anything about that time except that the complete German translation of Proust had appeared. She sounded tired when she said it, not a trace of her pert manner, not a spark of provocation: "Just the Proust, nothing else."

Nonetheless, the first time she said it she surprised me as much as the others in the group: despite the lack of sparkle in her eyes, I couldn't tell whether she was joking. A dry, wicked, dark joke, since I knew what memories were associated with the fifties for Klara, for Klara and me.

If anyone failed to grasp that the conversation was repugnant to her, Klara would describe to them in detail how the volumes with their sand-colored covers had reached her hands one by one. This one she had acquired on a visit to West Berlin, that one was lying on the table in the morning on her birthday, two others had emerged from a parcel Klara had thought contained tinned sausages. "The Proust," that was her memory of the fifties, Klara only ever talked about "the Proust," for her there was no *Captive*, no *Fugitive*, and no *Time Regained*.

In case the company was not satisfied with this, she went so far as to state that above all it was the famous scene where the narrator washes his hands that had driven her on to read all of Proust, in fact it was the first detailed hand-washing scene in the novel that had initially given her access to this epoch-making work. The lukewarm water in the enamel bowl, whose temperature is checked once more by the grandmother — or is it the maid? — before the narrator is permitted to dip his delicate, waxlike fingers into it, the fragrance of the soap, the lather, the right hand embracing the left, and all the while the boy's long, wondering look out of the window, before he's called to the table.

The conversation was moving toward the period following Stalin's death, the secret speech, on to the doctors' plot, back to Slánský, and Klara recoiled, it wouldn't be long before they were looking to her to contribute a remark. She could feel their eyes resting on her, felt the challenge to initiate a diversionary maneuver, listened carefully until she found a key word, the right key word—afterward, nobody could have said how she managed to change the subject so elegantly.

After the first great hand-washing scene, Klara said, she had waited expectantly for any little scene featuring this everyday occurrence, however slight the reference, subordinate clauses, minor characters, one of those innumerable soirées, somebody leaving the company briefly to wash their hands—perhaps the whole secret of Proust lay in such fleeting moments, which the reader had to fill out for himself if he wanted to absorb them. Why, for example, Klara asked, does the painter, receiving an unexpected visit from the narrator, clean his hands with spit rather than turpentine before greeting his guest?

And what lies behind that scene where, after an evening in company, Swann leads Odette out to his coach to take a nocturnal drive through Paris—why is the coachman not on the spot at this moment, why don't we see him dutifully jumping down from his box to open the carriage door as soon as Swann and Odette appear in the street? There he is popping up behind the horses, embarrassed, muttering, his master doesn't even deign to glance at him, so the coachman redoubles his efforts to look keen. But Odette and Swann have eyes only for each other, the coachman keeps his hands hidden behind his back, once the pair have got in he acts as though he's reluctant to touch the door handle, and we, the readers, are the only ones to notice that in this scene Swann's coachman—for whatever reason—isn't wearing gloves when he shuts the carriage door from the outside. What was it that he put forward by way of excuse, we ask ourselves, wasn't it something about "opportunity to wash," didn't he say "quickly" and "unfortunately" and "unsuccessfully"?

Wasn't it in this connection that a formulation had occurred that caused Klara to stumble, something like "just a bit of dirtiness," hadn't Swann's coachman muttered "just a bit of dirtiness," a phrase that must sound odd to any reader? Was Proust using servant language here, was he descending into a kind of argot? No, it seemed too mannered for that—so perhaps it was just a not very felicitous point in the translation? Nobody had an answer for Klara.

People recalled anxious nights by the radio, tanks in Budapest and grotesquely twisted bodies lying on the torn-up pavements, which handed Klara a key word, enabling her to avoid the question of whether she too—yes, we had—spent sleepless nights sitting by the radio. From the pavements of Budapest—or was it Prague?—she moved effortlessly on within a few sentences to the uneven pavement over which Proust's narrator once stumbled on his way to a reception. Wasn't he thinking at that very moment about when he'd last washed his hands, and whether he shouldn't take the precaution of visiting a toilet before meeting his hostess? A moment in the balance, with quiet restraint ushering in one of those lengthy reflections which leave our hero standing as though frozen in the flux of events, when he almost trips on a paving stone. His hands, his feet, his attention takes a leap, one kind of irritation overlays another, and soon we too are stumbling, straight into the famous description of an unbidden memory.

The talk now dwelled on events nearer home, the demolition of the ruins in Rampische Strasse in 1956, Professor Manfred von Ardenne and the Dresden Club he founded in spring 1957, later known as the Intelligentsia Club—Klara countered by recalling that brief moment, tucked away in an interpolated sentence, where you get the impression that, as if by a prearranged signal, just for two or three seconds the group of young ladies on the beach at Balbec bend down, with their backs to the promenade, to the viewer, as though—unseemly behavior in public—to feel seawater flowing over their hands for once in their lives. Everything is happening at a great distance, the gentle waves, spray, the salty smell, taste, the faint odor of starfish and marine life. Wishing to confirm this sight, you look down again at the receding waves, but the girls have already resumed their afternoon walk, as if nothing had happened. You can't even be sure the narrator observed the incident, so you're left alone with the question of how four such refined young ladies could simultaneously, no, how they could get their hands dirty in the first place, perhaps the sand, sticky sweets, perhaps they have been touching the skin of girls, of boys.

Klara could be sure that after such a description her listeners would follow her willingly, and so she went on to talk about the strange passage in Proust where the narrator secretly watches a stranger washing his hands. The scene takes place during the First World War, one of the few set in Paris during this period, at any minute the sirens could sound the alarm, there might be another air raid, but the narrator goes on lurking, peering through a half-open window into an unlit room on the other side of the courtyard, perhaps into a corridor, where a young man in a singlet appears, letting a door close behind him and yielding to the urge to hold his hands under the nearest tap. A rough stone sink, the kind normally used only for filling cleaning buckets, no hand towel, no soap, but the man in the undershirt clearly can't wait until he has found a toilet.

"There's something obscene about it," Klara maintained, after yet another evening of anecdotes about their youth. "I can't bear it. Something obscene, and something desperate as well, this dogged determination dressed up as chat, as though by talking about the old days you can make yourself innocent."

Klara couldn't stand the gravity of these tales, that's the only way I could explain it to myself. This gravity which gradually disappears the longer a story is turned this way and that, the more details are brought to light, so that in the end a whole quite funny complex of happenings seems to lie behind every tragic event. But because I know how she looks when she sits brooding for days on end at the kitchen table, Klara never needed to explain to me why she escaped into talking about her Proust wherever possible.

2

―――――

HAVE YOU HEARD the news?" Four months had elapsed
since our chance meeting by Bird Island, we hadn't spoken to each other in the meantime, when to my surprise I
heard the interpreter's voice on the telephone that afternoon, near
and yet unfamiliar. After announcing herself with her full name,
she immediately went on to talk about the news, which had just
that minute ended with the weather forecast: "Did you know? Your
friend Knut Sieverding has died. On Friday. His family announced
his death today."

My instant reaction was a great sadness that in the intervening
years I'd had only sporadic contact with Knut, we had kept in touch
for the most part only by exchanging Christmas cards, after main-
taining a lively correspondence until the end of the eighties, and often visiting each other once the border was open. Now I didn't even
know whether he had died suddenly or after a long, difficult illness,
and Katharina Fischer couldn't enlighten me either.

Klara and I at the Sieverdings in southern Germany, we were
coming back from Vienna, I had been to see Ludwig Kaltenburg's
house, where jackdaws were nesting in the chimney, two years after
the professor's death. The birds approached me as trustingly as if
they were distant relatives of the Dresden flock. I bolted. We took
the next train to Munich. Knut met us at the station. On one of the
mild spring evenings that followed, as we sat on the terrace late into

the night, I was strangely moved by a photograph showing Knut and the professor on the occasion of an awards ceremony. The diploma is on display, floating in midair against the dark background, the two men are looking at each other and laughing. And yet the viewer is held by a gaze, the fixed stare of a gorilla that appeared to be thrusting itself into the foreground between the two portrait sitters. A stuffed ape, with glass eyes and open jaws, the dark coat, the shine around its nostrils—it makes you think that a memory of Knut Sieverding's year in the Congo, now in the distant past, had materialized as the negative was being developed.

Knut and I in the Lausitz brown-coal area, Knut and I on the former border strip—but while I was telling the interpreter about our last excursions, a thought was hammering away in my head: "You know nothing about Knut Sieverding in later years, there's a gap of nearly fifteen years." I asked Frau Fischer whether she was busy that afternoon, if she'd like to come over for coffee. Then I phoned Klara, who was spending the weekend with friends in Berlin, and told her the news.

In the following two hours I paced up and down the kitchen, fed the sparrows, the titmice, looked out the window at the oak that was shedding ever more leaves, cleared up the desk in my study, couldn't get it sorted out, let my distracted glance range over the books. Proust had been standing here in the bookcase for almost half a century without my ever touching him. Actually, sometimes when Klara was away I had carefully picked out one of the volumes, opened it, and read a few pages, hurriedly, keeping an ear open as if indulging in a forbidden pleasure, as if I had broken through a protective cordon thrown around the shelf reserved for Proust. I felt like an interloper, I was spying on Klara when I opened at a page that had a bookmark in it, and when I read a passage she had underlined or put an exclamation mark by, I was reading something that was none of my business.

Perhaps Klara would have liked me to read the book, to join in with her enthusiasm for Proust, which had been there since we first met. But to me the novel seemed sacrosanct, Proust was entirely

Klara's thing, and it never occurred to me to read him in order to share him with her. Perhaps that was a mistake. But maybe it was enough for her that when she made certain remarks—half to herself, half to me—while reading passages in the early volumes that I believed I could tell who she was reminded of, who she saw sitting in her parents' drawing room, who was exchanging a few words in English by the hall stand—people I myself had got to know at the Hagemanns' but knew even better from Klara's stories.

Likewise, watching her reading, over time I thought that I could tell which incidents from our life together were passing through her mind's eye, inevitably and even against Klara's will when—on holidays, perhaps, or in the short days around the turn of the year—she took the Proust volumes down from their shelf, determined to lose herself in the prose. At such moments, when Klara glanced up from the flow of printed lines, distraught, as if a dangerous insect had distracted her, I vanished as well, I was no longer sitting opposite her at the kitchen table, no longer lying next to her on the beach, but saw myself, without having read more than a few sentences of Proust, being taken back to scenes both of us would prefer to have forgotten long ago.

So it was that I found myself sitting once more, wedged between Klara and Knut at a pub table, in a noisy, smoke-filled hostelry, opposite us Martin and Ulrike, who for some time had no longer wished to be called Ulli. Was it the same day that Knut, after weeks of fevered work, had put the last touches to his Congo commentary and read the text out to us after lunch at the Institute? We hoped to persuade the professor to go with us into town that evening, but he declined: "That's not a pub, not a cozy tavern you're trying to lure me into, it's a dive." He just wouldn't listen. "You go, all you young people," he said, laughing. "You know I'm an old man." Was that the last time Ludwig Kaltenburg and Martin parted on friendly terms? It's possible that my memory has seamlessly fused together a whole series of scenes that are separated by many months or even years, it's possible that the very act of remembering precludes leaving any breathing spaces, and memory only conforms to reality where there is no chance of evading scenes of bewilderment and helplessness.

Klara talked about the young Soviet soldiers in the square that she could see every day from her place in the library. Sometimes one of them would wave when sweeping the parade ground, mending a machine, or standing by the garages and shuffling from one foot to the other, as though, by way of punishment, this child with the pale, narrow face had been banished to the furthest point of the barrack square. But Knut and Martin were feeling too high-spirited to follow such reflections, and all Ulrike could think of saying was, "Let's not talk about work, please, not today."

"You're right." Klara shook her head and smiled at her sister. She turned to Knut: "In your film, will you be telling the story about how the aardvark tricked you?"

Her hand felt for mine under the table. It was as though she could foresee that this evening was not going to end well.

At some point a couple we didn't know joined us at our table, with an apologetic gesture, there were no other seats free. They were our age, the woman was wearing a pale-colored suit, not particularly well cut, the man a washed-out shirt and a carelessly knotted, prewar tie. Two people, you think, who had lost their way in the dark and come in here at random, at any rate it didn't look as though they got out much. When a glass of beer was placed in front of them, they were startled. When there was a racket over by the bar, they turned around timidly and followed with widening eyes the two rough types who had just agreed to go outside to "discuss the matter further," as they say in these parts, meaning a fistfight.

They were no less amazed to hear us talking about tree pangolins and rhinoceros birds, they must have thought these were fictional animals, and for them the story of Knut turning up unshaven and unwashed after weeks in the tropical rainforest and walking into the lobby of a luxury hotel must have taken place in a part of the world not yet marked on the atlas.

"I know that man," muttered Klara next to me. Knut had finally turned to the strangers, no, they didn't usually go to the cinema to see wildlife films, no, they didn't know what an okapi was, the man asked politely whether he could stand us a drink, and Klara thought, *I know that man from somewhere.*

Nobody could hear her but me, not Martin, not Ulrike, not the strangers, but just as Knut was about to embark on another anecdote about the Congo, she broke in.

"Excuse me, but didn't you play the part of a prisoner?"

"A prisoner?"

"Yes, you were there on the truck in the jubilee parade, I remember clearly. As a camp inmate."

"I didn't play a camp inmate."

"Now you're lying."

Klara hardly raised her voice, her tone was not accusing, more disappointed, the man was reading Klara's lips, and then I remembered too, there was a rather plump young man that we noticed at the time, he didn't dare raise his arm because his jacket was stretched too tight across his shoulders, while the other characters' prison garb hung loosely about their frames. Yes, I recognized the well-nourished camp inmate, he tried to vindicate himself, said something about "allocated," he said "duty," as if he wanted to avoid the term "compulsion."

"Hermann, I want to leave."

All at once she was exhausted. There were some things, she said, that simply weren't right, it didn't take courage, all you needed was a bit of backbone, and anyway he knew himself how many jubilee participants failed to present themselves at the assembly point, even though they had been told it was their duty to do so. No, I heard him saying, he really wasn't brave, we were already on our way out, Knut was chasing after us, "Klara, just hang on," then we stood in the summer night on the pavement, the strangers, Ulrike, Martin, with Knut trying to mediate between the two of them. The man couldn't take in what had happened. "No, I've never been brave," he repeated, it was the first time I'd heard anyone say such a thing. Klara nodded distractedly, put a hand out, apologized. But for what? She herself had no idea.

On the way home she apologized again, she had ruined everybody's evening, Knut reassured her, "It's okay, really," Martin shrugged his shoulders, "It can happen to anybody," the two of them consulted, maybe we could drive out for a picnic in the country the following weekend.

I don't think we actually went on that outing, at least I have no mental picture of the five of us rambling through "Saxon Switzerland," each with a rucksack on our back. Perhaps Klara or perhaps Ulrike was not very keen on the idea, yes, I reflected as I heard the doorbell ring, perhaps it was the same evening when, after a long silence, Ulrike turned to Klara, as though the moment had come at last to address a sentence to her sister that had been going around in her head for many years: "I don't understand you anymore."

There was another ring, and only then did I grasp that the interpreter was waiting at the door. I heard somebody take a deep breath to free himself from the net of images, I left Martin standing there on the pavement as well as Knut, who was looking at the two sisters with a troubled expression, and lost sight of Ulrike too, just as we literally lost sight of her at some point, when she turned away from her family and started a new life with her husband in the north, without spelling out her motives for taking this step, either to her parents or to Klara. It may be that she wanted to move out from Klara's shadow, or maybe she simply realized one day that the time when she and her sister played together on the swing doors in their nightdresses lay far back in the past.

3

———

I TOOK KATHARINA FISCHER'S coat, showed her the living room, the kitchen, the view out onto the street, the view over the garden, led her along the book-lined hall to my study. On the desk I had placed a small, well-thumbed book, the cover had a design of white feathers with sand-colored, brown, and blue stripes, from the top edge a stain ran down as far as the title—a cocoa spill? I don't remember. Colored plates showing native songbirds and their nests, I opened the cover and let Frau Fischer read the inscription: "A book about your small friends, from your parents Christmas 1937."

She spent a long time studying the illustrations of egg clutches, twigs and wool interlaced, moss, drawn with a fine feel for the play of light and shade, creating an almost three-dimensional effect. I helped her to decipher the names written in old German script, "The Bullfinch," "The Goldfinch," "The Siskin," "The Yellow-hammer," "The Chaffinch," all perched there on twigs by their nests looking as though they had just preened themselves carefully, as though they had inspected every single feather on their bodies and rearranged each one especially before posing for the drawing. Whether the effect was what the illustrator intended or was the result of the uniform darkening of the paper, the interpreter remarked that all the birds struck her as being both alert and shy; she was particularly impressed by the blackbird, poised over the open nest with feathers slightly spread and tail fanned out, as though it had spotted the observer at that precise moment.

We talked about the relationship between the phases in which blackbirds are seen and heard everywhere and those during which they lead a secret life, we talked about diurnal and nocturnal animals, trust and timidity. About how one of the great tits here on the balcony, having turned up one afternoon in early August and without hesitation landed on my outstretched hand to take the proffered sunflower seed, had declined to accept any more feed for the last few days. The way that, from the edge of the balcony, as if it felt sorry, as if it were as surprised by its own fear as I was, it eyed this person who had suddenly become a stranger to it. If I hadn't known that great tits become tame again in the spells of freezing cold weather, then perhaps this familiar young bird might have struck me as weird.

"And you really haven't ever found out how Ludwig Kaltenburg's jackdaws died?"

As a matter of fact this question came up early on in the conversation, in fact with her very first words of greeting the interpreter started to draw me—or actually both of us—into an inquiry. Although initially it wasn't about the jackdaws at all. When I brought the coffee back to the study, where Frau Fischer had settled down on the couch that was once part of the inventory of the Loschwitz Institute villa, she inquired again about Knut, about Martin, about the period of silence between Kaltenburg and me.

In those six or eight years during which I never wrote the professor a single line, never telephoned him, would have done anything in the world to avoid meeting him—to do so would have been impossible anyway—it was Knut Sieverding who regularly supplied me with news of Ludwig Kaltenburg. The duck colony at the new zoological station had now grown to about four hundred birds. The research projects were dragging on. Environmental protection was becoming more and more central to his activities, big photos in all the papers, the previous day the professor had even appeared on the TV news because he had taken part in a sit-down blockade, old Ludwig Kaltenburg with a beaming face in the midst of young eco-activists, his attitude to the power of the state as stubborn as ever. Appearances. Speeches. Interviews. Once again the professor had used the opportunity to demonstrate his negotiating skills by extracting from the Austrian federal chancellor, in a personal discussion, a promise to help save the Danube water meadows. Knut once sent a postcard from Madagascar: "I can't help thinking what it would be like if you and the professor could be here to admire the amazing diversity of wildlife with me."

And one day, as I was engrossed in studying our gray-headed goldfinches, Martin Spengler suddenly turned up on the doorstep as if from nowhere, leaned across the table, and said, "Reminds me of a piece I was once planning for Venice."

That must have been in 1980. Martin, who was already world-famous by that time, bowed and introduced himself with a strange, Dutch-sounding name. He had come from Amsterdam, the sole male participant in a tourist group which, after an intensive sight-seeing itinerary, was now enjoying a coffee break, allowing Martin ostensibly to take a stroll along the Elbe while actually visiting me in the Ornithological Collection. He wanted to see everything, every drawer containing skins, the nests, the mounts, wanted to meet my colleagues, was astonished by the pigeon's nest behind the toilet, admired the snapping turtles in their aquarium in the corridor. Nothing was beneath his notice, no detail was lost on him, the tinned milk, the chipped Meissen cups, the coating of a tabletop, the curtain at a little window overlooking the courtyard, the smell in the stairwell—Martin soaked up these impressions as if it were high time he revised his idea of art.

Just as it's difficult to identify a bird when you see it in surroundings where you wouldn't expect it, so it didn't occur to any of my colleagues, nor to his traveling companions, nor to the tour guide, nor to the border officials, to suspect that the old friend unexpectedly calling on me was the famous Martin Spengler, although his clothes, his figure, and his posture differed in no way from his usual appearance. He hadn't even bothered to disguise himself by growing a beard or wearing glasses, he knew he could get by perfectly well as an art-minded tourist among other art-minded tourists.

The art historians, on the other hand, wonder to this day why Martin Spengler's late work bears so many obvious traces of local life in this area. Noting the dull, earthy, and industrial colors, the biological references, the worn but almost lovingly assembled functional objects of his later installations, they have interpreted them as imaginary extensions of 1950s perceptions into the present, but so far nobody has thought of looking at the register of the Dresden Interhotel, the Newa, for a supposed Dutchman signing in under a pseudonym.

He stayed for about two hours, which seemed like a whole long day to me, we said not a word about complicated travel arrangements or nerve-racking border checks, not a word about the worrying condition of the building, the ruins around us, or the miserable appearance of the city in general. We were completely wrapped up in the world of the collection's holdings, every drawer revealed new natural marvels, the blue jays, the shore larks, the blood-red, white-spotted parts of the strawberry finches, and under Martin's thorough scrutiny, alert to every shade of gray and brown, even the close-packed rows of house sparrows, whose live counterparts were regarding us from the windowsill, radiated a glow that few people ever notice.

"These faces—every sparrow here has an individual face," cried Martin, he exclaimed, "What I'd really like to do is take the whole case and set it up in a gallery."

It was also thanks to Martin that I started writing to Ludwig Kaltenburg again. When I showed Martin the great auk among the exhibits recently returned from the Soviet Union, he stood speechless before the bird, reverent, overwhelmed, stunned, torn this way and that between the different eras. Finally he stepped up closer, viewing the great auk from all sides, stammering, "He must have been pleased," and again, respectfully, "It must have given him enormous pleasure to hear about this," and although I knew what he meant, I wasn't quite sure whether his respectful tone related to the great auk or to Professor Kaltenburg.

That same evening I took an envelope, addressed it to Professor Ludwig Kaltenburg, Vienna, Austria, and placed in it a carefully folded sheet of paper on which I had written nothing but "The great auks are back."

I was glad at the time I had taken this step, and I'm even gladder now. Otherwise I would never have heard about the doubts the professor had to struggle with in his final years, nor about the worries he probably did not care to divulge to anyone around him. Many things never went beyond the letters, letters to a very distant country, letters to somebody who had never become a disciple of the great Ludwig Kaltenburg.

"I'm sure you'll let me have a detailed description soon," he replied. "Meanwhile, it's reassuring to hear that all the exhibits are clearly back in place, insofar as they survived the war unscathed, and weren't scattered all over the landscape by disappointed looters in the first days of peace. And don't ask me how I am. You know I'll always make an effort to appear cheerful for your sake."

I respected his wish, and so it was only through incidental remarks in the course of our correspondence that I managed to piece together some idea of the professor's physical condition. For example, when I asked him whether he still loved to spend his days in the open air as he had always done, he wrote back that those long walks in the country, where his animals had always kept him company, were now a thing of the past for good and all. For more than two years he had been confined to a wheelchair and mostly stayed indoors, or in the garden if the weather was fine. The less mobile you were, the more sensitive you became to the temperature. Storms, rain, and blizzards—he saw them now only from the terrace window.

"I have started getting rid of old documents," he wrote, "but don't worry, I have no intention of discarding incriminating material, as you might assume, what matters to me is completing my public break with ideas which I supported for many years without being aware of the madness that underlay them.

"Everybody wants to protect me," he wrote. "But when I listen to my protectors it often gives me the creeps, as though I were surrounded by people who doggedly insist there's no conclusive proof of evolution. Even the noise, the noise they create, you know, that's a betrayal in itself."

My father had always been wonderful to argue with, wrote Kaltenburg, without my raising the subject. "Your father was never a National Socialist—any more than I was—he had no connection with those people and refused to have any truck with them. Hence the misunderstanding, our quarrel, if you like, when I joined the Party without sharing its convictions. No, I certainly never appeared at your place wearing a Party button in my lapel, your parents would have shunned me a lot sooner if I had. It's always puzzled me how he eventually found out. Somebody must have reported it to him, some malicious person to whom our friendship was a thorn in the side. He had a hard time with his university colleagues, in fact he once confided to me that he was afraid they would stop at nothing to get rid of him."

When I cautiously followed this up with a question, he responded, "Your parents were deliberately frozen out. I was very sharply attacked at the time for persisting in visiting you. As a small boy you won't have noticed the depressed mood in your family. Your house seemed desolate, and I almost think that was why your parents acquired their first birds. Yes, they did it for you, though not for the reason you've always assumed. No, an atmosphere of death—I wouldn't call it that today."

Certainly, he wrote in a letter at Christmas 1988, sooner or later, like him, I would become aware that at an early point in my life, almost too early to identify, I had involuntarily begun to discriminate in terms of human and animal encounters. "Your early confrontation with a bird, for example, in whose company you spent an afternoon in your drawing room, will be strictly separated in your memory from the following events, the entry of your nanny or your parents on the scene." Every zoologist, maintained Kaltenburg, had a similar story to tell. True, our mentors also stood out in our mind's eye, the figures under whose direction we channeled and refined our animal observations, but such a mentor came into the picture only as a secondary step, when his attention was attracted by a young person absorbed in the world of animals.

Perhaps you could even say that at first every child makes a sharp distinction, animals here, human beings there, two worlds that are interwoven in a mysterious way that the child hardly recognizes as yet, as though there were openings somewhere through which you could slip from one to the other. Except that most people, especially those who confuse retrospective self-observation with the transfiguration of their own youth, can later not remember the time when they regarded people and animals equally with a mixture of curiosity and anxiety, as though it was very far from decided in which of the two spheres you would eventually make your own life.

You could even observe this phenomenon in animals, Ludwig Kaltenburg had discovered: "The jackdaw which courts its human friend at lunchtime, trying to stuff mealworm mash into his ears, and then flies off with its friends, the hooded crows."

I had expected Kaltenburg to return to the subject of his Dresden jackdaw colony, I knew it preoccupied him as much as ever, I heard from the people around him that he brought it up more and more often, but it was never mentioned in his letters to me. When he did describe to me the distinctive behavior of his favorite jackdaw, Taschotschek, for me it was a sign: the professor did not have long to live.

4

D ID THEY EVER find out how the professor's jackdaws
were poisoned?" she asked at this point. "And by whom?"
Not for certain. There's been plenty of speculation over
the years, of course, there have been suspects—Eberhard Matzke,
no less, personally ordered them to be killed, so thought the professor when he was already in the West and wanted to believe in a
conspiracy aimed at getting rid not just of Reinhold but of him too.
In his less dark hours he was inclined to see it as a mere oversight:
stupidly, his jackdaw flock had fallen victim to an illegal pest-control operation carried out by some collective farm organization.

"Is it difficult to poison a jackdaw, then?"

Not at all, and it's happening all the time. The odd bird had already unaccountably disappeared in previous years, after all. In the
nineteenth century the farmers put out poisoned voles to deal with
the crow problem, the corvids were regarded as nothing but pests,
and jackdaws mingling with the great flocks of foraging crows were
affected too. In Kaltenburg's day, when bird poisoning was on the
increase again, there's no doubt they had begun large-scale experi-
mentation in secret to develop plant protection through poisoned
grain crops.

"Poisoned grain?"

Grain that had been contaminated with an agent called Hora. At
the end of October 1964, for example, it was openly planted near

Fürstenwalde along with drilled winter wheat. Right up until the following March dead birds were being collected from the area, though in fact very few of them were jackdaws or crows. The majority, over a hundred specimens, were skylarks that had no doubt been looking for food in the fields as the thaw began.

"Large-scale anti-crow measures—sounds terrible." Katharina Fischer shook her head. "And surely that sort of thing was prohibited?"

It might never have been discovered if ornithologists on their routine rounds had not come across an unusually high number of dead birds. Late in February 1984, at a crow roosting place by the former gravel pit near Ichtershausen, forty-five jackdaws and eighty-five rooks were found. Subsequent investigations showed that the Rudisleben plant production collective had illegally soaked wheat and corn in the plant protectant Dimethoate and scattered the grain across the freshly plowed fields, which eventually led to the death of over a thousand birds.

"So poisoning operations took place mainly in winter?"

Yes.

"And yet according to your account, Kaltenburg's jackdaws died in late summer?"

That's true. And at that time of year you don't see massive raids by crows. What always matters is protecting the winter sowing.

"Therefore, if I've got it right, we can't be looking at either plant protectants or any other way of treating grain? Perhaps you've got to approach the question from a different angle altogether, and consider who had close contact with Kaltenburg's jackdaws."

Too many to allow the circle to be gradually narrowed down. Countless people. Workers at the Institute. Visitors. Neighbors. And strangers never seen by anybody but the jackdaws themselves.

"Is it conceivable that the jackdaws were poisoned by a stranger?"

It's possible they were. Jackdaws are pretty inquisitive birds, after all, willing to engage with new people and new situations—but I'm not quite convinced. I'm assuming that Ludwig Kaltenburg's jackdaws were duped by somebody who was around them every day.

"So we can rule out Eberhard Matzke, then."

333

After all that man has hatched up, I'd be the last person to want to defend him. But by that point he had long since achieved all his aims; he had cut Reinhold out and had succeeded in deeply humiliating Kaltenburg as well by harshly rejecting the peace offer from Dresden, that is to say, by behaving as though the offer never existed. When I think what care Ludwig Kaltenburg took over planning for the peace negotiations, how important he thought it was to consider every possible reaction on Matzke's part. In fact he didn't even want to divulge precisely what his offer consisted of, he thought it essential that nobody should know the substance of the forthcoming talks, this was a matter between him and Eberhard Matzke above all. No doubt he still had Knut's objections ringing in his ears when he decided not to go to Berlin himself—but none of his precautions did any good in the end.

He handed me a pile of documents. "Krause will drive you, and he's going to drop you off at the Tierpark, all right? I promised to send over a bundle of papers, that's this large envelope here, don't get it mixed up with the smaller envelope you're going to give to colleague Matzke in the afternoon. You know everybody there at the zoo, go straight to the boss, I've told them you're coming, pass on our greetings, get the business over as quickly as possible without seeming impolite. Then make your own way to the Invalidenstrasse. Don't worry about Krause lurking around, he won't wait for you—when we're in Berlin he always goes to see his sister, he gets well fed there and he can shoot his mouth off about how he's treated in Dresden. He'll pick you up again at the Tierpark at five o'clock on the dot."

There's nothing to report about my appointment with Eberhard Matzke. He didn't even offer me a seat. He laid the envelope aside without thanking me. He just muttered, "Funk, Funk—and you say I supervised your microscope work?" as though he couldn't remember a thing. I was idiotic enough to mention his bike, his cardigan, Martin Spengler in the practical lab, I wanted to smooth the path for him, and all the while I had no idea that I was looking into the face of an SS man.

I spent only about ten minutes in his office, and I still recall how surprised I was not to run into any of the museum assistants, either in the corridor or on the stairs. When Kaltenburg's limousine arrived at the Tierpark, I had been walking up and down the path for more than an hour. Krause switched the heater on.

"Did he quiz you?" the interpreter wanted to know.

He wouldn't have been Krause if he hadn't. But you had to get used to his way of questioning. He dispensed with question marks. We chatted about the weather: "Yes, it gets pretty cool after sunset," he nodded, offered me a cigarette, an S-Bahn train passed by, I sat at the back of the limousine and let myself be driven to Dresden. We discussed Kaltenburg's attitude to vodka, vodka was always said to harden you against the cold, but the professor was strictly opposed to the usual practice of giving zoo animals alcohol with their drinking water in winter. "I reckon he's right there," said Krause, glancing at the rear mirror, "Think of that nasty business last year," after drinking several bottles of vodka an elephant in the Moscow zoo had torn a radiator from the wall and turned on its keeper.

Thanks to Kaltenburg's careful planning I was well prepared for this bait. I praised Krause's driving, remarked yet again how well the heating worked in the car, and asked him a personal question: which did he prefer, vodka or mulled wine? "Mulled wine, the way my wife makes it," he answered promptly—and that was the end of a cunningly contrived attempt to find out something about what he thought had been my stay of several hours in the Tierpark.

We tore along in the outside lane of the dark autobahn. "Pull yourself together," I said to myself. "Don't tell him anything about Kaltenburg, don't tell him anything about your visit to Matzke." Then it went quiet. Krause was concentrating on the road, nothing out there but night, I was feeling drowsy.

"Did you drop off to sleep?" asked Frau Fischer. "Not a bad way of avoiding the chauffeur's probing."

Perhaps I actually did fall asleep. No more steady hum from the engine, no rumbling as we drove over the joints between the slabs in the road. I heard Ludwig Kaltenburg's jackdaws calling quietly. I sat stretched out on the back seat, my hands resting on the upholstery, I blinked up at the roof of the car and heard in turn the various gradations of jackdaw calls, depending on whether the birds were in a mood to fly off or felt the urge to head homeward. I opened my eyes again and looked out at the landscape. There was no landscape. The jackdaws went on calling. I looked around in the car, the rear shelf, the floor beneath my feet, the armrests, then somebody said, "Mating calls are really quite easy to imitate."

Krause was making jackdaw noises. Or was it the professor I was hearing? Yes, the chauffeur wasn't so much imitating jackdaws as imitating Ludwig Kaltenburg's jackdaw calls. In the rear mirror I saw Krause nodding. He was obviously pleased to be able to continue our conversation over the last fifty kilometers. Of course you could sometimes see when the professor was worried or a particular person was bothering him—he, Krause, could tell that not from his expression, nor from any bad-tempered tone of voice, but simply from the fact that the professor was spending even more time with his fish than usual. He had never in his life met anyone like Professor Kaltenburg, although he had got to know quite a few famous zoologists over the years. He started listing names, I could see who he was going to name next—so far he had never yet seen Professor Doktor Eberhard Matzke in Loschwitz. "Follow Kaltenburg's example and wear a neutral expression," I said to myself. "Pull yourself together, for goodness' sake, you've got to distract him, do what Ludwig Kaltenburg does, talk about animals."

I told Krause about the jackdaws. But this may have been exactly the wrong move.

"And now you're asking yourself whether that was the wrong move," said Katharina Fischer at the same moment that the thought occurred to me.

It was possible that I had put an idea into his head.

"Even if we assume that this man was responsible for poisoning the jackdaws, people like that arrive at such notions sooner or later without any outside help, and you shouldn't reproach yourself," the interpreter protested. "Whether he was just nursing the desire for revenge because he thought Kaltenburg despised him, or whether he was brooding over his reports, disappointed that the professor wouldn't indulge in any disparaging remarks about the regime or

336

the closing of the border which Krause could have passed on to curry favor for himself—seen in a sober light," she declared, "that has nothing to do with you."

It was to keep Krause at a distance that I told him about the jackdaws. "Yes, they love cherries," he said, "I know that."

Even better: redcurrants.

"Really?"

Hadn't he ever watched that game involving the little shed butting onto the villa, a game whose attractions nobody could quite make out but which seemed to give Kaltenburg as much pleasure as it gave his jackdaws? "I must admit, I don't often go there, that raven is always hanging about." But the raven wasn't interested in slipping into the shed. The jackdaws, by contrast, were always intensely curious about what might be hidden in this lean-to. But Ludwig Kaltenburg couldn't bear to see them coming out disappointed each time because there was nothing new for them to find, so several times a day around harvest time he hid redcurrants among the clutter.

I can't remember now, did Krause seem surprised, or did he make out that it was coming back to him that he himself had once observed this odd form of bonding between man and bird? We would have talked at some length about other things; for example, Krause was far more interested, or so it seemed to me at the time, in the function of the yellow spot that magpies have on their third eyelid than in the question of currants, black or red. In any case, as far as the chauffeur was concerned, what the professor did with his animals in order to study their behavior was totally suspect, and the goings-on at the tool shed must simply have confirmed his opinion. Nonetheless, talking to Katharina Fischer now, it was above all this particular story about the jackdaws that sprang to mind.

I was tired when Krause dropped me off at home, and I was—I admit—just a little proud: not a syllable about Matzke and the peace offer. Kaltenburg was waiting with Klara in the kitchen, as we had arranged—in Loschwitz, they might have wondered what was so important about my trip to Berlin that it kept us talking late into the night. Unfortunately, I didn't have much to tell Kaltenburg. It's possible that at the time I was still convinced matters would come out right in the end, but I think Klara could see that my meeting with Eberhard Matzke had not exactly turned out well. The professor enjoyed his dinner, he said, "Difficult, difficult," and "We shall see," looking at me across the table with a look that you reserve for an ally. There was no mention of the jackdaws that evening, or redcurrants, or least of all Kaltenburg's driver.

5

———

FINALLY, ON THE WAY to collect her coat, we passed the Proust once again, and casting a last glance at the volumes, Katharina Fischer inquired whether I wasn't a little hurt when Klara maintained that all she could remember when she thought of the fifties—our early days together—was the newly translated, complete *À la Recherche*.

No, Klara certainly didn't want to forget our early years, didn't think of them as having no value in her memory. What there was, though, unforeseeably, time and again throughout the decades, was fits of jealousy, mixed with wistfulness, which Klara would have experienced as much as I did—not jealousy of a person, but of a world which belongs exclusively to the other, an inner world in which they move alone, can only move alone, and to which at times they devote themselves with the kind of dedication, of patience, which their partner too might well love to possess at that moment. Therein lay the pang, that was the Proust, and that's another reason why I never touched him.

And wistfulness, because we knew we couldn't accompany each other into the other's world. For a companion is surprised at phenomena which in terms of that world are accepted as self-evident, asks questions where they ought not to be asked, tries to engage the other person in conversation when they should be doing nothing but observing. If, on the other hand, you take on the task of guiding your loved one through this world, you'll find yourself concentrating more on your partner than on the things around, you'll want to point out details to them that they ought to be discovering for themselves, and you'll reveal connections which you yourself will begin to doubt again as soon as you put names to them.

Slight disturbances. First misunderstandings. Everything needs to be explained. At some point the mystery will begin to retreat step by step from your inner world, and with its retreat the need to explore this world decreases. Soon you start to enter it only as a matter of habit. But we couldn't have borne such emptiness, such loss, whether alone or together. So we resigned ourselves to the fact that the other person seemed submerged for days, weeks even, in his or her own world, barely accessible, as if he or she would never surface again. That was our pact. That's how we protected each other. That's what held us together.

We spent hour after hour at the kitchen table, Klara immersed in her Proust, I in my ornithological writings, surrounded by a succession of members of Parisian high society and representatives of all the bird families scattered across the globe. It is conceivable that over the years some of the individuals populating these inner spaces might have met, despite their differing origins and nature, on the edges of our world, far out there, without our being able to witness their encounters. I believed in such encounters when Klara said she was surprised by the transformation of the *blondschopf,* the "fairhead" she knew from Schottlaender's version, into the *Goldspatz,* the little golden sparrow in the new German translation. Together we reflected on whether there was some real bird lurking behind the original expression in the French, perhaps a yellowhammer, a citril finch, or maybe a canary—and it struck me that Klara may have come across the *Goldspatz* on the very same evening that I was preoccupied with the earliest form of canary, *Serinus canaria,* the wild canary, and its distribution. But she had not interrupted me, the two birds did no more than recognize each other from a distance, and a little later, when Klara was observing a young woman going on a journey with her "young linnets," the *Goldspatz* and the wild canary were no longer acquainted with each other.

The same thing happened to Klara when she couldn't help thinking about the "pitch-black jay feathers" on the narrator's head which he smoothes down, which refuse to lie flat, and which he has a young maidservant admire, while I was telling her how many subspecies of jay there are, each distinguished by the most subtle characteristics. And Albertine's laugh, which sometimes sounds like little cries and at other times resembles the cooing of pigeons—it's possible that when I tried to reconstruct how, independently of each other, *Columba junoniae* and *Columba bollii* conquered the Canary Islands and made them their living space, that rather indecorous female laugh accompanied me.

Indeed, it seemed from time to time that the paths of related people and animals were crossing in our kitchen knowing nothing about each other. The figure of Moreau, for example, whom Klara suspected of harboring a secret of some sort, and whom she held on to for far too long, though he is granted only one brief appearance in the novel, could have been a distant cousin or the late uncle of the ornithologist of the same name, when we sat together at the table reading and the kitchen beyond the lamplight lay in darkness, where nothing moved except shadows. There between the door and the sink a certain Monsieur A. J. Moreau handed the opera-loving narrator his ticket for a gala evening, while Reginald E. Moreau, without noticing the two figures frozen in a strange attitude, crossed the room as he followed the red-breasted flycatcher, the greenish warbler, and the arctic warbler en route from distant Asia toward the west, across Siberia, northern Russia, and Finland as far as Sweden, where no memory remained of their origins in India or Malaysia.

On our trip to Vienna, when we visited the Natural History Museum and were at last standing in front of the twin eagles that Ludwig Kaltenburg had always wanted to show me, I experienced—and so did Klara, as she later confessed—an almost indescribable moment in which I couldn't have said whether everything around me was slipping out of kilter or whether for the first time in ages I was filling my lungs with air right down to their finest artery branches. And we both felt that these mounted sea eagles, these sad-looking birds of prey with their drooping wings and bowed necks, were imbued with something. Was it a threat, a dark premonition, an unrealizable hope from a long-gone past? We found it hard to be more precise about our impression.

It no longer even seemed necessary to put a name to what we were leaving behind by the time we moved out of Room XXX into the stairwell and it dawned on Klara that the Crown Prince Rudolf whom Professor Kaltenburg had obviously mentioned often, judging by how frequently I talked to Klara about him, must be the same figure that she had known for nearly forty years as Archduke Rudolf, without ever connecting the two. The melancholy heir to the throne, passionately interested in bird life, who died in dubious circumstances on January 30, 1889, and who used to argue with his friend Alfred Edmund Brehm, on their deer-stalking expeditions in the marshy woods by the Danube at Draueck, about whether the *Steinadler* and the *Goldadler* are two different types of golden eagle or just different colorations of the same species: Rudolf is twice mentioned in passages of Proust that are chronologically far apart.

6

THE INTERPRETER ALREADY had her coat on when she announced she was now determined to read Proust's novel, about which, after a few failed attempts to tackle him, she was as ignorant as I was. And she knew in advance that when she was reading him she would always think back to our conversations over the past six months. Mind you, I warned her, as far as the hand-washing scenes were concerned, she shouldn't expect too much—they don't exist. If Katharina Fischer really does pick up her Proust and not put it down until she reaches the final sentences, she will find that at no point in the novel does a character close a window, say "Good morning," or wash his hands. Klara had already revealed as much to me during our first boating trip in the Great Garden.

"Not once?"

Not once.

The interpreter laughed. We shook hands, she got into her car, I watched her go until the taillights disappeared around the corner. I cleared up. At exactly the moment, by the clock, when Klara must have been getting on the train in Berlin.

I can see myself again on an early mid-November morning sitting alone in an unheated carriage smelling of yesterday's cigarette smoke in a train standing at one of the outlying platforms of the Dresden main station. Feverish, still in my coat after being torn from a deep sleep, still barely conscious, I had left the house early and was now waiting endlessly for the train to set off for Berlin, on my way to an appointment about which I remember nothing except my half-sleep-drugged, half-impatient waiting while the sun rose over the city.

From the Ostragehege district dark spots are moving through the dawn light, the crows have left their roosting places and landed on a builder's crane, whose arm stretches far out across the roof of the main concourse. They're casting an early-morning eye over the inner city, more birds are constantly arriving, joining their fellows on the latticework of girders, they inspect the Wiener Platz and Petersburger Strasse, Fritz Löffler Strasse, Budapester, Strehlener and Prager Strasse, before work begins on the building site below. The crane operator doesn't disturb them as he climbs up the tower and into his cabin, shutting the door behind him. A circular saw swings on the suspension cable in the morning wind.

Not until the arm of the crane slowly sweeps to one side do the crows take to the air. I follow their flight across the roof of the station, the platforms, the November-dulled green of the park. The continuous breaking away from the formation, the little pursuits, the way individual crows drop out, wheel around, looking to slot in again, as though each morning they had to reassert that the skills they were practicing yesterday until the hour of sunset have not been lost overnight, as if they could shake off sleep only through their play.

Now a crow is heading toward the imposing building on the other side of the embankment, fluttering as it nears the dark stripe of crows marking off the clear composition of the facade, with its large windows, against the sky. At the instant the crow settles on the parapet, the black line is torn apart at one point, the bird's close-packed fellows become agitated, and I can hear somebody calling out, "We're not in Dresden here," I can hear Ludwig Kaltenburg, laughing: "We're in Moscow, can't you see?"

There stands the professor on the roof of the Institute for Transport Studies, bending his knees, leaning over, spreading his arms, he begins to run, slowly straightening up and croaking at the same time. Most of the crows observe this performance without moving, just here and there a bird is infected by Kaltenburg's flying motions and follows him, as though to humor him. The crows commandeered the building shortly after it was completed, the city pest-control people didn't know what to do about it, even the Society for Sport and Technology turned out to be helpless, Kaltenburg was called in, offering to try to tempt the birds away from the building.

He's not going to pull it off. He makes another round of the roof, but he can't disperse them, the first crows are already returning inquisitively from the station, Kaltenburg is attracting the birds. He could see it as a defeat, but he regards it as a triumph, his last carefree winter in the city—"They're simply familiar with this architecture"—his breath clouding in front of his face—"and why would you want to chase them away when you know they come from the Soviet Union? We should welcome them every year, our feathered friends, and joyfully allow them whatever space they want."

I have opened the window. Soon a taxi will pull up in front of the house, Klara will get out carrying her small suitcase, glance upward, and spot me up here. The air smells like snow.

With sluggish wingbeats a single crow moves through the light flurry of snowflakes.

They come from Siberia, from the Urals, the Baltic, and with the approaching cold once more this year they will gather in the Elbe valley. Hundreds of rooks, along with carrion crows, hooded crows, jackdaws, will form huge clouds of birds that will pulsate above us, fray at the edges, then reform as patches of black.

Acknowledgments

My thanks are due to the following bodies for supporting my work on this novel: the Fund for German Literature (*Deutscher Literaturfonds*), the Saxon Ministry for Art and Science, the Leuk Castle Foundation (*Stiftung Schloß Leuk*), and the Municipality of Leuk, Canton Valais.

Among the many people who have shared their knowledge, observations, and memories with me over the years, there are two in particular whom I wish to thank: Renate Glück, for a conversation continued since 1996 about a Dresden I could never have discovered without her; and Dr. Siegfried Eck, custodian until his death in September 2005 of the Ornithological Collection at the Museum of Zoology, State Natural History Collections Dresden, who awakened my interest in ornithology.